# AFTER TH[E] WAR

A decade ago the terrible demigod, the Kinslayer, returned from his long exile in darkness, leading an army of monsters and laying waste everything in his path.

The nations of the world rallied, formed hasty alliances, fought back the tide. A small band of heroes, guided by the enigmatic Wanderer, broke into the Kinslayer's palace and killed him.

But what happens when the fighting's done? When the old rivalries are remembered, when those who are hungry and broken turn to their neighbours in need?

*After the War* is a story of consequences.

## THE AFTER THE WAR SERIES

Book One: *Redemption's Blade* by Adrian Tchaikovsky
Book Two: *Salvation's Fire* by Justina Robson

*The Tales of Catt & Fisher* edited by Justina Robson

Also from Solaris
by Mark de Jager:

## THE CHRONICLES OF STRATUS

Book One: *Infernal*
Book Two: *Firesky*

# HOMECOMING'S FALL

MARK DE JAGER

First published 2022 by Solaris
an imprint of Rebellion Publishing Ltd,
Riverside House, Osney Mead,
Oxford, OX2 0ES, UK

*www.solarisbooks.com*

ISBN: 978-1-78618-721-5



A CIP catalogue record for this book is available from the British Library.

Designed & typeset by Rebellion Publishing

Printed in the UK

Tell them of us and say,
for your tomorrow, we gave our today.

# CHAPTER ONE

SLENN SHIVERED AS he picked his way across the battlefield, making his way back to the area he had left the night before with the aid of macabre markers. There was No Head, one severed arm still raised to ward off the blow that had claimed both hand and head. They turned left, following the line of his stump until they came to Third Eye, a hulking Yorughan warrior felled by a crossbow bolt sunk up to its fletching square in the middle of his forehead, drawing his eyebrows in to give him a look of startled disapproval. It had been a fine shot, and Slenn often wondered what had become of the archer who'd loosed it; although chances were he was lying dead somewhere close by.

As battlefields went, Tulkauth was almost claustrophobically compact: a shallow, natural bowl in the landscape. It wasn't his first battlefield by any stretch, and he'd picked over enough corpses to know that the fighting had been fierce and brutal. The battle had ended with some sort of explosion that had tossed the living and the dead into great heaps, and those corpses that hadn't been dismembered or charred beyond recognition all bore evidence of heavy and sustained combat. He'd had to cut the fingers from more than a dozen bodies where they'd died with sword in hand, still fighting even as their guts slithered out.

He paused as he reached his area, turning to wave at the three others who had followed him through the silent landscape. They returned the wave and raised their hands in a gesture of good luck before heading off to their patch. As a rule, none of them spoke while they worked; it wasn't as much of a concern here since there were no survivors, but on other battlefields that Slenn had harvested he'd had to run the gauntlet of stray carrion beasts of every description—or worse, the provosts of the victorious army and their equally vicious dogs.

Slenn waited until the morning mist rendered the others into shapeless shadows before turning aside and picking his way past the body of a mostly fleshless Yogg, its right arm draped across its barrel like rib cage and its bony fingers just as he'd left them, silently pointing the way back to where he'd ended his search the previous afternoon. He smiled at his handiwork and made his way to the edge of the crater, the familiar thrill of excitement starting to course through him. The ground here was glassy and brittle, and punished the careless with clouds of glittering dust that got in everywhere and quickly abraded skin. The bodies of the fallen had been unceremoniously dragged away and dumped in hastily covered pits in the aftermath of the battle, making for a truly treacherous landscape where a single misstep could spell disaster. But that same danger had kept the others away, which meant the centre of the battlefield was his for the picking, and his alone. This was where the blast that had crisped so many of the bodies had originated, which meant the bodies with the best kit were likely to be close—assuming that they had survived the conflagration. All he had to do was keep to the narrow ridge that wound between the pits and avoid falling into any of them. The steep walls were as crumbly as the dirt that covered them and climbing out would be all but impossible. He shivered at the idea of drowning in sand, slipping deeper with every struggle until he became one with the dead below.

He pushed past a particularly bloated body, wary of disturbing any of the vermin within lest they interpret it as an invasion of their territory, but nothing stirred. He paused and squatted on his heels a few paces beyond the corpse, studiously avoiding looking at its distended features.

It was quiet here, silent save for the intermittent dripping of unseen fluids and occasional dull whuff of escaping gases within the piled bodies. A few yards in front of Slenn's boots the ground began to visibly slope away, but to reach that he'd need to pass through a pearly layer of mist, a far denser barrier than what clung to the rest of Tulkauth, and one that stubbornly defied what little sunlight managed to pierce the clouds above.

Nothing stirred around him. No flies, no flesh borers, no crows. No rats, not even the warped and scaled ones that were so prevalent in these parts. *There should be something.*

Battlefields were normally a banquet for vermin, and the absence of one kind was normally an invitation for another to swarm in even greater numbers. He chewed his lip for a few moments more, on the cusp of turning away when a pattering sound reached him. He glanced down and caught a glimpse of a small, mottled shape running up the slope before it disappeared between two bodies, a long and hairless tail leaving a brief trail behind it.

Slenn exhaled and stood up, shaking his head at his own paranoia before heading down the slope, placing his feet carefully as he pushed into the unmoving mist lest he tumble forward and impale himself on some discarded weapon or ragged bone. He had a good feeling about the morning, that his luck would finally turn. All he needed was one good find that would pay off the last of his debts and put him in Boris' good books. The man was a felon of the highest order, but he looked after those that proved themselves.

He didn't look back, and so didn't see the same mottled rat reappear between the corpses, thrashing and biting at itself in mindless agony in the moments before its skin sloughed off; nor how its rapidly liquefying organs poured from it soon after.

He moved down the slope, treading carefully as he passed through the heavy, clinging mist. It stirred lazily as he pushed through, the touch making his skin tingle. It felt like thick smoke in his throat, but cool and soft at the same time, a balm after the choking dust and not entirely unpleasant.

An alien landscape awaited him beneath it. The light was softer, diluted by the mist so that it seemed to come from all directions at once, leaving no shadows at all, the lack of contrast making the blasted ground look stark and unearthly. Twisted corpses that the gravediggers had missed lay scattered about, skeletal arms and bare ribs thrusting from the ground like burnt shrubs. He slowed as he came to a dozen or more ash-coated figures that lay in an untidy heap, legs and arms intertwined as if they had turned to flee at the same moment. He edged closer, suddenly convinced that they were about to turn on him; but when he was a few yards away from the silent tableau they collapsed with a soft sigh, falling into themselves and leaving only a fine soot that was almost indistinguishable from the mist above.

He covered his mouth with his neckerchief and moved on through the pall of silence, closer to the heart of the crater. The occasional boulders that he passed resolved themselves into clumps of fused flesh and metal, the tangled and unrecognisable remains of the gods alone knew how many Yogg and human soldiers, all finally equal in death.

He'd be the first to admit he was no warrior, but he'd seen his fair share of fights and the aftermath of even more; yet nothing compared to what he saw now as he slowly edged forward. Fiery blasts left bodies broken and shrunken, so he knew that the melted remains that he saw were the remnants of many such bodies, so closely packed in their last moments of life that they had fused together; but in so doing some had defied the full ferocity of the blast. His gaze lingered on a nearby lump, following the strange, folded contours before he finally understood what he was seeing. He looked away as he saw it for what it was, but he knew the fleshless face, mouth open in a silent scream, would haunt him for some time.

He stopped and rubbed his own face with tingling hands. He had a job to do and hadn't come here to gawk or scare himself like some wandering child. He set down his pack and adjusted his belt, slipping a pry bar and sharpened chisel into the loops. There had to be something good around here. If flesh could survive, metal and gems certainly could too.

He adjusted the neckerchief as he moved to a pile of dust-covered flesh. He planted a foot on it and plunged the pry bar into the centre of the mass, grunting with effort as he began working it back and forth. There was a reason that the gravediggers hadn't bothered trying to move them, and he was sweating heavily before he managed to pry the first of the bodies apart.

The diffused glow around him brightened marginally as he worked his way across the crater, the only sign of the day passing outside of that strange and hidden world. He stopped when his arms were starting to ache and sat down to drink greedily from his canteen, sighing at the cool relief it offered. He hadn't realised how painfully parched his throat was, and the beer tasted cooler and fresher than it had a right to—not that he was complaining about that. He had a few things to show for the morning, mostly deformed jewellery and few dozen gold teeth, but nothing like what he'd been hoping for and certainly nothing that justified his aching arms and the danger he was putting himself in. He stashed the bag and canteen and stood again, disappointment weighing heavily on him as he made ready to make his way back to the patch he was supposed to be clearing. He looked around one last time, and with the sun having moved further across the battlefield, he saw an odd shadow cast where he'd only expected a heap of spoil from the pits. He cupped his hands next to his eyes and squinted at the shape the shadow had outlined, and the hitherto formless mass slowly resolved itself into what looked like several figures encased in a mound of sand and grit. Intrigued, he swung his pack over his shoulder and carefully made his way over to them, picking his way between two of the larger pits and testing the ground ahead of him with a thin rod. It was slow going, and despite his careful approach his footsteps were making the sand run from the figures entombed within it, revealing a small group of ash-covered figures that the diggers must have missed. He could see sheets of ash sliding from them as he drew closer, tiny avalanches steadily eroding their features into anonymity. When the ash eventually crumbled, it was to reveal the remnants of blackened skeletons and armour, some of which still held equally blackened flesh. That wasn't what interested him, but rather the figure they had been facing when their world ended.

The Yogg wasn't particularly large for his kind, although he would have towered over Slenn in life. The explosion had torn away at least half of his torso and his pose echoed so many of the other figures that Slenn had seen, arms raised in a vain attempt to ward off the fatal blow. The ash had cascaded from his face at Slenn's approach, leaving his skull exposed, and Slenn smiled under his neckerchief as he noted the fine, gold inlaid carvings that decorated the tusks jutting from its heavy jaw. Work like that fetched a good price among certain collectors, especially if it came from a Heart Taker.

It wasn't the explosion that had slain the Yogg mage, though; Slenn's money was on the four-inch crescent that had split its forehead. Without flesh to hide it, he could even see the canyon that bisected its cheekbone and nasal cavity, probably when the sword had been drawn back after the deadly blow. He shivered at the thought of the level of violence that went into delivering a blow like that and turned to look at the skeletons around him. Had one of them delivered the fatal stroke? He turned back and studied the ground around him, noting the scorch marks that radiated outwards from the body like a star, the melted and reformed rock gleaming like scar tissue. *This was it, the origin of the blast.*

Slenn shivered as he looked at the Heart Taker again, noting how both forearms ending just below the elbows. Whoever had delivered the killing blow had chopped through both in the same stroke instead. He paused with one hand on its tusk, scuffing the melted rock with the toe of his boot. Whatever had killed so many here had happened quickly, even before the body had a chance to fall. *At least it was quick.* He pulled the tusks and patted the Yogg's broken forehead, which shattered at his touch, making him start.

Shaking his head at his own foolishness, he moved past the gruesome figure and turned his attention to a clump of largely unidentifiable remains behind it. He pulled the loose parts away with his hands, then dug the pry bar in. It was hard work separating them, but one good thing about the bodies having being baked hard by the fire was that they weren't bloated and leaking like those he'd had to contend with on other sites. Dealing with aching arms and sweat was far easier than working amidst a cloud of bloatflies.

He'd just pried a warped breastplate from the mass when he caught the gleam of something wedged beneath it. He set the gilded breastplate aside; whole, it might have fetched a good price, but it was hard to sell armour that had so clearly failed its previous owner. He eased the bar back into the pile with far greater care, working it back and forth until he could get a better idea of what he was dealing with. Something round and golden. A crown? Slenn grinned under his handkerchief and fought the urge to rush. One careless stroke could halve the value of something—or worse, attract Boris' ire.

He sat back on his heels and rubbed his tingling arms. It wasn't a crown—not that he'd ever seen one in real life—but it was clearly something special. He would have liked there to be a few nice gems, but it only had what looked like silver or perhaps iron plates bound to a golden headband with copper wire of some sort. He lifted his canteen out and poured a small amount of beer over some of the small plates, washing at least one layer of muck from them, just enough to reveal the angular script carved into each. It was definitely Yogg. He licked his lips and moved to carefully slip a small knife under it, but even with such caution he still yelped like a kicked dog when a purple-hued spark leapt from the band to his blade, numbing his fingers. He squatted back and tried to shake some life back into them, the discomfort lost beneath a rising excitement. If it had magic, this was the find that would make him.

He wrapped the knife handle in cloth and tried again. This time there was no spark, and the congealed muck released the rest of the crown without too much of a struggle. He shuffled back a few paces and set it down on some clear ground, then sat back and tried not to weep.

It was a fantastic piece, clearly valuable, only it would have been more so were it not for the smooth-edged break in what he took to be the front, largely because of the two cloudy gemstones on either side of gap. He glanced over to the Yogg wizard's broken skull and back again, the images of what must have happened on that day assembling themselves in his mind. He nodded to himself and lifted the crown as carefully as he could, wincing as another spark arced between the broken ends. His smile returned as he carefully set it down and began wrapping it, tucking at least two layers between the broken ends to stop them from touching. Once that was stowed, he drew his knife and set to work on the rest of the dead wizard's teeth.

# CHAPTER TWO

OREC CASUALLY NUDGED the wooden stag forward then sat back, his beard hiding the smile that played across his lips as 'Grandad' immediately leaned forward, deep lines creasing his forehead as he studied the unexpected move. Even the nurses had started calling him by his nickname, to his endless ire and everyone else's amusement.

'Your finger's going to regrow by the time you make a decision.'

'Don't rush me, Orec. I didn't rush you.'

'I didn't take half a day to decide what to do with my stag.'

'Yes well, playing wolves is a bit more nuanced.' His finger hovered over a token, the crude etchings marking it as one of the earliest ones that Orec had carved. 'It requires strategy and patience. Cunning.'

'Of course. I just thought that the wolves were hunters.'

'Will you shut up, man?'

Orec held up his hands in a placating gesture. The old man hated losing at anything, a trait that wasn't at all mitigated by the fact that he rarely won. *The old man*. Orec smiled into his beard at the thought. As he reckoned it, Tomas was little more than five years older than him, but that and his prematurely grey hair had sealed his fate when it came to names. Going by the names you'd been given or earned by your brothers had become second nature to them, even the Cheriveni amongst them, who had bridled at what they considered to be an insult to their family names at first. It was endemic in the company though, and that resistance was soon eroded. At the end many of them were slow to react to their given names, and even their bursars had taken to calling men by both to speed things up.

He looked down as Tomas completed his move, pushing the pack leader in closer to his alpha stag. It wasn't a bad move, and threatened at least half of his pieces, but it also left his own flank exposed.

'You sure you want to do that?' he asked.

'Damn right I do,' Tomas said, sitting back to sip from his cup of morning beer. 'You sweating a bit there?'

'Not really,' Orec replied, tapping one of the smaller stags across and knocking two wolf tokens off the board. 'Double move.'

Tomas stared at the board, the cup still raised to his mouth, giving no sign that he was remotely aware of the beer running down his neck and darkening his shirt. Without warning, he threw the cup onto the board, hard enough to send both spinning from the crate that was serving as their table, scattering the pieces. They were still spinning on the floor when the door he'd marched through slammed behind him, doing nothing to muffle his curses on the other side, nor the thump of his fist hitting what Orec hoped was just a wall.

'You could have let him win,' said a voice behind him.

'I could have,' Orec said, pleased that he hadn't given any sign of being startled. 'But then I'd have lost, and he'd be even more insufferable.' He'd have been more surprised if he'd heard Hayden's approach, but even so, the man had a habit of being where you didn't expect him. 'Fancy a game?'

'Sure,' Hayden said, hooking Tomas's chair with his foot and pulling it back towards the table. Short and slight, he wasn't the first person anyone would picture if someone was talking about war veterans, but his slender frame hid a wiry strength that had surprised more than a few people, Orec included. He'd borrowed Hayden's bow once, and had been entirely blasé about using it, having shot his fair share of small game in the past. He'd managed to draw it for about a third of the arrow before it felt like he was either going to dislocate his shoulder or lose his fingers, and having done it in front of half the company had only made the indignity of it worse.

They played in silence for a while, each winning in turn, occasionally looking up as the doors at the end of the room opened and admitted another of the patients. Oren knew most by name, and waved to several. The number of faces he recognised was dwindling as the inflow of battlefield injuries tapered off and the remaining soldiers in the halls were replaced by civilians with mundane ills, taking pressure off the surgeons and letting them apply their hard-earned skills elsewhere. The hall they shared was emptying steadily, and it didn't take much to turn his thoughts to going home.

*Home.*

'Are you going to move that piece, or did you die?'

'Sorry,' Orec said, setting the stag back down on the board. 'My mind jumped me.'

'Tulkauth?'

'Home.'

'Ah.' Hayden's mouth quirked into a smile. 'That's a dangerous thing to dwell on.'

Orec toyed with one of the pieces he'd already taken off Hayden, rubbing his thumb across the nubs that passed for the wolf's ears. 'It shouldn't be,' he said. 'It's over, isn't it? He's dead, his armies are scattered. That's all I signed up for.'

'You don't have to sound so furtive about it. As you say, the war's over.'

'The way you were staring I thought there was a provost behind me.'

'I just can't imagine you wanting to give all this up.' He gestured to the row of narrow beds along the wall, most of which were empty, and the repurposed crates that served as all other furniture in the draughty hall. 'We even have the fireplace to ourselves.'

'And we didn't even have to fight for it this time.' Orec's smile was wry. When they had first been moved to the hall it had felt like luxury, and not just because their wounds were finally healing, the repeated stitches and ointments they had been suffering finally taking hold. It had been busy and loud, with every bed occupied by other recovering soldiers, talking, laughing and occasionally singing, and hot food whenever they wanted it: the perfect tonic after so many long weeks in isolation, lost to their own thoughts and only the rasping breath of dying men for company. They'd had to lie, cheat and fight their way closer to the fireplace over several weeks, and although that had largely been a bloodless struggle, it had been a fine game to keep them occupied. The celebrations when the news of the Kinslayer's death had come had been as raucous as so many injured men could manage, but things had slowly begun to change after that.

'Positively decadent,' Orec added, sitting back and surveying the hall again. It was true too, for despite the Yogg's rampant vandalism and the damage that the mansion had suffered when they'd liberated it, it was still the nicest place that he'd bunked in since he'd been dragged into the war. Once upon a time he would have been awed by opulence of it and the wealth that the owner must have had at his disposal to build or even keep such a home, but he wasn't that person anymore. He'd often wondered what happened to the owners. Were their bodies amongst those in the pit outside, or had they fled?

'Do you think they've just forgotten about us?' asked Hayden. He too had given up any pretence of finishing the game and was staring into the beer he'd helped himself to as if expecting to see his future revealed.

'Forget the heroes of Tulkauth? Impossible.'

Hayden's laugh was short and bitter edged. He didn't care for waiting at the best of times, and the hospital had begun to feel like a cage as soon as he could walk again, an impression that only grew stronger with every day that bled away. He'd taken to speaking to most of the other patients here, but even amongst soldiers to whom the need to gossip was as insatiable as his own curiosity, few had even heard of Tulkauth, much less what had happened there.

And yet someone did know. He'd found their files in the chirurgeon's office, which he had discovered was rarely locked, which by his reckoning meant it was fair game to enter. He didn't sleep much anymore, and spent the quiet hours exploring the mansion and grounds. The folder he'd found with their names on showed that someone was taking great care to record their recovery, far more so than any of the other patients. He'd yet to discover why, but whoever was responsible for it had written 'do not release' on the first page.

Hayden watched Orec over the rim of his cup, wondering how he'd react if he told him all of what he'd read. Of all of them, he had escaped with the lightest injuries, although he hadn't felt particularly blessed in any way. The burns had been agonising and had taken an age to heal, and he could only guess at what Orec, whose injuries were far worse than his, had had to endure. That wasn't what had stood out in the neatly-annotated notes as much as the burns that the doctors who had treated them had suffered. Blisters, rashes and illness had dogged all who had tended to them in the healing wards—so much so that none were permitted to spend more than an hour in their company.

He didn't understand all of it himself, and so he'd kept it quiet. They were all doing well, so he saw no need to sour things. *Let sleeping dogs lie, as the old saying went*. The sergeant was a good man at heart, and with his strength now all returned it would be interesting to see how they would stop him if and when he decided to leave.

'Can you imagine Tomas if someone gave him a medal?' he said, conscious of the silence.

They both snorted at the thought. The only thing the axe man liked more than talking about himself was other people talking about him. It was bad enough listening his blow-by-blow accounts of every fight he'd been in without others chiming in. Hayden took another sip and then kept his voice carefully neutral.

'Would you go straight home?'

'Straighter than any arrow you've ever shot.'

Hayden sat forward. 'Then let's do it.'

'Do what?'

'Go home,' the soldier said. 'You said it. The war's over. We've done what we swore to do, so let's go home.'

'We haven't been released from our oath,' Orec replied.

'We swore to fight him and to protect our home. He's dead, so we've done what we swore to do.'

'Maybe.'

'We've heard nothing for months. No one has,' Hayden said, sitting back and feigning nonchalance. Orec could be as stubborn as a mule, but what had made him such an effective leader was that he wasn't blind to his own failings and listened to ideas. He'd planted one now, and just needed it to take root. Across from him, Orec shook his head but didn't say anything.

'Fine, I'll leave it. I'm going to go see how Stef is getting on with his new leg.'

'See if you can rustle up some bread for toasting too,' Orec said, brightening.

'I'll go see what there is.'

Orec watched Hayden walk away, pleased to see that his limp had faded to an extent that only those who knew him could see how he favoured his left leg. It was a remarkable recovery but then aside from Stef's leg, they all had defied the surgeon's expectations at every turn. The healers' ministrations had stopped them from dying, but for reasons that no one had yet explained to any of them, that was all they could do. No prayer brought any relief, and in the end it was old-fashioned flesh and blood doctoring that had saved them. It had meant a long and painful recovery compared to others, but they had finally turned to corner on the path to recovery.

He reached under his shirt and ran his fingers along the ridge that marked the point where the silvery, new skin that now covered most of his right side met his mostly undamaged face and neck. Had it not been for his helmet, chances were that he wouldn't be alive, and his only regret was that the rest of his harness hadn't been of the same quality. He felt a stab of guilt at the thought even as it crossed his mind. More than fifteen hundred others had perished in the conflagration that had scarred him, all their dreams and potential ending between heartbeats as their bodies became so much ash and charcoal.

That he and the others had survived was a miracle, but the memory of the pain that had followed once the initial shock had passed made it impossible for him to think of it as that. The agony had been all-consuming, like looking into the sun and not being able to see anything else for it, and he had lost his mind for some time. That madness had been a blessing, and in the rare moments when he felt strong enough to look back on it, it was almost as if he had been on the outside of his own body, watching himself writhe and scream as soon as the sleeping draughts began to wear off, the bandages that wrapped him making him look like some Tzarkomani totem.

He shuddered anew, then sat up straighter and raked his fingers through his regrown beard. What was done was done, and brooding in such a way would only stoke his melancholy and unbalance his humours. It benefitted no one to dwell on it now, and he pushed the memory back into the chest within his mind as the healers had taught him to, then buried it once more.

Aside from two men sitting talking a few beds away, the hall was quiet. Tomas had taken himself off into the gardens and was no doubt talking the ear off some unfortunate nurse that was too slow to slip away, and Hayden had gone to find Stef. He shifted in the chair and slipped his little crafting knife from where it hung around his neck. His thumb brushed over the smooth surface of its handle, tracing the outlines of the face he'd carved on it what felt like a lifetime ago.

*Martina.*

She'd been an impossible dream when he'd carved it, as bright and vital as a star, and just as unreachable for an apprentice carpenter, something which had not stopped him from falling hopelessly and desperately in love with her. Not for the first time he wondered whether she would even recognise him now, much less want him back. He flexed his scarred hands, smiling as the firelight picked out the curving scar he'd given himself with a chisel. He'd been so self-conscious of it once, and now it was all but hidden under a cross hatch of newer scars, none of which had healed nearly so well.

*And what of the rest of you?* whispered the voice in his head. *What of when she sees how your skin ran like melted wax and hears how you begged to die?*

'Shut up,' he hissed, relieved there was no one around to hear him. Saying it aloud had become the only way to silence that treacherous voice, and he had uncomfortable but fortunately hazy memories of screaming at it during the worst parts of his healing as it tried to convince him to give up, to abandon all thoughts of returning home. It had been a rare day when the burns hall wasn't filled with screams or pleading, so no one had paid him much heed then, other than as a prompt to force another of their bitter potions to his lips.

He'd thought about going home so many times, letting it sustain him when things were at their bleakest but now, with so little preventing him from taking to the road, his legs felt leaden. He'd seen men who'd gone home on leave, only to return a shell of themselves, hollowed out by the trauma of finding their homes and families devastated. Those men fell into two categories on their return; they either succumbed to their melancholy and became a burden on their fellows until a Yogg mace ended their suffering, or they stopped caring and lost themselves to the violence. The end of the war would not treat either well, assuming they had survived it.

He rubbed at the stiff ridge that marked the transition from his living skin to the silvery scars. Who was he to complain, when Stefan was condemned to a cripple's life? The blast had stripped Orec's skin away, but it had taken fingers and half a leg from the young standard bearer. The only thing more miraculous than his recovery was that the battle priests hadn't simply given him peace in the field, perhaps because they had found so few alive. Orec smiled at the memory of his first conversation with Stef during their treatment. Rather than sobbing or wailing like so many of the others there, the young Cheriveni spent the time arguing why he shouldn't look forward to a half-price discount from cobblers.

He decided that sitting alone by the banked fire like an old man was not going to do much other than fuel such maudlin thoughts. He'd put off seeing Stef for too long already, and with a sigh that became a groan, Orec stood up, grimacing as he felt the edges of the new skin pull and stretch as he straightened. The only thing he knew to compare it to was the feel of an enormous scab, and while it wasn't painful, it wasn't pleasant either. He waited a few moments, tilting his body this way and that, until the sensation faded. That part was at least getting easier, and once he was up and moving he hardly noticed it.

He made his way between the rows of empty beds, pausing only to exchange greetings with the men playing cards near the door. There'd been a time when he wouldn't have dared to leave all their gear unattended, but the camp-following vultures who'd set themselves up in the gardens had dispersed almost a month past, whatever loyalty they may once have had having been eroded by the drop in injured men to help on their way home, most of whom would have been quietly relieved of any remaining valuables on the way. He knew all those who remained in the hospital now, and few if any were in any condition to make a run for it. It didn't stop him from keeping a good knife tucked into his trousers, but as he saw it, that was just common sense.

'THE WEIRD PART is that it still itches.'

'What does?' Tomas asked around a mouthful of stew.

'My foot,' Stef replied, tapping his newly fitted wooden peg against the floorboard to underline his answer.

'You don't have a foot, though.'

'I think he knows that,' Hayden said.

'But then—'

'That's why it's strange,' Stef interjected, somehow resisting the urge to roll his eyes. 'I can still feel my toes.'

'It's even weirder 'cos you hardly have fingers,' Tomas said, waving his spoon towards Stef's still bandaged hand. 'You know, to feel things.'

Hayden saw Orec compress his lips in irritation, but Stef only shrugged and lifted his injured hand, the stiff black stitches hidden by the linen, and stared at it as if seeing it for the first time. He waggled the two fingers that remained. 'Well, at least I've still got your sister's favourites.'

Even Orec grinned at that and nudged Tomas before he could give voice to his retort. Unlike Stef, who was grinning as he took a drink, Hayden didn't miss how Orec's playful nudge nearly sent Tomas spilling from his chair, and as much of a lunk as Tomas was, he registered enough in Orec's expression to know better than give voice to the retort on his lips.

'I'm impressed that you can walk on that thing already,' Hayden said, tipping his own cup at the peg. 'I reckon by the week's end you'll be vaulting on it every other step.'

'I'd be satisfied with not falling on my face every ten yards.'

'I can fit a foot of sorts to it,' Orec said, leaning forward and tapping his knife against the wood. 'It'll make it more stable, especially on soft ground.'

'That'd be fantastic.'

'Easy enough. And when we get back to mine, I can sort something decent out for you, maybe fit a hinge to it so that there's a bit more of a flex.'

Even Orec seemed surprised at his words, and for a moment they all simply looked at each other.

Hayden sat back. 'We're going home?'

Orec pursed his lips, then nodded.

'Yes!' Tomas cried, shooting to his feet. 'I'm so sick of this goddamned place.'

'Once Stef is able to travel,' Orec added, leaning away before his drink was knocked out of his hand. 'We go together.'

'Yes, but that's fine, he's got a leg now, right Stef?'

'Most of one, yeah.' He turned to Orec. 'I'm happy to put this place behind me, sarge.'

'I'm sure you are, we all are, but you need to build your strength. Get some meat and good wine in you.'

'But we're doing this?' Hayden pushed his chair in closer and leaned his elbows on his knees. He looked around, then continued in a low voice. 'If we are, we're going to need to start pulling some things together.'

'You've got some ideas.' Orec didn't pose it as a question.

'A few,' Hayden conceded. 'I've been nosing around, speaking to a few people. There are some opportunities.'

Tomas grinned and sat down again. 'Of course you have. So what do I need to do?'

'Just be yourself,' Orec said.

'What's that supposed to mean?'

'It means if they're trying to stop you being an idiot, they're not looking at Longshot over here.' Stef grinned. 'Right, boss?'

'Couldn't have said it better myself.' Orec reached out and tapped the wooden peg. 'Your job is to walk. We'll sort out the rest, you just need to rebuild your endurance.'

'I won't let you down.'

'And try not to lose any other bits in the meantime,' said Tomas.

'Screw you,' he snapped back, but his mouth was already twisting into a smile, and soon their laughter was echoing down the passage outside.

# CHAPTER THREE

BORIS SIGHED AS he leaned back in the chair, closing his eyes as the supple leather took his weight. He'd scraped a living for far too many years to be an ostentatious man, but his chair was an indulgence he could not deny himself. It was an exquisite piece, and every component was a masterpiece on its own. Together, they made something extraordinary. He stretched out his fingers and ran them across the serpent's heads carved into the end of the arms, fingertips lingering on the precious stones that served as their eyes, so dark as to appear black, at least until they caught the light at just the right angle. It was as much art as it was furniture, and the price that the former owner must have paid for it was staggering to imagine. In truth, it was the only thing in his life that Boris hadn't weighed in terms of coin. The moment he saw it, he knew he had to have it, and the man who'd brought it to him had been canny enough to recognise that and gift it to him: in doing so, ensuring that he had Boris' support and friendship, and also keeping his own personal liver entirely knife free.

A short knock on the door broke his reverie and he reluctantly pulled himself free of the chair's embrace as the door swung open at a measured pace. He disliked loud noises as much as he did surprises, with either likely to fracture his mood and send it to the dark place. There was no good reason for it that he could recall, but his men knew him well enough to take care around him, a consideration he appreciated. It also meant that despite their activities late into the night, their neighbours never had any cause to complain.

He adjusted the lamp to spill some more light as Ratigan stepped in and pushed the door shut behind him. Few people knew him as Ratigan anymore though; from the first day they'd met Boris had dubbed him Ratty, and the name had stuck.

'Brought you some wine,' he said, setting a squat bottle and two glass cups down on the desk. 'And the count.' He reached into the ridiculous brocade jacket that he was wearing and dropped two folded sheets in front of Boris, who pushed them aside and reached for the dusty bottle instead.

'Very nice,' he said, fishing a small knife out of a drawer and setting to peeling the thick wax from the top. 'How're the figures?'

'Good, mostly.'

Boris raised an eyebrow but didn't say anything as he turned his attention to prying the cork out and sniffing it cautiously. He knew Ratty well enough to be patient, and in turn the lanky rogue knew him better than to try hide anything.

'I say mostly 'cos there's a bit of a problem,' Ratty said, picking at a loose thread on his sleeve. 'At Tulkauth. The figures are way down, and we have a few men off ill.'

'Tulkauth.' Boris filled their glasses and set the bottle down. 'It should have been a sure thing but I'm rapidly starting to think it's not worth the trouble. Is it corpsefly fever? We still have tonic in the stores.'

'Cheers,' Ratty said, raising his glass and taking a generous sip before hissing through the gap in his front teeth as the liquor lit a fiery trail down his throat. 'Looks a bit like it, but they're vomiting, not shitting themselves. The sawbones says it's some sort of magic disease.'

Boris lowered his glass and savoured the heat that radiated

outwards from his gut. It passed quickly, leaving a sweet and smoky taste. He smacked his lips in appreciation and topped up his glass only. It was some of the best he'd had, and he wasn't about to waste another glassful on Ratty's ungrateful palate.

'Where are they now?'

'I've put them in rooms at Sindy's and told the crew you've given them a few days off for finding good stuff.'

'Smart,' Boris said, genuinely pleased. His crew were loyal, but by the gods, they loved to gossip and it would be a merry hell getting them back to work if any word of a magic curse spread. He took another sip and unfolded the written report that Ratty had brought, scanning the neat columns, silently tallying the likely resale of them items noted. In another life a Cheriveni tax collector would have been proud to have him as a clerk, at least until his propensity for taking things that didn't belong to him manifested. He tapped a nail against an entry near the bottom.

'These three, they're the sick ones?' A nod in reply. 'I see you've marked their finds as junk?'

'It is. A few nice fittings, scrap gold, and a broken headpiece. Nothing much that doesn't need to be melted down first.'

'And that's all?' He took another sip and held the liquor in his mouth before swallowing, watching Ratty closely.

'That's it,' the man said, eyeing the bottle but taking no move towards it. He knew the look on Boris's face, and really didn't care to have it levelled at him. He carefully leaned forward. 'Slenn, he's the one in the middle there, he's got it by far the worst. He looks like one of them dead ones from the south. He hauled the most out, but I reckon that's all because he went into the centre. You know, where everything went boom.'

'What did he find?'

'Um, just junk I reckon.'

'In other words, you don't know.' He drummed his fingers on the desk and then stood up, enjoying how Ratty flinched.

'We're going to Sindy's, and I hope for your sake we don't then have to have a private conversation about your record keeping afterward.'

'Of course, boss. I mean, and no, of course not.'

SINDY'S WAS TYPICAL of the places that had sprung up since the war ended. With threat of annihilation at the hand of the Kinslayer gone, the yoke of fear that everyone had lived under became a torrid desire—a desperate need—to celebrate the life that had been returned to them, especially in towns that the shadow of war had fallen across directly. Boris slowed and took a moment to savour the sight that greeted him as he and Ratty emerged from a side street.

A few months ago the centre of Maybury had been a churned mass of mud bounded by empty, ransacked buildings, impassable save on foot and then only if you didn't mind losing a boot, if not both. Now it shone with vitality and life, the darkness driven away with gaily coloured lanterns hung on the overhanging porches and pools of amber light that spilled from shutters that were thrown wide, venting the sound of laughter and a score of shouted conversations into the street.

People attract people. It was a simple maxim, and he only wished that he'd taken it to heart far sooner than he had. But any regret that he felt was dampened by the knowledge that if he had, he would have lost so much more when the war came, rather than finding his fortune. He'd fought for everything he'd ever owned—which hadn't been much, at least not until the war had trampled over everything. Poverty, cunning, and an abusive father who took too long to drink himself to death had ensured that he would never stand on the right side of the law. He'd been hauled out of prison and conscripted into a company of the condemned when it all began and would probably have been crow food years ago if he hadn't taken a club to the head in his first battle.

He'd woken up amongst the heaped bodies of the fallen, some of whom were wearing fine armour and lucky rings and tokens, for all the good it had done them. Officially listed as dead, he'd thrown off his uniform and taken the name of his childhood cat, a scarred tom that had survived his father's every attempt to kill it out of sheer spite, and remade himself as a trader. The troubles were everywhere, and everyone wanted armour back then.

With law and order cracking under the horror that the war unleashed, those who had no reliance on those structures could thrive, and he had never been one to miss an opportunity.

And now, thanks to an abandoned town hall and its unguarded vault of land deeds, he was becoming a rich man. He didn't harbour any fantasies that he would ever be considered respectable by the monocle-wearing gentry, but being feared had much the same effect.

He nodded to Ratty, who was nervously twirling the threads he'd plucked from his sleeve, and headed across the road to the inn, smiling absently as he recognised the bawdy tune spilling from the windows. He acknowledged the handful of greetings from passers-by, most of whom hastily doffed their hats and continued on their way, not wanting to cause offence but also not wanting to be seen with him. He shook his head, wondering who they were trying to impress, and continued on his way, bypassing the main porch and stopping outside of a nondescript door set into the side of the inn with no handle. He rapped his cane on it, and before he could land a second blow a small panel opened and shut almost as quickly. Two heavy bolts were withdrawn and the door swung open revealing a stocky man with a scarred face and broken smile.

'Evening boss. Wasn't expecting you.'

'I thought I'd pop in and check on the boys,' he said. 'Which rooms are they in?'

'Two and four, boss.' He rubbed his hands. 'Slenn's in four. I have to warn you, he's in pretty bad shape.'

Boris put a hand on the doorman's shoulder. 'That's why I'm here,' he lied smoothly.

He'd never been one to rule by fear when it came to his own men. He'd worked for bullies in his time, mostly out of necessity, and there'd never been one he wouldn't have betrayed at the drop of a hat if he thought he could get away with it. Fear was necessary, but it needed to be tempered with loyalty to keep men together and bound to a purpose. No one wanted to betray their friends, nor the man who was looking out for them; but if one did, the others wouldn't feel aggrieved at the traitor's punishment because then the dirty spug had betrayed them too.

He made his way up the stairs and paused outside of Slenn's room, carefully schooling his features and steeling himself for whatever waited within. He knocked once, then opened the door.

Boris pressed his fingers against the leather satchel and felt the hard contour of the wooden case within, then hastily pulled them away again as if expecting to be scalded. He had no hard proof that it was the circlet that had inflicted such a cruel death on Slenn, but it had been clear from his broken testimony that it was the most likely culprit.

Telling Boris about it had cost Slenn the last of his strength. The effort he'd put into forming the words in between coughing up mouthfuls of blood had been too much, and at the end they could only watch him suffocate as the softened tissues of his throat eventually collapsed in on themselves.

It was a hard death to watch, let alone experience, and he'd been moved enough to waive the cost of the cremation from the balance that his widow owed for his rent, food, and palliative care. He adjusted his coat again and smiled at the man who had boarded the coach at the last stop, who gave the briefest of nods in reply before turning his attention back to the woman sitting alongside Boris, clearly oblivious to the fact that she was, in fact, his bodyguard for this little trip. He could sense Lona's amusement too, and settled back in his chair, grateful for the distraction after two days of staring out at grass and rocks and mentally putting a bet on how long it would take her natural demeanour to win through any residual novelty of being dressed as a lady. Anything that kept the images of Slenn's suppurating body at bay was welcome, no matter how forced.

At some point he managed to doze off, and was woken by a tap on his wrist. He blinked the dregs of an ill-formed dream from his eyes and sat up, clutching the edge of the seat as the candlelit interior of the coach came into focus, and with it the memory of where he was. His hand drifted to the satchel at his side.

'Don't worry, it's still there,' Lona said. 'We're coming up on Cinquetann.'

'About time too. I can feel every pebble and branch we're riding over and not in a good way.' He glanced at the man opposite, taking in the bloodied handkerchief clutched in his hand, and didn't bother trying to hide his smile. 'Got a bit bumpy there, didn't it?'

'I'll be reporting you both to the sheriff,' he said in a nasal voice. 'You'll—'

'Funny thing, war,' Boris interjected, leaning forward and letting the needle-like tip of his knife dig into the inside of the man's leg. 'It shortens tempers and desensitises men to things that would once have horrified them. Take, for example, a man's body found on the side of a road.'

'Terrible business,' Lona said, moving to sit next to the now-silent man and smiling as she dipped her hands into his pockets. 'But these days, who even cares? Especially if he has no name.' She lifted out a carefully folded travel permit and tucked it into her bodice before moving back to Boris' side. 'Terrible indeed, wouldn't you say?'

'Very,' came the reply, half gasped as the knife dug in. 'Please, I have a family.'

'I had one too,' Boris said. 'Until the likes of you left them to be slaughtered.'

'No, I haven't done anything,' he said, edging as far back as the stiff seat allowed. 'I won't say anything either, I swear.'

'If I have any trouble in town, even so much as someone spilling my drink, you will be the first to die. Do you understand?' A nod. 'Good. Now sit there and behave like a gentleman, eh?'

Boris sighed as he slipped the thin bladed knife back into the sheath along his forearm and sat back, marvelling at the weight that the altercation seemed to have lifted from his shoulders. He felt more at ease now, freed of the need to check his buttons every time the man glanced in his direction, and despite the long hours he'd spent on the coach, he really quite enjoyed the last hour of the journey.

It was still bitterly early when they reached the coach house, the sound of the metal rims meeting the cobblestones jarring after the bumps and creaks he'd become accustomed to. A groom opened the door and he stepped out, ignoring Lona's tut of annoyance. It was her place to go ahead of him, but this was Cinquetann, not a war-ravaged border town where every second man had a blade and a grudge, and appearances mattered. It was a different game, but one he'd played before.

He turned and helped Lona down the stairs, and was pleased to see that a convincingly demure smile had once again replaced her usual stony expression. In the soft morning light she was quite beautiful, and certainly enough to keep most of the grooms' attention on her, rather than him. It served her as well as it did him, for it took a rare and peculiar sort of man to look past all of that and see the knife before it struck.

He passed the driver and his mate a handful of coins and waved away their mock protest, and then did the same with the grooms who brought their baggage from the racks. As grand as any city was, it was the invisible people that kept everything moving, and if they were on your side, it opened a whole world of opportunities. For that reason he never moved against them, not directly, and operated with a generosity that was carefully calculated to be memorable but not suspicious.

Bags in hand, he led them from the coach house with a confident step that was the envy of many others who made their way along the poorly lit roads. He had no doubt that he was being watched and in truth would have been more surprised if he wasn't, but they reached the inn he sought without incident. He was well met and before too long they had secured rooms and he was enjoying a padded seat next to a carefully banked fire, while Lona paid for their supper and a single bottle of decent wine.

In the morning they'd head to the shop and present the circlet, and he'd need a clear head for that. He'd dealt with Catt and Fisher in person a few times when his men had recovered something particularly interesting, and he'd left each time unsure as to who had actually come out on top in their discussions. It always felt as if they were having four separate conversations at the same time, at least two of which he wasn't participating in.

This time would hopefully be different. He had a better grip on them now, and had written to them directly, suggesting that he had something which may be of interest but was clearly and obviously broken. He'd kept the language light, almost apologetic, and the speed with which he'd received the reply and invitation to visit had confirmed that he'd used the right bait. He smiled as he stared into the flames. If he played this right, they'd owe him a favour, and for what he had in mind, that was far more valuable than coin.

'FASCINATING, WOULDN'T YOU agree?' Fisher sat back and pushed the various lenses of the cumbersome spectacles he was wearing out of the way, blinking owlishly as his pale eyes refocused. He drummed his fingers on the edge of the table as Catt pulled the velvet cushion towards him, the broken circlet that rested upon it gleaming under the silvery light of the arcanist's lamp that hung above them like a trapped star. Which, Boris mused, it could well be.

Catt lifted his own set of spectacles, a less cumbersome contraption than Fisher had used, but still impressive in that the lenses seemed to move by themselves.

'Did you see it?' pressed Fisher, moving to lean over Catt's shoulder. 'The arcs?'

'Perhaps I could if you weren't breathing on my neck and blocking my light.'

'Don't be so fussy,' said Fisher, looking to Boris as he rolled his eyes.

'So, it is of interest then?' Boris asked. They'd been taking 'a quick look' long enough that the tea they'd offered him had a skin across it and the lantern had brightened to offset the dimming light outside. He briefly wondered how Lona was coping, but then dismissed the thought as Catt lowered his spectacles too.

'Well, it is an interesting piece,' Catt admitted. 'An antiquarian curiosity, in the vernacular.'

'Broken though,' added Fisher, pursing his lips. 'Terrible shame that.'

'Such a shame,' agreed Catt. 'Rendered entirely non functional, its magic squandered. It's clearly not much use to anyone now.'

Boris kept his expression carefully neutral. 'But of course you already knew that from the description in my letter.'

'Quite,' agreed Fisher. 'But words are one thing, and seeing it is another.'

'Are you telling me this was a wasted journey then?'

'Not at all,' said Fisher. 'Travel is a tonic for the mind, and it's still a fascinating piece. The workmanship is certainly not

Yorughan: the internal structure is far too delicate for that, which begs the question of where it came from.'

'Quite right,' Catt added. 'The Kinslayer was quite the collector in his own brutish way, with fingers in all sorts of pies, as the saying goes. I'm afraid we may never know the provenance of this piece. Which pie it came from, in other words. We've not been able to find any information about Tulkauth, other than someone applying for a mining licence there. Tin, I believe. And when it comes to military records, it seems even the most paltry trinket or shiny bauble prompts the chronicler to plaster the title of sorcerer upon the wielder of said trinket. It's quite ridiculous.'

'If you've read the accounts, then you know whoever or whatever wore that certainly wasn't some apprentice,' Boris replied. 'My men dug it out of a crater, and whatever force that was held within it was still potent enough to cause them some health issues.'

'Perhaps, if that conjecture holds true, but provenance aside, I'm afraid it's no more than broken jewellery now.'

'I'm afraid you're both quite wrong,' Boris said, falling into their way of speaking with the ingrained habit of many years. He couldn't help the smile that tugged at his lips in response to their puzzled expressions. He held up a finger to silence the protest that was already on Catt's lips, which earned him a raised eyebrow. He had hoped that the circlet would have reacted to their examination, saving him from having to do what he was about to do, but they seemed entirely fixed in their opinion that it was essentially a junk piece. And he hadn't travelled that far, and at that expense, simply to be dismissed like some naive mudlark.

He tugged his gloves back on as they watched, licked his lips, then reached over and lifted the circlet from its box. Carefully, with slow and gradual pressure, he eased the two broken ends towards each other. At first, nothing happened, as it had when he'd first asked the jeweller in Maybury to attempt a repair. The resultant reaction had stripped the flesh from several of the man's fingers, and he had no inclination to share the same fate.

He felt the first vibration through the metal soon after, a brief flutter, as if he'd caught a moth in an open fist. It strengthened almost immediately, and he touched the bottom of the circlet to the table, letting them hear it. Both were leaning forward, and the only sound aside from the tapping of the circlet was the soft clicking as they both flipped the lenses on their spectacles. He kept the pressure steady, and a heartbeat later an arc of plum-coloured energy leapt from one end to the other, stabilising for the briefest of moments into a twisting helix before snapping back out of existence.

Boris released the pressure and did his best not to simply drop it onto the table, but as clumsy as he was, neither of the other men at the table noticed; both were staring at the circlet, their lips pursed. He tossed the gloves aside and hastily checked his fingers, a sigh of relief escaping him as they all reported for duty.

'Fascinating,' Catt said. 'It's broken, but yet it retains a charge of some sort.'

'But is it a charge?' asked Fisher. 'Or perhaps a chemical reaction in the metal?'

Both flinched dramatically as Boris flipped the lid of the box shut.

'But as it's of no interest and I have other parties to visit, I shall not detain you any longer. Thank you both for your time.'

Fisher's hand shot out to grab his, quicker than he thought the old man possible of. He glanced up, startled, and saw something like embarrassment flicker across the doctor's face as he let go just as quickly. Boris patted the box and pursed his lips, as if considering the choice that he didn't actually have.

'Should you wish to examine it further, perhaps we should discuss value?'

'Of the monetary kind?' Catt actually looked affronted.

'The very same. While I share your curiosity, I am not running a museum, nor a charity.'

'Of course, of course. Would you excuse us? We need to discuss these matters.'

'Of course, gentlemen. I might have a look at your showroom.'

Catt moved to the pull the heavy curtain that separated the office from the front of their shop to the side, nodding to Boris as he passed.

'We won't be long, I'm sure. Oh, and please don't touch anything.'

THE SHELVES WEREN'T very interesting, and at least a third of the pieces that drew his interest were items he had sold on, either directly or by way of subsidiaries that he used to simulate competition. Only two other people knew of their association with him, and even they didn't know the whole truth, which was how he preferred it. It was a tricky balance to strike: staying distant enough that no one pieced it together, while also keeping a careful eye on progress to keep his apparent opposition in check and free of any notion that decisions were theirs alone to make.

'Are they nearly finished?' Lona asked from her perch in the deeper shadows as he stepped outside for some much-needed fresh air.

'Well, we've finally got to the subject of a price if that helps.'

'Gods.' He didn't need to see her to know she was rolling her eyes. 'I tell you what, if another of these so-called gentlemen offers to walk me to my lodgings I may just say yes. Sitting on a barrel for four hours isn't as much fun as it sounds.'

'You can practise your lurking.'

'I don't lurk,' she said, cracking her neck from side to side. 'I loom.'

'Well, we're both still alive, so keep it up.' He fished a flask from his coat and unstoppered it in one motion. 'Drink?'

'Maybe later.'

'Suit yourself,' he said, taking a long swallow and smacking his lips in appreciation.

'They're back in the room,' she said.

He looked over his shoulder and caught a glimpse of the curtain swaying through the small window.

'I'll finish as quickly as I can.'

'Promises, promises.'

He went back into the shop and sat back down in his chair, his expression once again entirely neutral.

'How is your companion?' asked Catt. 'She is of course most welcome to take a seat inside.'

'She's fine,' he said. 'If I made her come inside, she'd only spend her time pacing up and down, or touching those fine pieces on display.'

For a moment Catt looked like he was going to say something, but instead he only smiled at Boris, holding his gaze for a moment longer than was comfortable. He wanted to ask what the matter was, but Fisher was already talking and he found himself trying to catch up with the stream of words instead.

'Which of course means that it's not likely to be something we could trade or sell on, you understand? It's a curiosity, and a dangerous one for sure, and it needs a professional touch to be kept safe. To protect the man in the street, if you would. If you follow me, as I am sure a gentleman of your quality certainly would, then you understand that it is tantamount to being our duty to relieve you of the responsibility and render it safe.' He spread his hands and gave an apologetic shrug. 'You do understand, don't you?'

'It was a long and tiring journey, and the night is drawing in. Perhaps you could summarise it for me.'

'We'll proceed with the acquisition,' Catt said, still watching Boris and ignoring the exaggerated look that Fisher shot him.

'Less a modest fee for our services,' Fisher added.

'A fee?'

'To be deducted from the price we agree. For making it safe, you see. A dangerous business this.'

Boris fought the urge to rub his forehead and instead settled for folding his arms. 'Do you have a net figure in mind?'

'Indeed we do,' Fisher said, opening a thin, leather-bound ledger and turning it as he slid it across to Boris, who scanned the neat columns before tapping a finger on the total at the bottom of the page.

The truth was that he had no idea how much a broken trinket like that was worth, and he could only compare it to something of equal weight that they'd paid what he thought was a very fair price for in the recent past. The figure they were proposing wasn't far off that, even allowing for the ridiculous costs they'd deducted, a clever mechanism to argue that they had in fact offered a higher price and setting out the reasons why they couldn't negotiate a higher value, all in one neat package. He pursed his lips, then tapped a figure on one of the deductions.

'You're deducting carriage costs? I have delivered it to you at my expense.'

'Have we?' Fisher asked, turning the ledger around to face him again. 'My apologies, it's a typical cost for us. If I add that back in, can we mark it as agreed?'

'An honest mistake,' Boris said, a wry smile pulling at his lips. 'And yes, we can proceed.'

'Capital,' Fisher said, smiling. 'We knew you were a gentleman of reason and quality, didn't we, Doctor Catt?'

'Indeed we did,' said Catt, inclining his head. 'Indeed we did. I'll draw up the banker's draft directly, if you will excuse me.'

'And I shall get us some sherry, to toast another successful venture,' Fisher added.

It was another hour before Boris finally stepped back out into the night, pausing at the doorway to draw in a great lungful of the cool air to try displace the sherry fumes that seemed to have taken hold of him.

'You alright there, boss?' asked Lona, hopping down from her barrel.

'Yes, I'm fine. It's all done.' He didn't pat the pocket where the promissory note sat in case someone was watching, but he could feel the stiff paper against his chest. 'Just had to have a drink with them to seal the deal.'

'Right you are. Let's get you back to the inn.'

'Food first, I think.'

Neither of them looked back, and even if they had, chances were they would have missed the face watching from the edge of the window.

'I STILL THINK you've overpaid for it,' Catt said, twirling a small crystal glass in front of an unwavering flame, a dozen prisms playing across the planes of his face.

'It's only money,' Fisher said, draining his own glass without much ado. 'If he's satisfied that he's got a good deal, he's both going to forget about it and be motivated to find something even more interesting. And in his defence, it has been a fairly fruitful partnership so far.'

'The man is a thug.'

'A surprisingly useful thug, and his manners improve each time we see him.' He set the glass down. 'Besides, I know you saw it too.'

'No, we both think we saw something that could be a planar echo. Don't forget that some oaf chopped in half. Those sparks could simply be a symptom of an imminent and quite catastrophic collapse.'

'Precisely. To enable that sort of energy surge when the circuit is broken, it must be drawing power from somewhere. Even the Kinslayer's crown couldn't have functioned after a blow like that. It's fascinating.'

'And dangerous. If it is planar in origin, do you have any idea what it's collapse would look like?' He raised a finger to forestall Fisher's reply. 'And if it is drawing power, it is doing so unpredictably. The discharge could be anything from a mere spark to something that could erase this city.'

Fisher pursed his lips in thought as he refilled both their glasses. 'We'll have to be very careful.' He smiled suddenly. 'At least we didn't have it resting on our lap for three days in a coach.'

A smile creased Catt's face as he raised his glass. 'Absolutely, my dear Fisher.'

# CHAPTER FOUR

'THEY'VE BEEN WASHED, so stop whining.'

'They're still dead men's clothes. It's not right,' Tomas grumbled, not looking up and so missing the archer rolling his eyes. 'I could get better stuff, not goddamned grave goods. We're begging for a curse, wearing these.'

'You seemed happy enough to collect armour from the quartermaster. Where do you think the surplus came from?' asked Orec, who was actually quite pleased with what Hayden had managed to scavenge. 'There's no difference.'

'Well, if anyone's going to be haunted, it would be you,' Stefan added. 'It's a fact that thinking about spirits draws them to you like stale breath does mosquitoes.'

'That's not true,' Tomas replied, pausing at the last button of his shirt. 'And what do you know of such things anyway?'

'I was going to be a priest before all this happened,' the young standard bearer replied, gesturing vaguely to the bulk of the requisitioned hospital. 'It's one of the first things we learned.'

'Bollocks.'

'Not talking about it all the time couldn't hurt though,' offered Hayden from his perch on a nearby crate, studiously avoiding looking anywhere near Stefan's infectious grin. 'Better safe than sorry.'

'I'm just saying, it's not right.'

'It's what we have, so we'll work with it,' Orec said. 'Longshot's done well to scrounge all of this. And it actually fits, which is more than anything we were offered in the last three years, so quit griping.'

'Before you bring the spirits down on all of us,' added Stefan, earning a glare from Orec.

'How's the food situation?' Orec continued, turning to Hayden.

'Good news, and some not so good.'

Orec folded his arms. 'Sweet before savoury for me.'

'The kitchens are still receiving supplies based on full wards, so there's a plenty in the stores, even after the staff have helped themselves.' He hopped off the crate and lifted the lid, revealing four marching packs inside. 'The downside is that most of it is fresh, rather than trail friendly. We've got enough for three, maybe four days. After that's it's foraging or buying stuff from towns.'

Tomas folded his arms. 'By foraging you mean your usual war effort of stealing chickens at night?'

Orec ignored him and lifted out one of the packs, opening the top and peering inside. 'Everything's in waxed cloth?' he asked.

'I repurposed some of the original packaging. Figured this time of year we're bound to be rained on sooner rather than later.'

'Very good.' Orec smiled and closed the pack. 'So, we have four days to disappear.'

'Four's plenty,' Hayden said. 'There are four viable routes out of here, so we've already got a one in four chance of losing them.'

'More like three days,' Tomas said, the words muffled by the hangnail he was trying to bite off. 'Remember Stef's a cripple.'

'Get stuffed,' Stefan said, but his words had little venom behind them. His leg was gone, and even with the improvements that Orec had made to the stump, the thought of walking on it day in and day out set a cold sweat beading across all of him. The truth was that he was a cripple.

'You're being a dick about it, but sadly you do have a point,' Orec said. 'Until we can get him a decent leg we'll have to pick our paths with a bit more care.'

'Or you can leave me here, sarge. It's not like they'll be sending me on anywhere else. They'll get around to letting me go eventually and I'm sure I can hop on a wagon or something.'

'No,' Orec said, almost cutting Stef off. 'No. We all go together, or we don't go.'

Even Tomas knew better than to say anything in the silence that followed. He'd heard that tone before and had no inclination to face what would follow after.

'Sarge, I—'

Hayden stepped forward and laid his hand on the his shoulder. 'The sarge is right. We all go together. The weather's been alright, and the path is firm. You'll be fine with the leg, especially with the new crutch. And besides, Tom will be carrying your pack.'

'The hell I will.'

'The hell you won't,' Orec replied, steel still in his voice. 'He's your brother.'

'My crippled brother,' he amended, then raised his hands in a gesture of peace as Orec's gaze pinned him to the spot. 'Alright, calm down, I'm just joking around. It's not like anyone here's going to chase us anyway. The war's over, and I can't see a bunch of nurses charging after us.'

'Probably not,' Hayden said. 'But since when did the army make any sense?'

'Amen to that,' Stef said. 'They'd probably looking to charge me for losing a boot.'

Orec's smile matched theirs as the tension in the room fractured. 'Pursuit or not, we're going home.'

'I'll drink to that,' Hayden said.

'Maybe try pick a path with a decent inn at the end,' Tomas said. 'I'll even let you buy the first round.'

'So, when do we go?' Stef asked.

'After the bed check tonight,' Orec said, setting the pack back in the crate. 'Get your kit together, keep it ready for Hayden's call. We'll meet here.'

He waited until the others had left, not hearing whatever new complaint that Tomas was trying to get the others to agree to, and made his way towards the gardens. They'd been churned into a morass by the cavalry when they'd first arrived, the formal arrangements quickly vanishing into an indistinguishable muddy mass, and remained that way for some time after the army moved off. But the dung had at least also fed the ground, and with boredom clawing at so many of the injured, it had become something of a shared project to restore them, albeit with a more practical purpose. He sat down on one of the rebuilt benches and stretched his legs out. Spring had returned, and the green of young life was dotting the plants and filling the air with the scent of turned earth.

The gardens would never be the same as they were before, but they were alive. Scarred, but alive. *Like me,* he thought quietly. He too carried his fair share of scars, but felt no shame about them. They had all been earned honourably, and he remembered the story of each one vividly, and if he traced them with his fingers he could see the men and beasts who'd inflicted them. They were all dead now, their bodies rotting in the ground or scattered by the winds.

He rubbed at the crescent that marked the back of his right hand like a moon tattooed in silver and smiled, but not at the memory of the Yogg who'd sliced him to the bone. It was more at the thought that Martina would like it; she always did like the moonlight, and always insisted on going for a night walk under the full moon.

'I'm coming home,' he said, the words escaping his lips

before he'd even realised he'd said it. He closed his eyes and saw again the long path to their cottage, mentally following its meandering track to their door and watching it open. It was a daydream that had kept him sane far too many times for him to count over the recent years, a private refuge that was his and his alone, and the thought that he would be playing it out in real life sent a sort of jittery excitement through him that he hadn't felt since he'd first worked up the courage to ask her to accompany him to the fair.

His smile faded as he remembered that day, or more accurately, the younger man who'd sweated so profusely before clumsily daring to take her hand. He didn't recognise that man with his thick waist and rosy cheeks, nor could he picture him leading a hundred men into battle. His smile faded as the excitement within him withered into something bitter and sadly too familiar. That man was who she remembered, so what would she make of the scarred brute who wore his face now? Physical scars were one matter, but like the others, he didn't carry all of his scars upon his skin.

Why would she welcome such a man into her home? She had tearfully waved a carpenter named Orec Martinsson off to war, but what would she make of Orec Blackblade returning home? A sense of dread rose within him, but he ruthlessly quashed it. Thinking of such things was a pointless exercise. He'd seen stronger men eaten away on the inside by fears that they had no control over, and had long since disciplined himself against it. He forced the fear down and buried it with the rest of its kind. He'd find out soon enough, and what would happen, would happen. She was his everything, and he would do whatever it took to work through it.

He stood up and took one last look at the garden he'd help plant, then turned on his heel and headed indoors. It was time to go home.

OREC DRESSED IN the dark, and even after the month of inactivity, his fingers didn't fumble once as he buckled his harness on. He could hear the soft clink of the others doing the same around him, each working quietly and efficiently. The long rest and good food had left its mark though, and he had to pause and let the straps out by another notch before reaching for the leather-wrapped shape waiting at the end of the bed.

He rested his fingers on it, hesitating for a moment, then undid the bindings and unwrapped the sword. The mottled scabbard was sturdy but plain, unadorned by decoration, the only patterns upon it of the accidental sort caused by blood flying amidst the heat of battle. The sword itself was another matter. The hand guard was plain enough, two tapering steel bars, notched from use, protecting a handle of greyed leather bound with wire and capped with a gleaming black pommel. He slowly slid a few inches of the sword out, telling himself it was just to make sure that it wasn't sticking after neglected for so long. The charcoal-coloured blade emerged without much resistance, the silvery sheen of the cutting edge gleaming against the thundercloud hue of the steel. He exhaled slowly and slid it home again, then rested it on his legs.

He'd never found out the name of the man who'd given it to him, but that didn't stop him from lighting the occasional candle in his memory. He'd only found him because he'd vaulted over a fallen horse to evade a volley of crossbow bolts, half sinking into the mud that waited on either side of the causeway and making himself as small as possible as the bolts slammed into the dead flesh. It was only when he opened his eyes that he saw the man's face looking at him from the muddy waters, moments away from being dragged completely under by the weight of his archaic armour.

'I'm sorry, brother,' he'd said to the man, knowing he couldn't reach him in time, and certainly not without catching a bolt in the back.

The man had only nodded, the water already bubbling around his nostrils, and with what must have been a superhuman effort, pulled his arm free of the cloying mud and held his sword out to Orec, hilt first.

Orec had stared at him for a long moment, and even now he remained in awe of the calm courage in the dying man's pale eyes. Even though he was moments from a horrible death, there was no fear in those pale eyes. It had felt as if the dying knight was looking *into* him, not just at him and in that moment, Orec felt unworthy, and his face had burned with the shame of his own cowardice. All he wanted to do was be worthy of respect in those eyes.

He didn't look away as he reached out for the sword, not even when a bolt missed his head by mere inches, and not until the face had entirely vanished into the bloody waters.

The encounter had taken mere moments, but had felt more solemn than any ceremony he'd ever attended. The warrior's calm dignity had become a touchstone for him, and when he held the sword, it was never far from his mind. Fear lost its grip on him when he held it, and the keen blade had saved his life more than once. Together it was a debt he could never repay, save to honour the memory and try to live up to the quiet awe that it still engendered. It was the standard that he judged himself by, to make himself worthy of the gift he had been given.

He dispelled the memory with a shake of his head and quickly strapped the sword on, the weight and feel of it instantly familiar and reassuring. He coaxed a single candle back to life with an ember from the fireplace and checked the footlocker and bed one last time before snuffing it out. It was time.

He set the candle down and turned away, picking his way between the cots at the end of the room, the snores of the men there masking his footsteps. He stepped outside, scanning the area for any guards but finding none, and as much of a relief that it was, it angered him as well. The war was over insomuch as the Kinslayer was dead, but it was complacency of the worst kind to assume that everything had suddenly gone back to normal. His legions had scattered, not disappeared, and it would be long years of work before they were all hunted down and eradicated once and for all.

Which was precisely the sort of mission and commitment he wanted to avoid. He had left home to in a naive quest to seek vengeance for his brothers' deaths, and he had spilled enough blood to fill both their graves many times over. That thirst had long since been slaked, and he only wanted peace.

The others stepped out behind him, moving as cautiously as he had, but then straightening as they too took in the empty grounds.

'You couldn't keep a cow out of this place,' muttered Tomas.

'Or good men inside it,' answered Hayden. 'Nor even the likes of you.'

'Quiet,' Orec admonished them before Tomas could reply. Hayden could tell him that the sky was blue on a summer's day and the axe man would still argue with him. Loudly. 'Let's move.'

They saw two guards on their way to the meeting point, each carrying their spears like hoes, and talking loud enough to provide even the clumsiest attacker with ample warning of their presence. He hadn't realised that he was staring at them until Hayden tapped his arm.

'Not our problem today, sarge.'

'Let's go before they hear you grinding your teeth,' added Tomas, unwilling to let the archer have the last word.

Orec snorted and moved across the final stretch of yard in one burst and quickly opened the door to the supply shed, the others on his heels.

'Stef?' he asked into the darkness, but no reply came, prompting a curse from Tomas.

'He's probably got caught with that leg and all.'

'Not helpful,' Hayden replied. 'Remember, he's coming around from the east wing. We've got time.'

'My thoughts too. Get the packs ready in the meantime,' Orec said.

'Do I really have to carry his as well?'

'Since I knew you'd whinge about it, I redistributed his across the three,' Hayden replied. 'That way even you can manage the extra weight.'

'How do I know you didn't put extra in mine?'

'Suck it up,' Orec said, holding the door open and peering out across the moonlit yard. 'You carry it, or you find your own food.'

'No need get testy about it,' came the muttered reply. 'I'm just saying—'

'I see him,' Orec said with no little relief. He'd had his doubts about Stefan despite the work he'd seen him do to try and get used to his wooden leg. It was a rare day that he hadn't finish his day's exercises with a grey face and sweat-soaked shirt. But here he was, moving carefully from shadow to shadow, quiet despite the crutch he was using. Orec opened the door and waved him inside, where Hayden and Tomas boisterously welcomed him.

'Alright, calm down,' Orec said. 'It's almost time. Is everyone clear on the route and rally points? I'm not expecting anyone to get separated, but who knows with you lot.'

'Side gate by the elm, stay on the path for two miles straight,' Hayden started.

'Right at the crossroads with the grave marker, then straight on again, keeping the river to the right,' Stef continued, then looked to Tom.

'This is stupid,' he said, folding his arms. 'We all know the route and we're not going to be chased.'

'Humour me,' Orec replied, waving Hayden to silence. For a moment it looked like Tomas was going to dig his heels in, but then he shrugged. 'Move through the woods, two left forks and then the right. Rally at an old well. There, happy now?'

'That's the longest I've ever heard you speak without complaining about something,' Hayden said.

'Screw you.'

'Stow the bickering, both of you. I'm not getting slammed into a military prison because you turned out to be fishwives disguised as soldiers.'

For several long heartbeats the only sound was the shuffle of moving feet, but then Stef spoke up from his seat near the door. 'Mind you, Tom would be quite fetching in a sundress.'

'Screw you, cripple,' he replied, but there was no venom behind his words.

'How about you get those well-turned calves to leaving,' Orec said. 'Hayden, you lead.' He didn't bother waiting for a response and slung his pack over his shoulders, the too narrow strap almost immediately uncomfortable. Behind him the others followed suit, save for Stef who was only carrying a sling bag with a leather tube protruding from it.

He stepped back out into the night air and felt a familiar thrill coursing through his veins, and with it the heaviness fell from his limbs. He took a deep breath and, without a backward glance, moved off along the side of the building, pausing only to check that the guards were still where he expected them to be before racing to the gate in a crouched run.

It opened silently on lard-greased hinges, courtesy of Hayden and his midnight visits to the kitchens, and he quickly moved through, pausing a few feet along the path while the others caught up with him, impressively quiet after their long convalescence. The gate was closed just as quietly and Hayden made his way past Orec, checking the string of his longbow.

When he was thirty paces ahead, Orec moved off after him, staying low until they had at least two hundred yards of shrubs and hedge between them and the perimeter of the hospital. He knew he was quite likely being overcautious, but they had a long road ahead and it would be hard enough to keep a standard of vigilance until the end already without eroding that discipline right from the start. He'd happily trade their complaints for reaching home in one piece any and every day.

CATT SET HIS glass of wine down and stared at the book in front of him, not really seeing the neat writing or even the elaborate drawings that decorated half of the page. It was a masterpiece, both as an object of art and in its content; the philosophies set out within radical enough to have seen the writer executed barely two centuries past, but still volatile enough to ruin friendships. And yet he'd been reading the same page for what felt like hours.

He closed the book and pushed it away. His heart just wasn't in it, nor in the other half a dozen or so ongoing projects dotted around his desk, each a silent reminder of his tardiness.

He took another sip of the wine, forcing himself to savour the taste of it. That he could still do, but it was clear that something was upsetting his humours. He knew what it was, of course, but he'd expressly promised not to do anything with it until Fisher was back. It shouldn't have been that much of a bother to him, but ever since he could remember he'd always wanted to know how things worked. He swirled the remaining wine in the glass and smiled as he remembered his father's incandescent rage when he'd discovered his son sitting amongst a starburst of cogs and lever springs, the automaton that he was proudly expecting to show off at that night's dinner lying gutted before him. It was the one time that he'd seen his father properly angry, his scholarly discipline forgotten for a few terrifying, speechless moments. He'd been unable to reassemble it, of course, a child's enthusiastic curiosity being no match for the work of master craftsman—all of which had first led to a truly miserable week of utter dejection, and then to a burning drive to discover more.

And he had come a long way since then, and had in his time

rebuilt a handful of automatons for grateful customers, the satisfaction it gave him even more welcome than the invoice he submitted for his services. The truth of it was that he was something of a master craftsman now himself, and a scholar too, and the more he thought about it, the more unseemly the idea of having to wait until Fisher's return felt. He was no apprentice needing a chaperone to observe and tut at him. And besides, he wasn't about to wear the circlet, simply examine it and make some preliminary notes on his observations. If anything, it was the proper way of doing things and would provide a suitable foundation for further investigations.

'Why yes, I think that's very proper indeed,' he said, tipping his now empty glass towards the carefully preserved head of a three-eyed serpent in a mock salute. 'And yes, I shall of course take every precaution.'

He took a moment to refill his glass, then made his way to the furthest corner of the back room. His hand found the switch almost of its own accord and the stone wall in front of him shimmered and faded away, exposing an ornately carved door. It was older than the city and the potential locked within the swirling runes carved by its unknown creators was still palpable. It opened at his touch and swung shut as easily behind him even as a warm white light filled the room, the faint thud of its closing giving no hint of the insurmountable effort it would take for the uninvited to open it again.

The room itself was unremarkable once you looked past the rune that marked each and every stone in the walls. *Spia*. Strength. A spell so simple that even a child could understand it, but effective nonetheless. They'd both seen their share of mishaps over the years, and that the room even existed was testament to that. As their collection grew, so did the chance of encountering something malicious or, as it was now, broken and dangerous.

He lifted the box from a shelf and set it down on the single, sturdy workbench in the centre, then set down his notebook and writing set. He opened the box slowly, relieved to see the circlet lying inert and cold within. Looking at it now it was hard to imagine it was anything special, but his instincts were saying something entirely different. He dipped the quill and began his notes, handwriting as steady as ever. The first task would be to record its appearance, and with that in mind he lifted it out of the box and began the painstaking but entirely satisfying business of sketching the band, noting every mark that adorned it and unconsciously tutting when came to the break, the flared edges almost vulgar in contrast to the intricate workmanship that led up to it.

He turned the band to better follow the tiny symbols that wove around it like a vine around a pillar, his focus fixed on not losing his place in the sequence, and in so doing twisted it further and further, so much that he needed to rest it on the table to get a better grip. He almost had the last few that hadn't been ruined, and as he pressed in he felt the circlet shiver in his grasp, the faintest of tremors that he would never have perceived had his attention not been so intently fixed upon it. He flinched back as a flicker of violet light no thicker than a hair arced between the two broken edges, an even finer filament branching off and striking his closest finger.

*The room vanished, and another world rose around him, a world of towering stone pillars rising into a titanic thunderstorm above, where clouds the size of continents were lit from within by the same violet light.*

It was there and gone again before he could finish blinking, the circlet rattling on the table before settling again like a flicked coin, the sound of it almost as loud as his breathing. He rubbed his blessedly unmarked finger and took a slower, steadying breath.

Then he reached for the quill, but hesitated. It should be recorded, but the thought of Fisher's admonishment loomed large, and the idea of handing him the moral advantage was quite insufferable. He drummed his fingers on the table, equally curious and wary about touching it again, but in the end curiosity won, as it so often did. He would finish his observations, and if it happened again, he would note it down.

He reached for the circlet gingerly, but it was cold and still again, and he lifted it carefully, slowly turning it until he found the last mark he'd noted. He glanced at the journal and then mouthed a short, bitter curse. A forked scorch mark marred his careful sketch, the blackened edges curled and the damage quite permanent. He stared at the page for a few more moments, lips pursed in irritation, but there was no saving it. He cursed as he carefully cut the page out and tossed it aside.

It was nearly dawn before he'd finished, but the annoyance of losing his first draft had long since been swallowed by the gentle pleasure of study. It was only once he'd finished and had stretched the kinks out of his back that his mind returned to the vision that he'd glimpsed; it was still quite vivid in his memory, the shadowy outlines imprinted in a hundred shades of purple. Violet, he corrected himself. He'd never seen anything like it, and to have visualised something like that was quite beyond the scope of his imagination.

He lifted the circlet and turned it over and over in his hands, taking care not to bring the broken edges too close to each other. It fascinated him how something that was so undeniably broken, and which had no right to be anything more than an interesting artefact, could still be so potent.

He ran his finger along the inside of the crown and the paused. There! He moved his finger back until he found it again. A tiny prong of sorts, except this wasn't some defect created by the explosion or its rough excavation. It was deliberate, as was the matching mark on the opposite side. Small, but sharp, like tiny teeth which would bite into any scalp it was placed on.

He rubbed his finger again and sat back as an idea took shape in his mind. He'd seen such things before in simple enchanted items, mostly weapons, which would lay inert until they were taken up. With its workmanship and provenance, he'd simply assumed a level of sophistication about it, but what if the opposite were true? What if wearing it was enough to complete the pathway? Both times that he'd seen it do something had been when someone was holding it.

There was, of course, an easy way to prove his theory. It carried a risk, but he was wearing both Ankov's Protective Pendant and the Redstone bracelet, each an effective layer of protection in their own right, and the fact of the matter was that whether Fisher was there or not, the only way they were ever going to learn more about it was by testing it. A simple test would suffice, enough to prove he was correct, and then he could present his findings with suitable authority.

'It's an entirely reasonable course of action,' he said, setting the circlet down in front of him. With exaggerated care he reached down and deliberately pinched each of the broken ends. He felt it buzz under his fingers, and had enough time to muse that it was no worse than he'd expected before he fell through the world.

THERE WAS NO transition that Catt was aware of. He inhaled the air of the secure room, and exhaled the same breath into a dark and jagged world, surrounded by monolithic spears of rock that skewered the black mass of cloud above. The only light came from the arcing bands of violet light that pulsed their way down those same spears of black rock, dimming with each leap until they reached the gravelly surface he was now standing on, whereupon they flashed one last time and sent a new pulse of light rippling outwards through the equally black gravel that covered the surface.

He took a cautious breath, mostly as a gasp of astonishment, and bent over coughing as the alien vapours filled his lungs, leaving a distinct metallic tang that quickly became almost unbearable. But he wasn't dead, and more pointedly, he'd somehow had the presence of mind not to release his grip on the circlet. Even as he took a first, wobbly step backwards and looked around him he could feel the sharp edges of the torn metal between his fingers, buzzing against the tips like trapped bees.

He looked down and saw the circlet in his hands, now glowing like molten gold, the only steady light that he could see. He kicked a leg out, half expecting to feel it connect with the table he'd been sat at, but instead he only stumbled forward. *This isn't a vision,* he thought. *I'm not in Cinquetann. I'm actually here, wherever* here *is.*

An apocalyptic blast of thunder on a scale he'd never experienced before shook the world around him, lifting gravel three feet in the air while nearly throwing him to the ground, and as he regained his balance he looked up and watched as violet lightning surged across the sky in a tidal wave of elemental power. He shook his head as the sound rolled away into the unfathomable distance and turned to watch it pass.

That's when he saw it for the first time, even though he dismissed it as the flicker of a shadow thrown by the flickering lightning. That illusion lasted until it appeared again on the other side of the pillar, a dark shape moving in obvious defiance of the rules of light. He squinted at it, trying to make sense of the triangular shape, then gasped as eyes the same colour as the circlet blinked open, suddenly giving perspective to the tapering predator's snout that was pointed right at him. The taste of metal was sharp and bitter, burning his throat and chest and he staggered back as a coughing fit seized him, feet sliding and sinking into the gravelly surface and making him stumble.

He kept his arms close to his chest as he fell, pinching the circlet even tighter lest it be jarred from his grip. He twisted, looking over his shoulder just in time to see the creature emerge from behind the pillar, tall and sinuous, like a centaur whose equine part had been replaced by that of a long-legged crocodile. It was watching him with quick, birdlike movements as he pushed himself to his knees.

*No*, he thought, *it's not watching me, it's watching the circlet*. Fear offered his curiosity a brief struggle and then he was lifting it, watching as the creature's gaze followed the glowing ring. It bent low, and for a moment he thought it was bowing, but then it hissed and shook its head violently from side to side, like an angry dog trying to shake off its leash. In his hands the circlet trembled and a long arc of that cursed violet light leapt between it and the beast with a sharp crack. He could feel the metal growing hot under his fingers, which was never a good sign with artifacts, let alone damaged ones—but he was so close to understanding the puzzle!

The creature, whatever it was, dashed across the uncertain surface as if it were a paved road, a tapering tail whipping behind it, and was upon him before he could do more than think about standing, let alone running, the wind of its arrival carrying the scent of ozone and ocean spray, oddly pleasant despite the terror that now gripped him.

Its head tilted to the side, giving him a view of the altogether vicious teeth that lined its jaw, at which point he released his grip on one side of the circlet and watched the fabric of the world tear open next to him, the familiar lines of the secure room visible between its tattered edges.

The predator lunged for him but he leapt away, diving through the glowing rift as if it was a pool rather than a gateway to another world. There was moment of infinite cold and then he was rolling across floorboards rather than the midnight black gravel, with air that now tasted sweet filling him. He rolled awkwardly, then turned and edged backwards to stare at the violet-edged scar that marked the opposite wall like the pupil of a monstrous, disembodied cat's eye.

He spotted the circlet a moment later, laying several feet away, its glow diminished by the brighter lights but still very much evident, curls of smoking smoke rising from the scorched floorboard beneath it. The tear in the wall crackled and a black shape dropped from it, falling to the floor in a heap of sharp angles, dark enough that it seemed to defy the light, making it impossible to discern one part from another save for its molten eyes.

Catt could see those clear enough as he scrabbled towards the door, unwilling to turn his back on it but desperate to put eight inches of ensorcelled iron wood between them. In the confines of the room the creature seemed far larger than it had in that strange landscape, and the claws it dug into the floorboards looked as long and keen as razors. The kite-shaped head swung towards him and he felt the strange chill of its utterly alien gaze, if only for a moment. He reached up and pulled himself up by the door handle.

Ignoring him, it snatched up the circlet and shook it, sending a burst of violet sparks leaping along its forelegs and dancing across the floor.

Its jaw opened and a series of loud clicks sounded from it, the last dissolving into something more glottal. It tried again, and this time he could pick out words amidst the sounds. It tried again, and this time there was no doubt in his mind. It was speaking, or at least mimicking it well enough. As he watched, unable to tear himself away from something so fascinating, the molten light that suffused the circlet flickered once, then again, and the light in the monster's eyes copied it. The pattern repeated, and then the light in both its eyes and the band faded completely.

It screeched like metal tearing and tossed the circlet against the wall, the impact snapping the band into two pieces. A final burst of violet light spat from it, leaping along the walls until it reached the flickering tear and vanishing into the darkness beyond, pulling the ragged opening shut as it went as cleanly as an upholsterer's stitch.

The creature shook its head again, barking a single word over and over again until it devolved back into a series of sharp clicks, its movements slowing as it did so. Catt recognised the Yogg word, one of the few he knew by rote. *Zhak*. Kill.

He slipped around the door and pulled it shut behind him, quickly running his fingers across the runes that would lock it, then fell into a nearby chair. He wasn't sure how long he had sat there before his composure finally rallied itself, but when he did sit forward again the first light of morning was beaming into through the shutters.

'Well, this simply won't do,' he said. He made his way back to his study and poured himself a glass of port. It wasn't his usual choice of morning fare, but then the sun hadn't quite risen yet and in the circumstances certainly lent themselves to some leeway. It was only after the warmth of the first mouthful had spread through his chest that he remembered that his journal was locked in the room with the creature, and that more than anything else made him curse. It was no doubt already ruined, possibly eaten; all those hours lost. It was a tragedy, especially now that the circlet itself was destroyed, rendering unknowable numbers of the symbols unreadable.

*You have more pressing problems than missing notes.* He grimaced and shot the serpent's head a filthy look. 'It's contained, and no harm has been done.'

He took a longer sip of the port, then stood and walked back to the safe room, pausing in front of the door. He found the pattern he was looking for easily enough given how long he'd taken to find it the first time. He traced it, pressed an innocuous-looking knot and closed his eyes. There was no sound or sign of anything changing, save that when he opened his eyes again, there was a small slit in the door, a viewing port not unlike that which you would find in any decent gaol.

He leaned forward cautiously, wary of being poked in the eye, but his fears were unwarranted. The creature was hunched in the corner of the room, its tail coiled around its clawed feet and the broken circlet in its long fingers. It was sniffing the metal and occasionally tasting it with rapid jabs of a pale orange tongue, clicking quietly in its throat after every dab. What was more concerning was the wall behind it, the same that had played host to the rift, was scored with several parallel claw marks—something which he had assumed was impossible, or at the very least highly improbable given the magical reinforcements that had made it all but impervious to anything they had tested on it thus far. For raking claws to mark the stone deeply enough that he could clearly trace the gouges from the door suggested that something far more deadly than horn or enamel was at work.

The wall was suddenly replaced by a mahogany-coloured eye with a clover-shaped pupil and he flung himself back without thinking, his heel catching a box that he'd meant to put back on the shelf for months, sending him sprawling. A snout was pressed to the slot by the time he'd scrambled back to his feet, sniffing and snorting like a pig hunting truffles, swiftly followed by long fingers tipped with curved talons that twisted that way and this.

'Get back!' he shouted, gathering up the nearest book and swatting at its claws, startling it as much it as himself. The claws vanished back through the slot and he punched the knot as quickly as he could, sealing it once more. He stared at the door, breathing hard and holding the book close to his chest, half expecting it to burst through the door. He thought he could hear its clicking call, but the sound was too muffled to be sure. He set the book down and took a steadying breath, quietly reassuring himself that there was no danger. It was definitely dangerous—the gouges in the wall attested to that—but even if it could damage the stone, it would take months for it to dig through, assuming it didn't die from thirst or starvation first.

Suitably mollified by his own reasoning, his thoughts turned elsewhere. He and Fisher weren't the only collectors by any stretch of the imagination, only the best, but there were others with a penchant for more exotic finds. Exotic, and organic. He'd never seen a creature like it before, and something so rare would without doubt be of interest to someone. He drummed his fingers on the table, then went over and sat down at his writing desk.

# CHAPTER FIVE

STEFAN KNEW THE others were checking their pace on his behalf, and though it grated on him to see it, he also knew there was no point in protesting it. Not only would it only encourage Tomas, who was already doing more than his fair share of complaining already, but the bitter truth of it was that he needed them to. His leg was aching, every impact sending a jolt straight up into his hip and all the way up his spine, as if his backbone had no gristle left in it.

Orec had done his best to carve the bowl that cupped his stump into something more comfortable, but as much of an improvement as it was, it was still just wood, and he wasn't looking forward to seeing the state of his leg when they eventually stopped. That's when it would really hurt.

*Cripple.* Tomas's words echoed in Stef's mind. The axe man was a miserable bastard who hadn't stopped complaining since Stef had first joined the company, forever questioning Orec's judgement despite having survived so many times because of it. He'd almost punched the old man on their first meeting, having been in no mood to stand there and endure the older man's diatribe about how such a young fool, barely weaned from his mother's teat, would surely lose the company standard and flee back to his books at the first sound of trouble.

Fortunately, he'd looked past the axe man and seen Orec watching them with that wry grin on his face. He'd unclenched his fist and instead asked the company in a loud voice if anyone had lost their grandfather, setting Tomas off in a fresh tirade but raising a good laugh with everyone else.

Their relationship hadn't changed much since, but he had learned to see past the bluster and Tomas's complete inability to think before he spoke: a trait that sabotaged his constant efforts to portray himself as an unappreciated mentor to anyone younger than himself.

But despite knowing that he hadn't spoken with real spite, the epithet still stung. *Cripple*. Even thinking it evoked images of the wretches that had ebbed and flowed on the city streets. He'd always felt sorry for them, offering a coin whenever he could but never looking directly at their empty trousers or twisted limbs, and yet here he was now, one of them. It could have been worse, he knew that, but what comfort that offered was scant and easily forgotten when he was left to his own thoughts for too long.

He looked up and saw that he'd fallen further behind and redoubled his efforts, setting his jaw against the hot ball of pain that had now lodged itself somewhere just behind his hip.

'How's it going with the crutch?' Hayden asked, seemingly appearing from nowhere at his side.

'Walk in the park,' he managed through gritted teeth.

'Glad to hear it. We're stopping about a mile and a half along, there's a good place for a camp.'

'Bit early isn't it?' Stef replied, glancing up at the sky. There was still good three hours of light left and he felt both shame and anger warming his cheeks at the thought of their pity.

The scout pursed his lips. 'I need the time to backtrack and clear our trail. No point in leaving our intentions signposted.'

'That's good thinking,' Stef offered, hoping the relief he felt wasn't too obvious.

'I'll see you there,' Hayden replied, stepping off the path and turning back the way they'd come. 'Don't let Tomas finish all the toast.'

Now that he knew there was a rest coming up it was easier to push the immediacy of the pain away. He looked ahead as far as he could and picked a tree, promising himself that once he reached that point, he'd take a minute to relieve the pressure on the stump. It was the kind of lie that Orec had once been very good at, breaking up long, dull marches with promises of a beer ration if they could just make it to that rock or tree or whatever within the hour. Everyone knew what he was doing, of course. No one but the rookies actually believed his promises, but the rest of them had found their own humour in it. Hayden had actually made one of those promises come true once though, and that had been a good day. Orec had promised each of the company a pint of ale if they could make it through a canyon by nightfall. In truth, they all knew it that if they were ambushed by the enemy between those tight walls it would be nothing short of a massacre, and so hadn't really needed much motivation to grit their teeth and pick up the pace.

Unbeknownst to them and Orec, Hayden had come across a supply wagon with a broken wheel that had been left behind by the rest of the logistics division, the lightly armed rear echelon troops having panicked at the rumour of a Yogg raiding party closing in on them. The relief of the four crew members had at the sight of a soldier, however, quickly turned to sullen resentment after he'd helped them with the repairs and proceeded to commandeer the wagon and its refreshing cargo. He'd managed to guide it down two steep trails, arriving at the rally point not ten minutes ahead of the company's arrival, by which time he was perched on the first barrel, a foaming cup in his hand. That had been a good night, and even now Stef found himself smiling at the memory of it. They'd come across a couple of stray goats who had soon found themselves gutted and hung over fires, the sizzle of the fats lost to the songs and increasingly ribald stories being traded across the glowing embers. He'd felt part of something greater that night. It had no longer mattered that he was young, or that he'd been a cosseted clerk whose soft fingers had bled and blistered so badly during his training. He was one of the Company, and sometime in those long hours the men around him had woven their own kind of magic, freeing him from the fear that had been festering in him for so long, and he hadn't even felt it leave. As long as he had his brothers, he'd feared nothing since.

He looked up to find himself at the tree he'd been steering towards and sighed. They were all gone now, their stories silenced and their faces fading from memory. He took a swig of water but resisted the urge to sit down. Instead, he looked up and forward, picking another tree, and began walking again.

TOMAS LOOKED OVER his shoulder, just long enough to watch Stef round the corner, then hiked his pack to a marginally less uncomfortable position and resumed walking. Up ahead, Orec and Hayden were talking as they walked, their voices low enough that he couldn't quite make out what they were saying. He supposed that it may just have been a precaution, and he may even have believed that if he hadn't seen the archer casting the occasional sideways look back at him, usually followed by a laugh from one or both of them.

He hawked and spat into a nearby bush, almost catching a bee with the greenish wad. *Now that would have been funny,* he mused, *unlike whatever childish crap those too were spouting.* He'd grown a thick skin when it came to them making fun of his age, but by the gods, on days like this he really felt the extra years. None of them would even be alive if it hadn't been for him, but they were too damned blind to see it. All he had to do was look at them now to know it for sure. Chatting like schoolchildren, with neither sparing so much as a glance into the undergrowth that grew so close to the path.

Anything could be hiding in it, and the gods knew he'd seen the worst happen more than once. If they were lucky it would be Yoggs, but if it was alone it would probably be some nasty grabber, bursting from its hole like a groundhog with a hot poker up its arse, although groundhogs weren't generally hairless things with the bodies of moles and the legs of a spider. If you were taken by one of those it was all over bar the screaming because no one went down into their burrows by choice, at least no one who had any thought of coming out again except as a turd.

No, he'd take an honest band of Yoggs any day. They were unrelenting and brutal, but they were polite enough to die when you chopped them properly, preferably in the head or neck. Too many of the Kinslayer's playthings were full of dirty tricks or too many limbs and faces, and by the time you finally got them to stop squirming you had no real idea what had actually killed them. He rubbed his thumb along the fine patchwork of notches scratched into the haft of the axe and smiled to himself. He hated Yoggs, but he at least understood them.

He glanced back again, but Stef was still hobbling along on his half leg. If anyone was going to get taken, it would be him first, but the boy didn't have the good sense to realise it and stay close. He hiked his pack up again and watched Stef walking, his gaze wandering to the wooden peg, as it had so often done since the boy started his recovery, and he looked away as quickly. He'd broken his leg once, and he'd never felt as vulnerable as had in the months it took him to walk again, and the idea of it being permanent was enough to make him go cold inside.

And yet Stef seemed to have taken it in his stride, so to speak, and it hadn't stopped more than one nurse paying him more attention than she probably should have. Had it been any other man but Stef crippled like that, they would have been polite and apologetic, but he seemed immune to it, and the truly infuriating part was that he probably wasn't even trying.

'I'm going to backtrack a bit,' said Hayden, stopping next to him and startling him back to reality.

Too damn close by half, as Tomas saw it, almost indecently so. He took a half step away and fought to contain his irritation at being having been caught napping.

'Tell the pup to keep up before something catches up with him.'

'See? You do care, you big softy.'

'Just shut up and do it,' he growled, his temper rapidly fraying. 'For the sarge's sake.'

Hayden looked back towards Orec and sighed. 'We're going to camp at the next big clearing.'

'Bit early, isn't it?'

'Well, we know all this walking doesn't help your old joints,' he replied cheerily, striding off and leaving Tomas to stare daggers at his back before he vanished into the same undergrowth he'd been watching.

He spat again, then started walking again. He'd seen his share of men like Hayden, brash and overconfident in their own abilities, and he'd seen almost as many fall on their faces when the truth of the world caught up with them. They were the ones who didn't know how to cope with failure, or without the adoration of every other farmer's daughter or barmaid tripping over there every word. They were the ones that more often that than not ended up in in the ditch, bawling for their mothers while they tried to stuff their guts back inside themselves. Hayden had defied his expectations, and it wasn't that he wished such a thing on him, quite the opposite, but his kind had always rubbed him the wrong way. What made it worse it that the archer had somehow sensed that and, despite his attempts to be a mentor and share the experience that years on the town guard had given him, his only thanks had been increasing levels of disrespect. Orec had at least paid him some heed, and he liked to think that those first few weeks under his wing had kindled the sergeant's leadership instincts. It had rankled him that Orec had been given a promotion despite Tomas's seniority, there was no denying that, but such things had always been half political, and that was part of a world that a simple soldier like him could never negotiate.

*Not a soldier anymore though.* He puffed out his cheeks at the thought. He'd never wanted to be a soldier and hadn't even wanted to be a town guard. The truth was, he'd never known what he wanted to do, and hadn't been good at anything he'd tried before. Letters and numbers always had a life of their own when he tried to put them down on a page, and his tutors had the same intolerance with his inability to sit still as he did with their constant nagging. He'd taken to becoming a woodsman both for the solitude and the pure physical satisfaction of a hard job well done, and when veins of silver had been found in the nearby hills he thought his fortune had finally found him. That had only lasted as long as it took for the labour gangs to move in and force independents like him out.

The years of hard work had left him with good shoulders though, and he'd fallen into helping out in a few of the drinking holes that had sprung up in the rapidly expanding town, working at several until the Cheriveni need for law and order reasserted itself and he suddenly found himself with a uniform, a steady salary, and a purpose. He'd had a healthy respect for the law beaten into him at a young age, so it seemed a natural progression.

The good thing was that even with the war over, there would always be a need for someone with a strong arm and a willingness to step in where others would shy away. The neat hatchwork etched onto his axe was testament to the folly of underestimating him because of the grey streaks at his temples and in his beard. With the bit of loot he'd managed to accumulate, he was looking forward to going home and enjoying some time as a patron, rather than employee, at least for a while. His wife had vanished a year before the war swept him up, abandoning their life together in favour of some bastard coach driver, and he quite liked the idea of finding someone new to share his bed.

He smiled as he walked, quietly picturing the women he'd known, trying to remember their names and wondering if he'd see any of them again. That would be something, and would certainly be a welcome shortcut to get around the tedium of small talk. He could picture the regulars' faces as they recognised him, astonishment and wonder writ large on each, and taste that first sweet pint as he took his seat back.

Either way, he had no doubt that it would be quite the party when he finally got home. He smiled as he walked, the undergrowth forgotten.

HAYDEN SETTLED HIMSELF under the shade of a neeba tree and took a long drink from his canteen, a quiet sense of satisfaction settling over him. They were finally underway, and making good time. He'd had a real fear that Orec would change his mind and opt to delay matters until Stef was in better shape, but both he and Stef had come through in the end. He suspected that Stef had regrets, but despite the obvious strain he was under, the standard bearer was holding up well. He'd certainly picked his pace up after he'd been told of the night's camp, which meant he still had some fight left in him.

He quietly admonished himself at the thought. Of all the tasks in the Company, standard bearer was the one that he himself dreaded most. To stand in there in the centre of the field, hemmed in on sides and holding aloft a prize that every enemy wanted to seize, one that you were oath bound to never let fall, seemed a death sentence to him. And yet Stef had done just that, time and time again, holding his own against the most vicious of killers, his defiance rallying the men around him. It was no wonder that they loved him, even those who had almost mutinied when Orec had first given the pale clerk such a revered position. He'd seen something that no others had, and Stef had grown into the role better than anyone but Orec could have imagined. There was plenty of fight left in him, and anyone who thought he would be an easy mark because of his leg were probably in for a rude awakening.

He shrugged the thoughts away and did a quick check of his equipment, making sure that the fletching of the few arrows he had left weren't snagging, then stood and dusted his leggings off. Despite what he'd suggested to Orec, he really wasn't expecting a pursuit. He'd gotten to know the hospital and its staff very well during his night-time wanderings, and as hopelessly undermanned as it was, even if they'd managed to muster more than half a dozen men for the task, none of them would have the motivation to venture more than a mile or two from their base. But he also knew from bitter experience that complacency killed, and he had absolutely no intention of end up rotting in a nameless field just because assumptions were easier than actual work.

Only he and Orec knew the truth of how he'd come to be attached to the Company. The men he'd marched off to war with had fed the earth years ago, slaughtered in their sleep by the same raiding party they'd been sent out to find, all because one vainglorious bastard decided that a cold camp was beneath his dignity. He'd voiced his objections to the idea and had been banished to the edge of the camp, almost to the edge of the picket line, a punishment that had saved his life.

He'd been troubled by vivid dreams as long as he could remember and he had taught himself to wake whenever the dreams took a disturbing turn, which was more often than not, something which had left him a very light sleeper. The first screams had woken him, although his waking mind had tried to convince him it was part of whatever nightmare had been stalking him.

That uncertainty lasted as long as it took the next man to scream, a piercing cry whose echoes he still heard on particularly bad nights. He'd struggled into his jerkin, desperate to join the fight, to help, but by the time it was settled and his bow was strung, the campfire had spread to the tents, the ruddy light revealing the pitiless slaughter that the darkness had hidden. What resistance his comrades managed to muster was short-lived, their formation ripped apart by the enemy's billhooks and the darting, savage attacks of their direwolves, pulling men out of formation and swarming over them, tearing them apart like ragdolls.

He'd fled when four of the wolves had turned in his direction, no doubt catching his scent but thankfully losing it again amidst the carnage. It had taken him weeks to navigate his way back to another fortified camp, weeks in which his fear had slowly subsided. He'd learned a lot about himself in that time, including the enormous debt he owed his father for the hours spent in the woods and at the archery butts. Those skills had kept him alive, and by the time he walked back into the camp, he was so far removed from the rank-and-file archer who everyone believed had died in the massacre that he didn't feel any compunction to correct them. He'd taken his father's name and officially become a scout, so ensuring that he would never again be beholden to the whims of the kind of entitled lordling who would risk the lives of forty men just to avoid a night's discomfort.

He'd been assigned to the Fourth shortly after Orec had been promoted to the rank of captain for the first time, and had at first pegged him as just another ambitious try-hard. That initial opinion had changed as soon as they were out in the field. Orec not only listened to advice, but also led from the front, refusing to order men to do anything he wouldn't do himself, giving the Company a spirit and cohesion that Hayden hadn't experienced before. Under his guidance, the Fourth Company had become the Fighting Fourth, able to hold its own against any of the mercenary companies that the local lords had brought in, which was no mean feat for a ragtag company first raised as a local militia.

Those same qualities had infuriated the officers of more prestigious bands, whose men now judged their own reticence to take the lead in the same way, and that resentment had led to campaign of sabotage and false accusations being levied against him. In the end, Orec had been brought up before a tribunal because of it. The sneering inquisitors appointed by the Duke had insisted on it being public to ensure his humiliation was complete, and the memory of Orec telling that same tribunal to get stuffed if he was expected to put his personal comfort ahead of his men's safety was one that Hayden treasured. Their plain to humiliate him backfired spectacularly, because the same men they'd gathered to witness his fall had cheered his even word and made it clear that any punishment would be met with open mutiny. All they could do was strip his promotion away, and Orec robbed them of that too by tearing the braid from his sleeves before they'd even finished delivering the judgement.

Hayden pushed the memory away as he finished the sweep of their trail and turned back once more, trying not to think of the strange void that would be left when they all parted ways.

'WHAT HAVE YOU done?' Fisher asked, his coat held out in front of him like a shield, several inches away from the peg on the wall. 'And don't say nothing, because I can feel it.'

Catt opened his mouth, then closed it again. He'd expected to have this conversation with Fisher on his return, since stopping him from ever going into the strong room again wasn't a viable option. And he knew, because he'd considered it, along with a number of other equally unlikely scenarios. What he hadn't expected was to have to answer it before Fisher had done more than put his bag down and take off his coat. A hot bath and good dinner would surely have prepared the ground for a far easier delivery.

'Now, everything is under control, so there's no need to be so prickly. You've had a long journey, and you're probably both hungry and tired. How about some supper first? It's always nicer to talk with a full belly and a smidge of brandy in hand.'

'That's quite ominous actually, coming as it is from someone without the patience to boil an egg properly.'

'You can't judge me on that just because you prefer yours half petrified. Eggs—'

'I don't care about the eggs,' said Fisher, finally hanging his coat. 'Tell me what you've done.'

'I'll go pour some wine.'

Catt pursed his lips as Fisher followed him down the stairs, silent save for the bony click of his teeth grinding against each other, which was never a good sign. Dinner would have helped, but there was nothing to be gained by pushing the idea if he was already in such an unfairly fractious mood.

'See,' he said, uncorking the bottle that had been waiting on the table. 'Everything is in order.'

Fisher accepted the glass without comment and sat back in the chair, his sigh indistinguishable from the wheeze of air from the padded backrest. He took a sip, then set the glass down and looked across at Catt with eyes that were incongruously bright for the room, lit as it was by two conventional lamps.

'So, do you remember that chap Boris, from Maybury?'

'The gentrified thug.' He narrowed his eyes. 'You did something with that crown.'

'Now, we don't know that it was a crown as such. The truth is, we didn't know much of its nature or purpose at all and that surely was a more dangerous approach, having something so unpredictable on the shelf.'

'Stop prevaricating and tell me what you did.'

Catt sighed and reached back onto the table behind him to retrieve a journal with a bad scuffed and stained leather cover. He weighed it in his hands for a moment, then slid it across the table to Fisher, who sat forward.

'What's this?' he asked, not really expecting an answer as he opened it to the first page of writing, the lambent light in his eyes fading slightly as he followed Catt's neat copperplate writing.

'As you see there, I—'

Fisher hushed him without looking up and continued reading. He would have preferred a straight answer, but he'd known Catt for long enough to recognise that this was the straightest version of an answer he was likely to get. He skimmed the first page, and turned to an illustration of the main band of the crown, the artistry of it impressive, but something was off. The ink had dried in two shades, but not in a way that suggested he'd changed pots. It was the same ink, but the one page had been inked later than the other. He ran a finger down the centre binding and felt the rough edge of a missing sheet, which was unusual. He thumbed the page, noting the denser writing that followed, and looked across to Catt, who was watching him closely.

'Shall I read the next part, or do you want to tell me?'

Catt topped their glasses up, then took a steadying sip from his. 'I discovered that the circlet was a planar key of sorts. They were using it to summon and control beasts from another realm as slaved weapons.'

'Fascinating,' he replied, tracing the stem of the wineglass with a finger. 'I must say you sound very sure of that given that we have no idea what the symbols or language are.'

'Well, that's the funny part, you see. Do you remember what

that man Boris did?' He paused long enough for Fisher to nod, somehow infusing the motion with a tired acceptance. 'Well, it activated again. I think you may have jammed it in a bit when you put it away, but setting that aside for now, what happened was quite extraordinary.'

'What did you do?'

'Me? I did nothing. If anything, I was trying to stop it. It pulled me through, you see, into a strange plane. All towers of rock and grit, with purple lightning. I've described it in there.'

'Yet you're here, so that wasn't the problem.'

'Yes, well. One of their beasts was waiting. Now this is just conjecture, but its eyes were the same shade as the circlet, you see, as if they were attuned. We've seen that before of course, with Nilfur's Beastly Brooch, and—'

'What did you do?'

'I did nothing,' Catt replied testily. '*It* chased *me*. I was lucky to get away given how ferocious it was, and all with the cast of a chimera about it.' He sighed dramatically when Fisher simply kept staring at him with the same slightly pained expression. 'Obviously, I got away. But, here's the thing, it sort of followed me through the rift. It was unstable, you see. The circlet should have been an anchor, but since some thug had chopped through it, it couldn't stabilise.'

Fisher sat up straighter, the strange energy he'd felt as soon as he'd passed through the curtains suddenly making more sense.

'It's not here,' he said, a statement rather than a question.

'Define *here*.'

'Oh, for love of everything holy, will you just tell me the rest,' Fisher said, barely aware of his eyes brightening again.

'Fine, yes, I was getting there,' Catt replied, taking another hasty sip. 'It, and I mean the creature obviously, was weakened from the transition and the circlet's misalignment. Stunned would be a good way to put it. I thought that perhaps we could contain it, even learn from it. It was intelligent, you see.' He leaned forward. 'It tried to mend the circlet, and not just that but to use it too!'

'Did it succeed?' Fisher pinched the bridge of his nose as he waited for the inevitable reply.

'Well, no, it was quite broken. But an attempt was made, and that's the point I was making.'

'So where is it?'

'It, um, got away.'

'It got away,' Fisher said, and the look of misery on Catt's face was almost enough to take edge off his mounting irritation. 'How, exactly?'

'It was on the ceiling, if you must know. I thought it had been drawn back to its own realm as the energy faded, but the cunning thing had been watching me. It hid where I couldn't see it, then dropped down as I opened the door.' He noticed Fisher's expression and lowered the glass without taking sip. 'I thought it was gone, you know. No harm done.'

'No harm done? You've no idea what that thing was, or what it's capable of. And now it's on the loose.'

'It was meant to be used as a weapon,' Catt replied. 'It'll probably starve and die soon enough.'

'Maybe,' Fisher said. 'But if it doesn't? What if it's like those poor Vathesk and goes on a spree, killing for a hunger it can't ever satisfy?'

'Then there's something else out there prowling the woods,' Catt shrugged. 'And there's only one of it, so it's a lesser danger than the Vathesk. It really is just a shame that we couldn't study it properly.'

Fisher studied him for a few moments. 'There's something that you aren't telling me. Something that has to do with this new devil-may-care attitude.'

'I was getting to it,' Catt replied. 'I did try and track it after I'd recovered. I used the glasses, as well as the Wind Taster.'

'And?'

'And nothing. Both failed after barely half a mile. All I know is that it was keeping to the alleys and headed north.'

'I can't believe that both failed, not if they were being used appropriately.'

"You think I—'

'I think that perhaps you were trying too hard, or moving too fast.' He stood up. 'I'm going to have a soak, and then get some sleep. Come morning, we'll try find a trace of this beast of yours and decide how we're going to fix this mess.'

'Take this then,' Catt said, sliding the notebook over to him. 'Read the rest.'

Fisher took the book and weighed it in his hand as he considered Catt for a moment more, before turning and heading to the stairs.

Catt watched him go and then finally slumped back in his chair and allowed himself to finish his wine. It had gone better than expected, and with a sliver more of luck, they'd be able to find and trap the creature in good time before the collectors wrote back to him.

# CHAPTER SIX

OREC SET HIS pack down and slowly straightened, wincing as various parts of him began protesting at the unexpected exercise they'd been subjected to. There was a time not so long ago when a walk like that would hardly have set his heart to beating any harder, but he'd grown soft at the hospital in every sense of the word.

It was a good kind of ache, he reckoned, the same that came from a hard day's work well done. He'd always been happier when he was busy, although the last few years had given him a fundamental appreciation for how glorious boredom could be. Doing nothing was immeasurably less of a burden than having something trying to disembowel you and the gods knew, he'd had more than his share of days like that.

He walked back to the path, although calling it that was generous, and saw Tomas coming up. He gave a quick wave then moved back and began walking around the edge of the clearing, picking up deadwood and checking for tracks.

'Hey,' he said as Tomas dumped his pack alongside his. 'How're you feeling?'

'Not too bad, but I wouldn't say no to some cheese on toast.'

'Then you're doing better than me,' Orec said, dropping the wood he'd collected. 'I'm half tempted to go back and get my bed.'

'It's too heavy to carry.'

Orec watched him, hoping for a sign he was joking, but his expression remained entirely serious as he squatted and started sorting through the firewood.

'Yes, well, that's why I haven't done it.'

'Some of these are damp. I'll stack them on the side.'

'Wouldn't want to attract grabbers.'

'Don't be ridiculous,' Tomas replied testily. 'They're underground. It's the rest of what's out there I'm worried about.'

Orec nodded in agreement and scratched at his stubble to hide his smile. 'Sure. There aren't any tracks around here, not even old ones.'

'Well,' said Hayden, stepping into the clearing from the opposite side, 'the bad news is that you're wrong, but the good news is that there were enough to follow.' He proudly brandished two large, field dressed hares. 'Unless of course you prefer old cheese on older toast.'

Nobody did, and by the time that Stef arrived both hares had been skinned and hung on improvised spits. Orec waited until they'd all settled back down before reaching into his pack and lifting out a bottle of wine, eliciting a round of cheers. He'd thought to keep it to lift their spirits after a few days, but quite honestly he was looking forward to getting rid of the extra weight. He pried the cork free and took a swig before passing it to Tomas; by the time it had done the round and returned to him it was considerably lighter, but so was the mood around the small fire.

'How's the leg?' he asked, passing the bottle across to Stef.

'Boot's a bit tight,' he said. 'But otherwise not bad.'

'You've done well.'

'He needs to keep up with us,' said Tomas. 'Something's going to pick him off.'

Stef watched Tomas over the fire as the man purposefully ignored his outstretched hand and purposefully took a longer drink.

'I'm right here, you know,' he said when he eventually lowered it.

'Most of you anyway,' said Orec, without looking away from the fire.

The silence that followed stretched for one heartbeat, then two, and on the third Tomas began to chuckle. Stef followed suit, and when they looked across at each other it quickly turned to outright laughter, the infectious kind that quickly drew Orec and Hayden in before they were even aware of it.

When it finally spluttered away Hayden jointed the hares, pausing only to wipe the tears from his cheeks as he passed the pieces around.

'What was the name of that kid with the bushy red hair?' asked Orec around a mouthful of meat. 'The one who wanted to grow the moustache?'

'Daniel,' offered Tomas.

'Yeah, that's him,' Orec said, shaking his head at the memory. 'Remember when he trapped that tellac and then insisted on eating it?'

'God, yes,' answered Hayden. 'I've never seen anyone get the shits like that.'

'It tastes like chicken,' Tomas said in a piping voice, which set them all to laughing.

'Is that what you sound like at home?' asked Stef, earning himself a rib bone to the face.

'Good times,' Orec added. 'Now get some sleep. Wake me when you're done,' he said, looking across at Hayden, who nodded absently. How the man managed to stay so alert on so little sleep amazed him. In more than three years together he'd not yet gone to sleep after him, nor woken before him, but it didn't seem to have any effect at all. They weren't far apart age wise, but if he'd tried to keep to the same regimen he'd be a wreck within a week. He laid his bedroll out and tried to make himself comfortable, but only seemed to succeed in finding more rocks and roots to dig onto his back. How he'd ever come to complain about the beds they'd been given was lost to him now as he finally wriggled into a position that didn't hurt in more than one place at a time. He closed his eyes and took a deep breath; by the time he'd exhaled the last of it he was asleep.

Tomas likewise had no issue falling asleep but unlike Orec, he welcomed the feel of the earth beneath him. It felt more honest and gave him a certain peace of mind he hadn't really know he was lacking. It was, however, a peace that neither would enjoy for very long.

Orec first became aware that he was dreaming when the lightning hit him. He'd seen men struck by bolts smaller than the ones that struck him, and he knew that he should have been dead, his core burned out, leaving the shell of him standing there like a hollowed-out oak until it fell in upon itself.

The bolt had sent him sprawling, but it hadn't hurt, and as he rose again he found himself looking out upon a desolate plain, the surface dry and pockmarked with the scars of centuries of lightning strikes. It was dark, but he couldn't tell whether it that was because night had come, or the clouds that ebbed and flowed like stained sea foam above him were too thick to permit any light whatsoever to pass. The same violet glow that had overwhelmed his senses moments before swelled within the clouds, illuminating them from within, and it took everything he had not to fall to the ground again. But no strike came, and he watched it ripple away into the distance, eventually silhouetting what appeared to be a forest of tall stone columns that pierced the clouds.

He turned and looked around, but the light had faded and the darkness was again pressing close. He looked down at himself and was reassured to see that he was dressed as he remembered, with the reassuring weight of his sword firmly at his hip. He rested his hand on the hilt and, with no other point of interest to worry about, he began walking towards the stone columns. It felt like he'd barely taken ten steps but suddenly he was at the foot of the nearest of them, broader as any of the great redwood trees in the Southlands and rising higher than anything that heavy had any right to.

He felt the hairs on his arms rising and smacked his lips as a metallic taste filled his mouth. A moment later the skies brightened, violet light visible in the gaps between the thickest cloud, and felt rather than saw a bolt strike the column next to him. He stepped back as arcs of it raced down towards him, but they weren't what set his heart to racing. That honour belonged to the creatures that clung to the column like parasites on a rose stem. He hadn't seen them until they lifted their heads in perfect unison, their eyes lighting with the same light as was racing towards them.

He backed away rapidly, his sword filling his hand almost without conscious thought, the blade barely clearing the scabbard before the creatures sprung at him, hissing through the air with their silvery teeth bared. He managed one swing before they tore into him, biting and twisting like swamp lizards, tearing his flesh away to the bone, ramming their tapering snouts into his ribcage, tearing away his organs with a frenzied abandon. His scream became a wet wheeze as their now-bloodied bloody teeth ripped his lung in half.

Which is when the waterfall hit him, the unexpected and icy blast momentarily overwhelming the agony. He gasped once, then again as his lungs inflated normally, and pushed himself away. He wiped his very wet face and looked around with wide eyes as his heart hammered within him as if surprised to find itself still within his ribs.

'What the fuck!' he spluttered.

'You alright, sarge?' A figure squatted in front of him, silhouetted by flame.

'Hayden?'

'No, it's me, Martina,' the figure replied, then stretched out a hand.

'You sure got ugly,' Orec said, taking the proffered hand and sitting up, the fear fading quickly as Hayden and the sparks from the campfire reasserted themselves around him.

Hayden set the canteen down and threw another branch onto the fire, sending a swarm of sparks swirling towards the stars. 'What was that?' he asked.

Orec was deciding whether to lead with weird or intense, but at that point Tomas rolled onto his side, his hands clenched into fists and a pained keening escaping through his bared teeth.

'What's happening here?' Hayden asked, his voice a whisper.

Orec passed him the canteen and nodded towards Tomas, who took a single, convulsive breath as the water hit him and surged to his feet, fists swinging wildly, before crumpling to the ground and just sitting there, breathing as if he'd just sprinted up a hill.

'You alright, Tom?' asked Orec.

He looked around and sat up a little straighter. 'Fine,' he said. 'Just a stupid dream.'

'She must have been quite something,' Hayden jibed, earning himself nothing more than a two-fingered salute from Tomas.

Orec and Hayden both looked across to Stefan, who was wrapped up tightly in his blanket and sound asleep, his face slack and his breathing slow and regular.

'Go back to sleep,' Hayden said. 'I'm good for another couple of hours.'

'Love to, but some idiot wet my blanket,' grumbled Tomas, who had shuffled closer to the fire, the same blanket draped over his legs and part of it already steaming.

'Think of it as a taste of your upcoming dotage,' Hayden replied.

'At least I'm not building a signal fire to bring every Yogg in fifty miles.'

'Shut it, both of you,' Orec said, the thought of sleep warring with the memory of the biting jaws that may be waiting behind his eyelids. Knowing that it was a dream should have made it easier to bear, but if he dared dwell on it he could still feel those silvery teeth scoring his bones. He went and sat next to Tomas, spreading his blanket out as well.

'Why're you awake anyway?'

Orec didn't look away from the embers, ignoring the instinct that told him to look away and preserve his night vision. 'Just a stupid dream.'

Tomas grunted and continued peeling the bark from a twig. 'Something was hunting me,' he said eventually.

'Grabbers?'

'Oh, shut up,' he said, flicking the twig at Orec. 'Not bloody grabbers. They're real, you know.'

Orec smiled and set the twig on the embers. 'I had something similar,' he said, 'except they caught me.' In his peripheral vision he saw Tomas turn and look at him, but he just watched the twig smouldering. He licked his unexpectedly dry lips. 'They ate me.'

'Well, shit.' He poked at the fire, sending another flare of sparks spiralling away. 'It got me too,' he said in a quiet voice. 'I tried running, but it was too fast. I tried to fight, but it was a slippery bastard. Went low and cut my tendons.' He almost rubbed the back of his sock but stopped himself. 'Couldn't do anything much after that. It had just opened me up when Longshot woke me.' There was a dull snap as he closed his fist around the stick he'd been using to stir the fire, but his voice didn't change. 'Hate to say it, but I owe him for that. It was way too real for my liking.'

'Same here.' He gestured to Stef's blissfully unconscious form. 'Never thought I'd be this jealous of a one-legged man.'

That got the laugh he'd hoped for. 'Hold that thought,' Tomas said, climbing to his feet and going back to his pack. When he sat down again, it was with a battered silver flask in hand. He unstoppered it and took a swig before handing it over.

Orec followed suit, grimacing at the coarse burn of the hooch inside. 'What is that?'

'Best you don't ask. But it's good for taking your mind off things.'

Orec ran his tongue over his teeth and spat into the fire. 'And cleaning mail.'

'That too,' Tomas grinned.

The axe man was true to his word, and by the time the second hit had lit a fire in his gut, the memory of the helpless fear he'd felt so acutely was slipping away like smoke, and with it went the half-formed idea that he was missing something important.

It only took half the flask before they were asleep again, back-to- back, unaware of Hayden having to pull their smouldering blankets out of the fire.

'I SWEAR I can smell it,' Tomas folded his arms as if daring any of them to argue with him.

'If the wind changes, I'm pretty sure they'd smell you though,' Stef said. He wasn't looking out towards the town though, but at the twisting path that would take them down to the trade road that led into the town. It looked even worse than the glorified goat trail they'd been travelling on for the last two days, something he didn't think possible short of stumbling across a tar pit. It was steep too, and he could already feel the blisters he'd have by the time they reached the bottom.

'I just want a bath,' Hayden said. 'And proper bread.'

'With butter,' added Orec. The very idea of it lent him new energy. 'So, let's go. It's almost dark, and I don't want to have to spend a night camping outside the gates if we can prevent it.'

He waited until Hayden and Tomas were on their way before turning to Stef. 'It's pretty steep.'

'I'll manage.'

'Alright. Stay close, and call if you need a hand.'

'Yes, mother.'

In the end, he didn't need a hand, even if he had to bite his lip twice to stop himself from entertaining the idea of asking for help. Tomas and Hayden were already at the bottom, and he knew the smug old bastard would be watching him.

The flat, even road was a welcome change and they managed a decent enough pace. Now that they were on level ground, the palisade around the town looked far more formidable than it had from the hill, but then for the town to have endured for so long its defences would have been well-tested and proven. As they drew closer, it became apparent that the war's end hadn't slackened their vigilance. There was minimal commotion but they all noticed that another handful of archers had made their way to the wall on either side of the gate, and the gleam of metal inside its shadows left little doubt that trying to bully their way past the two guards posted outside wouldn't be a great idea.

Orec kept his hands clear of his sword as he approached them. 'Good day,' he said.

'What do you want?' the guard on his left asked, leaning on his spear in such a way that it would take little more than a determined twitch to level it at Orec's chest.

'A roof and food,' he said, tilting his head towards the dark clouds that had been relentlessly following them. 'We've got coin.'

'Where'd you come from?'

'Does it matter?' Tomas asked from behind him.

The guard shifted his feet and looked past Orec, who was fighting the sudden urge to turn and slap Tomas. The guard was probably the same age as Tomas, and from the look of him, possessed of the same wiry strength that the careless and short-lived were prone to underestimate.

'It matters because I say it matters.'

'Ignore him,' Orec said with an exaggerated shrug. 'It's past his bedtime.'

That got a snort from the guard and, more importantly, brought his attention back to Orec. 'We just want a drink and a proper bed, in that order. We've no intention of causing trouble.'

The guard spat off to the side and looked Orec over, silently noting the battered but well-maintained chainmail and unadorned weapons, but it was the look in his eyes that finally quietened his suspicion. He saw his own weariness there, and the conscious effort of someone working hard to rein in the easy violence that their appearance suggested.

'Change your mind about that and we'll have a problem,' he said, waving the other guard to the side.

'We won't.' He meant it too, which is why he spat a curse as Tomas added 'About bloody time too' from behind him. He turned on his heel and took a step, putting his face mere inches from Tomas'. He didn't say anything, and didn't need to.

Tomas took a step back, then another. 'It was just a joke,' he said, holding his hands up. 'You know, lightening the mood.'

'Don't,' was all Orec said.

Behind him the guards watched closely, arrows nocked to strings but their weapons not quite levelled. The guard who'd stopped them shook his head and offered Orec a nod as the sergeant turned again. He'd had to deal with his fair share of loudmouths and if anything, the incident had made him feel more confident that he'd made the right call.

'Alright, let's close up for the night,' he said once the one-legged man had passed. 'No one else in or out.'

THE ANGER DRAINED from Orec as he made his way along the road. From number of bare plots that marked the high road like missing teeth, the war had clearly visited the town several times. Even in the fading light it was clear that none of the buildings had been spared its touch. Windows were boarded, roofs patched with tent canvas or simply leafy branches as a rough thatch. Unsmiling faces watched from those few windows that still had shutters, closing as soon as they saw Orec watching them.

The most impressive feature of the town was the palisade, which the townspeople had clearly prioritised over any other repairs, an approach that he quite agreed with; as he saw it, a nice house could swiftly become a nice tomb. The ruined plots had been cleared to some extent, more likely stripped by the neighbours, and most of these hollow shells now sported tents or shacks amidst the blackened stone, usually with a brood of children sitting out front, watching them pass with wary eyes and pinched faces. A few of the bolder ones stood and started following them, but keeping well out of reach.

The inn was a square, two-storey building with the look of a fortress about it, and the bottom half of it was most likely the oldest building in the town, formed as it was of enormous stone blocks that fitted together too tightly to slip even the narrowest blade between. Age had softened the corners, but Orec had little doubt that it would still have taken a siege engine to get through them. The single door was standing open, and in the light of the lantern that hung outside the gouges and scorch marks that had been added to the stone's ancient patina were obvious.

He ducked and stepped inside, relieved to find that the ceiling height hadn't been sacrificed when they'd added the floor above. The interior was as plain as anything else he'd seen here, but there were at least enough benches spare, albeit in the furthest corner from the fire smouldering in the fireplace, the one original feature that was rounded rather than square. He dumped his pack on the floor and sat down heavily, stretching his legs out in front of him with a sigh.

'What a dump,' Tomas set, sitting down next to him. 'Bet the beer tastes like piss.'

The men at the nearest tables were already watching them, and Orec saw more than a few start muttering amongst themselves.

'Why don't you go get us some,' Orec said. 'Your round, since you can't keep your mouth shut.'

'I'm not the last one in.'

He rubbed his eyes. 'Hayden's sorting out a room, and Stef can't exactly carry four pints now, can he?'

'I have to do everything,' he grumbled, setting his own pack down.

'And Tom? Don't speak to anyone.'

'What's that supposed to mean?'

Orec recognised the tone and opted to simply shake his head. 'Just get the beer.'

Stef sat in the seat he'd just left, not bothering to hide either the wince or the sigh as he took the weight off his leg.

'How is it?' Orec asked, trying not to stare at the dark patch that marked the bandage.

Stef massaged his thigh for a moment before replying. 'It's been a rough day.'

'We're going to hole up here for a day. We'll see about getting some salve and fresh dressings.'

'Right now I'd settle for a pint and a bed.'

'Amen to that.'

Tomas returned a few moments later, Hayden in tow, and passed the drinks out without comment. They drank deep, finishing half outright, then sighed as one.

'That almost tastes like beer,' Tomas said, wiping his mouth on his cuff. 'I've had worse.'

'High praise,' Hayden said. 'So, we have a room.'

'One?'

'One,' Hayden said. 'And there aren't any baths, unless you fancy hauling well water.'

'So be it,' Orec shrugged. 'It'll be a good night to have a roof.'

An hour and three pints later he lay listening to the rain

throwing itself against the roof, which admittedly wasn't hard given that the tiles were less than an arm's length from his face. The room wasn't more than a supported floor dividing the roof space, accessed by a ladder that he had to climb over three other sleeping figures to reach. It was however, both warm and dry, and compared to the apparent ferocity of the storm, it was entirely luxurious. He settled again and let his thoughts drift, and soon enough all concerns he had about Tomas' snoring, the route, their rations, and Martina's face when she opened the door faded away.

He only became aware of anything else again when he was standing in the open, watching the play of the lightning in the distant clouds and trying to ignore the cool night breeze that kept finding its way under his coat. There was something familiar about the shape and size of the hills around him, and as he turned to trace them in the fading light he saw the churned fields that spread out behind him, pockmarked with craters and crossed with trenches whose depths now gleamed with pooled rainwater. And there, in the distance, squatted the outline of the fortress of Dal Tulkauth, its mighty towers now little more than ziggurats of fallen stone and a gaping frame where its once-proud iron doors once stood. He'd not seen it after the battle, nor anything else for a month for that matter, but the sight of it was nevertheless indelibly imprinted upon his mind from the week of vicious close quarter fighting that it had taken them to simply get within striking range of it.

He was still staring at it when he noticed the figures moving across it. There were three of them, and what he at first took to be axes resolved themselves into shovels and picks. He watched as they unerringly picked their way through the ruined landscape until they reached a particularly wide trench. They spread out and pulled back a large canvas before descending.

*Scavengers.* They were as familiar a sight as crows after a battle, only less welcome. He had resolved to go and confront them when something exhaled noisily behind him, a bear from the sound of it. He turned slowly as so not to spook it into attacking but staggered away as he caught sight of the angular head and whipping tail of the lithe creature perched behind him. Eyes the colour of the setting sun narrowed, and before he could do more than think about reaching for his sword it had sprung forward and a line of cold agony had crossed his gut with the sound of paper tearing.

It circled away and made a throaty, clicking noise as it watched him. He took another unsteady step, not wanting to look down but unable to stop himself. Ropes of steaming intestine spilled from the long gash as he did, surely far too much to have come from inside of him. He lifted a length of it in bloodied hands and stared at it dumbly before the strength bled from his legs and the night swallowed his vision.

He sat up with a gasp that turned to a curse when his head smacked into a roof beam. He fell back onto the bundled cloak that was serving as his pillow and rubbed his head. It hurt, but the sharp knock had at least driven off the dregs of the dream, if that's what it was. It had to be though, didn't it? He kept rubbing his forehead, willing it to make sense, but in vain. The gods knew he'd felt the back of his father's hand enough when he was a child for getting distracted when he was supposed to be helping in the workshop or around the house, but the bored daydreams of a youngest son were an entirely different matter to concocting something so devilish. And so real. He rubbed his fingertips together and would have sworn that he could still feel the warmth and weight of the guts in his hands. He glanced over to where Tomas lay sleeping, his snoring at a low, even pitch and tried to get some sleep.

Boris waited until Ratty had finally settled in the chair before pouring them each a drink. He was more fidgety than usual, which never preceded good news, a trait that he was actually strangely grateful for as it at least gave him a little time to brace himself.

'Thanks boss,' Ratty said, lifting draining half the cup without so much as a perfunctory toast, which set Boris' eyebrow climbing further up his forehead. He took a more modest sip from his own cup and sat back in his chair. Lona was lounging near the fire, no less menacing despite her outwardly languid appearance. She was likewise familiar with Ratty's mannerisms and was doing her best not to look as curious as she no doubt was, although that may have simply be because she was bored and eager for an excuse to go out and bang some heads together.

'Just tell me,' Boris said after watching Ratty turn his cup too many times as he tried to decide how to break whatever news he had. 'Get it over with.'

'Sorry,' he said, flashing his yellow teeth. 'We got some problems up by Tulkauth.'

'Again? Is the sickness back?'

'No. I mean yes, one or two of the guys are ill, but not very. It's come down since I told 'em to quit if their hair starts falling out. But no, it's not that.' He finished the rest of his wine before continuing. 'A crew got killed the other night. Outright murdered.'

Boris sat up straighter and leaned his elbows on the table, fixing Ratty with a look that justified the cold sweat he always felt when delivering anything other than good news. Dealing with the side effect of the Burns, as Boris called it, was one thing. But having men killed was another matter entirely.

'By who?'

'I don't know, boss. Someone got them all, sliced them up but good.'

'All of them?'

'Yeah. I saw the bodies, and it wasn't pretty. Some were gutted, the others looked like wolves got hold of them.' He reached for the bottle and filled both their cups. 'Freaking direwolves, boss. Necks were bit to the bone.'

Normally he'd have been bothered by Ratty helping himself to what was an expensive bottle of wine like that, but from the unhealthy pallor of his already pale face, he wasn't trying to spin the story. He let it pass and took a steadying breath. Things like this happened sometimes. It hadn't been that long ago that a particularly ambitious gang had tried to pass themselves off as werewolves to try and muscle in on one of his protectorates, leaving torn up bodies in their wake. They'd been little more than thugs with a theatrical flair, tossing trussed up victims into a pit with hungry strays. When he and his men came for them they'd pissed themselves and died without ever even seeing a bit of silver, and he'd bet his own back teeth that this was the same kind of stupid stunt.

Killing a scavenger team was hardly an impressive feat, especially at night, but it was the fact that it was his team that got his blood going. It was clearly a message, but from who? You had to get in front of these things as quickly as possible otherwise you'd constantly be reacting and handing them the advantage.

'Who do we know that would have the balls to try something like this?'

Lona made her way over to perch on the end of the table, giving no outward sign that she had any idea of the effect she had on Ratty.

'None that come to mind,' she purred.

Boris made an effort not to roll his eyes. 'Be serious.'

She shrugged. 'I am,' she said in her usual tone. 'After that business with Tanu no one's dared to take a bite at the apple.'

'Yeah, she's right,' Ratty said, 'There's some low-key peddling stuff, but nothing big. Nothing organised.'

'Clearly someone has a different idea,' he said. 'Get out there and turn over every rock you need to. Take some of the men and remind them why they're getting paid. Do what you need to, but find this bastard.'

'Yes boss,' Ratty said.

'I'm going to stay close,' Lona said. 'I've no doubt we can rely on Ratigan.'

Ratty actually sat up straighter at that. 'I won't let you down.'

'Then stop staring at her and go find them.'

'Yes boss.'

He waited until the door had shut again before turning to Lona. 'There's something off about all of this. Get out there and see what you can dig up.'

'You don't trust him?'

'Ratty? No, I think he's being entirely straight on this, but he's not the sharpest knife in the drawer. If someone has managed to worm their way in without anyone noticing, it's going to take more than tossing a few rooms to root them out.'

'I'll see what I can do, but I'm not happy with you going about alone, not until we know what's going on.' She finished the rest of Ratty's wine in a single gulp. 'It sounds like they've got a real killer on board, especially the whole throat thing. That takes some doing.'

He'd thought about that too, and was relieved to hear it voiced by another. 'I'll stay here until you get back, don't worry. Too much to do.'

'Lock the door,' she said as she tucked a pair of knives into the twin sheaths at the small of her back and adjusted her coat over them.

'Yes, mother,' he said drily.

'I meant it,' she replied.

'As did I,' he said, pushing out the door and locking it. He put his back to it and sighed. Things had been going too well recently, which was always a sign that his fortunes were due a correction. Even the ache in his bad leg had faded, perhaps for the first time in ten years. At least he hadn't lost weight and regrown a full head of hair, because that would have spelled an entire apocalypse. He snorted in amusement at the thought and made his way back to his desk where a stack of bills and letters needed answering, and soon lost himself to their banality.

He finished the pile sometime the next afternoon, having made the most of being undisturbed save for the occasional runner bringing fresh letters or news, most of which was entirely mundane. He ate alone in a booth downstairs and, despite the food being the best the cook was capable of and the fawning service it was served with, he found himself picking at it. Lona wasn't a conversationalist by any stretch of the imagination, but she could listen with the best of them and to his complete surprise he found that not only did he feel safer with her about, he actually missed having her stony expression watching him from the other side of the table.

He gestured for another glass of wine and enjoyed it slowly while turning the revelation over in his mind. Did he actually like her as more than an employee, and how did she feel about it? She was almost impossible to read, and he didn't want to risk her scorn. He'd witnessed it before, and if it could have been weaponised, the Kinslayer would have been dealt with years ago.

He finished the wine and thanked the innkeeper, whose relief at the compliment was no doubt matched by the relief that he was leaving, and stepped out into the night.

'ACTUAL BACON,' STEF said, cramming another rasher into his mouth but still managing to grin over the table. A series of grunts answered him, given that they were all doing the same thing, albeit with different combinations involving eggs and bread. They had most of the common room to themselves, having slept in well past sunrise, when the locals had begun their day. The innkeeper hadn't looked very enthused when they'd asked for breakfast but his eyes had lit up when they asked for a breakfast of that magnitude, which should perhaps have warned them of what would come after.

They sat there for some time after the last scrap had been eaten and the small beers had been drunk, all equally reluctant to be the first to break the spell of contentment. The clouds had emptied themselves overnight, bringing the promise of clear skies to compensate for the muddy paths, but the idea of another dry night and good food was tempting. In the end however, the decision wasn't theirs to make.

Once the serving women had cleared their table the innkeep made his way over and hooked his thumbs in his overworked belt.

'If you want the room another night, you've got to settle up,' he said.

'How's that?' Hayden asked.

'Let's say it's a lesson learned,' he said. 'Everyone pays daily. Keeps us all honest.'

'How much then?' asked Orec.

'Twenty for the room, ten for the breakfast. Each.'

The suggestion that they stay another day died on Orec's lips. An incredulous 'What?' escaped instead.

'You heard me. Thirty apiece.'

'You're having a laugh,' Tomas said. 'Thirty shillings apiece would buy this rathole.'

Orec was about to say something very similar, if potentially cruder, when a boot dug into his shin. He looked across to Hayden, and then followed the tilt of the archer's head to where six of the town guard had sauntered in and were ostensibly warming themselves by the fire.

'That isn't what we agreed,' Hayden said.

'Sure it is,' the innkeeper replied, folding his arms. 'Isn't that right, Clarissa?'

The serving woman who'd been hovering behind him took a

step forward. 'Yes, father,' she said, folding her arms. 'That's what he agreed.'

'Bollocks,' Hayden said. 'I'd sooner sleep in a stable.'

The guards made their way over as he spoke, spreading out to form a line between them and the door. They were fully armed and armoured, and Orec had little doubt that they knew how to use the weapons their hands were even now resting on. It had been a long time since he had felt as vulnerable as he did then, nor more acutely aware of what a poor threat four unarmed men presented.

'Is there a problem here, Stalsson?' one asked, the smirk on his face leaving little doubt that none of this was unexpected or unrehearsed.

'These men are refusing to pay,' the innkeeper replied.

'That so?' asked the guard, shaking his head. 'Can't have vagabonds stealing the food from honest men's mouths. How much do they owe?'

'A hundred,' the innkeeper said.

'And twenty,' Stef replied testily. 'At least get it right.'

'A hundred and twenty,' Stalsson growled.

The guard grunted. 'If you're unable to pay, our magistrate can weigh the value of your possessions.'

'Or your service,' said another. 'Make your decision.'

Tomas' face was colouring by the moment, and even as he watched, Orec saw a vein swell on his forehead. He scanned the table, noting the forks that lay near each plate, and the small eating knives that they'd each brought to the table with them. They were a poor match for the heavy bladed swords the guards wore, and would be entirely useless against armour. But none there were really expecting them to fight back, so they'd have surprise on their side.

He made a show of dipping the last bit of bread in the bacon fat and chewing it.

He'd been ready to act, and on the verge of moving before the voice had spoken, the same voice that had taunted him for his inaction and indecisiveness when he'd courted Martina, and then gone on to save his life many times in the years that followed.

*And then what?*

He was sure they could overcome the guards, although it would be a hard and dirty fight, but after that? The noise would bring more guards, and the innkeeper and his daughter would most likely be screaming blue murder by that time. Even if they managed to get their gear before the rest came, they couldn't fight a town, nor evade a determined pursuit.

He swallowed the mouthful, then stood up, turning as he did and stepping into the innkeeper's personal space, pressing his eating knife into the junction of hip and thigh.

'We can pay,' he said, digging the knife in. It wouldn't take much to drive it in and open the great artery in his leg, and from the ragged gasp that answered him, the man knew it too. He turned to the nearest guard, whose sword was four inches from clearing its scabbard.

'Put it away, son.'

The room fell silent as the guard licked his top lip. Orec knew that he'd seen the flash of the knife, and the sense of imminent violence that hung in the air, like oil awaiting a spark, was impossible to miss. Orec kept his gaze on the guard, almost daring him to look away. He felt, rather than saw the moment the man made up his mind, despite how he tried to hide behind sudden bluster.

The guard sneered as he slid his sword back into its sheath, and with that, time seemed to start again.

'It's almost a shame that you can pay,' he said, spitting the words at Orec, who for a thought he was going to do something stupid and draw it again, but whatever he saw in Orec's expression stayed his hand. Before he could think of anything else, Orec pushed the innkeeper at him, forcing his hand away from the sword.

The guard shoved Stalsson away. 'The cripple stays with us. To make sure none of you get any stupid ideas.' A passing grunt was the only reply he got as they filed past.

'There's a good boy,' he said as Tomas stalked by. For a moment it looked like he was going to swing at the man who'd spoken, but he turned away with nothing more than a murderous glare and thump his way up the stairs.

'YOU'RE NOT SERIOUS,' Tomas spat. 'I say we go down there and open those dirty, thieving bastards up!'

'Sure,' Orec said, shrugging his mail into a more comfortable position. 'And then we can torch the town.'

'What—'

'I mean, we don't want to be run down by the rest of them. I figure we drop a few of them in the square as an example and set some fires, just enough to keep them busy, then head straight out. Turn north by east, and lose them in the forest.'

'That's not what I said, and you bloody well know it.'

'But it is,' Orec said, his tone hardening. 'What did you think's going to happen after?'

Tomas opened his mouth to protest, then swore and hurled a discarded tankard across the room. 'Goddamned swine! That's everything we've got.'

'Not everything,' Orec said, fastening his belts. 'Just most of it. Now get your shit together.'

'We really going to let them do this?' Hayden asking, knowing the answer before he asked the question. His initial reaction had been the same as Tomas's, and if he thought about it, probably Orec's too. But Sarge was right. This fight was one to be avoided if it could be, however bitter a pill it would be to swallow.

They made their way back down the stairs with Hayden carrying Stef's kit over his shoulder, walking back into the common room just in time to see one of the guards slamming a fist into Stef's face, snapping it sideways while two of the others held his arms and grinned like children at fair.

'Oh fuck,' was all that Orec had time to say before his peripheral vision caught the motion of Tomas' arm. The throwing axe whipped across the room and bisected the eyebrow of the guardsman who'd hit Stef, the wet crack of its impact leaving no doubt that the man would never stand up after his spinning body hit the ground.

By the time that it had, the black blade of his sword was free of its scabbard and his shoulder was set as he charged across the room towards the guards who still had their backs to them.

The seconds it took for the stunned guards to move past incredulity and truly register what was happening cost them everything. The first was catapulted into the table by Orec's mailed shoulder, and the second could only gasp as the dark steel of Orec's sword chopped into the side of his neck. He fell backwards without another sound, hands trying to stem the tide of blood.

The last man managed to draw his sword, but he was overbalanced and moving backwards, and Orec was quicker. He recovered and lunged forward, sending the sword through the padded jerkin the man wore, skewering heart and lung before bursting from his back. Behind him, Hayden's long knives had found and opened the neck and wrist of the fourth guard, who staggered back, spraying them all with arcs of blood.

Of the men who'd been holding Stef, one was on his back, his hands flailing weakly at the grotesque gash that Tomas' axe had opened in his chest, and the last had his hands held up high above his deathly pale face.

'Please,' he said, pushing him backwards into the wall. 'Don't.'

Tomas only grunted and backhanded him with the axe, leaving him with a broken jaw, but unconscious and alive.

'Goddamn it,' Orec snarled, lashing out with a boot at the man he'd charged into, knocking him out cleanly.

Orec marched over to where the innkeeper was crouched and pulled him to his feet by an ear. Stalsson protested but didn't offer any real resistance as he was dragged over to where the bloodied bodies lay.

'This is your doing. Look at them.'

Stalsson looked away but Orec swung a fist into his ribs, doubling him over, then lifted his head with a fistful of lank hair.

'I said look at them.' The innkeeper wheezed, but made sure that Orec saw him looking. 'All we wanted was a bed and some breakfast.'

'This wasn't supposed to happen,' he coughed. 'You were just supposed to pay and go.'

'I say we kill them all and burn it down,' offered Tomas. 'It'll buy us time.'

'Tempting,' Orec admitted. He wanted to be angry with Tomas, but he'd felt the same surge of anger when he saw them laying into Stef. If anything, Tomas' act of violence was touching in a perverse sort of way that the man he'd been five years ago would never have understood. Orec Martinsson would probably be throwing up at this point, rather than weighing up the deaths of another three men. Murders, whispered the voice in his mind.

'What do you think?' he asked Stalsson, jerking the innkeep's head back, exposing his grimy throat. 'A few more deaths aren't really worth losing sleep over.'

'Sarge,' said Stef. 'Let's just rope them and go.'

In the end they settled for rounding up the serving women and locking them all in one of the storerooms. They waited outside as Hayden barred the doors of the inn and clambered out of a window. It wasn't a great deception, and Tomas was still arguing for the fire, but Orec's blood had cooled, and the morning's bloodshed was about all he could stomach.

They hurried through the streets, not running or barging their way through, but simply moving purposefully and trying not to be memorable in any way. It must have worked to some extent as no one troubled them and soon enough the gates were behind them. The grin that the guards there had flashed as they marched out wasn't encouraging though. If they'd been in on it, which they most likely were given how a shared barracks bred gossip, then they would be expecting the others back sooner rather than later.

'What do you reckon?' he asked Hayden as soon as they were out of earshot.

'No more than an hour.'

'Goddamn it,' Orec muttered.

'The forest is our best bet for losing any trackers. If we keep to the road any idiot on a horse could spot us from miles away.'

'Alright, lead us in.'

His wasn't the only sour face as they headed back along the road they'd come down the day before, each reassuring themselves in their own way that it was simply a detour and not them turning away from the path home.

# CHAPTER SEVEN

'A LETTER FOR you.'

Catt looked up as Fisher tossed the envelope to him, barely catching it before it knocked his ink pot over. He scowled, but Fisher had already turned away, apparently blissfully unaware of the carnage that had been so narrowly averted.

'Savage,' he muttered, fumbling in a nearby drawer for a suitable letter opener. He slid the page out and unfolded it, the quality of the paper stoking his curiosity even further. He loved the mystery of letters and the potential that an unopened missive carried. They could be anything, from the most mundane claim for payment (which paper of this quality certainly made unlikely) to great and terrible tidings that could change lives. He allowed himself a moment to enjoy the sensation before unfolding it and leaning forward under his desk lamp, unaware of Fisher watching him over the top of the book he was ostensibly absorbed in.

'Well?' he asked when Catt finally set the page down and leaned back in his chair, his hand raking his hair in an unconscious but futile attempt to put his fringe in any kind of order.

'Well, what?'

'What is it?' He lowered the book, marking his place with a finger. 'You've been reading that for almost a quarter of an hour. Not even you read that slowly.'

He could almost see Catt's inability to keep a secret warring with his habitual urge to try anyway and simply waited until the former won, as it usually did.

'It's from the Blackharts,' he said, smoothing the pages out on his desk. 'I wrote to them about our, um, missing visitor.'

'You'll simply have to tell them it's no longer for sale.'

'It wasn't an offer of sale,' Catt said testily. 'I wrote to ask if they had anything in their library regarding its morphology.' And it was true too, at least of the second letter he'd sent.

'My apologies,' Fisher said, his even tone stripping any sincerity from the words. 'And? Were they able to offer anything?'

'Yes, as a matter of fact. They've transcribed an entry from one of their journals.' He tapped his fingers on the paper. 'I really would love to see their library, you know? I must write a suitable thank you. Nothing too flamboyant, but enough to encourage a reply and establish a correspondence.'

'The letter?'

'Oh, yes. Apparently the description of the lightning struck a chord with one of them, and they managed to find a reference to something which sounds remarkably like our little friend.' He scanned the second page again. 'It seems that certain Heart Takers could bring them through rifts, and in their records, the done thing was to drop them in middle of the opposing army's rank and file. They're vicious predators, quite deadly from the sound of it.'

'That's interesting, but hardly ground-breaking.'

Catt held a finger up. 'But here's the thing. These creatures would eventually shrug off the compulsion and had to be returned before they turned on the summoner, making them a bit of a gamble to deploy. That might explain the rarity, or why it was the last trick the previous owner tried. In this example, the beast opened one final rift and vanished back into, and I quote, *a black land lit by great columns and bolts of lightning and swarming with such beasts, like ants about their destroyed nest.'*

Fisher replaced his finger with an actual bookmark and folded his arms. 'Now that is interesting. Well done.'

Catt accepted the compliment with the slightest of nods, his mind still dwelling on what other secrets the Blackhart library might be hiding. Given how remote the family holdings were, it was something close to miracle that he'd received such a comprehensive reply in so short a time. It was that same remoteness that made it so difficult to plead for access; they were unfailingly polite in their correspondence, but also unwavering in their stance. To trek hundreds of miles through an arid landscape that had been unwelcoming even before the Kinslayer had loosed his legions of monsters to request admittance without an invitation wasn't a journey that excited him, especially not if it was on foot. He suddenly frowned and picked up the transcription again.

'One final rift,' he said, lowering the page.

'What was that?'

'The beast opened one *final* rift. It opened a rift, my dear Fisher.' He rose and went to stand before the small fire. 'It stands to reason then that it had opened others, and apparently of its own volition. It wanted to go home.'

Fisher drummed his fingers on the back of his book. 'Extraordinary, for sure.'

'But why hasn't it done it now? It ran off, like a poor lapdog finally sensing freedom. How far did you track it? Three miles?'

'More or less, as the crow flies.'

'Well, if I could open rifts and go from one place to other, I certainly wouldn't be running around knocking over market stalls and stirring up such a hue and cry.'

'No, I suppose you wouldn't,' Fisher said, a smile pulling at his lips. If Catt could have found some way to animate the legs of his favourite chair, he would never walk anywhere again. 'It is a valid point though,' he conceded. 'I saw no sign of being wounded, and its pace was constant.'

'Yes, it was quite hale, I assure you.' He knelt and placed another log onto the embers, the memory of the creature looming over him playing across his mind once more, stirring up the ghost of how unmistakably mortal he had felt at that moment.

He stood up then, fast enough to send motes of light dancing at the corner of his vision.

'It wasn't injured, but the circlet was.' He gave no sign that he even heard Fisher's question. 'That must be it. The circlet activated, but it wasn't intentional. Whatever process that was meant to bring it over was incomplete.'

'An excellent hypotheses.' Fisher sat forward. 'It ties in with what you said about it trying to mend the circlet.'

'Yes,' Catt said. 'Tell me again, when you tracked it, which direction did it go? And I don't mean this way and that.'

'North by east. I lost the spoor on the King's Road.'

Catt dropped gracelessly into his chair, the leather puffing it and sending dust swirling. 'That's it,' he said, rubbing at his forehead. 'It has to be.'

'Fine, I'll ask. Has to be what?'

'If I'm not mistaken, Tulkauth lies to the north east. I think that's where it's going. That battle ended when the Yogg leader died in a great explosion, which was clearly the circlet being broken. All that energy was discharged there, and I think it needs that same energy it go home.'

'Hmm,' Fisher said, fingers absently tapping on his armrest. 'Perhaps, but Tulkauth was months ago. Even if we assume that it's sensitive enough to sense the location from so far away, whatever happened there would have been washed away by rain and time.'

Catt seemed to deflate along with his chair. 'Then why that way?'

Fisher leaned back and thought about it, recalling the memory of the two days that he'd spent tracking it. It had wandered widely at first, then steadily refined its course until it finally left the town and headed to the north without wavering far off course, only turning aside once near one of the inns, no doubt drawn by the light and smell of food.

When the answer came to him he sat up straight, his nails leaving a furrow in the armrest.

'The King's Road,' he said. 'It wasn't using it to travel, it was tracking something as much as I was it.' He mentally cursed himself for not seeing it earlier.

'Well? What is it?'

'It's tracking your man Boris. He came by coach, all along the King's Road from Maybury, perhaps even Tulkauth itself.'

Catt banged a fist on his desk and grinned. 'That's it. An excellent deduction, Fishy.'

'I fear it doesn't spell good news for Boris though. I can't imagine it wants to have a chat with him.'

IT HAD BEEN three days since they'd fled the town, and Orec's bleak mood was finally starting to lift. He wasn't naive to think that they'd gotten away cleanly, but they'd not seen any signs of pursuit as yet and it no longer felt that every break or hour spent asleep was bringing them closer to a hangman's noose.

He looked across the campsite as they readied themselves for another day's march and felt a stab of guilt at the realisation of how surly he'd been. *Not that it wasn't justified*. He pushed the thought away before it dragged him back down into a whirlpool of worrying and forced himself to focus on the here and now. Stef's bruises had faded well, and his leg wasn't bothering him as much, but other than that, they were all in relatively good shape.

They could do with a bit more to eat, but their depleted packs at least made walking a bit easier. He tightened his harness and walked over to where Hayden was fussing over some of his fletching.

He picked up one of the arrows and turned it in his fingers, testing the chiselled point. 'What do you think about trying that ridge for game?' He pointed to the shadowy bulk to the north, as yet untouched by the rising sun. 'We could do with something hot.'

'Could do.' He reached forward and snatched the arrow from Orec's hands. 'We crossed a few game trails yesterday. Can't promise anything though.'

'If anyone can manage it, you can,' Orec said. 'Did you hear that? Roast tonight, lads.'

Hayden have him a sour look and refilled his quiver.

'About bloody time someone else pulled their weight around here,' Tomas replied. 'My navel's near pressing against my spine.'

'Says the man I overtook twice yesterday,' Stef replied, settling himself on his crutch.

'It's called a rearguard.'

'Sure it is.'

'Ask a grown up to explain it to you.'

'Cut it out,' Orec said, his smirk hidden as he kicked dirt over the last of the embers. 'It's mostly uphill today, so save your breath.'

'I'll give it until noon,' Hayden said. 'I'll find you.'

'Be careful.'

'Yes, mother.'

With that, he turned and sauntered from the camp. Orec watched him go, not quite seeing the moment where he blended into the dappled foliage, then headed out.

The hills were deceptively high and the slopes constant, never offering a peak to aim for. Every corner simply revealed more of the same shrubbery and ankle twisting roots, and by the time that the sun was directly overhead, the monotony had eaten away at both their legs and willpower. Orec could barely remember the forced cheer of the morning, much less muster any more of it, and the wrinkled apple and tepid water that remained to serve as lunch didn't improve his mood any further. He swatted at whatever was crawling through the sweat on his neck and watched Stef making his way up towards him.

'He's doing good,' Tomas offered, wincing as he stretched his legs out. 'Be nice if we get can get some horses.'

'There's a proverb somewhere about horses and wishes.'

'How's it go?'

Orec shrugged. 'Don't remember, apart from that it doesn't make sense.'

'No horses,' Hayden said from behind them, making Tomas twitch as if kicked. 'But I can offer dinner later.'

'Creep,' Tomas said testily, but like Orec, his eyes were on the bulging sack looped over the archer's shoulder.

'How'd you get here so fast?'

'I got lucky. There were forest buck at the stream, and from the path just meandered along the ridge up there.' He gestured over his shoulder. 'A nice walk too.'

'Hey,' said Stef, finally arriving and lowering himself to the ground with a groan.

'So,' Hayden said, 'that's the good news. The not so good news is that there are horsemen on our trail.'

'You and your big mouth,' Oreo said, glancing at Tomas. 'How far?'

'A couple of hours. I couldn't see anything apart from dust, but judging by how much I'd reckon at least half a dozen.'

'They may not be on our trail,' offered Stef.

'We're better off assuming the worst,' Orec replied. Even at a walk, horses could conceivably close the distance before nightfall proper, assuming they had a half competent tracker.

'There's a good vantage back there. We'll know soon enough.'

'You good?' Orec asked Stef, who shrugged.

'Better than grandad,' he said, starting the three-step process to stand up again.

'You wish.'

The path Hayden lead them on was almost cruel in its contour, but just when they were ready to call for another rest the ground evened out and the trees gave way to wildflowers and the stinging flies were replaced with fat bees.

'As I said, it was a nice walk,' Hayden said, smiling at the look on the others' faces. He almost felt bad about sending them along the lower path, but it passed quickly. 'This way.'

He led them past a pool whose tranquillity was marred by the four rusted swords thrust into the ground nearby, the equally rusted helmets that had once rested on them laying nearby, each now home to seedlings, a stark reminder that death didn't care about nice views.

'The other graves are over there,' Hayden said, pointing further up the slope. 'Goblins, from the look of the bones.'

'You checked?' Tomas asked, slightly horrified.

'Yeah sure, I stopped to dig some out.'

'Foxes,' offered Stef.

'Or ghouls,' said Orec, which raised Hayden's eyebrows. He moved on past the pool to a slab of rock that jutted out some thirty feet over the edge of the ridge that the flowers hid so well and gestured Orec forward.

'Stay low,' he said, setting his bow aside before squatting near the tip.

Orec kept his gaze and thoughts fixed on the rock under his feet as he moved up to join him, but the thought of the void beneath it left him feeling strangely hollow. He hunkered down next to Hayden, who pointed off in the distance.

'There. Follow the line past those dead trees.'

It took a few moments for the haze to resolve itself into something specific, but once it did there was no mistaking the dust cloud for what it was.

'There's no trade road that far up.' Orec didn't expect a reply, and didn't get one. 'What are you thinking?'

'Well, I'd suggest we follow the river down.' Hayden swivelled and gestured to a dark strip that rolled out towards the grassland below. 'They can't follow that, not on horseback. Might win us enough time to lose them.'

'But Stef couldn't do it,' Orec finished for him.

Hayden nodded. 'What's the call, sarge?'

Orec sat back on his heels and looked out over the vista, his eyes picking out the form of a red-tail hawk circling over the same ravine. He watched the bird for a few moments, simply enjoying its effortless grace and letting all other thoughts fall away. To him, the hawk was a thing of beauty to be admired, coveted even, but to whatever it was watching in the vegetation below, it was terror incarnate.

'Come on,' he said quietly, rising and moving back to the others. An idea was taking shape in his mind, not necessarily a good one, but it was all he had.

ARMAND GARGLED A mouthful of water and spat it out before taking a long drink from his canteen. Gods, he hated this province. If it wasn't raining, something was trying to bite you, and once it dried out, which it did almost overnight, everything was soon coated in fine dust. How people lived here or, more to the point, why anyone would choose to live here in the first place was beyond his reckoning. He'd taken a job here out of necessity, not choice. The town had needed a firm hand to restore order, and he had the skills and, more importantly, needed the money. That money that had yet to find its way to his purse, a situation the Mayor had sworn to remedy once they brought the fugitives in. That was most likely because paying him what he was owed would be cheaper than an open bounty, but that didn't bother him. A deal was a deal, and with the coin in his pocket he could finally move on again. There were plenty of other towns that needed a provost's skills, and if the gods were kind he'd find one where everything didn't taste like dust.

The fugitives they were pursuing were on foot, and not half as clever as they thought they were, so it shouldn't be more than another day or two, especially if they were moving with a cripple. There was clearly more to the story than what the watch commander had reported, but sorting that particular mess out wasn't going to be his problem to solve. Once he had his money, he was going to put this dusty hole behind him and not look back. He slowed his horse as his tracker waved him over.

'These are fresh, no more than an hour, give or take a half,' he said.

'Good work,' Armand replied. Luc was the best tracker he'd worked with, and a good man to boot, and he'd been relieved when he'd managed to secure a matching posting for him. He turned and waved the rest of the platoon forward to relay the news. It was, as he had expected, taken as good news. A quick result was the best result, especially when it meant having a little extra time to cash in on the innkeeper's goodwill.

They took some time to ready themselves, stowing anything which could get in the way in their saddlebags while others strung their bows and checked that their weapons were readily to hand. He checked his own sabre and tightened the leg straps on his pleated mail before nudging his horse forward.

'You all know the drill. It's pretty tight in here, so keep your eyes and ears open. Don't wait for permission if threatened. They've killed three men already, and I don't plan on letting them increase that number.' He gestured to Luc to move out and glanced over his shoulder. 'Unless it's you, Gustav. Your wife deserves better.'

A round of laughter greeted that, breaking some of the tension, and he nudged his horse along the track. He didn't plan on losing anyone, not now, and not to a bunch of thugs. An hour passed before Luc signalled him forward.

'The path opens onto a small escarpment,' he said, talking quietly, more out of habit than for any good it did given the sound of their harness and the snorting of the horses. 'There's a campsite with two men, an old one and the cripple.'

'There should be four.'

'I didn't see the others,' Luc offered with a shrug. 'They might be off foraging; there's a ravine off to the far side.'

Armand sat back in his saddle and tapped the reins against his palm. Luc's suggestion was entirely reasonable, but the gate guards he'd interviewed had been clear that one of the killers had been carrying a leather-wrapped longbow, and the thought of them being out there, unseen, sat very poorly with him. A short bow he could have understood, as most companies had sported at least two, both for skirmishing as well as the off-chance of nabbing something for the pot, but a longbow was the weapon of a dedicated archer.

'Stay under cover,' he said, 'and watch out for the archer.'

Luc nodded and watched Armand head back to where the others waited, then slipped between two thorny shrubs and moved back along the edge of the clearing. He'd settled himself into a decent spot behind a forking tree when he heard the sound of the patrol moving in. The escarpment, which had seemed wide and spacious moments before, was suddenly crowded by eight horses. They split into three groups as they fanned out, each three on either side, two of these with swords drawn and the third with a distinctive red fletched arrow nocked to the string of their curved bow. Armand and his sergeant took the centre, with the latter carrying the now unfurled standard of the provosts, and Luc couldn't help but feel sorry for the two men who now stood with their hands held high as this imposing spectacle rode up to them.

'You are now bound by law,' Armand called, his horse

wheeling as he drew up mere paces before the two men, who hastily thrust their hands into the air. 'Lay your weapons aside and surrender.'

'What've we done?' the cripple called out.

'Where are the others?' Armand asked, ignoring the question.

'What others?'

He kept his hand on his sabre as he looked down on the man. He was younger than he'd expected, and the bandages on the stump of his leg looked weathered and grubby.

'Don't play games, son. It's over, so don't make it any worse. You'll get to put your case to the magistrate.'

'I'm not your son, and we've done nothing wrong.'

Armand felt his annoyance rising, and he was fairly certain he wasn't alone in that. No matter how you caught them, they all feigned shock and innocence, even if you found them elbows deep in a dead man's blood.

'Lower your bows.' The voice rang out from behind them, drawing a curse from Armand. 'Nice and slow.'

He turned and saw a lone figure standing some sixty yards behind them, a half-drawn longbow trained on the nearest of his men. Four arrows were thrust into the ground in front of him, and if he was any good, it wouldn't take long for all four to be in the air.

'Don't be foolish,' he called back, drawing his sabre. His two riders with the bows turned in their saddles as he spoke. As good as they may be, hitting two men at the same time wasn't an option. 'The war's over. No one else needs to die.'

'Last chance,' the archer called.

Armand opened his mouth to reply, then flinched back as something sprayed across his face, warm droplets finding his eyes and open mouth. He recoiled and spat at the same time, and through blurred vision he saw the shape of Harald, his second, tilt in his saddle and plunge to the ground, followed a moment later by the standard.

*Blood.*

Angry shouts filled the air as he furiously wiped his face, followed a breath later by the *whip-thump* of arrows finding their targets. He saw a shape reaching for him and lashed out with the sabre, a clumsy cut that would have earned him a good thump on the head on any training ground, but the figure yelped and fell back. He drove his spurs in and his horse reared, hooves flailing and sending the killers stumbling away.

He spun as it came down, his vision finally clearing and giving him his first glimpse of the pandemonium around him. The three men to his left were down, shot through with yard-shafts, while Harald lay on the ground with an axe where his nose should have been, his face a bloody ruin. As he looked, his two remaining men spurred their horses towards the archer. Only one made it more than thirty paces.

He heard footsteps behind him and barked a command, bracing himself as the horse bucked and kicked backwards, hammered its hooves into whoever was behind them.

'Yah!' he shouted, turning its head towards the path and slipping sideways, putting its body between him and the archer. What sounded like an enormous and angry bee flew through the space his chest had been a moment before and he clung on for his life, exhorting the horse to greater speed, trusting to its instincts and whatever luck remained in his life that it wouldn't stumble.

THE LAST EMBER of Qrec's hope died when Hayden came back up the track and shook his head. It hadn't been much of a hope, but he'd nursed it so carefully, telling himself that he hadn't been mistaken, that the arrow must have hit him. He'd seen him swing in the saddle from the impact. It had to have stopped him.

Except it hadn't, and the lawman had escaped, and would even now be coaxing his horse to greater effort. He'd be back at the town tomorrow if he didn't care about riding it to death, and from there the word would go out. Four local guardsmen was bad enough, but could be dismissed as a local incident, but the killing of seven, whether travelling under the standard of the provosts or not, would certainly cause trouble when word got out. That sort of thing made everyone nervous and galvanised communities.

The hunk of bread he'd been gnawing on no longer tasted like anything and he spat a mouthful of it into the fire, followed by the rest of what he was holding. He rubbed his face, pressing hard enough that whorls of light danced across his vision, and fought the childish but unbearably tempting urge to break something. Preferably Tomas's neck.

But he was in command, and the fault lay with him. He'd been unforgivably naive to think that matters would pan out as he'd envisaged, with nothing more than a few scrapes and some bruised pride left in its wake. From the moment they'd cantered into the clearing he'd felt it all unravelling. He clenched his hands into fists and tried to work his way past the frustration that was choking him, but it refused to give way. He was angry at Tomas for throwing the axe, and Hayden for miscounting their numbers, but the real venom was reserved for himself. He should have reacted before everything swung so wildly out of control, but he'd been too slow. *Too scared,* the voice in his head whispered. *You froze, and now you're doomed.*

He heard Hayden sit down but didn't look up.

'Did you find him?' Stef asked.

'Only my arrow,' he replied. 'He slipped it.'

'Damn,' muttered Tomas. 'I thought you were better than that.'

'Shut up,' Orec said, rhythmically massaging his temples, his eyes still closed. 'Just shut up.'

'I'm just saying that I'd have shot the horse,' Tomas continued. 'That would have—'

'Shut up.'

'What're you getting so worked up about?'

Afterwards he wouldn't remember rising and diving onto Tomas, burning logs spinning in all directions behind him, as he grabbed the old man's coat and slammed a fist into his stupidly surprised face. He would remember how good it felt, for at least one perfect moment, even though that memory would quickly be tempered by shame once Hayden had pulled them apart, and promptly slapped Orec meatily enough that the ringing wouldn't leave his ear for another two days.

'Get a hold of yourself,' the archer said, his voice cold as Orec staggered on his feet. A few feet away Stef was holding onto a snarling Tomas, his bared teeth red from the blood streaming from his nose.

'Come on, you chickenshit,' he growled, shrugging his arms from Stef's grip. 'What're you going to do? Huh?'

Stef stumbled after him but Hayden stepped between the two men. 'Stop it, for gods' sakes. Both of you.'

'What'd you think was going to happen, huh?' Tomas continued, swatting the archer's outstretched had away. 'Did you think we're going to give up? Take a chance with some district judge? You've lost it, Blackblade.' He said the last in a mocking tone before the snarl returned to his voice. 'This was always going to end like this. It always does.'

He spat at Orec's feet before turning and walking off towards the pond.

Orec watched him go, then turned and walked off in the opposite direction, stopping only to collect one of the flasks they'd taken from the dead men's saddlebags. He heard Hayden talking quietly to Stef as he did, but their words were low and clearly not meant for him. Which was good, because he wasn't listening and had no inclination to either. The anger and shame roiling within him felt like acid, sour and sharp, and ate at him as much as the truth behind Tomas's words.

He took a long swallow of the dead man's liquor, but barely tasted the cheap brandy as it burned its way into him. *You've lost it*. He looked down at his hands and flexed them, the blood that still clung to the creases of his knuckles stark against his skin. The problem was that he hadn't lost it. He couldn't even remember the faces of the man he'd killed, only that he'd taken his arm off as he dodged the sabre, then ended him with a cut to the neck as he reeled from the blow. He took another drink, holding the mouthful until the fumes made his eyes water.

'Hey,' said Stef quietly, coming to stand next to him. 'That any good?'

He passed it over without a word and waited for the cough.

'Gods,' Stef said a moment later, wiping his mouth as he finished coughing. 'I'm not even sure if that's actually booze.'

'Me neither.'

'Sarge, I think we should go.'

'I'm not a sergeant anymore,' he said, picking at the band sewn onto his cuffs.

Stef grabbed his wrist. 'You are until you get home.' Orec tried to shrug his hand away, but he held on. 'Until you walk through that door, that stays on.'

'And then what,' he replied, hating the sneer in his voice but unable to stop it. 'We live happily ever after?'

'That's up to you,' Stef said, letting go of his wrist. 'But you're not going to get a chance unless you stop staring at that damned bird and we get out of here. There's nothing we can do for these men. What's done is done.'

Orec looked away from the hawk, first down at his hands again, and then across at Stef. In his mind, Stef was still the awkward shipping clerk, drunk for the first time and extolling the virtue of reading to the men around him, but that boy, for that was what he had been, was long gone. Stef as a man would be a complete stranger to that boy.

He clapped him lightly on the shoulder but didn't say

anything as he turned back. Tomas was back already, having washed himself in the pond, and Hayden had busied himself in dragging the bodies into a line, affording them some semblance of dignity.

He walked along the line and stopped as he came to that of a man with a severed arm and gaping throat wound. He'd bled out and was a pale and cold as fine marble, a stark contract to the dark rawness of the gash that had torn his life away. His coat and boots were well maintained, and his moustache was neatly trimmed, and it may have suggested a vain man had it not been for the worn, functional gear that he'd carried. *Not vain then, simply disciplined*.

Orec squatted next to him and unfastened a silver coat pin in the shape of an oak leaf that had no place on his uniform, clearly a token of some sort, mostly likely from his woman. He turned it over in his fingers a few times as he tried to commit the man's face to memory, then pocketed the pin and stood.

'Let's go,' he said.

# CHAPTER EIGHT

LONA MOUTHED A half-hearted apology over her shoulder as the man she'd shoved went sprawling, but didn't slow down. There were dozens more like him ahead of her, nursing both their drinks and their own sob stories, as if the war had targeted them personally. Everybody had lost something, and no matter how bad the pain, the dead envied them all.

She heard shouts behind her as he picked himself up and began spitting insults at her back. He didn't follow after her though, which was perhaps the best decision he'd made for some time.

'Move,' she growled, pushing her way through the crowd. Why'd it have to happen tonight, when everyone had some coin in their pocket? She shot a look over her shoulder, not sure what she was expecting to see, but it was just a street full of milling men gathered around the light spilling from the gambling houses, bars, and pie shops like enormous, unwashed moths around a lamp.

But beyond the lamplight the darkness deepened quickly, and only a few isolated pools of light hinted at the rows of houses hidden within it. Something moved across one of those pools as she looked, a brief shadow, gone before her eyes could registered anything more than movement.

*It's just someone going home.*

The platitude sounded thin even to her, and she forged ahead with new speed, no longer bothering to offer anything akin to apology as she pushed her way through to the passage up to Boris' office. A hand landed on her shoulder, and a voice barked angrily at her, at least until she grabbed two of the fingers and wrenched them backwards, the gristly crunch preceding a shriek of pain. The hand fell away.

Ahead of her the guard at the mouth of the passageway stepped aside, a grin on his face as he watched the punter fall to his knees behind her.

'Heya,' he said.

'No time,' she said, pausing just long enough to lay a hand on his shoulder. He wasn't a bad guy, just dim and entirely transparent in his intentions, and deserved a warning. 'There's bad shit on the way. Gear up and warn everyone.'

'Wait, what?'

'Just do it,' she called as she flung the door open and pounded up the stairs. The door was locked, which she should have been pleased about, but now she simply hammered on it with a fist.

'What?' Boris' voice rang out in an unmistakably irritable tone.

'It's me,' she said. 'Open it.'

'One minute.'

She bit her lip and used the time to gulp in a few deep breaths. When it opened, she pushed inside and immediately locked it behind her.

'What's going on?'

'We need to get out of here,' she said. 'There's no time.'

'How bad?' he said, thankfully moving back to the desk and slipping several ledgers into a satchel rather than arguing. She moved to the window and peered out at the street below before closing and locking the shutters.

'Lona,' Boris said. 'What happened?'

'Whatever killed the crew at Tulkauth also killed the entire workhouse,' she said, sliding a panel open and taking out a sword and cursing as she fumbled with the strap. 'Thirty men.'

He stared at her, open mouthed and frowning as he tried to digest what she was saying.

'Something killed them all,' she said. She moistened her lips before the next part, hating the tremulous feeling inside her. 'And not long before we got there.'

'Hold on, hold on.'

'There's no time,' she said, swallowing hard. 'We have to go.'

'Lona, look at me.'

'We have to go!' Her fist crashed into the desk and the silence that followed was only marred by her heavy breathing before she fell back into the chair and covered her face with her hands.

In the darkness behind her hands shapes materialised unbidden, glimpsed in fits and starts by the light of a swinging lantern. Limbs bent at impossible angles, and silent, screaming faces paler than the splayed ribs protruding from their ripped flesh, and through it all, the heavy scent of pooled blood, cloying in its intensity. She ground her palms into her eyes until the images fractured into a thousand swirling motes of light and sat back.

'Sorry.'

Boris passed across a bottle, which seemed to be his answer to everything, but at the moment it certainly felt like the right one. The liquor burned its way down into her stomach and managed to dislodge the icy hand that seemed to have been gripping it.

'What happened?'

'They were slaughtered,' she said. 'This wasn't the work of a man, nor even a Yogg. This was something else. They were ripped open to the spine.'

He turned an old coin over in his fingers as he considered her. 'Where did you want us to go?'

'Away from here. Don't you see? Whatever this thing is, it's only taken our crew and our house. It ignored everything else.'

'You think it's coming after us. After me?'

'I think so, yes.'

'But why?'

The sound of something smashing in the alley outside paused the question on his lips. On nights like that, it would be more unusual not to hear something breaking as bets were lost and tempers were frayed, but they'd both developed a fine ear for distinguishing the hidden notes of bar fights. Fists on flesh sounded different to batons, and mirrors and windows each broke differently, as did tables and chairs. The wood that heard they heard splintering wasn't a table or a chair, but more like a door. Boris stood unmoving over his chair, straining to hear what would come next, but Lona leapt out of hers like a scalded cat.

She had hold of his collar and was pulling him towards the hidden door or the far side of the room when a scream echoed up the stairs, terror and agony rendering it genderless.

She pulled the lever and spat curses as she forced the stiff mechanism open and pushed Boris inside. What sounded like a horse was coming up the stairs, and she pulled the sliding door closed with all her might, only breathing again when she heard the catch engage again. The wooden veneer hid a strengthened panel, and despite having cursed its weight moments before, she now rested her back against its reassuring solidity. Which is why she heard the hiss on the other side, the sound tapering off into a series of chirruping clicks that reminded her of nothing more than the crickets that had invaded her childhood garden every summer.

Her left leg exploded into agony even as she wondered about the sound, and all she could do was stare dumbly at the tapering horn that was sticking out of it. Time seemed to slow, enough so that she could distantly admire the arcs of violet energy that skipped and danced across her thigh, and then it was pulled back through the wound and the agony redoubled and stole her vision away in a cascade of sun-bright flashes.

Boris caught her before she could hit the floor and was already half carrying, half dragging her to the narrow escape stairs before she could do more than try to shake the light from her vision. Behind them the creature threw itself against the barrier over and over again, every impact sending streams of dust falling from the ceiling. They spilled out into a side street, and she pushed him away. Blood was pouring from the gash but not spurting, so she had some time. She reached for a pouch and pulled out a bandage, wrapping it roughly around the wound. It wouldn't do much, but it was better than nothing.

'Go, I'm good,' she said through clenched teeth.

He pulled her arm over his shoulder and they started moving, both angling towards the stables. The problem with secret escapes was that your men weren't around to help, a fact that Boris was cursing when the door splintered behind them, panels tumbling across the street. He couldn't help but look over his shoulder, a short and sharp breath marking the moment he saw it emerge from the broken door, swift and angular and, save for its eyes, as dark as the night around it. It vanished amidst the darkness until moonlight caught some part of its gleaming hide, giving him a stuttering view of its progress as it turned and raced towards them.

'What is that?' he panted.

Lona didn't bother replying. Even if she did know, it didn't matter anymore. Her strength was quite literally bleeding out of her and her leg would soon give way.

She took a faltering step, then stopped and ducked out from under Boris' arm.

'Go,' she snarled, pushing him away. 'I'll buy you time.'

'Lona—'

She swatted his hand away. 'Just go, damn you.'

The series of clicks sounding from the darkness to her right and made his mind up for him. He gave her a last smile, then turned and ran.

She turned away and drew her sword and rolling her wrist to loosen the tendons and focused on the anger that was simmering somewhere between the fear and pain.

'Come on then,' she said to the darkness while her heart thumped against her ribs as if trying to get as many beats as it could in before it was ripped from her. 'You want me, you're going to have to earn it.'

It came forward then, head held low, serpentine muscles squirming beneath its oily hide and its eyes warming to molten gold. She squared up to it and filled her other hand with her dagger.

'What are you?' she asked breathily.

It circled her, blowing air from unseen nostrils as its head swayed from side to side, reminding her of something, but the thought vanished before she could focus on it. She readied herself for the lunge, but it never came. It sprang to the side, claws raking the wooden cladding as it ran along the wall like a gecko, safely out of her reach.

She spun and could only stand and watch as it sprang back into the roadway in a shower of wood splinters and vanished into the same darkness that had swallowed Boris.

'Well, fuck.'

She fell against the side of the same building and slid down to the soiled duckboards, her sword still clenched in her hand. The only part of her that was warm was her leg, but at least it didn't hurt anymore. She stared in the darkness, waiting and fearing what would come next. A groan escaped her lips, and tears filled her eyes, when his screams cut through the night. Boris was no saint, but he'd never been cruel to her and the sound of his agony pierced her more than she'd ever thought it could.

She could hear men running towards her, the good ones who ran towards trouble, and felt a stab of resentment at the thought of being denied a suitably tragic death. They arrived as Boris finally fell silent, bringing with them a tumult of questions and noise. She wanted to warn them not to go any further, but the last of her strength had poured from her leg and the warning left her lips as a wordless sigh.

It had taken less than an hour for Orec to remember why he'd been content with being a footsoldier. There was no comfortable way to sit in the saddle, and he suspected that the horse was trying to get its own revenge for its previous owner's misfortune. What made it even more unbearable was that the others actually seemed to be enjoying it, even Tomas, although the wineskin may also have played a part in that. Even so, it wasn't the old man who was wincing with every jarring step.

By the time nightfall found them it was all he could to dismount without help, and even then he had to hold onto the saddle until the trembling in his legs faded. He didn't bother with even a token protest when Hayden stepped in and took over removing the saddle and told him to go collect firewood like some neophyte. He could see Stef watching him but he wisely didn't say anything. He winced with every stick and log that he picked up, but it did serve to ease the ache slightly, not that he had any doubt that the morning would see him more crippled than Stef.

Once everything was set, he sat close to the fire and stretched his legs and firmly waved off Stef's concerns. There was nothing any of them could do, and once Hayden staked out the remaining venison over the glowing coals, his discomfort was all but forgotten.

'It's better terrain tomorrow from the look of it,' Hayden said once the last scrap had been wolfed. 'An easy slope, then into a valley. We can make good time, and hopefully get water too.'

'Good terrain for the men behind us too,' Tomas muttered around the stick he was picking his teeth with.

'Don't start that again,' Orec said, the good mood that the food had brought him already fracturing.

'I'm not starting anything,' he said. 'I'm just saying they'll be after us properly now, one way or the other.' He flicked the stick into the fire and watched it get consumed in a flare of light. 'Riding up the high road is as easy for them as it is for us. Well, maybe for most of us.'

He winked at Orec as he said the last, and flashed his yellow teeth in a grin at the sour expression that it provoked.

'It's a valid point,' Hayden said. 'They will be coming after us, and I don't think they'll be coming with a view to parley. But we need water, and these horses will need grain. There's a town somewhere downriver, perhaps three days. It's not much of anything, but they did have stables.'

'Somewhere downriver,' Tomas said. 'That's some high quality scouting.'

'It's there. I came at it from downriver, and only passed through once.'

'You think it's still in one piece?' Stef asked.

'It's by a river,' Orec said. 'People never stray far from a river.'

'We can get water, then climb back into the hills and move parallel to the road. That should buy some time.'

He looked to Orec for confirmation, but the sergeant's head was resting on his crossed arms and wouldn't be answering anyone until the morning.

'Is he going to be alright?' Stef asked.

'He'll be fine,' Tomas said. 'He just can't ride worth a damn.'

'I didn't think he was scared of anything until we had to pass through that gorge earlier,' Stef said. 'He looked green.'

'Get some sleep,' Hayden said, banking the coals. 'I'll take the first.'

Neither of them offered any protest, each knowing that it was futile. They both thought they knew what made Hayden sleep so fitfully when his body eventually forced him to rest, but neither ever spoke of it, not even among themselves, perhaps for fear of being asked the same question.

Orec's suspicions about his legs were confirmed in the morning when Tomas kicked his feet by way of a wake up.

'Sun's rising.'

'Gods and bells,' Orec swore as he sat up, his legs and back already screaming their protest.

'There's toast,' Stef called. 'If you can reach it.'

'Shut up,' he snapped in reply, slowly and clumsily pulling himself to his feet.

'Like a newborn foal,' Tomas said, making a show of sitting down. 'If it was drunk.'

'Would you like a hand?'

'Piss off, the lot of you.' He slowly straightened and ignored their mocking grins. Something crunched low in his back when he took his first step, which seemed to ease some of the tension. He lumbered over to the fire and snatched up a piece of toast.

'This must be what it feels like to be you, Tomas.' He ate standing up and watched the sun slip over the distant horizon, as orange as a yolk, while birds squabbled and wheeled through the cool air. For a few precious moments, he actually felt content.

'I need to take a dump,' Tomas announced, and stomped off into the woods.

'If there's any justice in this world, he'll wipe with thimbleweed.'

Stef and Hayden chuckled at that. Orec dusted the crumbs from his beard and turned to the scout. 'This river town. What's the chance they had barges?'

Hayden closed his eyes for a moment. 'I didn't see any, but there was a pretty sturdy pier.'

Orec nodded. The briefings on their move up to Tulkauth felt like a lifetime ago, but the commander's map had been a work of art that had probably cost several years pay, and he'd made the most of any chance he had to study it.

'I think that's the Andunin. If it is, it flows due south, and forks at High Town.'

'I think it is.' Hayden stood too. 'There's bound to be a riverboat from there.'

'To that dump? Are you sure?'

'Where there's trade, there's merchants. It's the circle of life.'

'I just can't imagine there being much trade in High Town,' Stef said.

'It used to be quite something,' Hayden said. 'Ever been in a treehouse?'

'Sure.'

'Now imagine one big enough for a whole town, with houses and shops joined by suspended walkways and every branch hung with lights and wind chimes.'

Stef frowned, trying to marry his memory of the ashen ruin with what Hayden was describing. 'Who would build, or even live in a town like that?'

'Mostly Aethani and Oerni, but also various river traders, foresters, and a fair number of Shelliac, although they tend to be clustered nearer to the shore.' He smiled briefly as he described it. 'It used to be quite something.'

'I didn't see it before either,' Orec said. 'But I heard what he did to it.'

'And to those who survived,' Hayden added, his expression falling into something darker. 'The people's misery is understandable.'

'Those that are left,' Orec added.

'Who's miserable?' asked Tomas.

'Us, now,' Hayden said, kicking dirt over the embers.

'Whatever,' was the short reply. 'You going to be alright to ride?'

'I'll walk for a bit to loosen things up,' Orec replied. 'You go ahead.'

'You sure?'

'I'll watch out for grabbers.'

Tomas shot him a filthy look but didn't say anything as he

set to packing his bedroll away. He knew what he'd seen, and it wasn't the kind of thing that he would forget anytime soon. And if he never saw it again, he'd be alright with that too. He picked at his teeth and watched Hayden helped Orec with his saddle before taking the lead out of the campsite.

Orec returned Stef's wave as they turned and left, then took up the reins and began to lead his mare.

'Come along, girl,' he said, 'You and I have a few things to discuss.'

As he had for the last week, Armand made his way to the east watchtower as the sun rose. He didn't care about the sunrise itself, and the play of golden light across the low clouds didn't even register with him. His attention was solely on the road his reinforcements were expected to ride in on.

The guards greeted him and left him to his own devices, having quickly learned that he had no inclination to participate in any kind of small talk. Everything was discussed in the barracks, and his return upon his frothing, dying horse and the subsequent tirade he'd launched at the watch commander had dominated every discussion since, whether over the morning oats or jugs of ale. He was civil but cold, and what sympathy they'd held for him had rapidly weathered away when he exhorted the commander into reinstating a daily training regimen that he led with unnecessary passion and a penchant for punitive tasks. The truth of it was that they were hoping his reinforcements arrived as much as he did.

On the eighth day since he'd sent the pigeons, the outlying watch post flashed a warning back with a mirror. *Riders approaching.*

Armand almost toppled the bench he was sitting on when he heard the warning bell, then scrambled to the front gates, pushing several men out of the way as he forced himself up the stairs. He leaned forward, gripping the spikes that adorned the wall, and watched the road. He could feel his heart hammering in his chest and tried to quell the excitement that was already coursing through his veins. *It may not be them but please, by all that's holy, let it be them.*

He didn't have to wait long. The pennants and disciplined formation told him all he needed to know. He punched the air in delight and quickly made his way back downstairs, the dark thoughts that had weighed so heavily on him since his return falling from him like rusted shackles.

An entirely unnecessary trumpet blast announced their arrival at the gates, and he paced back and forth as the guards and patrol commander exchanged greetings. Moments later the gates swung open and a dozen riders cantered in, quickly filling the space with noise and the comforting smells of leather, metal and horse sweat.

Armand grinned and moved forward as the lead rider dismounted and lifted off his helmet.

'Marshal Armand?' He extended a hand. 'Sergeant Quental and the fourth.'

'It's good to see you, sergeant,' Armand said, shaking his hand. 'You must have ridden hard to get here so quickly.'

'We were in the area already, so it was more of a redirect. Where can we get some chow?'

'Of course,' Armand pointed out the mess and stables, quashing what even he recognised as unreasonable, childish frustration that they weren't immediately heading out in pursuit. 'I'll meet you there for a briefing.'

Quental tapped the briefest of salutes against his breastplate and set to sorting his men out. Armand was smiling as he crossed the yard and headed towards the mess hall to warn the cooks. He like to think of himself as a good judge of men, in a manner of speaking, and the impression that Quental gave was one of hard-nosed competence. For the first time since he saw

Harald's head split by the axe, he felt something like confidence again. *Soon.*

In the end, they waited until the next morning to set off. The briefing with Quental had only reinforced his initial opinion of the man, and he'd been pleased to hear that the men in his patrol were all volunteers. The mission wasn't a burden or distraction for them, and from the way they had listened to his briefing and the questions they'd raised afterwards, they were quite serious about it too.

As if to reinforce the point, when he'd packed the last of his gear into his saddlebag and walked outside, he'd found them waiting for him, which was refreshing. He greeted Quental with a nod and slung his bags. A dozen or so of the town guard were watching them and talking quietly amongst themselves, which was nice too. He knew some of them had been reluctant when he'd started the training regimen, but he liked to think that by the end they'd come to appreciate it.

He settled into the saddle, adjusted his split coat, and settled his lance into the quiver, giving it a quick shake to ensure his pennant hung free.

'Ready to ride, marshal?' Quental asked, bringing his gelding alongside.

'That I am, sergeant. Let's go get these bastards.'

Quental tapped a hand to his chest and nudged his horse forward. He turned and gave a short whistle, and the troop began to follow behind Armand. The gates opened and he felt a welcome surge of strength as they made their way out in a rumble of hoofbeats and the jingle of well-kept armour. There would be no stopping him this time.

Lost in his thoughts, he didn't hear the cheer from the palisade and guard towers as he rode off.

Quental's tracker, a dour man who Armand would have taken for a bookkeeper rather than woodsman, came up alongside him half a mile from the town. Armand recounted what he'd told him the night before, pointing out the landmarks he described, and then watched as the tracker rode off without another word.

'Don't feel bad,' the rider behind him said. 'He's always like that.'

'I don't care as long as he does his job,' he called back over his shoulder.

'Don't you worry, marshal. He's like a terrier with a rat. They'll never shake him off.'

It was said matter of factly, and Armand found himself smiling for the second time that morning as he watched the tracker heading up the trail. The hunt was on.

# CHAPTER NINE

Orec made his way to the prow and joined Hayden in leaning his elbows on the railing. The archer grunted a greeting but kept watching the riverbank, a steaming mug of tisane cupped in his hands.

'Do barges have prows?' Orec asked. 'It seems a bit fancy for what is really just an overgrown raft. Is it just the front?'

'I can honestly say I've never thought about it.'

'Me neither. I do like it though.' He took a sip from the cup the matron had given him. She hadn't offered it as much as thrust it at him, but from the way that the hard-bitten crew, who he suspected had piratical tendencies when trade slowed down, deferred to her he had no intention of saying no, even if he hated the stuff. He grimaced as he swallowed. 'River travel, that is.'

'It's a bit more civil, at least while the weather lasts.'

Orec looked over his shoulder to where one of the crew was relieving himself over the side while talking to one of other passengers.

'Very civil,' he said, taking another sip and trying not to taste it. 'We've made good time.'

'Given how much she charged us for passage I would have hoped so.'

Orec shrugged. 'That wasn't our gear, and I'm just glad they took it in trade. We kept the horses, and that's the key thing.'

'It would have been nice to have something beside what we're wearing on our backs. But you're not wrong I suppose.' He sipped his tea. 'I just don't fancy being strung up this close to home.'

'We won't be,' Orec said, his tone purposefully confident. 'We just need to buy some time. We'll ditch the horses, get some clothes, and a haircut and disperse. They're looking for four armed and armoured mercenaries, not a clerk, a carpenter and whatever it is you do when you're not hunting Yoggs and stealing chickens.'

'If you shave that I doubt even we'd recognise you,' Hayden said, glancing at the thick beard that clung to Orec's jawline and sidestepping the question, not liking that he didn't know the answer to it yet himself.

'Martina won't unless I do,' he replied, unconsciously reaching up to stroke it. He'd never been one for beards, but he'd started growing it the moment he'd signed his name in the Duke's roster, and it had become a part of him in the years since and his only vanity.

They quietened as several deckhands made their way forward and dropped through the hatch into the hold, their voices echoing up. Others were readying ropes on the deck and Orec felt a trickle of excitement run through him. The next bend in the river would reveal the town, and from there the next and final leg of their journey. So close.

'I'll see where they are,' Hayden said, tipping the rest of his mug over the side. 'Gods, this shit really is vile.'

Orec snorted and took another sip of the concoction, willing himself to find something to like but swiftly pouring the rest out too. He waited there, watching the distant bank slide past as they barge tacked its way around the bend. Green, forested hills flattened out into wide, gently contoured bay, but where there should have been mighty red oaks and the bright lights of a living town within their boughs, full of light and the sound of life, there were only blackened stumps rising here there from amidst the haze shrouded shanty town clustered around their bases, giving the impression that the once mighty trees had sunk into to the earth, scraping off the town that had thrived within them like shit off a shoe. It was no worse than many of the towns they'd moved through in the way of the fighting, and had he not known of its former glory he wouldn't have thought much of it nor found the sight of it so bitter.

As it was, he was still trying to absorb the scale of its fall when the others joined him.

'What a dump,' Tomas said. 'Looks like the kind of place you wouldn't yawn in in case someone steals your teeth.'

'Just like home then?' Stef said.

'A bit, yes,' Tomas said, an unexpected smile playing across his face.

They were ushered out the way by the crew soon after and waited with the dozen or so other passengers while the crew members sprang into life with an energy that had absent for the last week. The apparent chaos quickly resolved itself into a newfound efficiency as the anti-boarding shields were dropped and cargo winch was rolled back into place.

'Ready to get back into the saddle, eh sarge?' Tomas asked, nudging him.

'I can't wait.' The lie came out in an even tone. 'I'm actually starting to enjoy it.'

'Sure you are.' He leaned in close. 'So, listen, I know we discussed the money and everything last night, but I was wondering if I could borrow a few coins.'

Orec fought the instinct to ask him what for, knowing the answer already and not wanting to hear it.

'Take some from the purse in your boot.'

'I don't have any,' he began, then shrugged when he saw Orec's eyebrow arc upward. 'Those are for emergencies, in case you get yourself robbed again.'

'Well, if it's not an emergency, it can stay in your trousers, can't it.'

Tomas stepped back and dusted his sleeve. 'When did you turn into a such a goddamned Redemptionist?'

'When we killed a team of provosts and stole their bloody horses,' Orec hissed, stepping in close to him now. 'So I'd rather spend whatever lead we've built up riding than waiting for you to finish having a good time with whatever two scit joy-girl is desperate enough to lay with you in the daytime.'

Tomas took a half step forward and closed the space, more out of instinct than any real desire to provoke a fight, especially when the proximity made it impossible to ignore Orec's height advantage and the unexpected bulk of his shoulders.

'Fine. Great,' he hissed back. 'I'll just go get hung with a hard on. What a way to go.'

Orec narrowed his eyes. 'And here I thought that was your dagger pressing into my thigh.'

Tomas shifted back with a look of disgust blooming on his face, one that was greeted by Stef's howl of laughter, while Hayden tried and failed to hide his behind his hand.

'Fuck the lot of you.'

'Is that a threat?' Orec asked, his own grin splitting his beard.

'Shut up,' Tomas said, his own smile robbing it of any venom. 'Bastards.'

'I'll get going,' Hayden said as the ramps were finally locked in place. 'It shouldn't take too long.'

'You sure you don't want me to come with you?' Tomas asked, holding up a hand to forestall Stef's quip. 'I can make sure your horse is still there when you're done.'

'Go,' Orec said. It was unlikely there'd be trouble during the day, not if they had good coin to pay with, but desperate times brought out the worst in people. 'But don't attract attention. Get the goods and get out.'

They nodded and made their way down through the disembarking passengers while Orec waited with Stef until the way was clear before following suit, a coin in hand to thank the boy holding their horses for them, and another two in his pocket if their saddles hadn't been looted.

If the horses were relieved to be on land again, they made no sign of it. Orec led them until they were clear of the dock before they mounted. Stef settled himself in the saddle and looked across the dock at the town, tilting his neck as he took in the girth and impressive height of the splintered and blasted trees, the charred remnants still twice as tall as any oak or elm he'd ever seen.

'I wish I could have seen it,' he said. 'You know, before.'

'Don't wish for that,' said a lilting voice behind them, startling them and the horses. A narrow face had appeared on top of what Orec had taken for a pile of discarded sacking, its thin lines dirty and lined with hardship, the blue of its oversized eyes more shocking for it.

'To have known its beauty is a curse, a burden of sadness that will make you wish for the sword.'

Orec quietened his mare. 'Avan mar, nollem,' he said in Aethani. The greeting was almost the whole of his vocabulary unless he had to swear. He tried not to stare at the shrunken limbs that jutted from the man's back like trembling, skeletal fingers, but failed.

The faint smile that pulled at the Aethani's face vanished just as quickly. He turned, hiding the outline of his maimed wings from view. 'Do not pity me.'

'Sorrow is not the same as pity, friend.' He leaned from the saddle and took three coins from his rapidly emptying purse and dropped them neatly into the man's lap.

Pride warred with need across the Aethani's face, but not for long. A delicate, pale hand pulled the coins under the wrap.

He didn't say thank you, but Orec knew just enough not to be offended by the custom.

'Come on,' he said to Stef, who was still staring intently at the beggar. 'We need to go.'

'Good luck,' Stef said as he turned his horse.

A'lori offered no reply and only watched them go, his fist clenched around the coins. He hated the shame of charity, and watched until the bearded man vanished amongst the ramshackle warehouses on the fringe of the town. He ignored the wave from the younger man and simply turned the coins over in his fingers as he considered the strange pair. He had at least offered a greeting, and the coin had been offered freely, not asked for, and that was something.

He settled back into position, carefully so as not to touch the bales with the stumps that marred his back, then turned his attention back to the docks, trying not to let his sharp gaze drift to the saloon and the temporary escape that it promised.

CATT TOOK A few minutes to compose himself once the carriage was safely stowed, then walked back out onto the road and through the gates of Maybury, although to call them that was quite generous. Only the gateposts remained, much like the rest of the other hastily constructed defences the inhabitants had attempted to put up. Maybury had become a town almost by accident following the discovery of tin and copper in the nearby hills, and so had evolved nearly unchecked into its current sprawling mess, most of it centred on the main street that divided it so clearly.

The Kinslayer's armies had simply marched straight up along that same street, having knocked the gates down in a matter of minutes. The survivors hadn't bothered trying to rebuild the defences, something which had probably contributed to the town surviving the war at all. Defences were a provocation to the Yorughan, to whom any kind of resistance justified slaughter. Once it was subjugated, the Kinslayer had moved his own slave army in to strip the mines and had simply repurposed the clustered buildings.

If was honest with himself, Catty had expected it to be as completely dreary and depressing as he imagined a ravaged mining town could be, and he'd dressed in a suitably understated manner. There was no getting around the fact that the town was one of those places that people lived in for a while before moving on to somewhere nicer, but as he made his way onto the main strip, he found himself having to re-evaluate his opinion of it once more. It was busy and the road suffered for that, but it was still entirely passable, and the shopfronts had been whitewashed recently and each bore the name of the enterprise above the doors in colourful, painted boards. He paused to appreciate the stone arches that let pedestrians cross the gutters without risking a boot full of effluent and made his way along, peering into various stores and generally appreciating the bustle of activity.

He was still dubious about renting a room in a hostelry, but having a recognisable place where he was staying would avoid any awkward questions, and besides, he'd packed a few home comforts to make the most of it. The woman who served him was polite enough and had good teeth, which was always reassuring. He paid in advance for three days, then made his way upstairs into a sparse but clean room, nicely aired. A serving girl came in behind him and prepared the bed with quiet efficiency that impressed him enough to part with some smaller coin in thanks. She gave a delightful curtsey and left, closing the door behind her.

He set his trunk down and took out a small box, and from that a tiny but intricately carved house which he set on the floor in the middle. He knelt beside it and pressed the two panels hidden in its roof, then sat back and watched as it lit from within, yellow light spilling from its little windows and quickly spreading across the floor in a golden flood. It raced across the floor and everything upon it, including him, before climbing all four walls and converging at a point above the tiny chimney before vanishing again.

Catt smiled as he picked the house up and set it on the dresser next to the bed. He'd have to tell the maids not to turn the bed in the mornings, but at least now he didn't have to worry about any light-fingered visitors. He donned a fresh, more comfortable shirt and then headed downstairs.

He caught the hostelry manager's eye as she sat sipping a tea and smiled as he joined her.

'Is there a problem with the room?' she asked, her nails tapping on the side of the cup.

'No, it's quite adequate, thank you,' he said. 'I wanted to ask you to carry a message for me.'

'We're not couriers,' she said, slightly testily. 'But I can arrange one for you, at a price.'

'I'm sure you could, madam.' He leaned forward. 'But it would be for Boris, not some distant cousin or sweetheart.'

'Boris?'

Catt winked. 'You know, *Boris.*'

She lifted a finger off her cup, then sat back. 'And assuming for a moment that I know who you were talking about, what sort of message would it be?'

Catt paused at the creak of a floorboard behind him, and a glance over his shoulder revealed a rather burly man in work clothes that were far too neat to belong to any real labourer.

'Simply that I wished to continue our recent conversation.'

'Well, why don't you make yourself comfortable while we go ask around if anyone knows him.' She gestured to the figure behind him. 'My friend here will keep my seat for me.'

'Excellent, thank you. And could I get a tea as well, if you don't mind?' He kept his expression friendly as the man sat down in her seat, his expression somewhere between boredom and idle malice. 'Make it for two.'

'Of course,' she said, her tone flat. 'And some biscuits too?'

'That would be positively delightful.'

As it happened, he barely had time for the first cup and to learn that his new companion was a former soldier named Obadiah before the landlady returned and asked him to follow her. He excused himself and pocketed two more of the biscuits, feeling quite pleased with himself.

She led him through a door near to what he expected were the kitchens, then out into a small, connecting alleyway that he wouldn't care to revisit in the dark before stopping at a door that looked incongruously new compared to the rest of the building.

A small panel slid open and a pair of dark eyes looked him over before two heavy sounding bolts were drawn and the door opened.

'Good luck,' the landlady said as she turned and left the way they'd come. He hesitated for a moment, then stepped inside with a smile for the mostly unseen doorman, who gave no sign of noticing. He started up the stairs as the door shut behind him with a dull thud that spoke of reinforced timber. The light wasn't good, but it was enough for him to see the tapering grooves that marked some of the stairs and walls. Someone had taken a plane to them in an effort to minimise the scars, but they were too pale against the darker panels not to notice.

He knocked on the door at the top and was heartened when Boris' female companion opened it. He wracked his memory for her name, but the introduction had been fleeting and his attention had been elsewhere at the time.

'Hello,' he said instead, 'it's good to see you again.'

'I hope I can say the same, Mister Catt,' she replied, closing the door behind him and limping back towards the desk that dominated the side of the room. He was about to ask after Boris when she lowered herself into the throne like chair behind it. 'Please, take a seat.'

'Thank you,' he said, looking around with naked curiosity as he did so. There were a pleasing amount of books, with a number of ornaments dotted between them, some of which looked quite interesting at first glance. 'Is, um, Boris unwell?'

'In so much that he's dead, yes,' she said matter-of-factly, watching him closely. 'Quite dead.'

'Oh,' he said, sagging back into the chair. 'I'm sorry, I had no idea.'

'No reason you would,' she said. 'Now, how can I help you? Or would you be more comfortable talking to one of the men?'

'Goodness, no,' he said. 'It's just a bit of a surprise.' He frowned and sat forward again. 'But my purpose may very well concern you too. Before I start, could I ask how it happened? I noticed you had a limp, which you didn't before, and I can't help but think they're connected.'

'Perhaps you should tell me why you're here first.'

'Very well,' he said. He had no idea how much she knew of their negotiations, or how such matters worked in the backrooms and alleys of the world, but if she had stepped into Boris' shoes so completely, then there was clearly more to her than being an unexpectedly pretty thug. 'It concerns the circlet that you brought to us.'

'What of it?' she asked, her tone flat and leaning towards boredom, rankling him slightly.

'You may recall that it wasn't entirely broken, as I believe you discovered for yourselves.' Now it was him watching her closely. 'I must report that it activated a few days after you departed, and manifested in a way that neither myself or Doctor Fisher expected.'

She sat forward as he paused. 'Go on.'

'To be frank, it seems to have created a temporary anomaly in the fabric of time and space. It opened a gateway, in the vernacular.' He leaned forward. 'To another world.'

'And something came through it.'

'Why yes,' he said, taken aback. 'You knew of this?'

'No, but that's generally what doorways are for,' she said, the indifference tempered with a hint of mocking amusement. 'What happened?'

'As you surmised, a creature came through it, something unlike anything I've ever seen, and we've seen a fair deal of things. We had it trapped, but then it, uh, engineered an escape. We tracked it as far as we could, and found its route was headed this way.' She leaned forward as he spoke, elbows resting on the table and her head resting on her steepled fingers, her lidded eyes boring into him. 'I don't know why it came this way, or how it even knew to, but the only connection we could extrapolate is—was—Boris. And you, my dear.'

'Call me that again and you'll leave here without your teeth,' she said, her tone even. 'And as for your creature, it looked oily. And when it moved, there was violet lightning.'

'Yes,' he said, also sitting forward. 'So, it found him.'

'It didn't come here first though,' she said, not looking up. 'It went to Tulkauth before it came here.'

'By the stars, it's fast.' He rubbed his chin. 'Tell me,' he said, and she did.

She wasn't a good storyteller, and spoke haltingly as if confessing some great and shameful crime, but for all of that, the way that she spoke of the slaughter she had seen told him more than enough. She only looked up at him again when her tale came to an end.

'So now I have become Boris, for better or worse.' She poured them each a cup from a silver ewer on the desk, and he was relieved to see that it was ackerberry juice. She looked at him over the rim of her cup. 'Now it's your turn.'

'My turn?'

'To tell me the rest.' She waved the cup at him. 'You didn't travel all the way up here, sitting on a barely padded plank, to warn a business acquaintance. You could have done that with a letter.' She sat back. 'And since all of this is your fault, you owe us as much.'

'That's hardly true at all. I mean, I did travel here to issue a warning, but I can hardly be held accountable for the actions of creatures from another world. The fact is that we were sold a defective item, one that could have killed me just as easily. If anyone should be aggrieved, it would surely be me.'

'But it didn't kill you, and here we are.'

'Quite right. Focus on the present, that's what I always say.' He took another sip of the juice, which was tarter than he normally took it but still refreshing. 'The truth of it is that while I'm certainly not at fault, I am not without conscience, and recognise that I have some obligation towards rectifying the matter.'

She set her cup down and wagged a finger at him. 'You're hunting it.'

He opened his mouth to protest, but closed it again. It was true enough that he had packed a few extras just in case he stumbled across it, but he'd never really thought of himself as hunting it. And yet, he was closing in on it now, wasn't he? His theory had been proven, and he had an eyewitness account.

'Yes, I suppose I am,' he said, matching her triumphant smile.

'I want in.'

MYRON TOOK A deep draw from his pipe and let the smoke curl from his nose and mouth as he leaned his head against the post. The pipe-weed was past its best, but it was still good.

'I don't see what you're complaining about,' he said, the words escaping in diminishing puffs of smoke. 'It's not raining, and there's nothing to do but eat and get paid.'

'It's boring as shit.'

Myron watched Luke pace back and forth and mustered a shrug. 'Boring is underrated.'

He'd been dragged into one proper battle, and that had been enough excitement to last him the rest of his life as far as he'd been concerned. The breastplate he'd complained about for so many weeks before had actually turned a javelin, and when he'd found his feet again he'd been roped into a stretcher bearing detail by a passing officer and hadn't looked back since. 'Anywhere but the frontline' had become his personal motto and had served him well since. He took another draw from the pipe and sent a smoke ring over the fence, quite pleased how things had turned out in the end.

'What was that?' Luke said, leaning onto the railing of the guard post. 'There, by the corner.'

'You'll need to try harder than that,' Myron laughed.

'I'm serious,' Luke said.

With a sigh, Myron made his way over and followed the other guard's pointing finger. As he squinted at the shapeless gloom he saw flicker of movement.

'What was that?' he echoed, tapping his pipe empty against his heel and stashing it in the sash he wore around his waist. Having a patient someone forgot to discharge go over the fence in the middle of the night was one thing, but a thief in the storehouse was another matter entirely.

'Let's go check it out,' Luke said, already heading to the ladder.

'Dominic can go.'

'He's on sick report,' Luke said as he sank from view. 'It's just us.'

'Shit.'

He followed Luke down and drew his mace, the weight of it suddenly making him regret abandoning any sort of training regimen. Yellow light suddenly flooded the yard as Luke managed to light one of the storm lanterns and opened the shutters wide.

'Who goes there?' Myron called. 'You are bound by law.'

There was no reply, just a strange chirping sound, as if a field full of crickets had gathered somewhere in the stubborn shadows that clung to the far side of the storehouse.

The light suddenly swung wildly, making the shadows grow and vanish in turn.

He swung around, irritation hardening his tone. 'Keep that thing steady.'

As he spoke, Luke dropped to his knees. 'Myron?' he said, his voice hushed.

He lifted the lantern and they both stared in horror as the dark line across his gut suddenly widened and vomited out what looked to be a pit of snakes. Myron staggered back, the breath stolen from his lungs, as Luke toppled backwards like a hinge.

He turned for the guardhouse but had barely taken a single step before something knocked him into the side of the storehouse. He heard something snap, but couldn't tell if it came from him or the wooden boards. There was no pain, but it felt like someone was sitting on his chest. He could only lay there, gasping for his final breaths, as the creature loped past him, paying him no mind at all, and vanished through an open window, its tail whipping once against the shutters.

# CHAPTER TEN

OREC HAD STOPPED listening to Tomas more than an hour ago, but that hadn't stopped him from talking. His words had become background noise as much as the wind in the branches above had, or the steady clop of their horses. He absently patted the mare's neck at the thought and it chuffed appreciably back at him. It seems that all it took for him to become a reasonable horseman was a fortnight with no other options and a litany of curses every time he dismounted or the horse tried to bite him, something which she had hopefully given up doing for good.

He flinched as a pinecone hit the side of his head and swung to glare at Tomas.

'Just checking you hadn't suffocated in that beard,' he said. 'Since you weren't bloody listening to a word I said.'

'You've told that story before,' Orec said, shrugging. 'And I still don't believe it.'

'I'm telling you, they're cannibals. The lot of them, all painted up to look like the bones they want to be gnawing on.'

'Plenty of tribes paint their skin,' Orec said, gesturing to Tomas's pauldron. 'And you've got skulls on there, so maybe you're one too.'

'Only if you count fingernails and hair as cannibalism,' Hayden said, bringing his horse up between them. 'Maybe he gnaws on ours too while we sleep.'

'Maybe I would,' Tomas said testily, 'if you ever slept.'

'And maybe that's why I don't,' Hayden replied. 'Nails aside, do you smell that?'

'Stars above, not you too.'

Hayden chuckled. 'No, in the air. Woodsmoke, and it's getting stronger.'

Orec slowed and stood in his stirrups, a recent feat he was quite proud of, and drew in a deep breath. 'Yes, it's there. Village, or maybe charcoal burners?'

Stef brought his horse around and moved ahead of them, twisting in his saddle as he searched the ground and surroundings.

'What is it?' Tomas asked.

Instead of a reply, he tapped his horse's rump with a stick and began cantering down the road.

'What's got into him?' Orec said.

'He's been squirrelly all day,' Tomas said, 'and most of yesterday.'

'Let's go find out then,' Orec said, tapping his heels back and heading after him, his reins held one handed while he checked that his sword was loose and ready in its scabbard.

They caught up with him quickly, and by which time Orec's curiosity had already given way to annoyance.

'What are you doing?' he said, slowing alongside him.

'I know this road,' Stef said with a smile. 'There's a small village just ahead, well more like an overgrown farmstead. The woods give way to an open track just past the next bend. It's less than half a mile.'

'Slow down, I mean it.' The hard edge in his tone was unmissable and Stef reined in, although it didn't stop him from rolling his eyes.

'I know these people, sarge. We're good.'

'You knew them. There's a difference. You don't know what kind of welcome we're likely to get.'

'And they may only remember you with two legs,' Tomas added.

'Get stuffed, grandpa,' Stef replied, then turned back to Orec. 'They're good people.'

'Makes sense for him to scout it,' Hayden offered. 'If they're the same people, he's less likely to spook them into a pitchfork party.'

Orec raked his fingers through his beard, then nodded. 'Fine. But you keep your eyes open and head square.'

'Yes sir,' Stef said, snapping a parade ground salute. He grinned at Orec's obscene reply and nudged his horse forward again.

They watched him until he disappeared past the curve of the path.

'Do you think he's expecting bunting and gleemaidens?' Tomas said, patting dust and grass off his tunic.

'Gleemaidens?' Orec said. 'Gods above, how old are you?'

It was Tomas' turn to voice obscenities, which only set the other men to laughing as they began to follow Stef in.

THEY RODE IN slowly, weapons close to hand but not drawn. Stef had been right in that it was barely a village, and more like a large farmstead with too many farmhands. The central farmhouse was a sprawling thing, the original stone house having sprouted two or three different extensions over the years, each one less architecturally sound than the last, and the barns too. There wasn't a fence as such, only the low kind that cattle farmers used, although there was a trench just beyond it. It may have been enough to foil a careless charge, but having the front open defeated the point of it.

There were a dozen or more people gathered around Stef, who hadn't yet dismounted, most of them shouting at him, although none were actively brandishing the farming implements they'd gathered up. At least not until they caught sight of the three horsemen approaching them and shouted a warning. One by one, the shutters on the lower floor were slammed shut and most of those who had gathered fled inside, leaving four men, two on either side.

Orec waved as they passed the fence, and despite the instruction he'd given Tomas, the older man sat with his hands resting on the horn of his saddle, a position from which he'd be able to draw and throw his axes in a heartbeat. Hayden followed a few paces behind Tomas, his longbow strung and the tip resting on his boot, but no arrow nocked.

'Good day,' Orec called out.

'Shove off,' one of the farmers called back. 'We want none of your trouble. Take it and go the way you came.'

'We're not bringing any trouble,' Orec replied, coming to a halt twenty feet away. 'We just want to water our horses and be on our way.'

'We'll kill him first,' another of the men called, lifting what looked like a boar spear to his shoulder, the angular point rising to Stef's chest height. 'You just try anything.'

'Easy, friend,' Orec said. 'Lower that pigsticker before anyone gets hurt.'

It wasn't a boar spear, now that he looked closely, but a cut-down Yogg pike, and the man next to him looked to laying on a war-scythe, an awkward but terrible weapon more suited to harvesting heads than wheat. But the pike was the immediate problem; with the counterbalance lost when the shaft was shortened, the man holding it would be feeling the strain soon, leaving him two options: lower it, or use it. And he didn't need to look at the men behind him to know that the latter option would see a lot more blood being spilled the instant he moved to do so.

'Where is Old Marek?' Stef asked, punctuating the tense silence that fell.

The man who'd first spoken to Orec shifted his weight. 'What do you know of Tante Marek?'

'Enough to know that she would be ashamed that her hospitality has come to this.'

The farmer moved around the horse to stand by Stef's maimed leg, his iron tined pitchfork now resting on the ground. 'Who are you?'

'As I said before everyone lost their mind, I am Stefan, son of Dumi, from Pulcek.'

The farmer was still eyeing him when the door behind him swung open and two women stepped out, one old and one young and fair, the younger woman's hair hidden beneath a brilliantly red scarf. A single glance from her ended the farmer's protest before it began. She helped the old woman down the stairs, and even from where he sat Orec could tell she was blind—and the very definition of what he imagined when someone spoke of a crone.

'Tante,' Stef said. He swung his good leg around with an ease that belied the painful practice that had marked his first attempts on the road. He held onto the horse in lieu of his crutch as the older woman stepped forward and embraced him. The men stepped back, their weapons lowering, and Orec felt the tightness in his chest loosen. She didn't say anything to the men, but in that simple act they swung from belligerent to apologetic.

'There is a trough yonder,' the man said as he hung his pitchfork from a peg set into the wall. 'Tend to your animals then please, come in and join us.'

'Thank you,' Orec said as he dismounted, sharing a shrug with Hayden. Tomas watched it all with a frown on his face and a hand on a throwing axe and didn't follow them to the trough until the last of the villagers had set aside their weapon.

'You trust them?' Tomas asked as he dismounted, not bothering to lower his voice. 'That's a witch if I ever saw one and they all look like they're two missed meals away from sticking Stef in a pot.'

'Let me do the talking,' Orec said. 'You two keep your eyes open and knives handy.'

Any notion of starvation was quickly dismissed as they entered the immaculately neat and cosy farmhouse. The table was laid with bread, cheese and salt, and cider was being poured for them as they took their seats. Stef sat by the old woman, leaning in close as she talked in a soft voice clearly meant for no one else. The woman in the red scarf stood behind them, an untouched cup of cider in her hand, watching them intently and ignoring Tomas' lustful stare.

'You came by river, then?' the man who'd had the pitchfork asked. 'How was that? Was High Town busy?'

'It's busy,' Hayden said. 'As busy as it can be now, possibly too busy. There's only so many mouths the river can feed.'

The farmer nodded. 'I agree. The Kinslayer's priests, if that is the right word, put something into the river. For a long time, there were no fish bigger than my hand, not even here, in our little stream, and the animals who drank directly from it sickened.' He smiled mirthlessly. 'We all did at first. But it is getting better.'

Tomas lowered his cup and looked into it, but the man only laughed.

'This is why we're making more cider and beer now. It makes the water good again and, of course, it is never a bad thing to have more beer in the house.'

'It's good,' Tomas admitted. 'Good and sharp. You should sell it.'

'We do,' he said with a tight smile. 'It's a good trade. Better than beets and tubers. But now I must go and ready your rooms.'

'Rooms?' Orec asked. 'We're leaving soon.'

'No, my friend,' the farmer said, but without menace. He looked across to the old woman, who was at that moment holding Stef's hand. 'You're not going anywhere.'

OREC SMILED ABSENTLY as Martina settled herself against him again, her knees tucked behind his thighs and a possessive arm across his chest. He sighed and settled his face deeper into the pillow, revelling in the sensation of being home. Nothing hurt anymore, and he felt completely at peace, as if he were floating on a warm, gentle ocean. He didn't even mind when Martina stirred behind him, the movement distant and equally dreamlike. He felt her weight shift.

'I need a piss,' she growled in a voice scarred by too many years of drinking cheap rakk, and then punctuated the statement with a wet burp that would have startled a mule.

Orec felt the bliss he'd felt only a moment away fall away, the peaceful ocean suddenly swallowing him and spitting him back out into a reality where Tomas had staggered to the corner and was groaning as he noisily filled the chamber pot. The air was thick with the odour of four drunk men with traveller's diets and no open window. He lifted his head, which was apparently the cue for an unseen smith to start using it as an anvil, and sagged back down with a groan.

'Fuck,' was all he managed.

'Good, you're alive,' Tomas said with unnecessary cheer, then opened the window and pushed the shutters open, flooding the room with morning light and cool air that couldn't yet penetrate the fug that hung within.

'Piss off.' Stef's voice came from across the room, followed by a groan.

'I can smell breakfast,' Tomas said, stomping across the room and digging his boots out from the pile in the centre. 'Goddamned bacon!'

Orec grimaced. 'I just want bread. Toast.'

'Too late to soak it up now. You'd be better off with a hair of the dog.'

'Gods, no.' Hayden sat up and clutched his head. 'Whose idea was this anyway?'

'I don't think we had a choice,' Tomas said. 'Good beer, that.'

Orec grunted as the splintered memories of the night began arranging themselves into some kind of order. Despite their protests, they had found it impossible to deny the old crone's edict that they join her household for supper and to share a cup of cider to celebrate both the end of the war and the return of a lost son to the valley. One cup had turned to two as they gathered in a spacious common room and heard how Stef was known to the locals as an incorrigible apple thief, clobbered by the men as often as he was kissed by the girls, most often in the reverse order.

By the time the conversation moved to the war and the havoc that the Kinslayer's raiding parties had wreaked upon the area, it was too dark to ride and they'd all developed a taste for the cider.

That memory made Orec's gut sour even further. They'd told them how the raiding parties had moved up from the south, most likely to have avoided the strong garrison and walls of Castle Falgard to the east. It had saved them from the worst of the devastation, but it was scant comfort to them, seeing as their road home was southward.

He'd always held to the hope that the worst had passed their small and nondescript corner of the world by, that the battle that had taken the lives of his older brothers would have deflected whatever ambitions the Kinslayer had held for the pastures and orchards surrounding the cluster of villages and small town that gave Cambry its name. The idea of raiding parties still plundering their way through the area was one that filled him with a dread and fear that he wasn't yet ready to face. The cider had silenced those thoughts, but now they were returning, and despite the hammering inside his head, he felt a restless urgency growing within him, one that would only grow more pronounced as the haze lifted from his thoughts.

He pulled on his boots, his groan echoed by Hayden, but otherwise readied himself in silence, content to half-listen to another tale of Tomas' unlikely exploits. He always had a story of having done something better or more extreme than whatever it was that someone had just spoken of or done, and yet seeing him moving about and talking with no sign of the gallons of cider he'd poured down his neck the night before made Orec wonder if perhaps there was more than a grain of truth when it came to his bar-room exploits.

They made their way to the kitchen, Tomas grinning as they picked their way through half a dozen sprawled and snoring bodies in the common room, and were welcomed by the smell of sausages and warming bread. The woman with the red scarf, Chiara, turned from the stove as they entered and shook her head.

'You've cost us an entire day's work, you know,' she said, turning the bread.

'I'd apologise, but today I can only pity myself,' Orec replied, quietly trying to gauge how his stomach felt about food.

Chiara flashed a smile over her shoulder, the gesture so much what Martina would do that he drew a sharp breath.

'Easy there, sarge, I saw her first,' Tomas said in an exaggerated whisper, patting Orec's arm.

'Get off me,' Orec growled, pulling his arm away.

'Gods, someone's cranky this morning,' Tomas said, holding his hands up in surrender. 'You'd best feed him first, darling.'

She did too, and by the time that they'd mopped the last of the grease from their plates, the pounding in his head had become a dull throb and he felt no worse than he had any night in the barracks. Stef had stumbled into the kitchen halfway through the meal, as pale and silent as he'd been after his surgery, and ate like an automaton, oblivious to Tomas' mocking. He remained like that even when Chiara and three of the other women came out to see them off.

'Thank you again for your kind hospitality,' Orec said. 'If you ever come by Cambry, you are always welcome to what I have.'

He glanced over at Stef. 'And please, thank your grandmother on behalf of Stef and all of us.'

He reached into a pocket and handed her a small object wrapped in linen.

'No payment is necessary, it was our pleasure,' she said.

'It's not a payment, it's a gift,' he replied. 'Something to remember us by.'

'Well, then I thank you,' she said, inclining her head. 'It is good to see that the old ways are not entirely forgotten.' She took the parcel, but then held his fingers.

He looked up, confused, but his question didn't make it past his teeth as he watched her hazel eyes darken, the pupil swallowing the colour before rapidly receding to a pinpoint in a honey-hued corona. Her grip on his fingers tightened painfully.

*'Something from another world hunts you, Orec Blackblade. Beware the shifting earth when it finds you.'*

'You're a witch,' he said, the quiet words a statement rather than accusation.

She released his fingers as if he'd stung her and crossed her arms, and if he hadn't known better he would have thought she was as surprised as he was at what had just happened.

'That's just your word for it,' she said. 'I apologise if I've offended you. That doesn't usually happen unbidden.'

'We are what we are,' he said, mustering a smile. 'And my offer stands.'

'Go in peace,' she said, returning the smile and moving off to where Tomas had just settled himself in his saddle.

Orec hoisted himself in his own, and then turned to see Chiara and Tomas locked in a lingering kiss. The axe man smiled as their lips parted and he settled himself back in the saddle as she walked away.

'What?' Tomas asked, with a shrug as he caught them watching. 'I am quite charming, you know.'

'The world no longer makes any sense to me,' Orec said

with a shake of his head, something he instantly regretted, and gently tapped his heels to his horse's flank. 'Let's move.'

CATT WAS SMILING as he finished his tea and watched the sun rise. It had been a busy night, and he wondered how the spies that Lona had sent after him were faring. By now they would have discovered that the campsite they'd spent the night watching had been a decoy and would probably be on their way to report this to her. He hoped she wouldn't be too angry with them, but for all the menace she'd radiated, she'd seemed sensible enough, and he'd actually enjoyed the hours they'd spent together poring over the various maps that Boris had collected over the years.

Indeed, without her authority to back him up, he'd never have found out what had happened to the beast after it hollowed poor Boris out. Clearly the promise of a broken arm or leg did wonders to refresh witnesses' memories. They were unanimous on one point, and that was that after gorging itself, the creature had flashed with lightning, shrieked like a scalded cat, then bounded off back towards the west. It seemed clear to him that whatever it had taken from Boris had not been enough to do what it needed to do, but he was in uncertain territory now.

It had been to both places where there might be lingering traces of the power it sought, so what lay to the west? He'd pored over the accounts and local maps that Lona had acquired for him, but there was nothing that stood out. Dozens of local skirmishes and burned farmsteads, each no doubt a tragedy for the people involved, but nothing that suggested a place where a Heart Taker of that power would have used the circlet or had need to.

He'd all but given up hope of figuring it out when Lona had passed him a terribly drawn and oddly pungent map. He recognised a few of the landmarks from the others he'd seen, and was about to move it aside when he saw the spidery annotation next to the marker for a local mansion that had been taken over and turned into a field hospital. That was interesting but hardly groundbreaking in itself, at least until he'd matched up the edge of the map to another and seen how close it lay to Tulkauth. He'd made of a show of dismissing the map but had surreptitiously made a copy for himself, and then spent the rest of the evening politely dissuading her from trying to pressgang him into her employ.

In the end he'd simply left in the darkest watch of the night. It hadn't taken him long to figure out that she'd expected him to do just that, and he was flattered by the skill of the spies she'd sent after him. Fisher would have spotted them from the start, and while it had taken him a bit longer, as he reckoned it, it was a good effort given how much he had on his mind. He'd taken an extra half day to change his direction before leaving them behind, just to muddle things up a bit, and a few terribly early mornings were the price he'd have to pay for that if he ever wanted to try and make up the time.

He rinsed the cup and stowed it away along with everything else, the little ritual reassuring in itself. He laced his boots, gathered his pack, and made his way back to the path, watching carefully to ensure that it was clear before unpacking the chariot.

He'd suspected that it was going to be a long day and in that, he was not wrong. He'd kept any breaks to a minimum, and despite the relative comforts the chariot offered, the long hours took a toll. And yet, his discomfort was not for nothing. The miles had vanished beneath the wheels, and despite his misgivings about the poor quality of the map, he found the converted mansion without too much trouble in the end. He stopped a way off to collapse the chariot and freshen up, then made his way back onto the path and up to the gates as if he had every right to be there, greeting the guards warmly.

The mansion was a nice country house, or certainly had been before it found itself in path of the war, and the only sign that it had become a hospital was the white flag that hung from the highest gable. Some good work had been done to re-plant the gardens, which were starting to bloom again, and he watched as a man in a drab tunic made his way between beds of neatly planted herbs, dusting his hands on his thighs as he came up to the gates.

'Can I help you?'

'Oh, yes.' Catt smiled. An orderly of some sort, from the grubby badge on his tunic. 'Sorry, I was lost in thought.'

'This isn't a public hospice.'

'Well, then it's a good thing I'm not sick, injured, or dying then,' Catt said, softening the rebuke with a smile. Might I ask what may seem a strange question?'

The orderly frowned. 'Go on.'

'I was wondering if anything unusual had been sighted around here recently? Peculiar creatures, perhaps, or even some dancing lights. That sort of thing.' The orderly's frown deepened. 'Or perhaps if there had been reports of animal attacks of some ferocity?'

'Is this some kind of bad joke?'

'Not at all,' Catt said. 'I'm quite serious.'

'Then you'd better come with me.'

Catt nodded his agreement and followed him through the gardens, quietly cataloguing the various herbs and tubers he could see, mostly as a distraction to still the self-satisfied smile that was tugging at his mouth in case it was misconstrued by his very sombre guide. But he couldn't argue that it wasn't satisfying to have put another piece of the puzzle together so neatly.

'Wait here,' the orderly said, gesturing to a bench in the hallway they'd just entered.

'Of course,' Catt replied. He ignored, ignoring the invitation to sit as the orderly knocked once on a nearby door and stepped inside, closing it behind him. This had evidently been a servant's entrance, but even so, the walls had been decorated with whimsical figures in rural scenes. He was still studying them when the door opened and the orderly beckoned to him.

The room was larger than expected, and from the size and sturdiness of the desk within it seemed that the room had been built around it. You could have slaughtered an ox on it, or had a family sleep on it.

The man behind the desk cleared his throat and Catt instinctively smiled.

'Good morning and apologies, I was admiring your desk. That's yellow wood, and from the shade of it, I'd say the tree was more than a few hundred years old.' He leaned over and ran his fingers along the grain. 'Quite impressive, and antique furniture isn't even my speciality.'

'It's not mine, but yes, it is quite impressive. I am Doctor Bonner, chief chirurgeon of this hospital.'

'A pleasure to meet you,' Catt said, taking a seat.

Bonner frowned at him as he rested his elbows on the edge of the desk. 'My colleague tells me you're asking about the recent attack on my men?'

'To be clear, I'd asked if there had been anything peculiar incidents recently, or perhaps an attack, not a specific attack. However, as there apparently has been one, then yes, I am now asking about it.'

'I have my own questions first, since so few people knew of it.' He leaned back and peered at Catt. 'How do you know of it, and what do you know about it?'

'Those are questions whose answers I will have to defer for now, since I don't yet know anything about the incident you're referring to,' Catt said. 'What I can offer for now is that I'm investigating and tracking a creature that is certainly capable of violent action, and one whose route suggested was heading this way. From your statement, it seems I was quite right.'

Bonner pinched the bridge of his nose. 'What creature?'

'We'll come to that in time, but tell me one thing first, please.' He waited until Bonner nodded. 'The men that were attacked. Were any of them opened.' He ran his fingers down his breast bone. 'Along here, to the spine?'

Bonner looked to the orderly, then back at Catt.

'None that I recall,' he said. 'They were slashed with an imperfect edge, which suggested claws, but with some force.'

Catt's expression fell into a frown and sat back. 'Oh dear. How many?'

'Men? We lost three guards, and six patients were injured in the ruckus.'

'And they all bore the same wounds?'

'What's this about, Mister…?'

'Catt,' he said. 'Doctor Catt.'

Bonner's eyebrows rose. 'A doctor?'

'Not of medicine, I'm afraid.'

'Then why such an interest in their wounds?' Bonner asked.

'An excellent question, of course. The creature that I seek has a specific pattern of behaviour, and certain habits.'

'Larsen,' the orderly said suddenly, moving forward from where he'd been leaning against the wall. Bonner motioned for him to continue.

'One of the patients, Larsen, he had a severe chest injury. It wasn't quite as you described, but it wasn't the same as any of the others.'

'Could I see his body? It would be most helpful.'

'I'm afraid not,' the orderly said. 'They've been cremated. But I saw the wound. It was here,' he placed two fingers under his breastbone and slid them upwards to his collarbone, 'to here, just under the bone. One rib was broken.'

'As if it stopped,' Catt said, his frown deepening as the orderly nodded. 'You must tell me everything you can about this Larsen.'

It didn't take long for them to retrieve a slim folder from the depths of the drawers that lined the desk. Aside from the way he'd died, the man named Larsen seemed entirely unremarkable. He'd been admitted with an arrow wound to the knee that had gone septic but was making a good recovery after the amputation. The rest of the file consisted of terse notes about his recovery. Catt set it aside and found himself drumming his fingers on the desk.

'Why him? He has no connection to any of this. Someone so mundane.' He hadn't realised he'd spoken out loud until the orderly replied.

'I don't know. Larsen was just a good man. He was a terrible card player, but quite funny and otherwise well liked.' He smiled. 'Blackblade even left his bed to him.'

Bonner chuckled at that.

'What's Blackblade?' Catt asked.

'Who,' Bonner corrected him. 'Orec Blackblade. One of four soldiers who, uh, discharged themselves recently. He was something of a hero, and quite a character, so he and his fellows had the beds closest the fireplace. Prime real estate here, especially in the cooler months.' Bonner shrugged. 'When they left, he left a note, written like a will, granting Larsen the rights to his bed. It was quite funny, if infuriating.'

'His bed?'

'Well, yes. There'd be a scrap over it otherwise.'

Catt waved him to silence. 'Out of interest, was this Larsen killed in Blackblade's bed?'

'Yes,' the orderly said. 'And with any luck, he didn't wake up.'

'What can you tell me about this Blackblade fellow?' Catt asked, sitting forward.

'THERE IT IS. The walls are new.'

They sat quietly alongside Stef as he looked across at the town walls, beyond which his home and family were waiting, and an end to the war.

'It feels like I'm going to throw up.'

'Only because you're downwind of Tomas,' Hayden said. 'You'll be fine.'

'It's my natural musk,' Tomas said, sitting back in his saddle. 'The boy will miss it.'

'There are many things I'm going to miss, but I'm not sure about that one.' He nudged his horse and turned to face them. 'Are you going to come in? I'd love to introduce you to everyone. Even you, Tomas.'

'Not this time,' Orec said, offering an apologetic smile. 'If we're being tracked I don't want anyone remembering four scruffy riders where one could go unnoticed. Once this all dies down, we'll arrange something.'

'A proper send off,' Hayden added. 'I'm game for that.'

'I'll bring the women,' Tomas said, leering.

'Deal,' Stef brightened at that. 'It's a shame though. I wanted to have at least one proper drink without someone dying.'

They laughed at that, if somewhat guiltily.

'We'll have it,' Orec said, moving forward and extending his hand. 'It was an honour serving alongside you.'

'Same,' said Hayden, moving forward once Orec released Stef's hand from a warrior's handshake. He leaned from the saddle and embraced Stef, clapping him hard enough on the shoulder that he coughed. 'I'll miss you.'

'Same,' Stef said, turning to look at Tomas, who rolled his eyes.

'Fine,' he said, pushing Hayden out of the way. He paused and considered Stef, before nodding to himself. 'You did good, son.'

Stef smiled as he shook Tomas's hand.

'I'll miss the sound of your little crutch.'

'Fuck you.'

When their laughter had died down Stef sat straighter in his saddle and, with one last look at the men he considered brothers, turned his horse towards the gates.

They watched him until he disappeared into the town, Hayden's eyes alone catching his last wave in their direction before the gates swallowed him.

'Let's go,' Orec said, flicking the reins. 'I've had enough of your musk.'

STEF MADE HIS way through the streets at a slow walk, the sound of the horse's hooves loud in the unexpectedly quiet streets. Wherever he looked he saw signs of the war's passing, small things like missing and mismatched shutters where house proud families once lived, boarded-up windows, and walls where hasty repairs weren't able to hide the scorch marks. And yet the town had endured despite all of that, and as he neared the central square, the sounds of life grew louder. The square had ever been the heart of the town, and it was there three years ago where he had signed the quartermaster's register for the first time and become part of the war.

He smiled at the memory of how entranced he had been when the company of halberdiers had marched in with the recruiters, splendid in all their finery and polished armour, at how unstoppable and fierce they'd looked. He knew better now of course, and if he'd dared to get closer to them he knew he'd have heard them muttering and complaining about the heat, or their aching feet, or that they'd had to spend their nights polishing armour just to impress some local simpletons. *They're probably all dead.* He pushed the thought aside and chose instead to focus on that he was one of them now. He'd taken Cherivel's coin, and by the gods, he'd earned it and his right to hold his head up proudly.

He patted the restive horse and let it carry him to the square. Now, as it had always done for three days of the week, the space had reverted to a free market where any and all could pay a day's rent to the registrar to set their tables out and offer anything for sale, free of the guild restrictions and tithes that controlled so many other markets. People had come from far and wide to offer their goods, and to browse and haggle. It had always been his favourite place, because there was never any telling what you'd find from one day to the next.

He slowed to a halt on one side and just watched for a while, not caring that he was smiling like an idiot at the smells drifting from the various stalls and the sight of the yellow bunting strung from the now fractured and broken statues of previous mayors. Given that each had portrayed a jowled and bearded man staring into the distance, few would miss their presence aside from their families, and he could only grin at the thought of invading Yoggs stopping to decapitate statues while leaving the buildings around the square largely undamaged. It was more likely that someone had taken the opportunity to express some long-repressed opinions of the high and mighty.

He skirted the edge of the market, still largely oblivious to the curious stares directed at him, and turned down the street that led home. It was different to how he remembered it, smaller, but then he had never ridden down it.

He stopped outside the house, the whinny from the horse announcing him as well as any trumpeter ever could. He saw the curtains twitch and smiled to himself. *That hadn't changed either.* He dismounted as the door opened and his mother and brother came out, she with a curious expression and his brother with a scowl that his fledgling moustache rendered ridiculous. He was taller though, much taller, the pale child having been replaced by a pale young man.

Stef swung off the horse and tucked his crutch under his arm with the ease of practice. He'd been thinking of this moment for weeks, practising what he'd say and how, but in the end he went with 'Hello, mum. I'm home.'

She stared for a moment, then clutched his brother's arm.

'No! It can't be my Stefan, can it?' she said, her eyes wide.

'They said you were dead,' Carl added, smiling until he saw the reason for the crutch.

'Well, most of me is alive.' He eyed his brother. 'That's my shirt.'

'It's a bit tight,' he grinned back. And it was true too, the realisation bringing with it a deepening sense of the time that had passed.

His mother pulled herself up and threw herself into his embrace and would have sent them both to the ground were it not for the steady strength of the horse behind him. His brother joined a moment later, and he gave up the fight against the tears that were burning for release.

'Come inside,' she said, finally releasing him. 'Come inside.'

'I need to tend to my horse.'

'Pish,' she said, her grip on his arm unbreakable. 'Carl will take care of it, won't you?'

'Yes mother.' He slapped Stef's shoulder. 'You'd better go, unless you want another war. Old Darrell will have space.'

'That bastard's still alive?'

'You mind your mouth,' his mother admonished, and he could only smile at the thought at how the language he was used to would make her hair curl.

'Thanks,' he called over his shoulder as he was led inside, where nothing had changed.

# CHAPTER ELEVEN

A'LORI EMPTIED THE rest of the carafe into his cup and took a sip, wincing as he had from the first taste to this one. It was thin and had needed at least another six months in the barrel to even be passable, but with his last coin in his pocket, he wasn't going to squander it on something that would only be marginally less disappointing.

'You finished it,' the man sitting across from him said, peering into the neck of the carafe. 'What about me?'

A'lori wasn't yet drunk enough to give voice to the first response that came to mind and instead tried to look as apologetic as he could by human standards. 'I thought you had some left.'

And he should have given that he'd refilled his cup twice already, but that was no more than he'd expected when the oaf had first sat down, and he supposed it was a fair price for being able to drink in relative peace. The oaf was a dockworker, as gruff and loud as any of them, but he'd traded in High Town before its ruin, and so wasn't afflicted by the same pitying looks or undeserved arrogance that the newcomers inevitably had. Having him sharing a table and jug was what he imagined it felt like to wear armour and a shield.

'It's alright,' the oaf said, rising to his feet. 'I'll get this one.'

A'lori's protest was lost in the noise as the man pushed his way to the bar, and he consoled himself with another sip. It could be worse. Tonight he would be warm and have a roof over his head, no bad thing judging from the sound of the rain hitting the shutters next to him. And fleas by the morning. He smiled at the thought. His mother had always warned him about spending time in human establishments, citing various ailments and infections he was likely to contract, but fleas were her favourite. *Had been her favourite,* he corrected himself. In the end, it hadn't been men that she needed to worry about.

He took a gulp of wine, letting the tartness of it drag his mind away from such thoughts. They'd smothered him for weeks the last time they had taken hold, and in the depths of their darkness he'd very nearly taken one last, wingless flight from the clifftops. He looked up and plastered a cheery expression on his face as the man, whose name he still could not remember, returned with another man at his side. This one was smaller, but even amidst the thickened air of the saloon, he smelled of horse and iron, and his smile was as empty as A'lori's.

The oaf banged a clay carafe onto the table, laughing as he did so as if it were some great joke, and quickly filled their cups. 'This gentleman here stood us for a jug,' he said. 'Cheers to that!'

A'lori raised his cups to meet theirs and felt the sourness in his gut return at the calculating look that the man gave him. A sober man associated with the drunk for the same reasons that a wolf watched sheep, and he did not care for his scrutiny. Unfortunately, one downside to sitting with your back to the wall was that he had no way to slip out, unless he threw himself out through the window.

'Cheers,' the man said, taking a minuscule sip from his cup. 'My friend here tells me you work on the docks. Watching things.'

A'lori kept his expression even and simply nodded. 'I see things. Sometimes I remember them too.'

'Then perhaps you can help me,' he said. 'I'm seeking four men who would have come by barge, perhaps a week ago. Mounted and armed. One has a great beard and a sword of black iron, and another had a half a leg.'

A'lori swirled the wine in his cup and watched the residue at the bottom form a neat cone. 'A lot of men arrive by barge, and your kind often look the same.'

'I see,' he said. He reached into his jacket and quietly set five gleaming pollys on the table, and from the glint of them A'lori knew they were freshly minted, making them worth nearly twice as much for their ability to stop traders arguing over historic values alone.

'One of the others carries a long bow, with green fletched arrows.'

'That's quite specific,' A'lori said.

'My captain has met them before.'

A'lori pursed his lips. There was a history there, and one that he wanted little or no part of. And coin was coin. He licked the wine from his lip.

'I think I have seen them, yes.'

'Do tell,' the man said, any pretence of a smile vanishing as another coin joined the pile.

'A week and a day,' he said. 'But I only saw the bearded and one-legged man.' Under the table, his fingers found the coin the bearded man had given him, still strangely warm to the touch.

'And?'

'And nothing. They stopped for a few minutes, then took the Domshall Road.' He reached out and took the money, half expecting it to be snatched away at any moment, but something like a genuine smile had crossed the man's face as he spoke.

'Is there anything else? A name, or where they were going?'

'No,' he said with a shrug. 'They weren't that interesting. What did they do?'

'They're murdering scum,' the man said, with no little

venom. He stood and gave a curt nod to both before turning and pushing his way through to the doors.

'That went well,' the oaf said, filling his cup again.

A'lori nodded and walked one of the pollys across the back of his fingers, a simple sleight of hand that delighted the oaf. He stopped and slid two coins across to him. 'Here. Your commission.'

The man beamed and quickly pocketed them. It was a good score for both of them, but A'lori couldn't help but feel some slight remorse, at least until the next sip of wine pushed it from his mind. By the time that the carafe was empty all thought of it was forgotten and he was stretching out on the bench watching as the innkeeper closed the doors for the night and banked the coals, with sleep quickly following.

'I'M JUST SAYING we should have gone in with him,' Tomas said, stroking his horse's neck as it drank from the stream.

'We discussed this,' Orec said, not pausing in his swordplay and enjoying the sensation of back and shoulders loosening up. 'It's safer this way.'

'You'll snap the blade if you hit that stump. And safer isn't the same as right.'

'I'm not going to hit the stump,' Orec said, finishing the pattern with a devastating swing that would have happily removed any superfluous limbs of those unable to dodge it. He rolled his wrists and, satisfied, sheathed the sword again. 'Stef's a capable warrior, even with his wound, and if he wanted four armed vagrants decamping at his mother's door he would have said so. So stop pining.'

'I'm just—'

'If the next word from your mouth is *saying,* I swear by the gods that I'll drown you in that stream.'

Something between a sneer and smile pulled at Tomas's lips.

'Saying,' he said, lifting his hands into a boxing stance and winking at Orec.

'I forget that you're actually twelve years old,' Orec said, ignoring the taunts that followed, baiting him to try anything.

When the company had been together, he'd often josh around with men or join them in the drills that he always insisted on despite their griping that no one in other companies were doing them. In all those times, Tomas had been the fly in the proverbial ointment, the same unwillingness to give ground or surrender that made him so effective in battle making any kind of practice untenable. He was fine as long as he was winning, but once an opponent tagged him once or twice he would do whatever it look to ensure they didn't land another blow, turning a practice match into a brawl that would only end once the other submitted or Tomas himself was knocked clean out, which in turn left him brooding for days after.

Orec felt a sense of relief when he saw Hayden riding back up the trail, having gone ahead to gauge the source of a column of smoke they'd seen.

'That was quick,' he said as Hayden eased his horse to a halt and dismounted with enviable dexterity.

He led it to the stream and looked the reins over the saddle. 'It's a turned-over camp. About half a dozen dead that I could see.'

'Yogg?' Tomas asked.

'Didn't see any Yogg tracks. Just boots, and these.' He pulled a broken arrow and tossed it to Orec. 'That's an old head and those are duck feathers, so it isn't any kind of military arrow. I wouldn't try hit anything more than thirty yards away with that.'

Orec rubbed his thumb across the pitted head and grimaced at the dark smear it left. 'Did its job though.'

Hayden conceded the point with a shrug. 'Bandits, is my guess. And if they're making those, they probably have a camp somewhere.'

'So what?' Tomas asked. 'It's not our problem.'

Orec weighed the arrow in his hand. Whether he liked it or not, Tomas had a valid point. They knew nothing more about the situation, and if was truly honest with himself, he had no desire to risk his life for complete strangers when home was getting tangibly closer with every day that passed. There also remained the question of whether anyone was still on their trail, and they had to assume that was the case.

'You're right,' he said, dropping the arrow. He was looking towards the fading smoke and so didn't see the surprised look on Tomas' face. 'Unless they decide to try their luck with us, it's not our problem to fix.'

Hayden hesitated, then shrugged. 'Fine.'

'Excellent,' Tomas said. 'Glad you've seen the light.'

'Keep your axe loose and your mouth shut,' Orec replied, hauling himself into the saddle. 'They may still be about.'

As it happened, it wasn't the bandits they needed to keep an eye out for. Hayden led them around the site of the attack, far enough that they wouldn't be immediately visible to any scavengers or lingering attackers, but not far enough to spare them the smell of burning flesh. They all wore the same grimace as they rode past, their attention on the myriad of places someone could be hiding.

When the man stepped out from behind the tree and hurled his spear at Hayden, the scout was already leaning away, the sudden movement having drawn his attention. The missile sailed through the space where his chest had been, and he swung back as quickly, drawing the green fletching of the nocked arrow to his ear and releasing it before the attacker had recovered his footing. He looked up as the shaft skewered him through the centre of the chest, punching the air from his lungs and sending him sprawling.

A wordless cry rose around them and another dozen or more men charged from hiding. There was no way forward and they were too close. Orec swung his leg over the saddle and dropped to the ground, ducking under a lunging spear, and scraping his hand across the forest floor, filling it with leaves and dirt which he promptly flung in the man's face. He drew his sword as the attacker flailed backwards. Footsteps sounded behind him, but before he could turn the horse kicked backwards and the steps vanished with a crunch and a scream.

He swatted the thrusting spear away and split the attacker's head with the return swing, then turned and faced a third man, armed with a cruel looking sickle and ramshackle shield. Off to the side, Hayden was controlling his horse with his knees, creating space for him to loose more shafts, and even over the screams of the man whose arm Tomas had just removed he heard the meaty slap of another arrow finding its mark.

He frowned as the man swung the sickle at him, swaying back out of its arc, and then kicked at the man's shield, his weight behind it. The man went over without much resistance and fell awkwardly, the impact sending the sickle spinning away.

'Hold!' Orec shouted, unconsciously reverting to his battlefield voice, the booming command even making their attackers hesitate. He laid the tip of the sword against his opponent's chest. 'Tell them to lay their weapons done.'

'Do it,' the man shouted, his tone shrill in comparison. 'For the love of the gods, do it.'

He heard the thump of Tomas dismounting, and a moment later the screaming stopped.

'Move,' the axe man barked.

Orec lifted his sword and gestured for the man to get up, turning to follow him. There were only four left alive and they stood there in abject misery, whatever fight they'd had in them entirely spent. Orec had seen the look before, but wasn't about to take chances.

'Who the fuck are you?' Tomas said, pointing at one of them with his dripping axe.

They flinched back but didn't answer. Orec picked up a fallen spear and examined it. The shaft was sturdy enough, but lacked a counterbalance, and the head was simple iron, moulded into the standard leaf shaped pattern common to most militia.

'Refugees of some variety is my guess,' Orec said.

'Refugees my arse,' Tomas replied. 'Refugees ask for bread, they don't try to kill you.'

The man Orec had captured looked up at that.

'Speak, and be quick,' Orec said when he hesitated. 'Your lives may well depend on it.'

'We're from Alsmoor,' he gestured vaguely towards the west.

'Never heard of it. You're lying,' Tomas said. He turned to Orec. 'This is a waste of time. Let's just finish them and go.'

The men flinched back as he spoke, and the sickle man looked to Orec, desperation writ large across his face.

'It's the truth, I swear it. We fled when the monsters came, and have been hiding in the forests since.' The words came out in a rush. 'But recently there have been more attacks. We thought you were with them, the ones hunting us. I swear.'

Orec considered the patched clothes they were wearing and tapped his fingers against the shaft of the spear, then took a step back and jammed the spear into the dirt. 'I believe them,' he said. 'Let them be.'

'Are you mad?' Tomas shot a glare at Orec. 'So that they can trail us and finish the job while we sleep?'

'Fine,' Orec said tonelessly, motioning Hayden to step away as well. 'Kill them then.'

The men fell to their knees at this, terror darkening the trousers of two. Tomas jutted his chin at Orec.

'Don't think I won't.'

'So do it,' Orec replied, squatting to clean the blood from his charcoal-coloured blade. Next to him Hayden bit back on whatever he was going to say and simply folded his arms to watch it play out.

Tomas raised his axe and stepped forward, his jaw clenched, and the men cried out again, voices overlapping in fear. He lowered the axe, his arms shaking as if he were straining against invisible hands that were trying to raise it once more, and snorting through his nose as he fought to understand what he was feeling. He glared at Orec, who matched his gaze impassively.

'Hurry up,' Orec said. 'We're wasting daylight.'

'Fuck the lot of you,' Tomas growled, spinning on his heel and stalking off between the trees, slashing wildly at any branch or sapling in his way.

The prisoners watched him walk away, not quite understanding yet that they had been spared. When Tomas didn't come charging back at them they slowly straightened up and looked across to Orec, who had now sheathed his sword.

'We're only passing through the area,' he said, directing the words at the sickle man, who seemed less hysterical. 'Bury your friends, and find somewhere safer.'

'Safer? Like where? This used to be safe, but now it's a graveyard.' He raised a trembling fist. 'Because of men like you.'

'There's a town a few days' walk that way,' Orec gestured over his shoulder.

'Where we can fight all these bloody northerners for a chance to beg for charity? And sleep in stables, if we're lucky?' He spat to the side. 'No thanks.'

'It's your choice,' Orec said, shrugging. 'Take your chances in the forest then, but don't come crying when the spider folk find you or the men you attack fight back.'

The man seemed taken aback by that, and looked at his feet, muttering something unintelligible under his breath.

'Let's go,' Orec said, mounting up once more. Tomas had returned and was standing sullenly by his horse, the pulsing vein on his forehead signalling that he'd be dire company for the coming days. Orec nudged the horse forward, then stopped and pulled the griddle cakes leftover from the previous night's camp from his saddle bags.

'Here,' he said, gesturing to the sickle man. 'At least take these.'

The man made a show of debating whether to take them, but only for a moment. He snatched them away as if expecting a trick, then looked up at Orec and nodded wordless thanks. The sergeant wheeled his horse away and didn't look back.

HAYDEN WATCHED THE star blaze across the night sky, a silver streak amidst the glittering pinpricks of the night sky, tracing its path until it faded into the distance, wondering where it was going to land. He'd heard of people finding the remnants of such things, but didn't really like the idea of them being something as mundane as lump of iron. They, like the stars themselves, were something greater than that. How could iron shine so bright, or hang so high? Maybe it was something they created when they hit the ground, like lightning making glass of sand.

He smiled at the thought and turned back to the fire, gently coaxing the embers into a little more life. It was the coldest, deepest part of the night, and the fatigue was settling heavily on him now. Soon it would be time to wake Tomas, and he was actually looking forward to idea of laying himself down and closing his eyes.

Perhaps tonight the dreams would stay away, deflected by the shield of his exhaustion. They had lessened of late, but they were always there somewhere, like the men who were probably following them, a presence that made carefree rest impossible. Even if they had lost the trail or otherwise abandoned the pursuit, it was likely they would never know, and the voice in his head, the same one that always told him he would die unless he woke immediately, would ensure that he was looking over his shoulder for the gods knew how many years to come.

He stood and faced away from the fire and shook some life back into his legs and waited for his vision to readjust. Staring into the embers was foolish, a rookie mistake that had cost more than one guard their life. He turned as Orec muttered something, his words slurred by sleep. He repeated it again, and this time the pleading tone was obvious. Hayden moved over and squatted next to him, ready to lay a hand on his shoulder, a gesture that he'd found stilled whatever troubled the sergeant. He glanced across at Tomas, but he was still breathing slowly, his severe features softened in the dim light. If the night was to follow the pattern of the last week, he would start muttering and grabbing at nothing in the next few minutes too.

It was strange, almost as if they shared the same dream, and every time he'd thought to mention it he'd shied away. In the light of day his worries seemed fanciful and foolish, and neither man seemed any the worse for it. The gods knew, he'd kept them awake more than his fair share of nights too, flailing his way toward the surface of an ocean of blood, lungs burning until he woke to stare into the darkness and wonder why he could still taste the iron and salt. Orec moaned again, a wordless sound, and clenched his fists.

'Easy now,' Hayden said quietly, pressing down on his shoulder. 'It's just a dream.'

Orec's eyes snapped open, and Hayden fell back with a gasp. Orec's eyes were two featureless black orbs, infinitely darker than the shadows the campfire fought against.

Hayden's slap cracked against his cheek, knocking his head sideways. Orec reared up, but stumbled backwards as his legs folded beneath him, leaving him on his hands and knees, his now-normal eyes staring about wildly.

'What? What?' he panted, sitting back and looking around the campsite.

Tomas too was stirring, ingrained habits pulling him from the depths of whatever dreams had held him fast.

Hayden tossed one of the bundles of sticks onto the fire in

lieu of replying and waited until the initial flare died down to a steadier light.

'We need to talk,' he said.

'Is it my watch?' Tomas said, rubbing his face. 'Or morning?'

'Yes, and no.'

'What is it?' Orec said, his bewilderment quickly turning into irritation. He rubbed his jaw. 'Spit it out before I lay you out.'

'Do you remember what you were dreaming of?'

'Dreaming of?' Orec asked. 'No, and what do you care?'

'It's, uh, you've been having bad ones,' Hayden said, his tongue suddenly feeling thick in his mouth. This was exactly why he hadn't broached the subject before and having a brain that was fixated on sleeping wasn't helping. 'And it's getting worse. It's affecting you.'

'For gods' sakes,' Orec growled, moving back to his blankets. 'That can bloody well wait for daylight. Do that again and I'll break your hand.'

Hayden opened his mouth but shut it again as Tomas shook his head. As much as Orec resembled a bear, he sometimes had the temper of one too, and arguing with him now would be like going into his cave and poking him with sticks.

'In the morning then,' he said, but received no reply.

'Get some sleep before he kills you,' Tomas offered helpfully.

Hayden stretched out on Tomas' blankets, the residual warmth he'd left in them adding weight to his already heavy eyelids. It felt like he'd barely closed them before a rough hand shook him awake. He batted it away and earned a slap in return, sending him scrambling from the blankets, eyes wide and staring as his senses returned.

'There he is,' Tomas said with a crooked smile.

Hayden swore and rubbed the grit from his eyes before massaging his stinging cheek.

'I'm making griddle cakes,' Tomas said cheerfully. 'Seeing as someone keeps giving them away.'

'Are you still bitching about that?' Orec replied, hardly bothering to glance in Hayden's direction as he picked the worst of the forest litter from his blanket.

'They were some of my finest.'

Orec snorted. 'They're probably wishing we killed them by now.'

'Your uncouth palate isn't my fault.' He looked up from the pan. 'You get to clean and roll the blankets, since you're the one who's slept past daybreak.'

Hayden looked to the morning sun, its light diffused into silver by the mists that still hung between the trees. By his reckoning, the sun had been up for well over an hour already.

'Why so late?' he said, standing up and stretching this way and that.

'Well, you seemed to be having such a pleasant dream,' Orec said, cinching his bedroll.

'Screw you,' Hayden said.

'Odd dream to have,' Tomas said, 'but then, you are an archer. Cakes are ready.'

They ate listening to Tomas describing how much better the coarse cakes would be with some honey and various spices. Despite their grumbling to the contrary, Tomas' food was actually far more than simply passable, not that they would ever tell him that openly. It was only once they were done that Orec looked at Hayden for the first time.

'Tell me what happened last night,' he said.

He did, as plainly as he could, omitting any mention of what he'd been thinking.

'I remember none of it,' Orec said when he was done, staring into the fire as if expecting to see the answer in the embers. Tomas was watching him closely, but didn't speak either. Neither did, not until they'd been on the trail for an hour or more when Tomas cantered up to him.

'Have I ever done that? My eyes, that is.'

Hayden sighed and looked over to him, expecting to see his usual mocking smile but there was no sign of it.

'No,' he said. 'Just the twitches, and mumbling.'

'Huh,' Tomas said, running his hands through his hair and the ragged braid that hung from the back of it. 'It's a strange thing to be relieved about.'

'Can't argue with that,' Hayden replied. 'But these are strange times. You remember the first time we saw the land dragon?' He smiled as Tomas swore. 'Exactly. It was half a mile away and I was shitting my pants at the same time as wondering if I was dreaming.'

'That was something alright. What's your point?'

'Just that sometimes things we didn't think possible might actually be true.'

'Like fair taxes?'

Hayden chuckled. 'Maybe not that.'

'So listen,' Tomas said, edging his horse closer. 'Since we're talking about all of this, there's something you should know.'

'I'm listening.'

'You do it too.'

'Do what?' Hayden asked, his tone even and giving no sign of how he'd felt the ground lurch at Tomas' words.

'Twitch like a dog that's been beaten too often,' Tomas said. 'And I'm not talking about the usual gasping and such like.'

Hayden's knuckles whitened on the saddle horn and he ground his feet into the stirrups, making his horse prance in confusion. He concentrated on bringing it back under control, which offered a moment's relief from the heat in his cheeks and churning in the pit of his gut. Tomas waited until his horse was stilled again before speaking again.

'Orec doesn't want to say anything, says you already have your own demons and all that, we all do, but if this is something besides another bad dream I figured you should know.'

'Grateful,' he said in flat voice. 'I'm going on ahead.'

He didn't wait for Tomas to reply and touched his heels to the horse, nudging it to a careless pace for the forest they were in. Mercifully Tomas didn't follow, and after the better part of a mile he slowed to a halt and just managed to dismount before throwing up across some ferns. He leaned on the tree as he spat the last of it from his mouth.

He was angry and ashamed to hear his suffering described and dismissed like that, but it wasn't strong enough to overpower the sense of violation that he swept through him. Tomas' words, careless as they always were, had dislodged something in his mind, like the pebble that starts a landslide. Perhaps he remembered it more than they did because he always slept with some part of his mind alert, waiting for the sleep demons that pursued him, but whatever the reason he could still feel the wrongness of it moving under his skin.

He salvaged a smile as the horse nudged him with its nose and huffed at him. He rubbed it and gathered up the reins.

'You're right,' he said quietly, swinging himself into the saddle. 'It's just a goddamned dream. Things will be better once we're home.'

He held to that thought as he headed back to the trail.

# CHAPTER TWELVE

'WHAT'S BITING THEM?' Armand asked absently, carving another slice from the apple and chewing it noisily.

Quental turned at the question and also rested his back on the railing as he watched the huddled crew talking. At least two of them were periodically clutching their foreheads and gesturing at the deck and water.

'No idea,' he said. 'That's the most animated that I've seen them since we shoved off. Whatever it is, she's watching them too.' He gestured towards the wooden ziggurat that acted as crew and passenger quarters, kitchen, and just about everything else, but mostly towards the imposing figure that stood on top of it. 'I'd be nervous too if I messed up in front of her.'

Armand glanced up at the captain and grunted his agreement. His first meeting with the tattooed Fornithi had gone just as bad as it could, short of violence. She'd ignored his attempts at small talk, rolled her eyes at his attempt to commandeer the barge, and had simply laughed in his face when he'd suggested that her refusal to help them could raise questions about the barge's ownership. *You're a long way from home, marshal.* She'd said it with a smile, but with the burly crew in earshot the message was clear enough.

In the end he'd been forced to negotiate the price of passage like a common traveller, a price that had gouged his purse given the cargo space that their horses took up. The men didn't mind, of course, and seemed to relish the opportunity to spend a few days sitting around—not that he begrudged them that. They'd worked admirably up to now, never questioning his orders and riding hard where they needed to, scouring the area for anyone who might have seen their quarry.

'Ever been to High Town?' Quental asked.

'No,' Armand said, cutting another slice of apple and offering it to Quental. 'Heard about it though.'

'Same,' the sergeant admitted, taking the slice with a nod of gratitude. 'But what I don't get is why everyone talks about it in hushed tones, as if what happened is somehow special. Dozens of our cities were razed, and countless towns and farmsteads. Why are they any less of a tragedy? Just because they weren't as pretty to look at?'

Armand chewed his slice slowly. It was the first time since they'd set off that Quental had sounded anything other than even-tempered.

'It's a fair point,' he conceded. 'I think the sympathy stems more from what happened after.'

'They're not the first people to be mutilated.' Quental said, the angry tone even more evident. He folded his arms and looked off to the side, watching a kite circling something on the shore. 'We gave them justice, and now it's up to them.'

'That's more than most got,' Armand agreed, tossing the core over his shoulder. 'I'm going to find out what's going on.'

Most of the commotion stemmed from the few civilian passengers who'd managed to cram themselves aboard and had been shooting the patrol filthy and fearful looks by turn ever since. There were five of them, two men and three women, all trying to talk to two of the crew at the same time, and none saw him approach.

'Yes, yes,' one of the crewmen was saying. 'I know, but things like that happen regularly. It's nothing to worry about.'

One of the women thrust a young boy of perhaps ten years forward and shook him. The boy took this silently, jaws clenched in the universal look of someone dying of mortal embarrassment. 'Tell them again what you saw.'

'A monster,' he said through his teeth, and pointed to the shore. 'It jumped onto the side of the boat from the shore.'

'It's probably just a water spider,' the crewman said, smiling down at him. 'They've been getting bigger, but they just want chickens, cats and dogs, not small boys.'

Some of the colour left the boy's cheeks and he looked down. 'It had four legs and a tail,' he said in voice that Armand had to strain to hear.

'What's the issue here?' he asked, stepping around the woman holding the boy. All five passengers began speaking at once, eager to make him hear side of the story. 'One at a time!' They shrank back and he turned to the crewman. 'You first.'

'The boy said he saw something large leap onto the barge, but there's nothing out of place.'

'I saw it,' the boy said. 'It made holes in the boat.'

'When was this?' Armand asked, hunkering down in front of the boy.

'Last night, just before supper,' he said, waving his arm in an arc. 'It came over in one jump and hit the boat. I saw it.' He pointed to the neatly wound ropes. 'I stood on those and I saw it.'

'You're very brave to have gone to check,' Armand said. 'Show me.'

He ignored the muttering of the passengers and let the boy take his hand and lead him over to the side.

The boy jumped onto the rope and leaned dangerously forward over the railing. 'There,' he said, almost tipping over as he pointed.

It took a moment for Armand to see what he was pointing at, but there were a series of parallel gouges in the thick timbers, the deepest of them not six feet from where the boy was.

'You were this close to it?' he asked.

'I told you I saw it.' The boy climbed down from the rope and Armand could see he was fighting back tears. 'It had a tail. Spiders don't have tails.'

His mother swept in and gathered him up, fixing Armand with a fierce stare. 'He's gone through enough.'

'Well, I wish my soldiers were as brave as him,' he replied, which silenced whatever she was about to say and made the boy smile as he rubbed his eyes with a grubby sleeve. 'Don't worry, we'll look into it. You have nothing to worry about.'

That seemed to mollify them and they headed back to the corner that they were occupying.

'What did you make of those?' Armand asked the crewman once they were out of earshot.

'Beats me,' the man said, peering over the side. 'The likes of you or me would need some serious works to gouge that much wood out of the old girl, even with an axe.'

'If it did jump, it must've done so for a reason. Is everything and everyone accounted for?'

'As far as I know, yes.'

'How long until we reach High Town?'

'About two days this time of year normally, so probably three now.'

'Water spiders holding you up?' he said it in a light tone, but the crewman seemed to consider it seriously.

'No, it's not breeding season yet, so I reckon the issues are further upriver. There's a lot of flotsam, so it keeps damming up, which changes the currents. Used to be all but a straight line down this way, but now you've got to watch for shifting sandbanks.' He leaned in closer. 'You don't want to get stuck on one of those around here, not at night.'

'Right. Well, we'll post a watch tonight as well.'

'The captain will be grateful. She won't want that lot running their mouth about monsters.'

'Of course.' He turned and headed back to Quental, who had recovered his usual calm demeanour.

'And?'

Armand told him, and felt better seeing the sergeant react the same way that he'd felt.

'Set a night watch. Short rounds.'

'I'll arrange a rota,' Quental said. 'It'll do them good not to get too lazy.'

'Let's hope they don't get too busy.'

TOMAS WATCHED THE crossroads grow ever closer. The last time he'd seen it he'd had three hundred clueless men around him and a beard that wasn't touched by grey. As soon as the recruiters had marched them across it, their demeanour had changed, as he alone had expected.

The cheery attitude of the sergeants riding alongside them had evaporated; they'd quickly increased the pace and kept it like that, whipping the legs of any man who lagged behind. He smiled at the thought of Oleg the baker's helpless rage as he began to realise that being the son of a town elder meant nothing anymore. The only time he'd ever run was when a stray dog had chased him for one of the pastries he'd always had to hand, a habit that he'd begun paying for in those first few miles. The soldiers had laughed at his request for a rest and had lashed his legs with their riding crops, briefly making him the fastest man on the road. Tomas tried to remember when he'd last seen Oleg, and his smile faltered as when he remembered the man's screams.

'So this is it?' Orec's voice started him and dislodged the bloody images, and he was glad for the distraction.

'It is,' he said. 'There used to be a few gibbets over there, but otherwise it all looks the same, which doesn't seem right.'

'Yes, I remember those,' Hayden said, looking around as if seeing it for the first time, which judging from how morose he'd been for the last few days, was entirely possible. 'This is the Turnandal Road.'

'Actually, Turnandal starts a stone's throw over there,' Tomas said, pointing over his shoulder. 'This side is the Harndul. So much for being the scout.'

Hayden ignored that and tied his hair back with a strip of leather. 'I hadn't appreciated we'd come this far to the east.'

'So when you picked that shitty goat trail for us to follow you were just guessing?' Tomas asked, looking back the way they'd come, and feeling every scratch and prick from the wild brambles they'd cut their way through again.

'I'm flattered that you think I have every path and streamlet in this entire nation mapped in my head, but I've been guessing since we set off.'

'You what?'

'I know the direction,' Hayden said, glancing up at the sun, 'so I just try and find the least offensive path going that way.'

'It's worked, hasn't it?' Orec said, then turned to Tomas. 'So, you're taking it? The road?'

'It's longer, but it'll still be faster.'

Orec sat back in his saddle and exhaled heavily. 'So this is it.'

'Don't cry now, sarge,' Tomas said.

'It'll be tears of joy knowing I don't have to wake to your stench.'

'Ride in with me,' Tomas said. 'Come on. One last drink for the road. The road takes us in the quiet side, it'll be fine."

Hayden looked across at Orec. 'The horses could do with some grain and rest.'

'I'm game,' Orec replied, looking across at Tomas. 'But you're buying.'

'Sure,' Tomas grinned. 'We'll keep it nice and quiet-like.'

The road was easy, and the stables that Tomas eventually led them to looked to be in better condition than the inn they were attached to, and that was a generous description. Orec had seen sturdier looking buildings in overnight camps and said as much to Tomas' obvious delight.

'The Lion's weathered every storm the gods have thrown at us for two hundred years, and she'll be here after they've had their fill of us.'

'Maybe so,' Orec said, 'but it wouldn't kill them to clean the gutters or replace the weatherboard once in a while.'

Tomas roared with laughter, drawing a few looks from the men sitting by the open windows.

'Now who's the old one? Come on, grandad. Get your chin out of the dirt, it's a celebration!'

He stepped into the gloomy interior that waited beyond the doorway and disappeared from sight.

'Watch my back,' Orec said, and followed him in, Hayden close behind.

It was better than he'd expected inside, with sturdy tables radiating out from a stone fireplace and a bar that could probably withstand a battering ram. The floors were mostly clean and it smelt no worse than they did.

Tomas was already at the bar already and waved them over.

'Three pints, you fat bastard,' he shouted to the stocky barkeeper, who turned slowly, looking like he'd just stepped in something unpleasant.

'God's teeth,' Orec muttered, setting his hand on his knife as the inn went quiet and several men stood up, the scraping of their benches the only sound. His sword would be a hindrance in the close quarters.

The barkeep flipped a hatch that sounded like it weighed the same as Hayden and lumbered over to stand in front of Tomas, ham-sized fists clenched.

'What'd you say?'

Tomas shrugged off Orec's hand and squared up to the barkeep. 'You deaf now as well, fatty?'

'Maybe I don't speak arsehole so good.'

Orec slid his knife out as Tomas squinted at the towering figure and didn't need to look around to know that Hayden had just done exactly the same thing.

Tomas and the barkeep both grinned at the same time and stepped forward into a backslapping bear hug while Orec and Hayden stared at them, and then at each other.

'My brother's home!' the barkeep bellowed, lifting Tomas from the ground and setting him on the bar as if he were a favourite child. Sound immediately returned to the inn, with half a dozen men raising their mugs in salute. His brother made his way back into the bar, slamming the hatch shut with a thunderous crash, and immediately began pouring ales.

Orec took a pair, passing one to Hayden while the barkeep downed his in two great gulps.

'Your brother?' Orec asked Tomas. 'This is news.'

Tomas shrugged the question away. 'Hey, Erik, I want you to meet my sword brothers, who have always stood by me. The hairy one is Orec Blackblade, the sergeant who refuses to be a captain, and the blonde is Hayden the Archer.'

'Good to meet you, and welcome!' Erik said, beaming. 'So it's you I have to blame for bringing this godforsaken wretch back?'

'Afraid so,' Orec said, offering a mock toast.

'Wait a moment,' Hayden said, leaning on the bar next to Tomas. 'Hayden the fucking archer? Are you telling me you don't know my name after three and a half years?'

Tomas paused with his pint halfway to his mouth, then shut it in favour of another shrug. 'It never seemed important.'

'You son of—'

'I mean it. You were always at our side.' Tomas said. 'It hardly seemed important. And it's not like I was sending you letters.'

Hayden's indignant expression deepened as Orec began to laugh, not entirely sure himself why he found it as hysterical as he did but unable to stop himself for all of that. It got worse as Tomas and Erik began to laugh as well, and when Hayden swore he found himself doubling over and gasping for breath in between slamming his fist on the table.

After that, his memories of the night would forever remain a badly strung together jumble of images, although he would be spared the memory of the hangover he woke to at noon of the following day, unable to remember where, and for a time, who he was.

He stumbled downstairs and was brought food that he ate mechanically, wincing at the first taste of the small ale that came with it. It helped though, and by the time that he was finished it no longer felt like the inn was a ship swaying at anchor.

The others had joined him midway through the meal, and they talked quietly, agreeing that he and Hayden would leave first thing the next morning, since even the thought of buying supplies that day felt like an impossible trial.

They did manage it in the end though, and for Orec at least the gentle exercise helped ease the pounding in his head. They hardly haggled over any prices, to the delight of the vendors, and returned directly to the inn to pack their kit and fall asleep before the sun had fully set, having refused Tomas' invitation to join him at the bar once more.

The eastern sky was a hundred shades of blue as they checked their saddles the next morning, watched by Tomas, who stood with a blanket draped over himself.

'Time to go,' Orec said, wiping his hands on his tunic before extending one to Tomas, who slapped it out of the way and stepped forward to embrace him.

'Stay alive,' Tomas said. 'And say hello to your wife from me,' he added with a leer.

'In your dreams, old man.'

'Every night.' He slapped Orec on the shoulder. 'Send for me when everything's done. And that goes for you too, Hayden the archer.'

'Arsehole,' Hayden said, grinning as he returned the embrace he was pulled into. 'Look after yourself.'

'Same, son.'

Orec mounted up and settled himself in the saddle, marvelling at how natural it felt now. He clicked his tongue and the horse began walking. He turned when they reached the gates, but Tomas had already gone inside.

'Let's go,' he said, and they nudged the horses into a canter.

A'LORI ROLLED HIS blanket and squeezed it into the bag he'd fashioned from a discarded cargo sack. The docks were winding down for the night, with most of the workers already filling the saloons. It was a good night and had been a hot day, so he felt relatively optimistic about finding something decent. The workers were careless with the locks when it was this warm, their thoughts either on shade or finding a drink, and there was every chance that they hadn't stowed everything correctly or locked up behind themselves. By his reckoning, their carelessness wasn't his fault, and if they left something lying about, it was fair game. It was risky going in when the sky was still light, but he wouldn't be the only one thinking the same thing and it was a chance he'd have to take if he wanted to find something half decent. He patted the coins in his belt, as he walked down the hill.

The return of the soldier who'd paid him had been unexpected, and he'd brought others with him, equally stern and mirthless but also equally generous, especially as didn't need to share these extra coins with anyone. The money was comforting, and if he could find something decent tonight, he wouldn't have to start using them. Combined with what he had stashed, it could be enough to start pulling himself out of the hole he'd been living in since the Kinslayer had laid waste to everything, both literally and figuratively.

He smiled as he squeezed through his usual gap in the fence, thanking the stars that he'd spoken out when the bearded man had stopped where he'd been sitting that day. Everything had gone well since that day, and if it continued to do so, he swore that he would have the coin he'd given made into a pendant. He slipped into a gap between two pallets of cut wood as pair of workers passed by, enjoying the scent of the sap as he waited to be sure they weren't coming back before hurrying over to a narrow walkway that ran behind the warehouses. It was reassuringly dark here, even for his eyes, and both ends were overgrown with spiky weeds, which served to keep most men from bothering to go down it.

He was a third of the way along it and making for a pair of windows that had been left propped open when he first noticed that the normally raucous gulls had fallen silent. He stopped and looked around, but there were only weeds and shadows. Something nudged his foot and he yelped as several wharf rats ran past him, as large as cats and infinitely more vicious. Silence settled over him again as they vanished into the darkness beneath the warehouses. He shivered, appreciating how distant and isolated the passage was for the first time since he'd found and begun exploiting it. *I have to get out of here.* He took two steps, then caught himself. *Don't be an idiot, it's nothing.*

He was turning back towards the window when he saw the arc of violet light snap from the side of the building and flip across his sleeve like a glowing caterpillar. He was still marvelling at the sight of it when something grabbed his ankle with a terrible strength and pulled, slamming him against the supports before dragging him into the crawl space beneath. He flailed, trying to find something, anything to hold onto, but the gravel was bare saved for crab shells and rotting seaweed. It stopped, and he finally gathered enough breath to scream for help, but the sound was thin even to his ears.

A strange noise answered his cry, something like a cat's purr but higher and sharper.

*'Reowan, sparian te ae!'* he pleaded, and gasped when the grip left his leg.

His relief lasted a single breath. Somewhere over the bay, which now seemed impossibly far away, the clouds parted to allow the moon's light to shine down, just enough for his eyes to pick out the angular mass of the thing crouched over his legs.

He wet himself, but what would once have been a mortal shame was now immaterial.

The creature snorted, blasting furnace-hot air across his belly, and he screamed as its claws followed, opening him from shoulder to hip. He reached for the wound, instinctively trying to stem the bloody tide that was already rising from it, but it batted his arms away as it leaned forward, snorting across him again, the sensation lost amidst the agony burning across his torso.

He wept as he waited for its teeth to finish him, a thousand images spinning through his head. Of soaring high above the grasslands, and banking through the trees, a fierce grin on his face as he fought to stay ahead of the others, their whoops and laughter loud behind him. Of meals taken high in the branches, a thousand silver lights burning around them, as if they dined amidst the stars themselves. Of his wife, whose smile he could no longer remember after the Kinslayer came and ripped her away from him. He sighed as he saw her walking towards him again, her hands held out towards him and her green eyes flashing with mischief.

'Is someone there? Come out.'

The image drifted apart at the gruff words and A'lori opened his eyes. A beam of yellow light was swinging this way and that. The creature lowered itself, making him gasp in pain, and the light swung back towards him. For a moment, he saw it clearly, but even in the light it had too many angles to make any sense of it. He saw its eyes flash with gold as it flinched away from the probing beam, and then it was gone in spray of gravel.

'Help,' he croaked.

CATT WATCHED THE stew slide from his spoon and pushed the bowl aside. The wine was at least passable, unlike whatever they'd managed to render into the glutinous mess lurking in the cooking pot. He took another sip and sat back, watching the others in the saloon. It was such a quaint term for something quite so wretched, but then that was only fitting for what High Town had become. The sight of it had stopped him in his tracks and laid a yoke of sadness on him that he would not easily shake off for some time.

Reading about it was one thing, but seeing it was another, which was why he generally preferred the latter. Writing about such tragedies was a soothing magic all of its own, each word another stitch in a bandage that hid the savagery of the wound beneath and making it easier to bear and think of the healing, rather than the agony. *I should write that down*. He shook his head and turned his attention back to his journal.

Blackblade and his band had to have come through High Town. Nothing else made sense, not if they were keeping to the direction they'd ostensibly set off in. The problem was that there were three roads that they could have taken, all of which generally led south or west, and even in its dilapidated state High Town was a busy nexus and whichever road they'd taken, it should have led them here. But even if it had, any trace of their passing would have long since been trampled into the mud that seemed to be everywhere.

A shadow fell across the journal and he looked up to see one of the locals pointing at him.

'That's him.'

The man he was being pointed out to wore the yellow sash of the mismatched group that he'd assumed to be the town militia, and stepped forward at his words, the swaying light of the lantern he'd bumped highlighting the red staining his hands and sash.

'You're the doctor?' he asked.

'Well, yes, but in so much as—'

'You're needed. Come with me.'

'No, hold on a moment, I'm not that kind of doctor,' Catt said. 'There's been—'

The guard held up a hand. 'Can you stitch?'

Catt knew he should say no. 'After a fashion, yes.'

'Then you must come. Hurry.'

'I need my bag.'

They waited outside while he hurried upstairs, quietly berating himself for not being sensible and staying in his room or keeping his mouth shut. He contemplated simply packing up and heading out the back door, but where would he go? Home to face Fisher and to describe his failure? It was unthinkable. He picked out a smaller leather bag from his luggage and made his way outside.

They led him straight through to a square building on the edge of the docks, the sheer functional ugliness of it a glaring insult to the memory of what High Town had been. The bars set across the windows told him what he needed to know about it, and he braced himself for the worst.

'He's bleeding badly,' the guard said, pushing a cell door open.

A woman was leaning over a thin, pale figure, her arms red to the elbow as she held an already soaked compress to his chest.

'You the doctor?' she asked, glancing over her shoulder.

'In a manner of speaking,' Catt said, edging forward. He gasped as he caught sight of the wounded man's aquiline features. 'He's Aethani?'

'Not for much longer if you stand there gawping.'

'We need more light.' Catt shrugged off his coat and rolled up his sleeves. He opened the bag and took out what looked like a river pebble and blew on it. Silvery light flickered around it for a few moments like kindling being lit, and then a steady light radiated outwards. He ignored the reactions around him and set it on a shelf.

'Show me,' he said, nodding to the woman, who lifted the compress. Catt gasped again, this time at the sight of the three parallel gashes that ran across the Aethani's chest.

'We don't know what did it,' the guard said from behind him. 'Can you help him?'

*But I do*. 'I've not helped an Aethani before, not like this,' Catt said, studying the pale body laid out before him. 'I could do more harm than good. Is there no hospice nearby?'

'He's beyond niceties like that,' she said. 'He'll be dead before we got him onto a carriage. We can't do nothing.'

He took another moment to consider the bleeding figure and rubbed his forehead. She was, of course, quite right. If he did nothing, the Aethani was as good as dead, and so was his next clue. He closed his eyes and counted to ten, calming himself, before opening them again and considering the bloody mess before him. *How long had it been?* The bowel looked intact, and the gashes could be sutured, and provided no arteries were damaged he had a fair chance of recovering. But the blood loss had been significant, and if their physiology was anything like that of a man, it was in the blood that the real problems would start.

'We best get to work then,' he said, offering her a fleeting smile. 'Tell me, are there any other Aethani nearby?'

He lost track of time after that, focused as he was on the messy business of putting everything back inside the Aethani in what he hoped was the right place and closing him up again.

'How is he?'

Catt turned as Tess, who he had found out was a midwife, entered the room.

'His breathing is steady and, more importantly, ongoing.'

'The men have brought some food in next door if you'd like a bite.' Catt waved the offer away and she stepped closer. 'I'm amazed that he's still alive. You did well, Doctor.'

'Me too,' he said. 'Amazed, that is. It would have been easier with a transfusion but I suspect his body's adaption to fly at high altitudes tipped the balance for us. There's a sad irony in that.'

His gaze found the stump of the Aethani's wings and he looked away sharply.

'Well, I don't know about that, but he's alive, and there's nothing more we can do for now. You should rest.'

'I can't,' Catt said. 'I have questions that he only he is in a position to answer..'

'And you both need rest before that can happen. Go now,' she said, her hand on his shoulder. 'I'll send word if he wakes.'

Catt sighed. The herbs fed to the Aethani while she was away would be taking effect soon, but it was true that he'd lost a lot of blood, which may delay the reaction.

'I suppose I could freshen up a bit.'

In the end, it was little over two hours before he was called back, time that he'd used to scrub the blood away (although his shirt was ruined) and update his journal over a nice cheese platter.

A burly dockworker was waiting for him inside the room when he returned, and before he could protest the man hastened forward and Catt found himself lifted off the ground in a crushing embrace before being set back down.

'Thank you, doctor,' he said. 'You saved him.'

'I did my best,' Catt said, quickly patting his pockets to make sure nothing within was missing or broken. 'You're a friend of his?' He couldn't keep the surprise from his tone.

'More than not,' the man replied. 'I'll get some air while you check on him.'

Catt raked his hair back into order and sat down next to the bed. The Aethani's pulse was still weak, but perceptibly stronger than it had been. The man opened his eyes as he released his delicate wrist.

'I'm alive,' he said.

'Quite. I can't imagine an afterlife that looked like this would make for an enthusiastic congregation,' Catt replied, eyeing the drab walls and barred window. He glanced over his shoulder to make sure that none of the watchmen were loitering in the doorway, and dragged his chair closer. 'Now perhaps you could help me in turn. Given your position, I will cut to the very heart of the matter, and I trust you'll forgive the brevity of my approach. When the misfortune befell you, was there a purple light?'

A'lori stiffened, his hands clenching into fists.

'Easy now,' Catt said, resting his hand on A'lori's fist. 'You're safe.'

'How did you know?'

'It was an educated guess, and while I'm sorry for your hurts, I'm pleased to see I was correct in my assumption. Simply put, I'm hunting the beast that tried to gnaw you. But it appears I am too slow once again.'

'Then you're a fool,' A'lori hissed. 'It's a monster, all teeth and claws. It's cunning, and strong.' He took a steadying breath. 'I might as well have been a child wrestling a troll.'

'I assure you that I'm not planning on wrestling with it,' Catt said. 'However I do need to find it. Is there anything you can tell me, however trivial it may seem? Anything could be useful now.'

A'lori closed his eyes and the memories filled his vision again. *The smell of the rotting seaweed under him, his blood, all mingling with the over-sweet odour of the creature itself. Then the sound of his skin tearing, so much like parchment that he'd looked around to find it before the pain arrived.*

'It didn't bite,' he said after a few moments. 'A mouthful of teeth like knitting needles, but it didn't bite. It tore me up with its claws, but stopped.' He grimaced as he focused on the memories. 'My purse. It tore my purse open and sniffed at it like a dog.'

'Your purse?' Catt didn't try mask his incredulity. The man

was half dead but already trying to scam a few crowns from the experience?

'It wanted the coins,' A'lori said, breathing out heavily and rubbing his face. 'Swallowed them all. Don't ask me why.'

Catt sat back, now entirely confused. *Coins?*

'I really thought my luck was changing,' A'lori said, staring at the roof. 'Coins being given when I didn't ask, and then being paid twice for the same information. If I'd scored last night I could have left this place.'

'Where there is life, there is hope, as I always say,' Catt offered. 'Out of interest, what information was it? And no, I'm not paying.'

A'lori smiled weakly as sleep pulled at him. 'The bearded one and the one-legged man on the Domshall Road. I felt bad telling them,' he said, his voice tapering to a whisper as he lost the fight to stay awake. 'He was nice. Gave me a polly and wished me well. But business...'

'Is business,' Catt finished for him. He sat back and fished his journal out of his coat pocket and flipped the pages back to his entry on the army hospital. Four men had escaped, led by a sergeant known as Orec Blackblade, a large man with chest length beard. And there: Stefan Alderg, a standard bearer and amputee.

He slapped the journal shut. He had his direction, and confirmed sightings of both, which meant it was no accident nor coincidence that their paths were converging. If the creature was sensitive enough to follow the trace of energy that this Blackblade had imprinted upon mere coins, then there was no doubt that it would follow him wherever he fled.

He smiled at the sleeping Aethani. He didn't need to track all of them. He only needed to find Blackblade, and the beast would eventually find its way to him.

# CHAPTER THIRTEEN

OREC WATCHED AS the distant figure of Hayden paused at the crest of the hill. He couldn't see if he had raised his arm in farewell like he had, but Hayden's eyes were keener than his. And then he was over the hill and gone, and Orec was alone.

He simply sat there for several minutes, listening to the countryside around him and experimenting with how it felt. Even in the hospital he'd been surrounded by other soldiers but now, finally, it was just him, and he felt strangely vulnerable. *Best watch out for grabbers as you go*. A smirk pulled at his mouth at the thought of Hayden's parting words and he nudged the horse onward, his sword a reassuring presence next to his leg.

Home was three days' ride, two if he pushed Goldie's pace. She seemed to like the name and, as if sensing the thought, the mare snorted and broke into a gentle canter and he patted her neck. He'd grown unexpectedly fond of her and despite his entreaty to the others to shed anything that could be traced to them, he was sorely tempted to keep her. Martina would certainly like that, plus it would be company for her nag, which was no bad thing. If nothing else, him finally being able to ride with a degree of competence would impress her.

He made a cold camp that night and ate smoked sausages from the generous parcel that Erik had packed for each of them, then laid and drifted off to sleep. He woke shortly before sunrise, dagger in hand, certain that someone had been standing over him, but the campsite was empty. He stood and checked again, rubbing the sleep from his eyes as he did so. There were no tracks, but his blanket was laying several feet away, balled up and covered in leaf litter. The frown didn't leave his face as he shook the worst from it and rolled it up.

Goldie nuzzled him as he strapped it onto the saddle once more and he smiled and rubbed her nose. The sun was rising, and if luck was in the air, he would be in sight of the valley by the time it set.

'Let's go, girl.'

The road followed a meandering contour as it skirted along the edge of what he knew to be Skanborg forest, dense enough that the floor of it had hardly seen sunshine in centuries, the trees within protected from the hungry eyes of loggers by fierce dryads—at least according to local tradition. As long as it wasn't Kelicerati, it didn't bother him. He'd never crossed swords with the spider people, but he'd heard enough about them around campfires to give thanks that he'd never had that particular pleasure.

A steady climb greeted him the next morning, and he let Goldie choose her own pace while he finished the last of the sausages. Slowly but surely the road evened out, and the sight that greeted him as he crested the hill drove the breath from his lungs as surely as if he'd been sucker-punched.

A huge swathe of forest on both sides of the road was simply not there anymore, unless he counted the blackened and cracked stumps that dotted it, each wide enough that families could have set out dinner tables upon them. The ground was dented inward and roughly gouged, the surface blackened and cracked as if it had not seen rain in a hundred years or more. Goldie whinnied softly and shifted under him as if sensing his unease, or perhaps simply more sensitive to the unnatural force that would have been needed to do such a thing.

He dismounted and led her forward, his hand on his sword. As he moved through the devastation, he began to notice that many of what he'd taken to be ashen branches were in fact bones, rendered as pale and fragile as those dug from ancient barrows by whatever had happened here. His mouth dried as he felt the ghost of the sun-bright and bone-jarring explosion that had ended his war.

Was this what Tulkauth looked like now? Were the bones of the men who'd fought beside him scattered across it like these were?

He remounted Goldie and took a quick sip from his canteen. What had happened here was one thing, but that it had happened so close to home was another entirely. This level of ruin wasn't something that a simple raiding party could unleash. That would need the presence of a Heart Taker of some skill, and that thought left him feeling hollow and fearful for what awaited him in Cambry.

Goldie needed no encouragement to put the broken landscape behind them. Once they were clear of the worst of it and the road was whole once more, he let her run. He normally exulted in the sensation of speed, but now it didn't feel fast enough. His mind was gripped by a dread that the voice of reason in his head could find not explain away.

He looked up the skies as he rode. 'I doubt any of you are listening,' he said, 'I don't care about anything else, just let her be safe. Do that and I'll swear a tithe to you.'

He hated saying it, not just because he had no time for the pious and all the trouble that inevitably followed them, but because it meant giving voice to the fear that had been growing in him for some time now. He'd written to her regularly, but hadn't had a letter in a year: something made all the more painful by it having been his task to distribute the correspondence to the company. Of course, it was an imperfect system to begin with, and most of the regular message carriers had either been dragged into the war or killed by it; so it was more likely that all those letters were a wordless sludge in a damp ditch somewhere. But it was the *not knowing* that bothered him like a sharp grain stuck between his teeth that he just couldn't dislodge.

He slowed the horse when he saw the lather on her hide, then dismounted and walked her for a mile, even though the slower pace chafed at him. He was moving through the fringes of the woods now, but, even with the dappled sunlight shining through, it felt menacing, a sensation he'd have dismissed had the back of his neck not been tingling with the sense of being watched. He made sure his sword was hanging just right and clearly visible as he walked, and while the feeling hardly abated, the road remained empty save for him. Night was falling by the time Goldie carried him out of the last vestige of the woods and onto roads that he'd once explored with his brothers.

'Just a little more, girl,' he whispered to Goldie, patting her shoulder. The light was fading, but not so quickly that he couldn't see the how the milestones had been smashed. The sound of running water made him sit up straighter in the saddle. He was close now, and his heart was beating as hard and fast as it had before any battle. He tried to lick his dry lips, but his mouth was likewise too dry.

He passed a familiar stone marker, then another, and as the road curved the path that led to his home came into view. He forced himself to stop and count to ten before he charged in. It would be the worst kind of stupidity if he survived everything that the Kinslayer had thrown at him only to be killed on his doorstep. He loosely tied Goldie to one of the trees in the unkempt orchard, then moved off into the deeper shadows and circled around the house.

The wall he'd spent an entire summer building had been knocked down in several places—by horses, judging from the fall of the stones—and two of the front shutters were missing. No light shone from the windows, and no smoke rose from the chimney. He moved into the front yard, crushing weeds underfoot where aromatic herbs had once grown. He drew a knife and held it in a reverse grip as he stepped up to the door, noting the distinct gouges that marked its surface. *Axes.* That it had taken so many blows to undo his work was of no comfort to him at all. He took a deep breath, pushed the door open and stepped inside.

He moved through the house quickly, checking for intruders while trying not to think about the scattered clothes and broken furniture that littered it. Only once that was done and he'd wedged the door shut did he put his back to the wall and slide down to the floor, and, for the first time since his brothers had died, he wept.

A SPLINTERING CRASH jolted Orec from the sleep that had finally claimed him. He rolled away from where he had been sitting and had his legs under him before his eyes were fully open. The noise came again and he stared about him wildly until the memory of where he was reasserted itself.

*Home. Martina.*

He drew his sword and held it in a two-handed grip as he moved to the side of the room and peered around the corner. He could hear men's voices now too, several of them talking at once. Shadows moved past the shutters, as others moved to encircle the house. Another crash at the door sent his makeshift wedge skating away across the floorboards as the door crashed open, silhouetting the forms of two men.

The inside of the house was dark and they had only taken one step over the threshold, squinting into the gloom, when they heard his footsteps. They both looked up just as he launched himself at them boots first, with all of his weight behind the kick. They flew back out of the doorway as if kicked by a warhorse, knocking two more men aside as they cartwheeled backwards and landed with a heavy crash.

Orec was on his feet again when they hit the bottom stairs, and out of the door before the others regained their balance. There were three more on the porch. Two had large, knotted cudgels in their hands, while the third had a sheathed short sword at his hip, and wore the flat-brimmed hat of a councilman over a suddenly pale face.

Orec extended his arm in a fencer's pose and rested the charcoal-coloured tip of his sword at the base of the councilman's throat, immediately drawing a bead of blood that the man's linen shirt greedily drank in.

The man backed away but Orec kept pace, and barely avoiding avoided spitting him when the councilman abruptly stopped, his attention diverted by the men fanning out around him.

'Where is she?' he said, tilting the sword so that the point dimpled the soft, plump skin under the man's jaw. 'I won't ask twice.'

The councilman waved the men back and stood on his toes in a vain attempt to alleviate the deadly pressure.

'Who?' he managed, and even that word cost him another rivulet of blood.

Orec lowered his sword enough to step around behind him and hold his starched collar, his sword rising to menace the men the councilman had brought. They looked like they'd been in a few fights of their own, but none had stepped in as leader, which meant some luck still remained with him and he had the advantage.

'The next words I hear better be about my wife or I by all that is holy, I will kill every last one of you whoresons.'

'Wife?' said the councilman. 'Who are you?'

'Orec?' He turned as one of the men stepped forward, lowering his cudgel. 'Guardians preserve me, is that you?'

Orec squinted at the man, who dropped his weapon and raised his hands. 'It's me. Max.'

'Max?' Orec asked, the angles of the man's face finally finding traction amongst his memories, although the face that Orec remembered hadn't had so many angles when he'd last seen it, only soft curves. The son of the baker, Max never gone without a meal in his life, which combined with his love of fine pastry had made him an outsider and a target for constant mockery and bullying. He and Max had both suffered the same abuse, Max for his corpulence and Orec for his crippling shyness and slow and deliberate ways.

'Fat Max?'

Max turned to the other men with him and gestured for them to lower their weapons before looking to Orec once more.

'Come now, let him go.'

Orec gnawed his lip for a moment, then shoved the councilman away from him and took a two-handed grip on his sword again. 'What are you doing here, Max?'

'Me?' He looked around. 'I still live here, dummy. What are you doing here, seeing as you're dead?'

Orec finally lowered his sword, to the obvious relief of the men closest to him. 'Dead?'

Max stepped closer and, carefully stepping past the sword, pulled Orec into an embrace. He tensed, instincts screaming at him that this was an attack, that he'd feel the bite of knife in his kidney at any moment, but there was no flash of pain, just a hand patting his shoulder. Keeping one eye on the other men, who now seemed more intent on attending to the little scratch he'd given the councilman, he returned the gesture, at least one handed.

Max stepped back and looked Orec up and down. 'Not dead, but not for a want of trying by the look of it.'

Orec grinned despite himself. The constant bullying had given each of them an ally, one person in the town who could understood and wouldn't simply tell them to walk it off or rise above it.

'What happened to the rest of you?'

Now it was Max who smiled, at least briefly. He jabbed a thumb over his shoulder in the general direction of the town. 'The war caught up with us.'

'Max, where's Martina?' His knuckles whitened as he asked the question, and as Max looked down and away it felt like time was slowing. Even though it only took moments for Max to reply, he wanted to grab him by the coat and shake the answer out of him, but didn't for fear of what that might be.

'When the letter came she, uh, didn't take it well, my friend.' Max took him by the elbow and led him away a few paces. He waited until Orec sheathed the sword before continuing. 'She mourned hard, and then opened her house to shelter some of the refugees that were coming in from the valleys. As a salve against the pain.'

'What happened? What letter?'

'The militia was called in to help face off against one of the Kinslayer's armies south of Chukker. It was a hard fight and we lost the town, but we blunted the worst of it. The main army turned westward, raiding the valleys as they did. We got back in time to face them here. You saw the forest when you came in?'

Orec nodded and fought to keep the lid on his impatience, but he was getting close to the point of shaking the answer out of Max.

'That was insane. They had one of their sorcerers, but we managed to spit him early. Took the wind out of them a bit, and—'

'Martina, Max. Where is she?'

'Sorry, sorry. After the battle, word spread that the town was whole, and hundreds of people came in. Unfortunately, word also spread to some unsavoury types. We'd heard rumours about people vanishing, crofts being raided in the night, and had assumed it was skirmishers. We were wrong. There's a band of them out there now, all deserters and worse. They keep moving so no one wants to take responsibility for rooting them out.'

He folded his arms. 'It's made them bold. They struck from the forest. They took her, Orec. Her and the women she had taken in. We came today because we thought you were one of them returning. I'm sorry, my friend.'

Orec turned away and walked to the edge of the garden. *They took her.*

He felt his anger stirring anew and raked his fingers through his hair as the councilman approached. 'You're coming with us until we sort this mess out and decide what to do with you.'

'Piss off,' Orec growled at the councilman, not even looking at him. 'Where are they, Max?'

'Somewhere in Skanborg.' He held up a placating hand. 'I know that look. Come on, don't do anything rash. Let's go back to mine and we can talk about it.'

'What is there to think about? I'm getting her back, and I will kill any man or beast that tries to stop me.'

'Gods, just wait a moment,' Max said, stepping in front of him. 'We need to think about this. There are too many of them.'

'I don't need to think about it. Or raise a committee to think for me.' He brushed past the man and unhooked one of the saddlebags and his canteen from Goldie's saddle. 'Look after my horse, Max.'

'Stop that man!' the councilman shouted. The men behind him shifted but none stepped forward.

'Stand down,' Max said tiredly, turning to the councilman. 'Let him be. If he's going into Skanborg, paying one of your stupid fines is the least of his worries. We tracked them to near the horseshoe lake,' Max added in a quieter voice, patting Goldie's flank. 'But it's not like you remember it in there. There are strange cries at night, and worse.'

'Is that why you stopped trying?'

'I stopped because I lost six men without seeing more than a cold campfire of theirs,' Max said in a harder tone. 'And if you charge off in there like a maddened bull, all you'll do is add your bones to theirs. Think about this, please.'

'I have and I've made my decision.' He took a steadying breath. 'I've no plans to die anytime soon. How long since they took her?'

'Nigh on three weeks now.'

'Fuck.' Three weeks in captivity was a long time, and he clung to Goldie's saddle as light-headedness and nausea warred for dominance within him. *Three weeks.* If they'd left the hospital three weeks earlier she would have been here to welcome him home. Max laid a hand at the back of his neck.

'Wait a day or two, let me organise some support. I can shut the bakery.'

'I can't, Max. I need to find her. I can't leave her at their mercy for a moment longer.'

Max nodded. 'I understand. But promise me one thing then. When you find her, be kind.'

'What's that supposed to mean?' He swatted Max's hand away, but the baker didn't flinch and moved closer.

'It means that if she's alive, she's had to do what she needs to do to survive. And if you storm in there and judge for it, you're going to lose her as surely as if you turned and walked away right now.' He said this in a low tone, ensuring no others heard it.

Orec's stomach churned as his meaning sunk in. Part of him wanted to lay Max out cold for saying it, but there was no spite in the baker's face.

'Do you really think so little of me?'

He didn't wait for a response and simply turned and began walking back towards Skanborg.

'Guardians protect you,' Max called after him.

The anger burned brightly within Orec for the first few miles back along the road and into Skanborg, miles in which he barely noticed anything around him. It took an unseen tree root to return clarity to his mind. One moment his mind was torturing him with whispers of what men like that would do to a woman, and the next he had a mouthful of dirt, and lungs without a trace of air in them. He rolled to his side and clutched at his chest until he remembered how to breathe, then lay there gulping air in great whooping breaths until the dull ache loosened its grip on his chest and allowed him to sit up.

*That could have been an arrow.*

He patted the dirt and leaves from his beard and stood up again. He was no good to her dead, and if Max was right, he was going to be hard pressed finding them, let alone overcoming them. He started walking again, this time with the care and caution of someone who knew he was in enemy territory and expected an attack at any moment. He'd learned more about moving stealthily in the hunts he'd been on with Hayden than he had in all his years before, and he was grateful for those skills now.

Growing up, he and Max had found a refuge in Skanborg. For all the taunts and bravado of the older boys in town, they feared the forest and its supposed guardians and wouldn't pursue the two of them beyond the edges of the woods. He now understood that it wasn't so much the fear of the physical threat that the dryads posed, but that they were supposedly able to see the evil in the hearts of those who entered their groves. Their tormentors knew their actions were wrong, at least on some level, and that guilt fed their fear.

A fleeting smile pulled at Orec's mouth as he mulled the thought over. Those days in the forest, although always the product of baseless anger and dumb prejudice, were nothing but good memories, albeit one that the war had driven from his mind.

Safe in the forest, they'd go fishing in pools and lakes where the fish had never known a hook or net, and seemed eager to volunteer themselves as their lunch. Max was the first one who he'd told about the torch he carried for Martina, although the baker's son had only laughed and told him that he and anyone who'd ever seen him in her proximity already knew that. He'd only laughed harder as Orec's cheeks had burned red, a laugh that was impossible not to avoid and soon the two of them had lain there in the mud of the riverbank, laughing like madmen, unable to stop. That was the first and only day he'd seen a dryad in the forest. She had risen from a nearby thicket, a lithe figure with skin like the bark of a birch, roots for hair, and dark eyes that glinted with green motes, as if fireflies lived within her head. She stared at them, head cocked to one side, as they howled and rolled in the mud. She'd vanished in a single, graceful leap when he stopped and stared back at her, and Max had never believed him.

*I wonder what they would think of me now.*

He didn't consider himself an evil man, but did such men think of themselves as evil in the first place? To a deer, a lion was an evil menace, mercilessly slaying its young; but the lion killed to live and feed its own young, not from malice. He pushed the thought away. It was something to chew over in front of a fire with a good wine in hand, not here amongst the trees where death waited.

Max had said that they'd tracked the marauders to an area near the Horseshoe lake, a name that they had given to two pools that had merged to form a crescent shaped body, and one of their favourite fishing spots when they went camping by choice rather than from pursuit. It was a good two-day walk into the forest with a boy's legs and careless energy, so three days with a man's weight and years. Three days to bank the anger burning inside him into something stronger and controlled.

He kept a steady pace, neither fast nor slow, but unwavering. The forest was easy to get lost in despite the relatively thin undergrowth in these parts, the heavy canopy creating shifting shadows that made it hard to track the direction you set out in; but while trees could grow and fall, the bones of the land were steady and unchanging if you knew what to look for. He brushed some mottled moss from the boulder he'd been looking for and patted the stick men scratched into its surface. This was their second marker, the place where they'd normally stop and devour whatever Max had manage to liberate from the bakery before they'd left.

A ripe smell reached him as he stood there, overpoweringly earthy and over sweet, and he stepped back, scanning the ground for some kind of animal carcass but finding none. The smell abated marginally, at least until he adjusted the strap of the satchel slung across his chest. He sniffed his hand and recoiled at the sharp tang of corruption, and hurriedly to kneel and rub his hands with needles and dirt before rinsing them off with a small dash from his canteen.

Once he was satisfied that the worst was off, he used a stick to scrape at more of the moss, which flaked away like an old scab and fell heavily. The smell redoubled as the moss hit the ground with a flat thud, filling the air with the odour something between old meat and spoiled milk. He backed away, a moue of disgust across his face, and moved off quickly, heading through the trees at an angle, aiming for a small, rocky gully that he would follow to the tip of the first lake.

He walked parallel to it, keeping far enough away that he could still see it but that anyone watching the gully, which was one of the few fixed landmarks in this area, wouldn't see him coming quite so easily. The trees were steadily becoming denser the further into the forest he went, and the dappled shadows were giving way to a gloom where rays of light were the exception rather than the rule. The smell came again when he stopped to relieve himself some time later, albeit not as strong, and he caught a glimpse of more moss coating the trunk of the tree he'd been aiming at. He buttoned his trousers with some haste and walked around the tree, which was covered in that same pale moss up to height of almost ten feet, giving the bark a furry appearance.

He noticed it more often now as he moved on, and tugged his neckerchief up to cover his nose and mouth as he walked, the smell of his own sweat a tonic against the reek as he sought a place to shelter for the night. The sun was slipping away, and the night came quickly in the forest. In the end he settled on a space between three trees that must have grown from the same pod of seeds and wove themselves into a massive network of branches high above him, their combined strength winning them a generous share of the canopy and the coveted exposure to the sun. He pulled himself onto two of the lower branches after checking them that they were moss-free and made himself as comfortable as he could, resting his back against one of the trunks.

He fished some of the food from his pack and ate mechanically, not really noticing either taste or texture, but stopped chewing when the doe walked into the clearing. It was small, probably no more than a few months old. It stopped in the centre and Orec kept still, knowing that it would scent him soon enough. It shook its head and turned towards him, revealing the second head that had grown out of the side of its neck, the slack jaws chomping at nothing. His indrawn breath sent the mouthful of half-chewed food into the back of his throat, and his sudden coughing fit was answered by both heads braying in alarm before it bounded away. He hit himself on the chest and few times until his airway was clear, and then shoved the rest of the food back in the satchel, whatever appetite he'd had now entirely gone.

He watched the clearing for a while longer, glad that he was off the ground, then leaned back and closed his eyes, drifting off to sleep with the soldier's gift of being able to sleep wherever and whenever the opportunity presented itself.

He woke sometime later, shaking off sleep's grip within a single breath, but didn't move and only sat there, waiting and listening for whatever it was that had woken him. At first there was only the sigh of the wind and the dry rustle of the leaves above him, but as he looked down to the forest floor he realised that he could see shapes and shades of grey. He sat up carefully. The tree he was in was a featureless black shape, but several others were bathed in what he at first assumed was moonlight until he realised that none bore the shifting shadows of the leaves above. The light came from the trees themselves, not the moon somewhere above. *The moss.*

He made himself look away from the softly shimmering trunks. As disturbing as it was, that was not what had woken him. He watched and waited, his eyes becoming heavier with each minute that passed, and they were almost closed again when the scent of pipe smoke reached him, the soft scent at odds with the earthier tones of the forest. He edged along the branch until he had a better field of view, and once he was certain that there was no one immediately around him, he lowered himself to the ground and quickly shrugged his satchel back on. He sniffed the air again and began following the smell, staying low and moving carefully, conscious of how exceptionally quiet the forest was.

It was hard to judge how long he spent moving forward like that, but it was long enough for his thighs to burn and a dull ache to settle into the small of his back. The smell of the smoke had faded as the smoker finished his pipe, so Orec settled himself down at the base of a moss-free tree and waited once more. It was unlikely that the smoker was alone, and the more men there were, the sooner it would be that one of them made a noise.

He didn't have to wait long in the end. While small in itself, amidst the strange black and white world of the forest, the flare of sparks as someone poked at a campfire was as good as a mountaintop beacon, and the cough that followed it was loud amidst the silence. He rose and began moving forward, his knife in hand.

* * *

'What are you doing?' Zelkof hissed at Andrei from across the fire.

'What does it look like? It's cold, and my blanket's still damp.'

'Leave the fire alone. You know the rules. We shouldn't even have one.'

'It's a stupid rule,' Andrei said, shrugging. 'There's no one for miles, there never is, and I'm sick of these fucking things crawling all over me.' He picked a pale, squirming shape from his sleeve and tossed in the fire, where it gave an almost human scream as its feathery wings ignited.

'They're just moths.'

'Keep telling yourself that if it makes you feel better, Zelkof.' He smiled as the other man shook another three of the things from his bedroll, his grimace making a lie of his statement. 'We're stuck out here doing nothing for no reason. I left to get away from bullshit like this, and now I'm back where I started.'

'Only with more money and an army of whores,' Zelkof replied. 'But if Dimka finds out about this he'll have our guts.'

'Dimka's not here though, is he? He's in his little palace with all the women. It's just us, sitting in this damned forest.' He paused to flick another moth towards the fire. 'With these fucking things trying to drink our eyes dry. Or worse.'

Zelkof gave a long, rattling sigh in reply, and then fell forward, his arm landing across the embers.

'What the fuck are you—' The words died on his lips as the bear like shape crouched behind the fallen shape of Zelkof stood up, the dim firelight bouncing from the wet blade held at his side.

'Oh gods,' Andrei said, scrabbling backwards and trying to kick the bedroll off his legs.

The figure took a stride forward and before Andrei could as much as lift his hands, a boot slammed into his jaw and laid him out flat. He felt the man pat him down for weapons, and the small hope he'd held that he would miss the dagger under his pack was quickly dashed.

'Talk or die,' the man growled, leaning his knee into Andrei's throat. 'Who's Dimka?'

Andrei sucked in a breath. He wanted to struggle, but from where he lay he could see Zelkof's still trembling body.

'He's in charge,' he said. 'Him and Hanna. Hey now, I didn't do anything.'

The weight of the knee pressed harder, choking off his words. 'Describe them.'

'Tall, over six feet, lean. Wears a red bandolier of knives. She's a witch. From Tzarkoman.'

The man grunted but didn't shift his weight. 'The women?'

'What about them?' Andrei panted and slapped the man's leg ineffectually. 'Can't breathe.'

The pressure eased fractionally. 'Is there a blonde? Straight hair, blue eyes. Scar on her chin like a small sickle.'

'Your sister?' he croaked. 'No. Your wife?'

Andrei felt, and worse heard, the point of the dagger grind into his breastbone. 'Answer me.'

'Maybe,' he gasped as the knife scraped into the bone. 'Long hair, yes, there's one.'

'Where's the camp?'

'Please. Breathe.'

The knee lifted and glorious air whistled into his aching lungs, the relief almost enough to make him forget the burning pain in the centre of his chest, at least until the man shifted his weight back and choked him again.

'Where's the camp?' He leaned forward, making stars explode across Andrei's vision. 'Tell me, or I'm going to open your gut and leave you for the wolves. I'll find it anyway.'

'That way,' Andrei said, his voice barely above a whisper. 'Fallen tree. Then ribbons. In the branches. Three miles. Please.'

'Did she say please?'

Andrei clutched at the man's leg and arm, but there was no strength left in his hands and the man swatted his attempts away. The pain in his chest flared brighter, and the sound of his breathing was drowned out by a terrible cracking that he felt as much as he heard before the darkness swallowed him.

OREC WASHED HIS dagger and hands using water from one of the dead men's canteens and then upended their packs. He picked out some dried sausage and pocketed the few coins that fell from them, and left the rest where it fell. He was annoyed with himself for giving into the anger. The bandits, or more likely deserters from the sound of it, were now two less, but how many did that leave? He could, and should have, learned more than he had, but what was done was done. He stamped the fire out and sheathed his knife. At least he had a direction now, and that was a good start if nothing else.

He checked his gear one more time before moving out in the direction the man had pointed out. In the grey light that had reasserted itself once the fire was smothered he could see pale shapes settling on the bodies, clustering around the wounds until they looked like boughs of cherry blossoms. He could hear their wings rubbing together, creating a strange sound that at times sounded like voices murmuring.

He shuddered and started walking away, swatting several of the moths out of the way when it looked like they were going to settle on him. It was an hour's steady walk to the fallen tree, by which time the skies had begun to lighten. The tree would have been a towering creation once, and its fall must have been felt far and wide. Even collapsed and rotted by age, the trunk was almost as high as a woodsman's cottage, and the hole left as its roots had torn free had become a pond since the year it fell. He didn't linger though; the water had an oily sheen to it, and rippled constantly although he neither heard nor saw anything that may have caused it.

He moved along next to the trunk as he scanned the nearby

trees, straining for any sign of the ribbons that were supposed to mark the path, his frustration growing with every minute that passed. He reached the end of the trunk and walked back on the other side, and groaned when he finally caught sight of the fluttering strip just above the caldera left by its roots. He silently chastised himself. Of course it was there. The trunk and roots were as good as an arrow, and the ribbon was the tip, pointing the way. He took a swig of water from the canteen and studied the path ahead, such as it was. He didn't want to keep to it strictly, as that would be inviting disaster, but equally there was no guarantee that it was a straight line or that the ribbons would be any easier to see from a distance.

He resettled his satchel and began walking again, placing his steps carefully and tracking from cover to cover, moving as Hayden had taught him to and willing himself to be unseen.

# CHAPTER FOURTEEN

CATT DRUMMED HIS fingers against his leg as he watched the comings and goings at the farmstead. It made sense that the men he was seeking would have stopped there, if only to water their horses, so the farmers might know something of use. The question was whether they knew anything truly useful; something that was of more use value than him simply continuing on his way and hopefully closing the distance.

But for all he knew, one of them may be right there, in the farmhouse. He only knew that they'd taken the road, not their destination. He made his way back to the road and carefully folded the carriage in on itself, then stowed it back in his travelling valise. Satisfied that he looked like nothing more than a well-dressed traveller, he picked the case up and began walking towards the farmstead, making no effort to hide whatsoever, exactly as a travelling merchant might.

They spotted him almost immediately, and while he was reassured by the fact that there were no whoops or cries of alarm, their silent scrutiny didn't bolster his confidence. One by one, they stopped what they were doing and watched him approach the house, a few giving the slightest of nods in reply to him tipping his straight brimmed hat as he passed. One of the men paused with a scythe over his shoulder, and as Catt passed he turned and began following him towards the farmhouse, the sound of those footsteps following his like an echo. Catt tried to ignore the itch between his shoulders and kept walking, certain that giving in to the urge to turn tail and run would only escalate matters, and make him feel entirely foolish in the process. It didn't stop the voice in his head, which always sounded like Fisher, from reminding him of all the anecdotal stories about cannibal families in the wilderness. He grimaced but maintained his pace and forced what he felt to be a friendly smile onto his face instead.

A woman stepped out of the farmhouse as he approached it, her clothing as utilitarian and dreary as the others save for the bright red scarf that held her hair up. Two other women followed her out and took up positions to the left and right behind her, their hands clasped before them. The footsteps fell silent behind him.

'Welcome, traveller,' the lady in the red scarf said. 'Peace be with you.'

'And peace be with you,' he said, the tension in his shoulders easing at the traditional greeting. It was an old custom and one that appeared in most cultures, and one that he assumed most murderous families of cannibals would not bother themselves with.

'Rest and be well,' she said with a smile. The women behind her both smiled at precisely the same moment, and with a quick bow, they made their way back inside the house.

'Thank you,' he said to the lady, doffing his hat. 'My name is Doctor Catt, and I am looking for someone.'

'Chiara,' she replied with the briefest of smiles, gesturing him towards a few chairs set on the porch. 'What kind of someone?'

He took a seat beside her and looked back to the courtyard, but there was no sign of the man with the scythe.

'Soldiers, actually,' he said, gratefully accepting a cup of what turned out to be cold cider that she had poured from a clay jug on the table. 'This is very good indeed.'

‘Thank you,’ she said, still smiling. ‘It’s safer than water around here these days. You’ll need to be more specific about these soldiers though. We’ve seen more than our fair share of them in these parts.’

‘Yes, of course. I’m seeking word of a smaller group, maybe as many as four travelling together, but I only have descriptions of two. A man with an apparently formidable beard named Orec Blackblade, and a younger lad with a missing leg named Stefan. I imagine they would be memorable.’

‘And what is your business with these men?’ she asked, looking at him coolly.

He took another sip of the cider and looked along the porch, his eyes picking out the little wooden figures bound to the eaves and what most casual observers would take to be simple decorative carvings on the sills of the windows but most assuredly weren’t.

‘You have a lovely home,’ he said. ‘It is fortunate that the war passed you by.’

‘Not entirely,’ she said. ‘But my grandmother has weathered wars before and precautions were taken. We look after our own, as we always have.’

‘Family is important.’

‘Family is everything,’ she said, swirling the cider in her cup, her gaze fixed on him.

He finished his and sat back, ignoring the creak of the chair beneath him. ‘I believe they’re in terrible danger. Mortal, even. Something pursues them, and I don’t mean me.’

‘Why do you care about soldiers who you’ve never met before?’

‘Well, therein lies quite the tale,’ he began, but then closed his mouth and looked across at her, meeting her frank gaze evenly. ‘The truth is, I don’t. Well, not really. I’ll help them if I can, but I’m more interested in the creature that follows them.’

She smiled, and he felt something inside him flutter for a moment. ‘Why?’

'Well, I appreciate how far-fetched this sounds, but some people believe that I may have something to do with it being set loose. Which is clearly nonsensical, and simply a symptom of the world we live in now that such aspersions can be bandied about with neither justification nor repercussion. The truth is far more prosaic insomuch that I am seeking it from more of a scholarly perspective.'

'Ah,' she said. 'Now it makes sense.'

'It does?'

She waved the question away. 'You and it are not the only ones pursuing them. A company of men passed by here not two days past, but they were only interested in Stefan and his companions.'

'What men?' Catt asked. 'Did they say why they were following them?'

'We didn't ask, and they didn't tell, but I can tell you that their intentions were not friendly.' She reached out and took his hand, then looked up at him with wide eyes. 'You must hurry. Stefan is in Pulcek, in a street close to the market square.'

The hand that she was holding felt tingly, as if he'd slept on it overnight, but he didn't try to pull it away.

'It's close, this creature of yours, and there will be blood soon.' She released his hand, pushing it away as if it now offended her. 'There is little time. You must go.'

'You're a Seer?' he asked, standing as she did more out of habit than a desire to set off again. 'I have so many questions.'

'This is not the time or place,' she said. 'You must go now, and not stop for anything.'

She looked resolute, and Catt knew better than to press his luck. He lowered his hands. 'Then I will be on my way,' he said. 'But, with your permission, I would like to come back and talk more. About other things, including those.' He glanced up at the figures on the eaves.

'Save the boy and we will consider it.'

Catt nodded his agreement to that and, tipping his hat to her, began walking back to the road, trying to piece together whether he was being duped or not. Chiara had seemed sincere enough, but that was assuming that she was in fact a Seer and not just mired deep enough in her own fantasy to believe the sort of dreams that living in a cider brewery helped to induce.

He made his way along the road until he couldn't feel himself being watched any longer before unpacking the chariot again. He had little doubt that Blackblade and his men had been there, but the men pursuing them were far more of a mystery. The dockworkers in High Town had mentioned them too, but he hadn't given it much attention at the time, a shortcoming that he would now add to his list of regrets.

'To Pulcek then,' he said, climbing aboard. 'And let's make haste.'

MARTINA LOOKED UP as the tent flap was pushed aside, hating how her stomach clenched at the sound of the heavy canvas, but it was only Magret returning. The flap fell back, and the tension released its hold on her by a fraction, although she gave no sign of concern either way. There were six of them in the tent, and, gods have mercy, the others all looked to her for support.

'They're drinking again,' she announced, making her way over to Martina. 'They sound angry.'

A murmur passed through the other women. When the men drank, they did so hard, as if it was a contest to see who could debase themselves first: a contest that Dimka often won. But then no one wanted to cross him; he was a bully who would cheat a blind man at chess, and then beat him to death for the temerity of having forced him to cheat.

'Let them drink,' she said, forcing a smile. 'The sooner they pass out, the better.'

'But what if they—'

'Then we'll deal with it, as we always do,' Martina replied, cutting in before Magret could finish the sentence.

They had all seen what Dimka was capable of once he was deep in the liquor. They were the ones who'd had to collect her body after all, and the ones who had to wash it. She had been a sweet and gentle girl, pretty too, at least until Dimka had taken his hands to her for fighting back. It was Martina who'd had to break her legs so that she could fit in the pitiful grave they'd been allowed to dig for her, and the thought of it brought a thickness to her throat and made her eyes burn with suppressed tears. She forced the despair back and concentrated on swallowing the urge to scream.

'Come on, sit down,' she said instead, patting one of the crude chairs that they'd made. 'We saved you some stew.'

'I thought you liked me,' Magret said as she sat, sending a rare ripple of laughter through the tent.

'I'm glad you're all in such good spirits.'

They gasped as one as they saw Hanna standing at the entrance of the tent. She was barely dressed as usual, unless you counted the swirls of clay and paint that decorated her skin as clothing. She smiled at their reaction like a cat knowing that its prey had nowhere to go.

'He wants you,' she said, pointing at Martina. 'And one more. You.'

The woman named Ailsa flinched away from the finger pointed at her. 'For what?'

Hanna's smile, cruel as it was to start with, fell into a sneer. 'For anything he chooses. Now go, or I will take your eyes.'

'Come on,' Martina said. 'Let's get this over with so he can make his funny face and go to sleep.'

'Watch your tongue,' Hanna said, rounding on her. 'If Dimka didn't like it so much I'd rip it out.'

Martina felt her cheeks burn with shame, but Hanna only laughed. 'Hurry now. You don't want to make him angry.'

She felt the touch of Ailsa's hands as she stood, and though it brought some small comfort knowing that she wasn't alone in this, stepping back out into the night made her stomach twist with nausea.

'Wait,' she said to Hanna's back. The witch, for Martina had no doubt that was what she was, turned, her mouth already forming a sneer. 'We need to freshen up. Please.'

She tilted her head toward the makeshift screen they'd put up next to the inlet in a mostly vain attempt to give themselves some privacy when making their toilet.

'You have until I count to fifty.'

Martina took Ailsa's hand and pulled her towards the water. They barely made it behind the screen before Ailsa fell to her knees and vomited into the water, and Martina joined her a moment later. There wasn't much to come out, but she felt better for it.

She led Ailsa a few yards upstream and scooped up a mouth full of water. 'Come on, rinse and spit.'

'I can't do this,' Ailsa said in a small voice. 'I just can't.'

'Yes, you can,' Martina said, cupping the younger woman's chin. 'You'll get through this. You smile and you dance, and you survive. It's not you in there. We'll get through this together, I swear to you.' She was pleased, almost surprised, at how even and reasonable she sounded, despite the utter despair that was steadily eating away at her like a canker.

It had all begun the day that Max had brought her the message about Orec. She'd known what it was even before he'd reached into his coat and handed it to her, and it had felt like she was watching herself from above as she broke the wax seal and opened it. The handwriting had been elegant, the work of a skilled calligrapher. She remembered because she had focused on its curves while she tried to delay reading the words that they spelled out. She couldn't remember what it had actually said; only fragments remained in her memory. *Courageous. Selfless. Sacrifice. Condolences.*

The days after had bled into one. She saw him everywhere

she looked, but it was the small animals he'd carved for her that made it feel like she was too broken to live on. They watched her from the mantelpiece, each telling their own little part of the story of the shy carpenter's courtship. The first few were her favourites, because those he had left for her to find as anonymous gifts on fenceposts and the doorstep. The first time she'd had an inkling that it was him was when he came in to hang new doors in their house. He'd seen them on her nightstand and, not knowing that she was watching, he had given such a smile that it seemed to her she had never truly seen him before. It seemed impossible to her that someone so large and clumsy could make anything so delicate.

Orec was a man ill-suited to war, but he had never broken a promise and until she'd opened that letter, she had hoped that he would keep his last. *I'll come back*.

Next to her, Ailsa took two hitching breaths, pulling her back to the present. Orec was gone, and all that mattered to her now was getting the others through their shared nightmare. Ailsa leant forward to splash her face and rinse her mouth, some colour having returned to her cheeks.

'We'll get through this,' she said, squeezing Martina's hand and even managing a small smile.

They emerged together as Hanna was striding towards the screen with her whip in hand. She looked them up and down, then turned and marched them towards the oversized cabin that Dimka called his hall and the braying laughter within.

SHE WOKE TO the touch of a cool cloth to her face, and even though the touch was gentle, the skin beneath was stretched and sensitive and she flinched. She made to sit up, but other hands touched her shoulders.

'Hush now,' Magret said softly next to her. 'It's not so bad. Just rest.'

'My chores—'

'We're taking care of them, don't worry.'

Martina sagged back against the spare blanket that served as her pillow and Magret pulled the one she lay under up a bit higher, tucking it under her shoulders as she did for them. The cloth dabbed at her face, and she was glad for the sting, the immediacy of it distracting from the other pains she felt. Images of the night before flashed across her mind and she felt hot tears spill from her eyes as her shame boiled over, but Magret didn't say anything and gently wiped them away.

'How's Ailsa?'

'She's fine, darling. She's strong.'

'He was the worst he's been last night,' she said softly. 'He made Hanna cut her.'

'We know, and it's all stitched. She'll be fine.'

She paused and Martina waited as the cloth was wrung out and placed on her cheek again.

'She told us what you did.' Magret's weight shifted and she felt the touch of her lips on her forehead.

The tears came again at the gesture, but this time they weren't from shame alone. She had known anger in her life before, but never hate, and certainly nothing on the scale of what she now held within her for Dimka. It almost felt corporeal, like a demon from the old stories riding her back: a dry voice constantly reminding her of the vile things that he demanded simply for her to have to the right to live, and suggesting the cruellest tortures that could be levied upon him when fate finally caught up with him. It was a voice that she no longer tried to avoid and she welcomed its return as she lay there, letting her mind escape into a world where it was she who sat upon the throne, laughing as he was repeatedly violated and cut to pieces.

When she woke again, it was dark and Magret was still sitting next to her.

'There you are,' she said as Martina opened her eyes. 'You

slept good and deep.' She leaned forward, a stub of candle in her hand and studied Martina's face. 'Much better. Now sit up, we've got some soup for you.'

She complied, and ate the soup with a hunger that she hadn't been aware of until she smelled it. One good thing about having to do everything in the camp was that the food that they made for each other was better than it otherwise would have been.

She looked around as she slurped it from the bowl, silently counting the women. They were all there, their conversations quiet and their eyes flitting to the entrance on every other word. She could hear the men's voices outside, but there was too much shouting for her to make sense of it.

'What's going on?' she asked.

Magret's smile was impish. 'It seems that some of their men have gone missing.'

'More?'

'So, it turns out that when those who were supposed to be back last night didn't arrive, he sent men out to fetch them this morning and they haven't come back either.' She looked to the entrance, then leaned in closer. 'Someone's found their bodies. Dimka thinks someone's trying to take over, but the others are whispering about rangers or even the dryads coming after them.'

'I wish they would.'

'Us too, don't you worry.' She patted Martina's hand. 'Liss went out earlier and they were all putting armour on. Whatever it is, it's enough to have gotten them really riled up. Personally, I don't care what happens to them, and the longer we're left in peace, the better.'

'Amen to that,' Martina said, setting the bowl aside. 'I need to go to the river.'

'I'll come with you.' She stood and helped Martina up, holding her as she slowly straightened and took the first few haltering steps.

The night was cool and clear when they stepped outside, and Martina felt the fog leaving her mind. It was still relatively early, and if it was this cool next to the water there would be mist later, the kind that made smudges of the lamps and clung to your legs like cobwebs as you walked through it. It was already gathering over the water and would soon roll across the campsite like a milky tide.

She'd been to the riverbank in those mists twice, and didn't care for its chill touch. She'd felt like a deer in a predator's gaze both times, her skin crawling, and any thought of attempting to escape into its milky depths had quickly evaporated. She was glad for Magret's company, but even so she did what she needed to do quickly.

They were halfway back to the tents when a shout went up on the far side of the encampment, one that sent the men running towards it, their weapons drawn. She slowed and pulled Magret to the side of one of the smaller huts.

'We should get back.'

'I want to see what's going on.'

The noise was growing louder, and she leaned out around the corner as six of the men carried another into Dinka's hall, leaving a trail of wet boot prints behind them.

'Was that one of Dimka's men?' Magret asked

'For his sake, I hope so.'

A boot crashed into Magret's back and she fell forward, hitting the ground as a hand sent Martina stumbling out into the open next to her.

'You two again.' They couldn't see Hanna's sneer, but they could hear it clearly enough in her voice. 'Get in there.'

'We've done nothing,' Magret said, rolling into a sitting position and scrabbling back at the sight of the whip in Hanna's hand. 'We were just peeing.'

'And now you'll tell Lord Dimka that yourself.' She shook the whip loose. 'Get in there.'

THE MEN CLUSTERED near the entrance of the hall turned, anger on their faces, as Hanna pushed them through inside. The air was charged with the potential for violence and heavy with the scent of iron, sweat and blood. Dimka was striding back and forth on the raised dais that held his 'throne', a plush chair looted from a previous raid, stopping on every turn to shake a fist at his men and swear that they would catch whoever did this.

Martina stopped as she reached the man they'd set down on one of the trestles. His limbs hung from the table and his shirt was open, exposing the horrific red trench that bisected his chest. It seemed impossible that he was still alive, but she could see his mouth moving, and, the gods help her, the movement of his lung in the depths of that bloody cut.

'They dare come here, and attack us? Kill our brothers? They've made their last mistake,' Dimka announced from his stage, voice cracking with emotion. 'We will find, and we will kill them. Slowly.'

A cheer went up from the score of men gathered there, several of them slapping the men next to them on the shoulder.

'What are those whores doing here?' Dimka had stopped pacing, and like every other man there, was staring at them.

Hanna pushed forward. 'They're good with bandages. And I caught them—'

'Bandages? Does it look like he needs a fucking bandage?' he roared back at her. 'Get them the fuck out of here.'

Martina gave the dying man a final look before Hanna roughly shoved her back the way they'd come, her anger at his dismissal lending her strength. She pushed and kicked them away from the hall, sending them stumbling through the gathering mist, away from the hall and any watching eyes, then unrolled her whip.

'We'll go, we'll go,' Magret said, pushing herself backward, but even as the words left her lips Hanna's arm jerked forwards and the tip of the whip cracked across her face. She rolled away with a scream, hands pressed to the already-bleeding slash on her face. The whip snapped forward again, catching her leg.

'This is what you deserve,' Hanna said, stalking forward. She muttered something under her breath and one of the swirling patterns on her arm began to glow as if there was freshly forged metal beneath her skin. Martina threw herself across Magret as the whip cracked and she felt a line of agony across the back of her shoulder, the pain too sharp not to scream.

'I'm going to flay that worthless skin from you one stroke at a time.'

Martina tried to push Magret away as the witch took another step towards them, the glow in her arm having now spread to another tattoo. She wanted to plead, and the words were right there on her lips, but then the ground behind Hanna moved and a figure rose up from it, dirt cascading from its shoulders, the sight of it stealing her breath away. Whatever features it may have had were hidden beneath a covering of leaves and mud, rendering it entirely inhuman.

'Martina,' it said in a voice barely louder than a whisper, the sound more suited to a wraith than anything living.

Hanna saw her look, and witnessed the open horror writ across her face, and at the sound of the voice behind her she spun on her heel. The thing behind her moved as she did, quickly shifting in two quick movements.

Martina watched Hanna's arm spin away from her shoulder, the hand still clutching the whip. She was still staring at the pale shape of it when something dark whistled through the air and clove the witch's head into two parts, ear to ear, the top half of her skull bouncing across the mud while the rest of her body still stood there, mouth open and braying wordlessly as her blood jetted from the savage wounds. Martina flinched as the witch's scalding blood sprayed across her and Magret.

The figure had vanished into the mist by the time that Hanna's body finally realised that it was dead and crumpled to the ground. Martina held onto Magret, who was staring at the draining corpse with eyes that were almost as wide as her mouth was at that moment, the seeping cut on her cheek forgotten.

'What?' was all she managed.

Martina finally blinked and let go as she pulled herself to her feet. 'We have to go.'

'No,' Magret said, swatting her hand away. 'What was that? Why did it say your name?'

'Get up, damn you,' Martina said, grabbing her elbow. 'Dimka will kill us if he catches us here.'

Magret let herself be pulled to her feet but couldn't look away from the still-draining corpse, even when Martina led her away through the rising mist. They hurried towards their tent and would not have noticed that the guards were missing had Magret not stumbled at the entrance. She caught herself before she could fall, and as she stood she looked at her wet and knee and hand, rubbing her fingers until the lamp light revealed its colour, the same as the dark arcs that curved across the front of the tent.

'Blood,' she said needlessly. They crashed through the entrance, expecting the worst, and found the women clustered together in the centre. Their shrieks quickly turning to concern as they saw who it was, and then a dozen questions sounded, all asked at once.

Martina held up her hands and waited for them to quieten. 'Where are the guards?'

'That thing must have got them,' Magret said, holding up her bloody hands. She turned to the others. 'It got Hanna too. Ripped her head and arm clean off.'

A stunned silence greeted that. 'Thing?'

'I'm sure it was a sword, Magret. We need to stay calm.'

'It killed Hanna?' another asked. 'Let it come then.'

'I didn't see any sword. How can we stay calm?' she asked, stepping back. 'It said your name!'

'It knew your name? Is it dryads?' asked Ailsa. 'Have they come?'

'That was no dryad.' Martina's chuckle was largely mirthless. 'I don't know what it was, and I don't care!' She straightened. 'I think we should go.'

'Go where? The forest, in the dark?'

'Dimka's going to go mad when he finds her, and what do you think he's going to do then, huh? We were with her, so he'll blame us.'

'We don't have swords, it can't be us!'

Martina snorted. 'Do you think that matters? He's lost men and his witch, and this is a man who'd attack his own shadow for daring to walk in front of him if he could. He'll be wanting to show off, to get their respect back.'

Magret knew the truth of it, as did the others; and the fear that something may be out there, lurking in the woods, was a possibility rather than the certainty that Dimka represented. She looked around at the others and nodded.

'We'll go,' she said, 'but we stay away from the water.'

Martina shuddered at the thought of entering the lake. She'd seen some of the malformed fish that occasionally washed up on its shore, and they had all seen *something* moving in the water, something that never broke the surface but was large enough to send ripples across the entire lake when it moved.

'Agreed a thousand times over,' she said.

There was no need to dress. Until the lights in Dimka's hall went out, they all stayed dressed in case he called for them, not wanting to attract punishment for being tardy. They rolled up the few possessions they had and moved to the entrance where Martina stood, one hand on the tent flap and a calm expression hiding the excitement and fear that was making her heart hammer so loudly.

'Ready,' Magret said.

Martina moved the flap aside and stepped back out into the

night, crouching outside the entrance. Down near the hall Dimka had led his men outside and was ordering some to move off to the far side of the camp, and she felt a cold hand grip her innards as he and six others turned and began walking towards her.

'Get back,' she hissed over her shoulder. 'They're coming towards us.'

'Who?'

'Dimka.' A babble of fearful voices greeted this and she heard them move back towards their bunks. She stayed where she was, confident that she was out of sight and curious to see what he was doing. As he walked, he gestured off to the side with his sword and three of the men headed off towards the men's huts. Dimka and the three remaining men were less than fifty yards away and she was easing herself back into the tent when a shout went up from the hall, stopping them in their tracks.

'Fire!' came the cry again, and now she could see the dance of flames inside the windows, steadily brightening. Dimka swore coarsely and broke into a crashing run back towards his hall, shouting for his men. Two figures staggered out of the blaze as he drew close, arms windmilling as the fire ate at their clothing and hair, and stumbled towards the dark waters of the lake.

She stayed where she was and so saw the three men Dimka had sent off come running back. The third had just passed the last of the huts when he stumbled and fell, and didn't get back up. The man ahead of him stopped and turned, cursing him for his clumsiness. He took one step towards the fallen man and she saw his head snap back as if he'd just been kicked by a horse. He fell heavily and didn't move again. The last of the three had seen this too, and he sped off, shouting for help at the top of his lungs.

Unlike her, he didn't see the dark figure step out between the huts, nor pause with the bowstring drawn to his ear. The bow didn't twang as she'd expected it to, but the running man fell with a sharp cry, tumbling but then scrambling to his feet once more.

The figure tossed the bow aside, and the matted cowl turned towards her. Even with the moon peering through the clouds she couldn't make out any features within its depths aside from beard that was caked with mud or worse. A man. He stood there, simply staring at her for several heartbeats before Dimka's bellowing intruded, then quickly turned away and ran back behind the huts, disappearing into the shadows again as Dimka and his men raced to where the fallen men lay.

She moved back into the tent but froze as he turned towards her, his small eyes catching the movement.

'Bring that bitch over here.'

She wanted to throw herself into the tent, but stood up straight instead. The canvas only offered sanctuary by his indulgence, and there would be none of it that tonight.

Gauntleted hands gripped her arms painfully and all but dragged her to where Dimka waited. He seemed even more imposing now, the mail he wore bulking out his shoulders. He rested the flat of his sword on her shoulder, the edge of the blade gleaming white under the moonlight.

'What happened?'

'A man shot them.' She pointed off to the side where he'd tossed the bow. 'Then ran off.'

He nodded to one of the others, who quickly found the bow and held it up. 'It looks like Rogar's.'

Dimka sucked at his teeth. 'One man?'

Martina nodded carefully. 'He was big.'

'As big as Dimka?' he asked, thin lips pulling into a sneer.

'Bigger.'

His lips flattened into a flat line and he tilted his chin to look down at her. She felt the blade come to rest on her shoulder and the sting of it as it touched her neck.

'Don't test me, bitch.' The blade pressed harder and she felt a rivulet of blood snake along her collarbone and down between her breasts. 'You're not that special.'

The urge to spit in his face was strong, but she was no use to anyone dead. 'He looked bigger. I didn't want to lie.'

He narrowed his eyes, but lifted the sword away. 'Useless cow.'

Whatever he intended to say next didn't make it past his lips as the sound of steel hitting steel tolled through the night, following a heartbeat later by an agonised scream.

'Go!' Dimka bellowed, punching a fist towards the sound. 'Find them!'

'What about her, boss?' asked the man who still held her arm.

Dimka didn't even look at her. 'Put her back with the others. Kill any that leave the tent before morning.'

The man yanked her away and started pulling her back the way they'd come while the others raced away towards where the scream had come from. Most of them had lit torches in hand now and were waving them at every passing shadow, making it more likely that they'd burn the rest of the camp down by their own hand. Could such chaos really be the work of one man?

'They're going to kill you all, you know,' she said.

'Shut your stupid mouth.'

'There's no shame in being afraid,' she said, wincing as he tightened his grip. 'If they were coming for me, I'd be scared too.'

She didn't see his fist, but her vision suddenly exploded into a shower of stars and she felt her legs buckle. A shove sent her sprawling, and then his weight was on her chest and her head snapped sideways as he struck her again.

'I warned you!' he all but screamed at her. 'This is your fault.' He leaned forward and wrapped his hands around her throat and pressed his weight down on her. 'This is your own fault. Always so fucking smug.'

She reached for his face, but he leaned back out of reach. Panic gripped her as her breathing shrunk to a thin whistling sound and then stopped entirely. She lifted her hips but he rode it out and bared his teeth at her in a feral smile.

'You like that?'

He leaned forward again, forcing her head back so that all she could see were leaves and the back of the men's huts. Her arms were becoming too heavy to lift. *So, this is how I die.*

A sense of regret welled up within her, her mind filling with all the things that she would never do again and all the harsh words she'd spoken, but with it also came the memory of joy, of dinners with her family filled with laughter, and days and nights of Orec's gentle smile. All were lost now. She forced her eyes open, wanting to see the stars one last time before the darkness swamped her.

She felt a tremor pass through the ground and looked over to see the cowled figure of Death approaching, the darkness within its hood only matched by the dark blade it carried. It broke into a sprint as the burning in her lungs grew to an inferno.

The pressure on her throat abruptly lifted and almost bestial grunting replaced the sound of her killer's impassioned panting. She turned her head in time to see Death yank its blade out of her attacker's head, and then chop it down into his already deformed face again, and again, and again as if it were an axe and the man's face a stubborn log, all but splitting him down the breastbone. A boot sent his cloven body sprawling, the stench of his emptied bowels competing with the coppery scent of blood and raw meat.

She watched it all with fogged eyes, every swing of the blade and arc of blood that followed it moving with dreamlike slowness, so much so that it felt like she could reach up and touch the blood as it sailed through the air. It seemed to take forever, but then an oak-hard arm lifted her from the ground, jarring her back to the present. and if she'd had the breath to spare she would have groaned as it brought her back to the searing pain in her throat.

There was a roof over her suddenly, and a gaggle of terrified voices. She felt her herself being lowered onto something more comfortable than the ground and looked up to stare at the hooded man. It was hard to focus, but she could see now that it really was a man, and a living one too, not the grim spectre she had imagined, his face blackened by soot and his bushy beard shaped into spikes with drying clay. Her gaze found his eyes, which were as green as spring ferns, and a smile split his beard. No fangs either. She stared up at him, trying to think clearly, but she felt like a drunk trying to will herself sober.

He rubbed a tear from her cheek with his thumb, leaving a bloody smear, then stood and spoke to the women before vanishing again, his voice deep but wordless to her. They rushed towards her, a dozen gentle hands propping her head on a pillow and fetching cool cloths for her bruised neck. She closed her eyes and tried to ignore the flood of questions coming from them.

The noise outside was still growing, the angry shouts having redoubled at the discovery of the bloody ruin of her attacker. She heard the distinct sound of Dimka's bellowing and the rush of boots. She knew what was coming, and so did the other women. Most scattered back to their bunks as the entrance was thrown open and three of them rushed in, swords ready.

Magret stood over her, but her friend's protest was silenced by the first of the men, who punched the pommel of his sword into the side of her head, dropping her cleanly. He grabbed a fistful of Martina's hair and simply turned and began walking, forcing her to scrabble off the bunk and stagger after him as his best she could. She had no doubt that he'd drag her through the mud if she stopped and would not care if it tore her hair out.

Dimka was waiting for her with four more of his men, two on either side, torches held high and swords in their other hand. She was pushed to the ground in front of Dimka and the men who'd fetched her stepped back, closing the rough circle around her.

'Why is it always you?' he said, hooking his thumbs over his sword belt. 'Everything that has happened tonight has been around you. Did you kill Hanna?'

She sat back and looked up at him, the ache in her throat momentarily forgotten.

'I see from your face that you thought me stupid, that I wouldn't work it out.' He drew his knife, curved and sharp enough that he shaved with it, and stepped forward. 'Call him. Tell him if he doesn't come out, I'll start cutting parts of you off.'

'I can't,' she rasped.

'You can and you will.'

She turned her head and showed him her already-darkening throat. 'I. Can't.'

He crouched beside her and jabbed a finger into the bruise, and the pain was such that she thought he'd stabbed her. She fell back, an agonised whooping escaping her lips as she rocked back and forth, not knowing how to soothe a pain like that.

'Seems genuine,' he said, rising to stand over her. 'Come out, you bastard!' he roared. 'Come out, or I start cutting her.'

At the sound of his challenge, his men turned to face outwards. Dimka paced within the circle, no longer even aware that he was grinding his teeth in frustrated anger. Once he'd killed whoever had done this, he's make an example of several of the women too, one that would ensure they'd never so much as breathe without his permission.

'Boss.'

He turned towards the sound and followed his man's outstretched sword. A single figure was walking up between the huts, a dark shape that may have been a sword held out to the side, although no light reflected from it.

He stopped ten feet from the line of swords that Dimka's men had formed before him.

'You're going to die,' Dimka said, enjoying the pleasurable shiver that came with knowing that he'd been right. Everyone had a weakness, and he'd found the killer's. He reached down and grabbed Martina by the hair, lifting her until she stood on tiptoes, his smile curving into a sneer as the hooded figure's posture shifted.

'Put the sword down or I'll gut her.'

'Let her go.' The man's voice was deep and steady.

Dimka's laugh was genuine. 'It's eight swords to one, and I have more men on the way. Put it down.'

'There are no more men,' the man said as he began to walk widdershins around them, forcing the men to turn and follow after him to keep their shape. 'Maybe you'll kill me, but I reckon I'll take another three, maybe four of you whoresons with me.'

'Stop moving and throw down your sword.'

He ignored the command and kept walking. 'You can throw their lives away, or you can face me, man on man.'

Several of the men glanced over their shoulder at Dimka. He tightened his grip on the woman's hair. 'Last chance.'

'So, you're scared.' He finally stopped walking. 'Hiding behind your last few men and an injured woman.' He looked the men in front of him. 'You'd die for a coward like this?'

'I warned you.' Dimka pulled Martina's head back, drawing a sharp gasp from her. He held up the knife, letting the man see it, and was turning to slide it into her belly when she lashed out with her fist, not caring how she tore her own hair, and caught him squarely in the groin. The pain and nausea were sharp and immediate, robbing him of his strength, and he staggered back, his grip loosening enough that she could throw herself away from him.

Half the men turned at the sound of his strangled yelp, and were thrown to the ground a moment later as the hooded man shoulder barged through them. Dimka saw the movement and threw himself back a moment before the black sword cut through the space where his head had been. The immediacy of the attack forced the discomfort of Martina's blow away and he threw the knife at the man, winning enough time to draw his own sword, but little more.

The man sprang forward, sword held in a two-handed grip. Dimka stepped away from his opening swing and met the lunge that followed it with his own blade, turning the thrust. Steel screeched as he was forced to maintain the contact to avoid a backhand cut. He shifted his feet, readying himself to push the blade away and open him up for a counter attack, but then saw that man's left hand was no longer on the hilt of his sword. *He was too close!*

A fist crashed into the side of his head a moment after the realisation set in, jarring his vision and knocking him off balance. He pushed away blindly, desperate to create space between them and win a moment to regain his equilibrium, but the damage had been done.

The man's sword crashed into his, forcing it down and away, and he saw the glint of the dagger a moment before it slid along the flesh of his upper thigh and into the junction of his leg and pelvis. The pain was like nothing he'd ever felt, even before the man sawed it back and forth, and when he felt the vibration of it across bone it broke him.

He didn't so much fall as throw himself to the ground, his sword falling from his hand as sudden and utter terror washed any other thought from his mind. He clutched at the gushing wound and screamed a wordless denial as the blood pumped through his slippery fingers, knowing it was mortal. He didn't want to die, he didn't deserve to die! Everything was finally going his way, and to have it stolen away like this wasn't fair. It wasn't fair!

He looked up and saw his killer standing over him. He didn't hear what he said, and didn't have time to think about it before that terrible black sword smashed through his teeth, the metal screeching against the shards before an awful, deafening crunch ended his every thought forever.

OREC SET A boot against the leader's neck and pried his sword free of the deformed head with another crack of bone that set the corpse to twitching. He took a hurried step back, sword rising to a guard position as he turned to face the others. It was seven on one, and if they attacked, he would die. But the head had been cut from the snake in every way, and he could see them wavering.

'I came for him,' he said, tipping the sword towards the trembling corpse. 'Go. Choose another path.'

He kept his voice firm and even, as he had in those times when it seemed that the line would break and the battle would be lost. In times like that, men looked towards authority; craved it, even. It didn't matter where they were from or what colour their skin was; courage was a universal language, and a man who spoke it well would ever have the advantage of those who did not. The men looked at each other, and he had to fight the urge to sigh loudly in relief as their swords lowered.

'We're taking our things,' said the one on the end, and Orec made a mental note to cut him down first if things turned.

'Take what you will, save for the women.' He kept his sword at a neutral angle. 'You're soldiers, not slavers.' It was an educated guess having seen how they stood and moved, and none of them protested.

The man sheathed his sword, and the others followed suit as they backed away. He kept his drawn and stood between them and Martina, unmoving and silent until they re-emerged from the huts and began walking away, packs over their shoulders. She didn't say anything for that time, and the wait was pure torture for him.

After what felt like an age, he was satisfied that they were truly gone and he moved back to the body and quickly cleaned his sword before sheathing it. Martina took this moment to scramble to her feet and snatch up the leader's knife, the same as he had intended to gut her with. She'd clearly been waiting for the moment. With the dawn not far off it was just light enough for him to see the blue of her eyes.

'Who are you?' she said. 'What do you want?'

He lowered his hood, suddenly conscious of the blood that was streaked across his face, arms and chest. He knew he should go and wash off in the river, and wanted to, but not as much as he wanted to hold her. He took a step forward and she flinched away, jabbing the knife towards him in fright.

He raised his hands. 'Martina.'

'What do you want?' she said, her voice hoarse. 'Who are you?'

The other women were slowly emerging from their hiding places, drawn out by the quiet. When no one stopped them they approached more boldly.

He stood a little straighter. Now that the moment had come, he was unsure what to say. She was watching him intently, hands shaking with tension.

She looked over her shoulder as the other women came to stand beside her, and saw that most of them had collected a fallen weapon along the way. Martina straightened and lifted the knife with new confidence.

'I asked you a question.'

Orec raised his hands and carefully reached under his collar, hooking a finger under the silver chain that hung around his neck. There was no way for him to undo it with his gloves on so he broke it with a sharp yank, then stepped forward, slowly so as not to spook them, and took a knee in front of Martina. He slowly extended his hand, turning his palm up and revealing the silver ring he held.

She lowered the knife and snatched the ring away, lifting it into better light.

'I gave this to Orec,' she said, amazement in her voice. 'You knew him?'

'I like to think that I still do, Tina.'

She turned at that and stared at him in wonder and confusion. He smiled, unable to contain it any longer, and she stumbled back, knife tumbling from her hand as she raised both hands to her mouth.

'It can't be,' she said, and burst into tears, the kind he'd only seen at funerals, and abruptly threw herself into the arms of the women around her.

He stood, hands at his sides, unsure what to do as they closed ranks around her.

One of the women stepped away and turned to him. 'Give her a few moments.' She looked him up and down. 'Maybe freshen up a bit.'

'But—'

'Trust me. Give her a little time.' She grabbed his wrist before he could go. 'Mind the water.'

With that cryptic warning, she rejoined the huddle, where at least two other women were now crying too. Confused and feeling oddly dejected, he left them to it and headed towards the lake. He'd been looking forward to that moment for as long as he could remember, and had not once imagined that that would be the reception he received.

He felt hollow and unwanted. If there was no joy in that moment, then what else was there? What had the point of all of it been? He knelt and began scrubbing the mud and gore from his face and beard. It took some time, and he felt more settled once it was done.

He looked up as he finally became aware of the ripples that were now rolling towards him with increasing regularity, and caught a glimpse of something dark and oily as it sunk back into the water. He scrambled backwards, the woman's warning coming back to him, and quickly headed back towards the huts. The women were still huddled together and weeping, and irritation was started to eat its way through his disappointment. Clearly being held captive and threatened with disembowelling was more palatable than your husband returning from war. Or perhaps she had taken the news of his death far better than he had feared, and seeing him alive had ruined the relief at her rescue.

He kicked a discarded helmet as he passed, sending it tumbling across the mud, and booted his way into one of the huts. There had to be something to drink somewhere in the camp.

THE SUN HAD risen well over the trees on the far side of the lake before they came looking for him. He could hear them moving about, clearly searching for him, but he didn't bother calling out and remained where he was, his back against a rock and a clay carafe propped against his leg as he watched the play of light across the lake. He'd finished the cheese and mildly scorched loaf he'd found, and the wine was remarkably good. He took another swig and felt the exhaustion he'd been trying to hold at bay creep closer. An inner voice was beseeching him to move away to a neutral location before he fell asleep lest the other bandits return when he was at his most vulnerable, but he was successfully ignoring it for now.

'He's over here. Drinking.'

Orec didn't bother looking up and purposefully took another long draw from the nearly empty carafe.

'Didn't you hear us calling?'

'I heard someone being called,' he said, smacking his lips. It really was the best wine he'd had in years. 'But not my name, so I figured maybe you were looking for someone else.'

A sigh and the sound of someone shifting their weight from foot to foot. 'She's ready to see you.'

'Well, tell Her Majesty that I need some time.'

'Don't be like that.'

'Piss off.'

She turned on her heel and marched off, which gave him a small amount of satisfaction. Let them wait and see what it was like to be dismissed like an unwanted pedlar. He finished the wine and tossed the carafe into the water, where it bobbed along for a few minutes before an errant ripple toppled it. He rested against the rock, half dozing, and was on the cusp of drifting into a deeper sleep when he heard soft footsteps on the stones and felt someone sit down beside him.

He didn't move or give any sign he'd heard them and they sat like that for a while.

'That's quite a beard.'

He opened his eyes at the sound of Martina's voice and rubbed the grit from them. Like him, she had cleaned herself up since he'd walked away earlier that morning, but it only made the bruises on her neck and cheek stand out more lividly. He stroked his beard and looked down with a half-smile.

'Once they stopped forcing us to shave I promised I'd grow it until we went home.'

'So you can shave now.'

He looked out across the lake. 'I had hoped so.'

She followed his gaze, her hand finding his. 'I hope so too.'

'I saw Max,' he said in a quiet voice, rubbing his thumb over her fingers. 'He and some townsmen tried to arrest me.'

'Fat Max,' she said, smiling. 'He's become quite the hero.'

'Not so fat now.'

'No, not so fat now.' She turned and looked at him with a ghost of her old smile. 'No one's the same anymore.' She took a deep breath and let it out slowly. 'Orec, I—'

'I don't suppose we are,' he said before she could continue, squeezing her hand. 'At least on the outside. But I like to think that the rest of us is still in there, waiting for the fires to die and the grass to grow back.'

'I'd like to think that too,' she said, resting her head against the rock. 'When I saw you last night, I thought you were a wraith come to fetch me.'

'A wraith.' He smiled at that. 'Not quite, but I did come to fetch you.'

'Do you regret it now?' She looked down and away across the water. 'So much has happened.' He heard her voice hitch.

'I couldn't stop him, but I tried, I tried so hard. But the others needed me, and. And…' She trailed into silence.

'I only have two regrets,' he said, lifting her hand and kissing it. 'Not leaving sooner, and not being able to kill that bastard twice.'

She shifted closer and he drew her close and held her tight against him, her trembling gradually stilling.

'Orec?'

'Hmm?'

'Your armour's pinching me.'

'Sorry.' He released his grip and shifted away slightly.

'So what happens now?'

'We go home and I make us some new doors.'

'So that's it?' She turned to look at him, brow creasing into a frown.

'That's it,' he replied. 'All I've wanted to do since I left the valley was come back.'

'You think we can just go back to our old life, just like that?'

Now it was his turn to frown. 'Why can't we? The house needs some work, but I've seen far worse.' He glanced down as he rubbed his thumb across the back of her hand again, only now noticing the stubborn blood that still darkened his nails and the deeper whorls on his fingers, and felt the old fears rise again. He looked across at her and sighed. 'I didn't want you to see me like that. Like this.' He gestured to the bloodied tatters of the tunic covering his mail. 'I just wanted to come home.'

She opened her mouth, but whatever she was going to say didn't make it past her teeth. Instead, she lifted her hand away and laid it against his cheek as she leaned forward to look into his eyes with an unsettling intensity. He heeded the warning in his mind and fought down the urge to pull her into a kiss.

'My gods,' she said after a silence that had almost stretched into something uncomfortable. A slow smile spread across her face, transforming her and making his pulse quicken at the sight of it. 'My Orec really is still in there.'

'Witch.' He smiled back at her. 'He'll never leave you.'

'The others are coming back with us,' she said, keeping her hand on his cheek. 'They'll need to somewhere to stay, at least for a while.'

He lifted her hand away and kissed it again. 'Good. I'll need help hauling timber.'

'Don't you dare,' she said, getting to her feet.

'Watch me,' he said, following suit with a groan. 'Get them ready. The sooner we're out of this damned forest, the better.'

'Amen to that,' she said. She gnawed her lip for a moment, then pulled him close and laid a kiss on his cheek. 'Thank you,' she whispered, and before he could put his arm around her, she slipped away.

He lifted his arms and let them drop to his sides as she hurried over to the others, looking over her shoulder with a grin. He shook his head and went to go fetch his pack. It could have gone a lot worse, and by the gods, he'd expected it to go far worse than it had. He'd rushed in like a boy with a head full of children's tales when he'd seen her, completely disregarding the plan he'd spent most of the afternoon rehearsing in his head. Had it not been for the mists, it would be him laying on the forest floor right now with those damn moths and the gods only knew what else drinking from his corpse.

He looked back to where he'd dragged two of the bodies and saw only grooves in the mud, grooves that led directly into the water. He shuddered and moved away from the bank with no little haste. To his surprise, the women readied themselves quickly enough, with most if not all of them having armed themselves from the fallen deserters in one way or the other.

'We're going to move fast and quiet,' he said. 'Stay together. The way should be clear but I don't want to take unnecessary risks. Any questions?'

'How long will it take?' asked a woman standing beside Martina.

'We'll walk through to nightfall and make a camp. If all goes well, we'll be out of the forest before the afternoon bells of the next day.'

He waited, and when no more questions came, he smiled at Martina and began walking, leading them back along the trail he'd come in on.

HE'D BEEN IMPRESSED with the pace they'd maintained throughout the day without word of an argument, but his instruction that they move quietly had clearly not sunk in quite as well. They'd lasted perhaps an hour before the conversations started and, like a pebble kicked down a mountain, they'd only grown louder and bolder. They ignored his reprimands and, in time, his pleas to keep it down. He didn't have the vocabulary to make them appreciate the sense of menace that was gathering around them and while the final hours before they made camp left him soaked in sweat and exhausted, they sat down around the small fire he'd lit with a carefree air that annoyed him as much as he envied it.

That bitterness abated slightly when they turned out the improvised bags that they'd been carrying and laid out the food they'd salvaged from the camp. He was genuinely surprised and impressed by the quantity of it.

'Come and eat,' Martina said, beckoning him over to join them. 'Before it gets too dark.'

'I'll just have something I can eat on the move.'

'Come and sit down, for gods' sakes. Take some rest.' The woman next to her moved along around the fire and she patted the spot that was now open. Her smile was real, and he made his way over, angling his scabbard as he sat down. He'd barely crossed his legs before he felt his skin crawling with the knowledge that they all had their backs to the forest and the fire in front, ruining whatever chance they had of spotting anything or anyone coming up on them. He flinched when Martina touched his knee and mumbled an apology that she only shook her head to.

'The larder used to be in the so-called hall,' she said. 'We moved it, so your fire missed most of it.'

'Is that salted pork?'

'It certainly is,' said the woman who'd moved. She passed the cutlet over to him. 'Excuse my fingers.'

He took a bite and couldn't help but grunt in pleasure, which made Martina laugh.

'This is so good,' he said between bites. 'Did you make this?'

'No. They stole most of this,' the woman said. 'We made the bread though.'

'From stolen flour,' Martina added.

He finished the meat and helped himself to some of the bread, drizzling it with oil from a small pot that Martina offered him, and washing it down with a wine that was almost as good as what he'd had after the battle.

'Thank you,' he said. 'But now I really need to get back out there.'

'Why? What's out there?' asked the woman.

'I don't know,' Orec replied. 'That's why I need to be out there. But thank you for the meal.'

He squeezed Martina's shoulder as he stood, then moved away from the fire, closing his eyes for a few moments to help them adjust. They had made good time by his reckoning, and if they kept the same pace, they would be back on the road by noon the next day. He settled into position next to one of the few trees that were still free of the creeping moss. The sound of the women's conversation was still a constant murmur, but aside from that the forest was far too quiet. The night should be alive with the noise of unseen battles of the creatures that called it home, and, this time of year, the ululating mating calls of the red fox and braying of the stags. Instead, there was only the sound of the wind sighing through the branches, which sounded too much like the breathing of some great beast for him to find it comforting.

He expected it to be a long night's watch, and in that he wasn't wrong. The sound of their conversation dwindled as the night settled across the forest and rendered the shadows impenetrable. He moved back to check on them and found them all asleep, some in pairs and others in threes. He smiled at the idea of Stefan and Tomas sleeping like that. There'd be a fistfight the moment either of them rolled over.

Martina was asleep with her head on her arm, and the woman he'd spoken to as they ate was tucked up against her, mouth slack. He knelt next to her and just watched her for a while, gently brushing a few stray hairs away from her face. Bruised or not, she was still beautiful and he felt something of the contentment he'd fantasised about on the journey rise inside him. He wanted nothing more than to tuck himself in behind her, and it physically hurt to stand up and turn away.

He was a few paces away when he heard a faint whisper of sound. He paused, and it came again, longer this time. He laid his hand on his sword and turned towards it. At first there was nothing, but then he saw a pale flash across one of the slivers of moonlight that had managed to penetrate the canopy. Then another, like a leaf caught in a wind he could not feel. He angled towards it, moving as quietly as the forest allowed him. The whispering was simultaneously growing both more urgent and more incomprehensible, as if scores of children were playing hide and seek, but there was nothing to be seen.

He flinched as something clipped the back of his ear and spun to see a moth with a wingspan the size of his hand tumble away before righting itself. And then clumsily circle back at him. He caught a glimpse of its feathered antennae and watched, dumbstruck, as half its head peeled back to reveal a pale tube that looked like nothing more than the fang of a viper. He only remembered to move when it alighted on his forearm and began scuttling up. His gloved fist crushed it as it passed his elbow, leaving a pale dusting and a smear of something dark and tacky to the touch. He stepped back, mouth pulled into a moue of disgust, and finally looked up.

The space beneath the canopy proper was alive with hundreds, perhaps thousands, of the moths, as they swirled around in a mockery of the great flocks of birds that came in the summer.

*HelpmeNoJonIthurtsRunHelpNoGodsEleanorComeback-ChildGetawayHurtsHelpmeGetthehorseRunGoHideHelpme-HelpmeHelpme*

He took a pace back, then several more as the swarm began descending, their dry wingbeats accelerating and the toneless stream of words once more blending into gibberish.

He turned and ran, breaking one of his own cardinal rules when in a forest, but at least some his luck remained intact and no roots tripped him, nor did any branches skewer his eyes. He all but skidded to a halt when he was back at the camp, and a quick glance over his shoulder was enough to confirm his fears.

'Up! Up!' he shouted, louder than he had since the fields of Tulkauth. He pulled Martina to her feet as she blinked and sat up, spilling the other woman onto the ground. 'We need to run, get up damn you!'

Around him the women had all sat up and were looking around. Several were clutching at each other, panicked by his tone.

'What is it?' Martina asked, trying to pry his fingers from his arm. 'Orec. You're hurting me.'

'That.' He released his grip and pointed towards the swarm, which was now almost at ground level and spinning towards them far quicker than he'd feared.

'What's that?'

'Goddamn moths. We need to run!' He reached for her again but she slapped his hand away.

'They're just moths,' the woman who'd fallen from Martina's lap said, dusting herself off.

Orec pulled Martina close, pinning her arms to her sides and resting his forehead against hers. 'Do you trust me?'

He felt her take a breath and release it before her eyes met his. 'Yes.'

'Then tell them to run, and don't look back.'

He released her and she stepped past him. 'Listen to him! We—'

The words she meant to say died on her tongue as the swarm dropped onto the campsite like a blizzard, blanketing two of the women almost instantly. They staggered and raised their arms, looking at the fluttering shapes in what may at first have been wonder.

Orec pulled Martina away. She was still trying to find her feet when the first scream rang out, a scream that was quickly muffled in a way that Orec knew would haunt him for years to come if they survived. More screams joined the first.

'We must help!' Martina shouted, pulling him at him to stop.

He cursed loudly but didn't release his grip. Several of the women were following them, scrambling and stumbling through the shadows behind them. The movement of the swarm had fanned the embers of the fire, unwittingly illuminating the scene as three human shapes staggered to and fro, swatting at their faces, necks and ears: but any gaps in the white blanket were quickly filled.

'There's nothing we can do,' he said, pulling her along and forcing her to look away. The gods knew, she'd already been through enough and he'd rather have her angry at him if it meant he could spare her one more horror. 'We have to go.'

He relented to wait until the other four women reached them and then hurried them all along. The swarm wasn't following them and the campsite was now pale and still, the screams muffled and lost to the night.

'Keep going,' he said, moving ahead of them and trying to pick out anything familiar. 'You're all doing very well. Come on.'

THE SUN HAD finally risen high enough to show their path again, and with it came the relief that the trees were thinning out. Their pace, which had slackened as the strength that their fear had lent them drained away, now quickened again to the thought of safety and sunlight. Another hour passed in which the surviving women finally began speaking again, something he wouldn't have thought he would be grateful for not a day ago, but they finally emerged from the treeline and simply stood in the sunshine and let its warmth seep into their tension knotted backs.

For his part, Orec was staring at the cracked and lifeless land ahead of them and trying force the memories of Tulkauth from his tired mind. Echoes of the sheer cacophony of the battle rang in his mind, underscored by the meaty crash as the lines met and tore into each other, the screams of men and beasts indistinguishable in their sudden agonies.

He flinched away as if burned as Martina touched him, his hand dropping to the knife at his belt before the ghosts fled his vision. She took a hasty step back but he raised his hands.

'Sorry,' he said. 'I was miles away.'

She nodded and returned to stand by his side. 'We were just asking if this is safe to cross.'

He looked across the shallow crater and, for the time it took him to blink, another image overlaid it. *Rings of purple light with a star-bright flash in their centre, the light somehow jagged and dirty, blackening the armour and flesh from the men around him with indifferent ease.*

He rubbed his eyes until starbursts of light overwhelmed the sickly purple.

'No,' he said. 'We'll go around. There's no point looking for more trouble.'

'I'm relieved you said that,' she said, squeezing his arm.

Once they were around what he had named the Blight, the road was waiting for them and familiarity and sheer normality of it brought no little relief to each of them. Their pace quickened again and even Orec felt a bit lighter on his feet as they came around the bend and saw the cottage.

'Orec.' Martina stopped him with a gentle hand on his chest while the others raced towards the sanctuary the house offered.

'What's the matter?' he asked, suddenly afraid she was going to tell him there was no place for him there anymore. No. Not just afraid: certain. This was her new life, and it had no place for someone like him anymore. She had been waiting for this moment, gathering the courage she needed to face him. He felt an unseen hand tighten its grip on his heart as she cleared her throat and looked up at him.

'Thank you. For coming home. For coming to get me. Us.' She looked up at him, and then away just as quickly. 'I don't know if I deserve it, or you.'

She looked up at him again, as tears cut two clean lines across her face, and whatever she saw in his expression was enough to make her take a step back and hug her arms to her chest.

'Tina,' he said, desperately trying to come to terms with what she said as opposed to what he'd expected her to say. He could understand fear and anger, and handle them without breaking his stride, but he was poorly equipped to deal with the depth of the emotions that rose within him now. He couldn't think what to say, so instead stepped forward and wrapped his arms around her.

'Don't be stupid,' he blurted, wincing as he said it. 'Stop. I mean to say, you're everything to me. You're home. Not those four walls, you.'

She said something that was lost against his chest and leaned into him a little more while the other women looked on.

'Come on,' he said after a little while, and kissed the top of her head. 'We've work to do.'

She only smiled at that and took his hand as they made their away along the path. There was a lot of work to do, that was true, but as they opened up the house and he had his first good look around with a clearer mind, it was not nearly as much as his mind had conjured from his first impressions on that troubled night of his return. The cottage was a mess from the rough looting of Dimka's men, but they hadn't had enough time to do more than empty out their dressers and trunks and rip out a couple of floorboards that had evidently squeaked and led them to think that the household silver was hidden beneath them. The women tutted and shook their heads as they explored the cottage, ushering him out of the kitchen as they convened there and began sorting through the wrecked cupboards.

He was too tired to make sense of it or even offer a token protest and instead made his way to their bedroom and pushed the bed frame back in place. The horschair mattress had been cut open during the raid and he cursed them for that; it was expensive, and not something he could fix on his own. He flipped it over and set it on the bed anyway, covering it with his camp blanket. It was better than the floor.

He unstrapped his harness and laid it and the sword on the bed, then unbuckled and shrugged off his armour and stood at the foot of their bed staring down at it. Being free of its weight was liberating, but he again felt vulnerable without it, a sensation that he fully expected would take years to pass. He stood there for a few moments, simply looking down at the war gear and wondering at how jarring it was seeing it in their bedchamber. He looked around, drinking in the familiarity of the room and silently assuring himself that he really was home, and that it was over. But even as he did so, his gaze would return to the armour draped on the bed, and it felt like he'd just found half a worm in the most delicious apple he'd ever eaten.

In the end, he draped it over one of the heavier chairs and hung the sword from the backrest, close enough at hand to satisfy the nagging voice in his head. His boots went beside the chair, and having found one of his old work shirts that the raiders had tossed aside, clearly thinking the threadbare linen not worth the effort, he peeled his shirt off, wincing at the sharp odours of sweat and old blood that saturated it. No wonder the women had kept their distance. He held the shirt out and would have thrown it out of the window if he'd had the choice. Instead, he simply grimaced and tossed it aside. He'd bathe in the morning and give it a wash at the same time.

He turned to pick up the shirt he'd salvaged and saw Martina standing in the doorway, her hand halfway to her mouth. He looked down at the pink and silver scars that streaked across his chest and shoulders like wax, the almost-smooth burn scars overlaying the earlier cross hatch of the claw and sword wounds that he had earned in the years before Tulkauth's fury splashed across him.

'They're just scars,' he said quietly, flexing his arms to prove the point. 'They pull a little, but they don't hurt anymore.'

She didn't say anything as she looked him up and down again. Disquieted by her stare, he slipped the shirt over his head and settled it across his shoulders. She was gone when he looked up again and he just sat on the edge of the bed, rubbing his face. He'd wanted to warn her, but had all but forgotten about them in his tired state. Even sitting there, he could feel the exhaustion weighing him down.

'Just an hour,' he said to no one, and lay back on the bed, closing his eyes.

When he woke, another blanket covered him and bright afternoon sun was streaming through the window. He sat up, rubbing the sleep from his eyes. He could hear the constant murmur of voices inside the house and the sounds of quiet industry. He didn't bother with his boots as he stumbled to the outhouse and back again.

The cottage looked far different already, and he was impressed by how Martina had rallied the other women and set them to work. She greeted him warmly, which was a relief, but also didn't come closer than arms' length to him, which immediately deflated whatever hope her greeting had fostered. He ate the food she set in front of him and excused himself, saying there was too much work for him to sit about. It was true too, and with a full stomach and his boots on he went to retrieve his tools from his workshop.

The raiders had been through it as well, but evidently didn't care much for the idea of making or repairing anything when they could simply steal instead. It was the work of a few hours to clear it, repair the door and take stock of what remained, and once that was done he set to work. He could hear the women in the house as he walked around it, and saw several of them watching him as he moved about the house, examine and collecting the damaged shutters.

Too many of them seemed to laugh at him, which did nothing for his already fractious mood, but that at least changed as he started working. He'd barely noticed the day passing as he set to repairing the shutters, even though his work was clumsy from lack of practice. He was trimming the edge of the front door by the light of an only slightly damaged lantern when he heard the crunch of heavier footsteps on the gravelly path behind him, and he quickly rose, his hand slipping to the knife he'd kept at his side.

'Gods' balls,' Max said, stopping and raising his hands in mock surrender. 'It is you! You did it, you crazy bastard!'

Orec only grinned in reply and took the hand that Max offered before being pulled into a rough embrace.

'Max!' Martina darted down the stairs and into his embrace. Orec kept his smile but felt his hand reaching for the knife again as something deeper than anger stirred within him as the baker caught and spun her.

'I saw the lights,' he said, setting her down. 'I didn't dare to hope it was actually you.' He shook his head. 'How in the name of the gods did you do this, Orec?'

Orec shrugged but kept his gaze level with Max's. 'They were dead the moment they touched her,' he said in an even tone, not breaking eye contact.

'He was terrifying,' Martina said, stepping between them and gently lifting Orec's hand away from his knife. 'Do you want to come in? We found a pot and some mint if you want a tea.'

'No, thank you,' he said. 'I only came to see what was happening before I raised the guards. Let me go fetch you some food and wine. How many are you?'

'Six,' Martina replied.

'I won't be long,' Max said, slapping Orec on the shoulder again. 'Goddamn.'

Orec watched him go, then turned to find Martina standing with her arms folded.

'What?' he asked.

'He's a friend, Orec. To both of us.'

'I know that,' he said. 'Now let me finish the door before it gets too dark.'

She raised her eyebrows at him but left him to it. He managed to finish it scant minutes before Max returned with a wicker basket in each hand and, Orec noticed, a falchion at his hip. Two of the women swept in to relieve him of the baskets and he lifted a bottle from one before handing both over. He pulled the cork with his teeth and sauntered over to where Orec was wrapping his tools up for the night.

He took a long swallow and offered Orec the bottle. 'Drink?'

Orec dusted his hands and took the bottle as he leaned against the railing.

'Thanks.' The wine was tart, almost sour, and he couldn't help wincing.

'It's a bit sharp,' Max said, grinning. 'But the second half is always better.'

Orec took another swig and handed it back.

'So how was it?' Max asked quietly, glancing away towards the forest.

'Rough.'

'Rough.' Max shook his head. 'You were never much of a storyteller.'

'They weren't expecting anyone to fight back,' he said. 'They got sloppy. Isolated guards, and too much drink in the rest.' He took the bottle back. 'If they'd been forced to drink this shit I'd probably be dead.'

'You know that wasn't all of them, right?'

'Guessed as much.' Orec leaned against a post. 'But I didn't need to kill all of them. Men like that have no honour, so they're not going to come looking to avenge their fallen leader. They'll squabble like spoiled children over who gets the big chair now, and then the knives will come out.' He extended a leg and tapped the end of Max's scabbard with his boot. 'Nice piece.'

Now it was Max's turn to shrug. 'No one walks around after dark here without some kind of protection anymore.' He drew it halfway. 'I realised pretty quickly that I was a lousy fencer so this seemed a good compromise.'

'They're handy in a tight spot.'

'And that?' He pointed to the sword that Orec had kept next to him as he worked.

Orec drew the sword and offered to him, hilt first, making a conscious effort not to keep his expression neutral.

'Wow,' Max said, weighing it in his hand. 'That's lighter than I expected, but also heavier. Does that make sense?'

'It's weighted slightly to the tip, but well balanced.'

'It's quite something,' Max said, raising it and peering at the steel from a few inches away before passing it back. 'I've never seen the like. It looks old. Where'd you get it, a barrow?'

Orec sheathed it, slightly annoyed at himself for feeling as relieved as he did.

'It was a gift.' He held a hand to forestall the next question. 'And that's a story for another day, and not anytime soon.'

'Sorry. I'm just trying to get it through my head that you're really back.'

Martina called them in to eat then, curtailing any further questions. To Orec's relief, the dinner wasn't the sombre and awkward affair he had assumed it would be, with Max prying at him on one side and the women either ignoring him or whispering between each other on the side. Instead there was a definite celebratory air to it, helped in no small part by the far more palatable cider that Max had tucked into the baskets.

For his part, spending the afternoon with his old tools in his hand had felt strange, as if he'd inherited them from a dead man. The old routines had helped his mind settle though, and from the look of the cottage and the laughter around the table, they had helped Martina and her women too. So why did it all still feel like such a hollow victory? He'd wanted this moment for so long, so why had the restlessness within him not abated?

He looked up from the bite of pie crust he'd been pushing around his plate and watched Martina laugh at some joke of Max's that he hadn't been listening to, and the sight of it was enough to lift the melancholy that had settled over him. He felt a hope rekindle within him that everything could still be all right. They were together again, sat at their own table in their own house, and that was little short of a miracle. He raised his cup to his lips and winked at Martina over the rim, as she used to do to him while they were courting, most often when they dined with her parents and her legs were pressing against him in unexpected ways under the table.

The gesture caught her unawares and she spat her own mouthful of cider across the table. Now it was his turn to roar with laughter, and the silence of the others didn't make it any less funny for him. Martina looked up at him as she wiped her sleeve across her face, and then began to laugh too while the others looked on in confusion.

'Long story,' was all he said when they had both recovered.

'Speaking of long stories, it's been a long day,' Max said. 'For me least of all. It's time for me to leave you to your rest.'

A chorus of protest greeted this, and he agreed to stay long enough to finish his drink. Orec followed him out onto the porch after and stood staring up at the sky while Max fastened his falchion's belt.

'It's too quiet,' he said.

'I was wondering if you'd notice,' Max said. He gestured out towards the road Orec had followed into the valley, barely visible as a distant, pale strip under the moonlight. 'Since all that happened there haven't been many birds or waterfowl, or even summer crickets for that matter.'

Orec grimaced. 'The forest felt strange. There are things in there now that don't belong, and there's something in the lake,' he said quietly, remembering the strange ripples that had marred its mirrored surface. 'Have you seen the moths?'

'The moths?'

Orec rubbed his arm at the memory of the creature's feathery touch. 'Count yourself lucky then. They're in there, great swarms of them, and drawn to you like midges in the spring. We lost two of the women to them on the way out.'

'Gods, that's a cheery thought to carry me home.'

'Sorry,' Orec said, holding out his hand and taking Max's in a warrior's grip. 'And thank you. I'm sorry I wasn't better company tonight.'

'You're most welcome, and don't fret on it. I'm sure it wasn't the homecoming you expected. Tomorrow will be better though.'

'Tomorrow will be better,' he repeated, nodding. 'I like that.'

Max smiled and gave a quick wave as he set off him, leaving Orec standing quietly on the porch where he remained, staring at the stars until Martina called him in.

# CHAPTER FIFTEEN

STEF SAT ON the edge of his bed, gently massaging the knotted scar tissue on his leg as he looked around the room. It looked the same as when he left it, if he ignored the holes left in the walls where Carl had boarded the windows up during the siege. He and Carl had sat by the fireside long after his exhausted mother had drifted off into the deep and satisfied sleep of a mother whose children were all safely home.

Carl had told him how the town had come perilously close to being overrun, and sounded far older than he should have as he did so. Every citizen, save the most elderly, had been called to arms to defend their home, and Carl and his mother had been no exception. The thought of his gangly little brother and mother forming into a square with their neighbours, all armed with spears made from hurriedly smelted and re-cast homewares, would have been funny if it hadn't been so damned terrifying.

But the gods had protected them, and they had been far enough away from the breaching of the gates that no harm had come from to them—at least not of the physical sort. The attack had been beaten back by the arrival of a cavalry regiment who had ridden through the night and had arrived in time to launch an assault at the mob's unguarded flank with no time to spare after the gates were breached, although they had paid a steep price for their heroism. Even as young as he was, Carl had helped with the clear up; and from his description of the cavalry's black and white pennants, Stef reckoned that they had been an Arvennir detachment, although only the gods knew what they were doing so far west. None of that had helped the dreams that had plagued Carl's sleep any though.

Stef sat back and looked around again. He had no idea what to do now. Aimlessly walking around the town would lose its novelty very soon, and didn't pay very well. He could hear his mother moving around in the kitchen and knew she would have been out already to buy food for a breakfast that could feed him for a week. The idea of going back to the coach service and drawing up travel documents for the rest of his life hardly filled him with joy, but money was money.

His door opened as he was considering this and he looked up at his mother, who was staring at him—or rather his leg, her hand over her mouth. She hadn't asked about it before, and he suspected she had been too overwhelmed to even notice it properly. The wasn't how he'd intended to approach any discussion about it, but what was done was done.

'It's fine, mama. It's still my leg, it's just been trimmed a little.'

'Oh, my beautiful boy,' she said. 'Look what they did to you.'

'It's fine, honestly,' he said, which he knew was ironic given how long it had taken him to even look at it without his own gut clenching up. He moved to the edge of the bed and pulled on his one boot. 'What's for breakfast? It smells good.'

'Breakfast?' she said, sniffing the air. 'Oh no, the toast!'

He shook his head as she bustled off back to the kitchen. He slid the cup of the wooden peg over the stump and slowly pulled himself up, bracing himself for the twinge as he distributed his weight again. *I got to come home, so I have no right to complain.*

The thought brought back a ghost of the dreams that had haunted his sleep, where the men who had died next to him were stood with parade-ground discipline around him, not flinching as a purple-tinged fire melted their armour and shrivelled their flesh, and only turning to stare at him with empty, smouldering eye sockets just before they finally blew to ash.

He made his way to the kitchen and stopped at the sight of the amount of food that awaited him. Carl was already sat by the table, grinning.

'Come on, before it gets cold,' he said.

'You should have started,' Stef said. 'The eggs alone weigh more than you.'

'That's what I keep telling him,' his mother said. 'He needs more meat on him. Girls like something to hold onto.'

'Mama, please, not now,' Carl protested around a mouthful of scrambled egg.

She waved her hands in mock surrender and came around to Stef. 'Do you need me to dish for you?'

'I can manage,' he said. 'I still have both hands.'

Carl chuckled, but she held her hand to her mouth and half turned away.

'No, I can't even think about it,' she said in a thick voice.

'Mama, please,' Stef replied. 'Sit down and eat with me. Come now. What's done is done. I'm still alive and not looking at me isn't going to change anything.'

'I don't like it.'

'I'm glad to hear it,' he said. 'I didn't let it happen just to be fashionable.'

She shook her head and sat down opposite him. 'The ideas you get in your head.'

He ate until he couldn't so much as look at another morsel, and was relieved when Carl suggested they go for a walk around the town to show him the changes. His mother dutifully resisted any offer of help in clearing the table, and after returning to his room to pull on his sword belt, he met Carl outside the house. His brother stared at the short sword as he came out.

'What's that for?'

'Combing my hair,' Stef replied.

'Funny. Why're you wearing it though? It's over, isn't it?'

'That doesn't mean bad things can't happen.' He adjusted the crutch. 'I want to go check my horse.'

They made their way to the stables. He was content to leave Carl to pointing out anything that may have changed since he was last there, but it only brought it home once more how close he'd come to losing them. A house two streets away had been smashed to its foundations by some kind of siege shot, and the houses alongside it showed signs of hasty repairs—although if he was any judge of such things, they'd need to be rebuilt in the near future. If whoever had aimed the weapon had nudged it upwards by a hair, it would have been their house that was turned into a tomb. Many of the other houses carried their own scars from the attacks, and not all had been repaired.

His horse greeted him boisterously but was being well cared for by Old Darrell, who looked entirely unchanged from the last time he'd seen him, which was unfortunate. He only grunted in reply to Stef's thanks and stared at him with his good eye as if he'd just crawled out of a hole; something which had terrified him as a boy. From there they made their way to the gates, where Carl excitedly pointed out where he and his mother had stood with their neighbours, waiting their turn to fight. The thought made Stef feel ill, and he dragged the still-jabbering Carl off to one of the benches set outside a new eatery that had been erected on the ruins of what used to be the guardhouse.

He waved to the server and ordered two morning ales before sitting down.

'How's the, um, leg?' Carl asked.

'It's mostly fine. When we first left the hospital I couldn't go very far, or fast, but it's toughened up and I've gotten used to it. Mostly.' He paid for the ale when it arrived and clinked his mug against Carl's. 'I still forget about it some mornings, so if you hear a thump from my room when I get up, you know it's happened again.'

'Did it hurt?'

Stef took a sip and lowered his mug before replying. 'At the time, no. But afterwards, well, that's a different story.'

'How did it happen?'

'There was an explosion.'

'Oh, come on, you can't just say that.'

Stef smiled. 'It was just outside this little place called Tulkauth, which none of us had ever heard of either, don't worry. We were pressing the Yoggs hard. The sarge was in the front, and I was behind him with the standard. We were going for their commander, who was a Heart Taker.' He paused at Carl's blank expression. 'A kind of sorcerer. We were outnumbered by hundreds more of them, and if we stopped, we'd be swamped, so we just had to keep going.'

He took another sip of the watery brew.

'Tomas jumped over the shield wall they'd put up to stop us like some kind of madman and cut a hole from behind, and we were through. Orec went straight at the commander like a terrier with a rat, and fought both of his bodyguards at the same time. I'll never forget the sight. He has this black sword, and every time he clipped their armour there were sparks and flame. He cut them down, and then bam!' He slapped his hands together, startling Carl. 'He chopped the sorcerer in the head, straight down, as the sorcerer was casting some new spell. And that's when it happened. Everything went sort of purple and white, like looking straight up at the sun, and I woke up on a stretcher minus a bit of leg.'

Carl was staring at him with wide eyes when he looked up from his ale again. 'Gods and Guardians,' he said in a low voice. 'That's awesome.'

'Awesome wouldn't have been the word I used,' he said, looking up at Carl. 'Five hundred men charged with us that day, and I was one of the four that left. Four. Many were the best friends I'd ever had, men who were as much a brother to me as you are.' *Perhaps more.*

'I'm sorry, I didn't mean it like that. '

'No, it's fine, don't worry. Some days it just weighs more on my mind than others.'

'So, what happened to the others? You said four of you survived?'

'Orec, myself, Tomas the madman, and Hayden the archer.' He could picture Tomas's response to that and grinned at the thought. 'They've gone home too, but you'll meet them one day.'

'Orec's the guy who killed the sorcerer?'

'That's him. He made my new leg too.'

'So, he's alive, even though the sorcerer exploded in front of him?'

'Very alive, yes.' He paused with the mug halfway to his lips. 'We were standing together, so it must've been too close to the centre of the blast. Like the eye of a storm. Anyway, drink up. I want to get some new clothes since you've stolen everything I had left.'

His mother seemed just as surprised to see him as the day before when they finally returned, Stef with a bundle of new clothes under his arm. He washed from a basin and tried the clothes on: clothes that smelled of sunshine and scented water rather than a combination of man and horse sweat, and he had to resist the urge to take them off again to keep them pristine.

One thing he did do was say no to was his mother's urging that he burned the clothes he'd come home in, reasoning that he had a horse and would need riding clothes, which was true but not the whole truth. He then displeased her further by knocking two pegs into the wall and hanging his sword from them, although this time she simply rolled her eyes and asked what visitors would think of this.

By the time the third morning dawned, his bed no longer felt strange and breakfast had become a far more humble offering. He knew his adventure was well and truly over when his mother scraped eggs on the toasted bread set before him and casually remarked that the widow Shipton's daughter had recently returned too, and perhaps he should go introduce himself, seeing as they clearly had much in common and neither were getting any younger. Stef simply nodded as if he were considering it and ignored Carl as he made exaggerated kissing motions against the back of his hand.

He'd had plans to take the horse out for a walk, and to then make his way around to a few of the traders, to see if any had need of a clerk. The idea of it didn't sit right with him, but while his mother would give him her last penny in the world if he asked for it, he had no intention of living off her or anyone else's charity.

He was scant yards from the stables when he heard the unmistakeable sound of other horses coming up behind him, and quickly stepped out of the way. He looked up as the lead rider passed him and then flinched away as if struck, his face paling and his breakfast churning unpleasantly in his gut.

The provost captain didn't look at him as he passed by, but there was no mistaking him. The last time Stef had seen him, he'd been leaning forward over his saddle as Hayden's arrow whizzed over his head. He waited until the last rider went by, then turned and walked back the way he'd come, shoulders hunched. It couldn't have been pure chance that they were there. And even if he dared hold to that sliver of hope, it would only last as long as it took them to take a look at his horse.

It wouldn't take much for Old Darrell to tell him who had stabled it and send them to his mother's door. He swore in a way that would have earned Tomas's approval and hurried along, ignoring his leg's protest.

His mother was sitting at the table with a woman he didn't recognise, and both looked up in surprise as he entered.

'I can't talk now,' he said, hardly pausing as he rushed to his room. He buckled his sword, dug out his purse and threw on his travelling cloak before turning and making his way back downstairs.

'I'm heading back north. I need to go see the others,' he said, bending to kiss his mother on her forehead. 'I'll be back soon.'

'Why?' she asked, grasping at the hand he placed on her shoulder. 'I don't understand. Why now?'

'Trust me. I won't be gone long. Love you.' He wriggled his fingers from her grip and made his way out through the kitchen, leaving the string of questions that followed him out unanswered. He made his way along the side streets, avoiding the few people he saw but trying hard not to make it obvious that he was. When he was close to the gates, he leaned against a wall and watched for a few minutes until he was satisfied that the guards were behaving normally and hadn't been reinforced with any of the riders. He fell in behind a family with a cart and made his way out, not bothering to even try keep up with them once they were past the guards, who were for now still more interested in who was coming in.

He had to warn the others, but if he was to have any chance of doing that, he'd need to persuade someone to give him a lift, or steal a horse. *Why not? I'm already a wanted criminal*. He doubted the provosts would care that he hadn't landed a blow on any of their fellows. He had been part of it, and that made him as guilty as any of the others.

'Pardon me?'

He stopped at the sound of the voice behind him, his hand dropping to his sword as he turned.

An older man stood there, dressed in a neat outfit that his grandfather would have approved of, a smart leather backpack riding high on his shoulders. He smiled as Stefan turned, and pointed at him with a cane.

'I don't suppose you're Stefan of Pulcek by any chance?'

'Who's asking?' He didn't look like any provost he'd ever seen, nor did he sound like one, but he wasn't about to take a chance.

'Ah, so you are,' the man said, his smile broadening. 'This is such a relief.'

'Look, friend, I don't know who you are, or what you think you know, but you'd better be on your way.'

'Speaking of such things, where are you going?' He looked Stef up and down. 'And in such a hurry too, it seems.'

Stef couldn't help looking back towards the gates, and thankfully all that could be seen were folk going about their daily lives. At least for now.

'From that look, I take it that those riders have found you.' He lifted his hat off and smoothed his greying hair. 'Which means that it won't be far behind either.'

'Look, I don't know what you want, but I don't have time for this.'

'Probably not. You can't outrun cavalry, you know,' the man said from behind him. 'Not even if you had your leg back.'

Stef ignored him and started walking. If he could make it to the woods, he had a chance. They were bound to have a tracker, but Hayden had taught them all a few tricks, and no one was infallible. And a small chance was better than none.

He hadn't gone far when he heard the rumble of a carriage behind him. He turned and saw the old man coming up behind him in a compact chariot drawn by two sturdy sheep the size of small ponies.

'Hop on,' he said. 'It's a bit of a squeeze but a damn sight quicker.'

Stef swore quietly and shifted his sword so that he could draw it seated if he had to, then climbed onto the chariot. A strange sense of vertigo gripped him as he took hold of the handle and pulled himself up, almost as if it were rising and falling. The sensation passed quickly though and the old man only nodded as he sat down, looking too pleased with himself for Stef's comfort.

'Who are you?' Stef asked once they were underway again, the sheep taking up the slack easily enough and trotting on.

'I'm a lawyer, as it happens,' the man said after a moment. 'Although one with a penchant for the esoteric. I find it all quite fascinating, you see. Exhilarating, even.'

'Right.' He braced against the footboard and looked back over the cart, but the road remained empty save for a man leading a pig. 'I appreciate the ride, but how do you know who I am? Why is a lawyer roaming the countryside with a sheep-drawn cart looking for me? I want answers.'

'So it would seem, and as it happens, we want the same thing so this is indeed a fortuitous meeting. And it's a chariot, not a cart. I'm not a farmer going to the market.'

'Well?'

'Well what? If you're asking after my health, then I am, thank you. As to the other, I've told you who I am but the why is a bit of a longer story.' He looped the reins over a nearby ring and fished a leather book from his coat pocket. He thumbed through the pages, giving Stef a glimpse of page upon page of neat writing that the clerk in him heartily approved of.

'Ah, here.' He held the book open, revealing two drawings. One was of a crown of sorts, a simple thing but finely carved with many symbols, and the other was a creature unlike anything he'd ever seen, its narrow jaw shown open and lined with small, sharp teeth. 'Now, do you recall seeing either of these?'

'Not in the slightest,' Stef replied, frowning. 'Should I?'

'I'd be a liar if I said that wasn't disappointing, but in the circumstances I suppose it is understandable,' he said, tucking the book away again. 'How much do you remember of Tulkauth?'

Stef felt a chill make its way down his spine. It was the first time he'd heard anyone outside of their circle say that name aloud in a long time. 'How do you know about Tulkauth?'

'I have wide range of interests, and I read a lot,' the man said. 'Almost as much as I listen. I'm afraid that time is against us, so

I have little choice but to sacrifice the fuller tale on the altar of brevity. The heart of the matter is this: your Captain Blackblade killed a Yorughan sorcerer there, one who wore that circlet and you're the first person I've met who was actually there at the time. An honest to goodness witness.' He smiled genially. 'I have questions too, you see. Perhaps we can help each other.'

'The sorcerer,' Stef repeated, rubbing his eyes as if they would dislodge the images that surged to the forefront of his mind. 'He's a sergeant, not a captain,' he added without thinking. 'He earns his pay.' He stood and looked back over the cart again. 'So what does that have to do with anything anyway?' he asked as he sat back down. 'Or why you're here?'

'I'm afraid that's the part that I've had to sacrifice, so you will need to forgive the truncated reply to your questions, as valid as they are. The sorcerer, for want of a better word, was summoning a creature before the sergeant struck him down, you see. A rather dangerous creature.' He tapped his pocket, making his meaning clear enough. 'It seems it's still here.'

'Impossible. There was no time for that.'

'My humble apologies, I hadn't realised that you were a sorcerer.'

'No, of course I'm not.'

'Well then it seems that you couldn't know that for sure, could you? Quite unlikely. The irresistible fact is that the creature has been seen, and it would appear to be following your trail. It is quite real, and it has already claimed several lives on its journey. It would have claimed another were it not for my timely intervention, but that part can wait for a quieter time.'

Stef stared at him, but before he could say anything he heard the distant sound of a whinnying horse. He stood hastily and watched the road behind them, and he was on the verge of dismissing it when he saw several dark shapes emerge in the distance.

'Shit,' he said. 'Shit. Shit. Shit.'

'The riders, I take it?'

Stef dropped back onto the seat. The verge sloped away steeply to the side, and he'd have to roll down it. After that though he would be in woods, which looked far too open for his liking. But what was the alternative?

'So, what is it that these equestrians think you've done?'

'Killed a few of their friends.'

'Well, that sort of thing would explain their agitation. Did you though?'

'I have to go.' He swung his good leg off the cart, but Catt grabbed his arm.

'I really wouldn't do that,' he said. 'You'll end up breaking your good leg, or worse.'

'If they catch me, it'll be my neck.'

'I'm afraid there's little if about it. They will catch you,' he said, and Stef's gut twisted at his words. It was true, and he'd known it. 'But come now, don't look so despondent. Not only am I a lawyer, as well reputed as I am well travelled, but I'm a fairly handy driver too, if I say so myself.'

Stef leaned against the backrest. 'That won't matter. I was there, and they saw me.'

'Did you kill any of them?'

'No, but—'

'Well now, that's a good foundation for a defence.' He tutted softly as Stef stood to look over the cart again. 'That's already plenty to work with. The greatest trees can grow from the smallest seed.'

'They're still gaining on us,' Stef said, frowning. He'd expected the riders to outrun the cart in no time. 'Slowly though.'

'Fascinating. Count your blessings, as they say. Come now, sit down and tell me about your companions, those vicious killers who stole you from your convalescence and forced you into the wilderness before making you a witness to such brutality by no choice of your own.'

'What? It wasn't like that.'

'And so the seed is planted, my dear Stefan. Tell me about them anyway. Help me water that seed. How were they on your journey? Did they seem any different in their behaviours?'

Stefan stood again and peered over the cart. There were five of them at least, and moving at a gallop if he was any judge of it, and yet they seemed barely any closer. He rubbed his forehead and felt another wave of vertigo wash over him.

'Oh, do sit down. If we hit a rock you'll fall out, standing around like that.'

Stef sat down and close his eyes until the sensation passed.

'Tell me about Sergeant Orec.'

'There's no time! I have to do something.'

'You're doing it. This cart, as you insist on calling it, is your best chance, and you know that. We'll make good time, you'll see. And should you persist in wanting to throw yourself into the forest and hobble to freedom, at least wait until there's a thicker bit of forest up ahead. It'll increase your chances of delaying the inevitable.'

Stef considered this with his head resting in his hands, fighting for calm. The lawyer was right though, and talking about something would be better than sitting there trying to imagine what it would feel like when they put the noose over his head. He lowered his hands and started talking, haltingly at first as he tried to find the words to describe how the sergeant's calm, stubborn demeanour had shaped the men around him.

'You're doing wonderfully,' the lawyer said. 'But I'm more interested in what he was like after Tulkauth.'

'Oh. Well, much the same, I suppose. Still stoic, just more tired, but then we all were. Having that knowledge that you had done it, that you aren't going to be marched into a battle tomorrow, is as big an idea to process as getting ready for your first one is.'

'I see. And Orec, he wasn't acting strange? Or either of the others?'

Stef scratched at his leg absently, remembering the nights on the road home where they'd all sat up at the same, woken by something at the same time, and laid back down again by unspoken agreement not to talk about it.

'There's something, isn't there?'

Stef made to stand up, to check on the riders, but the lawyer's voice hardened as he moved.

'Ignore them. Tell me what happened.'

For the first time since they met, Stef felt a prickle of apprehension, one that faded into the same sensation of vertigo, a sensation that now lingered.

'Did you see the purple light?' the lawyer asked, turning to glance at him. 'Any of you?'

Stef felt the vertigo turn to something else, something that made it feel like cold water was running through his bowels.

'You did,' the lawyer said, a smile lifting his moustache. 'We're making excellent progress.'

'I don't want to talk about it.'

'Ah, but you must! This is important, Stefan. I can keep the riders away from you, but I must know what you have seen. It is as much the matter of life and death as they are, and quite likely moreso.'

Stefan gritted his teeth and rose to look over the cart anyway. The road behind them was empty save for a swirl of leaves and needles, and he dropped back onto his seat, closing his eyes until the dizziness passed. 'They're gone.'

'I remain, as ever, a man of my word.' He tugged at the reins and Stef felt the cart slow marginally, the strange sensation abating as it did. 'So now perhaps we can converse without haste.'

'I'm really not sure what's going on.'

'There's nothing going on. We're just two travellers, having a friendly conversation as we pass through these interminable woods. Come now, it is just me.'

'I don't even know your name.'

'Ah, how tardy of me.' He held out his hand. 'I am Doctor Catt. You can call me Doctor, or Catt. Either is good but both is better.'

'I thought you were a lawyer,' Stef said, taking his hand.

'I am many things, as we all are.' He smiled as he looped the reins over the brake handle, then crossed his legs. 'Now please, tell me about what troubles you.'

'WOULD YOU CARE for some wine with that?'

Stef looked up with a mouthful of food and just nodded. The food was the best he'd had in a long time, but how Catt had managed to prepare it so quickly and on the small fire he'd built was beyond him. There were a few things that didn't add up around the lawyer, but he'd been unfailingly polite and generous, and so Stef hadn't pressed him on any one part of it yet.

Catt poured himself a generous glass of wine and sat down on the chair he'd unpacked for himself. The chariot was more comfortable than most, but that didn't make it fun to drive for hours on end. It had been a long day, and he could tell that Stefan had a dozen or more questions that he wanted to ask but hadn't quite worked out how to yet, which suited him. He took a sip of the wine, sighed contentedly, then took out his pen and journal. He reached up, lit one of the chariot's fog lamps and began to add to the notes he'd started earlier when he'd given Stefan the reins, more to keep him occupied while he spoke than anything else.

He didn't look up when Stefan told him he was off to wash the plates, only grunted, and didn't think anything of it, at least not until he glanced up at a particularly loud pop from the fire and saw the sparks drift upwards, their purple sheen stark against the shadows. He stuffed the notebook back into his one pocket and reached into another, taking out what looked like a fancy, if oversized, locket. He snapped the lid open and the glimmer of orange light confirmed it: something was nearby, and he'd bet his hat on it being the creature. It was faster than he'd feared.

He hurried to the back of the chariot and pulled out a long rod with several amber inserts and a copper tip, and quickly rubbed his sleeve across the inset amber, cursing under his breath as he did so. He felt it stir to life but kept rubbing as he moved towards the front, turning up the lamp as he did so.

'Stefan!' he called.

'Here,' the young man replied, emerging from the gloom a dozen yards off to his side, walking slowly and awkwardly, having eschewed using his crutch. He paused as he saw the staff in Catt's hands.

'What's that?'

'I'll explain later,' he said, finally satisfied that it was sufficiently charged. 'You should ready yourself. I believe the creature has found us.'

Catt winced as Stefan dropped the plates and drew the sword that was still at his side, holding it before him with a confidence that was reassuring.

'Are you sure?'

As if on cue, a sound like a box full of agitated crickets sounded from the shadows just outside of the lamp's light, followed swiftly by the rustle of something moving through the leaf litter.

'Gods,' Stefan muttered. 'What was that?'

The chittering sound came again, this time from the other side of the clearing, and they both saw a shape dash between the trees, moving closer. It was darker than the night that framed it, a trail of small purple motes briefly trailing it.

'What do we do?' he asked.

'It'll come to us,' Catt said with a confidence he wasn't entirely sure he believed in. 'All I need to do is give it a firm jab with this and it should be easy enough to capture.'

'Capture?'

'Ah, yes.' Catt tried to hide his grimace. 'There's a bounty on it,' he explained, satisfied that it wasn't actually a lie after all, seeing as the bounty simply wasn't the kind that Stefan imagined.

'I'll stick to my sword. I'm not risking my life on that fishing rod.'

'Just stay clear of it. It's quite dangerous.'

Next to them the fire popped again, a moment's distraction at best, but time enough for the creature to have stepped out between the trees not ten feet from where Stef stood. He took a step back, nearly dropping his sword as two hair-thin arcs of violet light leapfrogged down the blade. The rasping, clicking sound from the creature intensified as they reach the tip and vanished.

He watched as a lambent light woke within its eyes, giving shape to the otherwise pitch-black outline of its head for the first time. There was no pity in the gaze it revealed.

To his left, Catt was moving slowly to a flanking position, his staff held like a spear. Its eyes flicked to the side, and before Stef could do more than open his mouth to shout a warning, it had leapt onto a nearby tree, sending a shower of bark chips and splinters spinning through the darkness. They were still in the air as it leapt again.

Catt saw it move, or at least saw the needles and leaves erupt around its feet as it did. He turned too, silently berating himself at how slow he was moving. He saw it hit the tree and saw the same corona of bark that erupted around it, but it wasn't so much landing on the tree as using it as a springboard. It was there for a blink of the eye and then it was in front of him. He had a moment to think that it had missed, or merely meant to scare him away before its bony tail whipped around and slammed the staff back into his face. He flew backwards as if kicked by a carthorse, his limbs already spasming uncontrollably as the weapon discharged.

Stef recoiled as Catt hit the side of the cart and fell to the ground, wrapped in amber arcs of light, a long, incoherent groan escaping his lips. The creature was swaying from side to side as it turned to look at him, tail moving in counterpoint to its body.

He knew he couldn't outrun it, even if he'd had both legs. So instead he bellowed and swung at it instead, using an overhead cut that Orec had taught him a lifetime ago, changing to a one-handed grip anchored on the pommel to give him the extra reach he needed. It was a good swing, but the creature was moving too.

It swayed lower at the last moment, and the edge of the sword only clipped it, carving a furrow across its leonine shoulder. Then as it exploded upwards, driving with its rear legs and punching its fore claw into his chest.

Stef screamed as the claws bit deep, lifting him from the ground and dumping him down bodily again six feet from where he'd been standing. His head smacked into the dirt hard, knocking all thought from his head.

At least until it opened him up. He screamed then, as loud and shrill as the men he'd seen gutted on the battlefield and flailed at it wildly with his fists. It hissed as if in annoyance and leaned forward, snapping several ribs, then tore his throat out. His scream became a rasping wheeze, the trauma finally overwhelming his brain and making what was happening to his innards feel distant and unremarkable. His head, suddenly too heavy to hold up, lolled to the side and he died soon after, staring at an arm he could no longer move and the arcs of violet light skipping across the fingers he couldn't feel.

Catt remained where he'd been thrown by the jolt from the staff, not that he had much choice in the matter. It had felt as if every muscle in his body had been struck by night cramps at the same time and he couldn't do a thing about it. He'd never felt anything like it, and never wished to again.

The extreme discomfort of it had however at least kept him too busy to be afraid, because that was surely what he should have been, given how helpless he was and how the creature had torn into Stefan with no hesitation. Hearing about what had happened to someone and witnessing it were two entirely different things. He'd watched it all from where he'd lain, unable to do anything more than blink of his own accord.

Once it had knocked the soldier flat it had opened him up and begun ripping at his organs, tearing them loose and opening each with those terrible claws. The sound had almost been worse than the sight of it, at least until it started on his long bones. Those it had cracked against a rock, and Catt's morbid curiosity had sharpened into something else when the light had spilled from the marrow within. The creature reacted to this as well, splintering the rest and greedily scooping the glittering jelly into its mouth. Stef's head was ripped from his body and swiftly hollowed out too, and that for him had been the worst of it.

Whatever was going had an effect though. An irregularly spaced line of violet dots woke on the creature's flanks and, for a few moments at least, an intermittent glow lit the back of its throat as it stood victorious over Stefan's scattered remains. It shrieked then, the sound sharp and high enough to be painful and made a slashing motion with its arms, leaving a glowing trail in the air.

Catt stared open-mouthed as the glowing line hung there, vibrating silently and steadily brightening. He could smell a strange sweetness on the air and felt his hair rising as the air around the shimmering line grew opaque. Without warning, the line vanished in on itself like a rope pulled back through a hidden hole.

The creature shrieked again and threw itself forward into the oval shimmer that still hung in the air, stumbling as it passed through. He heard its harsh chitter from behind, and then the soft thump of its footfalls, rapidly vanishing. He exhaled noisily and slumped back against the canvas he was sprawled upon, relief washing over him.

That relief lasted as long as it took him to pull himself up into a sitting position and see that the opaque shimmer still hung in the air, but now rippling and twisting faster than it had been. He took hold of a wheel and pulled himself to his feet, now relieved that he'd been forced to leave the chariot out overnight. The ground beneath the twisting shimmer was undulating, as if it were more liquid than solid; and as he watched, the gory remnants of Stefan's body sunk into it, not so much disappearing as being twisted and folded into smaller and smaller pieces until the pieces were too small to see.

'That's not good, not good at all,' he whispered. He hurried to the side of the cart and threw whatever he could find inside it, chivvied along at every moment by the increasingly louder crackle coming from the light. Even the sheep were staring at him with something that resembled a sentient gaze as he climbed onto the driver's seat, cursing the lingering weakness in his arms.

'Go, damn you!' he called when he was mostly in the seat, and to his great relief they did just that, trotting forward with no little haste.

He braced himself in the seat and looked back over the chariot in the same way Stefan had. For a few moments there was only gloom and shadow, but then a disc of pale light exploded outwards, parallel to the ground, followed a heartbeat later by a thunderclap that lifted the rear wheels off the ground and came perilously close to tipping him under the front wheels. Not long after the rear crashed back down he heard the creak and snap of splintering wood, and the violent crash of several trees falling, their impacts a roll of muffled thunder. He hauled himself up again and looked back, and where the campsite had been there was now a bare clearing, awash with a rapidly fading pearlescent light.

He sat back and let the sheep pick their way back up towards the road while he rubbed his face, wincing as his fingers found the lump the staff had left. They had long since found the road and the sun had risen before his mind was able to put the pieces of what had happened back together, and he was able to stop hurrying onwards. He pulled to the side of the path and refreshed himself in a nearby stream, enjoying the rustic charm of it, and changed into clean clothes that weren't stained with arcing lines of dark crimson, each testament to the ferocity of the creature's attack.

Refreshed, he applied some salve to his forehead and helped himself to a glass of what he liked to call his morning tonic, then quickly put the cart in order before setting off again. They'd mostly spoken about the sergeant, Orec, and even then Stefan had been fairly tight-lipped, so he had little choice but to leave the archer and the thug to their own fates. At least with Orec, he knew the direction the man had been heading and had a decent description of him. He'd find him eventually, and the only question was whether he'd be the first to or not.

# CHAPTER SIXTEEN

THEY WERE COMING, pouring from the forest like ants erupting from a kicked-over nest, wave after wave of them, howling and screeching beating their swords and spears against their shields, a wall of noise, muscle and teeth. He suddenly, desperately needed to pee but the weight of the men marching behind him made stopping impossible, so instead he raised his sword and screamed his battle cry, a thin sound by itself, but midway through the Company roared with him, and to the rear the drummers began to punish their drums.

*Why were there so many? There weren't supposed to be this many.*

It was too late for such thoughts now. The gap between the two forces was closing rapidly, and he glanced up as a shadow fell over them, but it was only the arrows from the archers massed behind them. He watched them dip and then plummet into the ranks of the Yoggs, their deceptively lazy flight suddenly transformed into something deadly. The enemy's progress faltered as those with shields raised and hunkered behind them. Another volley scythed into them as they rose, punching more from their feet, but not enough, not nearly enough.

Orec brought the sword to guard position and charged, the company surging forward behind him. He wasn't more than six strides from first of the bellowing Yoggs when something snagged his feet and he felt himself falling into the mud. It was a death sentence, here where the battle would be fiercest, and his worse fear. He reached out to Stefan as he fell, but the young standard bearer only laughed and kicked his hand away.

'You deserve it,' he said, lifting the company banner higher, the standard now displaying a severed leg rather than the four crowns he remembered.

Then the soft mud welcomed him and he felt the first boot on his back.

'No!' Orec pushed himself away but he could feel the weight of the men above him sapping his strength with every heartbeat, slowly forcing his head down into the glutinous muck.

'Stop.'

It was a quiet word, yet somehow it found him amidst the cacophony of the butchery around him.

'Orec, stop.'

A woman's voice, here? Against every instinct, he closed his eyes. Panic welled up within him, but he knew that voice. He squeezed his eyes shut and as the stars exploded across his vision, the sound of the battle vanished as if he was falling off a cliff, away from it.

He opened his eyes and found himself on his back on the wooden floorboards, squinting up at Martina's silhouette on the bed, the remains of their bedsheet tangled around his sweat-slicked legs.

'Are you okay?' she asked.

He shook his head, but then realised she couldn't see the gesture. 'I'm fine,' he said, sitting forward and pulling his legs free. 'It was—'

'Just a bad dream,' she finished. 'Yes, I know.'

He freed his feet and scooted back slightly along the floor to look up at her. 'I'm sorry,' he said. 'It felt so real. I fell in the mud.'

'That doesn't sound so bad.'

He snorted. 'Unless it's in the middle of a battle. My own men were standing on my back, slowly pushing my face into it.' He rubbed his scalp, willing the images away. 'You know, it almost happened at Serbica Ridge. A javelin clipped my leg just a few paces before we met them.'

'Gods and stars, that's awful.' She lowered herself down from the bed and sat next to him, resting her head on his shoulder. 'I'm so sorry.'

'Stefan saved my life that day. I'd only known him for, I think, three days then.' He chuckled mirthlessly. 'That was the first time I ever pissed myself while sober.'

'Must you?' she said, although he could tell she found it funny too. 'Stefan again. I'd like to meet this mysterious man my husband keeps dreaming of.'

Orec laughed with her, but some of it was forced. Thinking of Stef while awake left him feeling strangely unsettled, the skin on the back of his neck prickling as it usually did before trouble hit.

'I think you'll like him,' he said, conscious that he'd been quiet for too long.

'Is he handsome?'

'What?' He glanced sideways and caught the curve of her smile. 'I wouldn't know.'

She laughed and kissed his shoulder before rising. 'Come on, back to bed. And no more battles.'

'How do you feel about wrestling?' he asked, accepting the hand she offered him, but she only laughed.

'Go to sleep.'

HE SPENT THE next day working on the new shutters, alternately cursing and whistling tunelessly as he worked, enjoying the feel and smell of the wood. His hands were slowly remembering their skills, and the women who they'd brought from the forest had gone their own ways over the last week, far sooner than he had dared hope. The cottage finally felt like home again, and once the shutters were fitted, it would look just as he had left it—provided he didn't look towards the forest, and ignored the deep gouges the raiders' axes had left in the doorframe. But time would finish smoothing those for him.

'Well, don't you look like the cat that got the cream.' He looked up and smiled as Martina came into the workshop, a tankard in her hands. She held it out. 'Here.'

He accepted the cool cider gratefully and drained half of it in the first swallow. 'Almost done with these,' he said, tilting the now-lighter tankard towards the frame in front of him. 'I just need to fit the slats and go get some oil for it.'

'It looks really good.' She perched on the edge of the workbench. 'How're you feeling?'

'Eh? I'm fine. The cider's good.'

'You know what I mean. Last night.'

'You need to ask?'

She laughed and punched him on the arm. 'I meant about the nightmares.'

'It's just a dream,' he said with a shrug as his smile faded. 'I'm fine. How are you, by the same token?'

Now her smile faded too. He wasn't the only one whose sleep was haunted by the ghosts of a personal war. She hadn't yet offered any insight into what she had gone through, and he hadn't pried, knowing how he felt about talking about his own experiences and—as he was coming to realise—out of fear of what she might tell him. What gave him the strength he needed was the simple joy of being near her, which had felt like an impossible dream only weeks ago.

'I'm fine too,' she said. 'I'm going into town to get some lavender for the front. I'll pick up bread too.'

*From Max*. He quickly quashed the thought. *Max is the baker, idiot*. 'That'll look nice. But take a knife.'

She lifted her tunic in a mock curtsey, flashing him a glimpse of the small knife on her waist.

'Very good,' he said. 'But I said knife, not a toothpick. That thing would just make them angry.'

'Oh really?' She drew the knife and looked at it, then at him. 'So you're not scared of it?'

With that she moved towards him holding the knife out in front of her, flicking the tip up and down so that the light caught and flashed across it.

'Don't.'

'So, you admit you're scared?' She stepped closer.

Orec's mouth dried as he watched the knife and he felt his heart beginning to race as if he were running up a hill. 'Put it away.'

'Yah!' she shouted, feinting towards him.

The light flashed off the blade, brighter than before, momentarily all-consuming, and he blinked it away.

When his vision cleared, he was straddling Martina's chest, her knife in his raised hand, his other hand pressing her head to the floor, exposing her neck.

He flung the knife away as if it were too hot to touch and scrambled backwards before lifting her off the floor and pulling her into an embrace.

'Oh gods, I'm so sorry.' He felt her trembling. 'I would never hurt you.'

'I'm fine,' she said softly, embracing him back. 'I'm sorry. I didn't think. About the knife, and you. I'm fine. Just startled.'

They both released the other and sat back, him looking down at his hands and feeling like an utter wretch.

'Hey,' she said, touching his face. 'Nothing fell off and no one died.'

Despite everything, he snorted with laughter at hearing his father's usual response to his complaints coming from her lips.

'You're too good for me.'

'That's what everyone insisted on,' she said, rising. 'I'm fairly sure they're wrong.'

'Only fairly, eh?' He bent and picked up the knife, offering it to her hilt first. 'I still want you to take my knife.' He held up a hand to quell her protest. 'The one with the wire handle. It's not much heavier than this, but will give you an extra four inches of reach.'

'Fine. You're the expert.'

'I'm just a carpenter.'

She stepped in and kissed him, harder than she had since he brought her back. When she stepped back, he would have sworn that she looked as surprised as he felt.

'I'm just a carpenter?' he said again, smiling at her.

'Nice try,' she said. 'You play with your wood and I'll see you later.'

'Be careful. And take the knife!' he called after her.

He stood in the doorway and watched her leave, then turned back to the shutters. He needed to work, to close down the thoughts of what he had just very nearly done. He'd never laid a hand on her, not in his darkest days—shaking his head at what he had once thought to be the worst days of his life. The so-called troubles he'd had then all seemed laughable now, and how the soft, clueless man he'd been had survived a war at all was beyond his ken.

He pushed the thoughts away, shoving them into the same box where everything else that he wasn't quite ready to face lived, and concentrated on the work in front of him. There was a lot to do yet.

'We found something.'

Armand brightened at Quental's words and rubbed his hands together. 'Is it him?'

Quental slowed his horse and brought it alongside Armand's mare. 'We're not sure.'

'How's that?' he asked, the hand on his thigh curling into a fist. *How hard could it be to find one goddamned cripple?*

'You'd best see it for yourself. It's up in the woods, about a half mile on.'

He knew they'd been close, so close to finding him, but the bastard must have spotted them first somehow. They'd shut the town down the moment he'd seen the horse in the stables, and the half-drunk stablehand had spilled everything he knew the moment Quental took the noose out of his saddlebags. The sheer audacity of it still woke a bitter anger within him. The little bastard had just gone home to eat and drink and fuck as if everything was well and good in the world and he hadn't helped to murder eight good men.

He felt a twinge of regret at how he'd treated the old woman and boy. It was entirely reasonable to assume he hadn't said anything about it to either of them, but they had nonetheless harboured a fugitive and they no right, none at all, to live on with a rosy image of their son and brother as some kind of war hero. They had plenty of time to think of it now though. Unlike his men, they still lived, but he took comfort that they would be cursing Stefan's name and memory every day that they walked past the gutted remains of their home. It wasn't the justice his men deserved, but it was a decent start.

'It's up here on the right.' Quental's voice brought him back to the present and he nudged the mare onto the track behind the other man, noting the ruts left in the mud by some kind of cart, which supported the outriders' reports. They dismounted a bowshot from the road, near to a clearing that neither horse wanted to get any closer to.

'Gods and stars,' Armand said in a quiet voice. 'What happened here?'

There was a bowl-shaped indentation in the ground, a good twenty foot across; and despite the risen sun and how shallow it was, the centre was blanketed in vapours that seemed reluctant to pay any heed to the breeze. Every tree within twenty feet of the edge of the bowl had been felled, the stumps smooth and the severed trunks of the trees flung outward like the petals of a monstrous flower. He walked around the bowl and ran his hand over one of the stumps, marvelling at how smooth and even the cut was.

'No idea,' Quental said, following him around. 'Definitely some kind of sorcery though.'

Armand grimaced at the thought. 'So what makes you think it was our man?'

Quental pointed back the way they'd come. 'Cart tracks in and out, and that.' He indicated off to the side.

It took Armand a few moments to pick out what Quental was pointing at. It was after all wood embedded in wood, but once he noticed, it became obvious enough. He knelt next to it, running a finger along the hand-worked surface of the peg-leg. He gripped it and worked it loose, silently wondering at what amount of force it would take to embed a wooden leg inches deep in the trunk of a birch, before deciding he didn't really want to find out.

He rose and turned the peg-leg over in his hands. There, carved into the surface, were four names, each carved in a different hand. Stef. Orec. Tomas Bigcock. Hayden. He tossed it over to Quental.

'It's our man, for sure. But it looks like he pissed someone or something off that he really shouldn't have.'

'The man in the cart maybe? The way he stayed ahead of the men did sound fairly unbelievable.'

Armand nodded. 'Possibly, yes. I don't know who that it is, but at least we have names for our faces now, so that's something.'

'That's true.'

He studied the clearing for a few more minutes, noting the eerie silence of that surrounded them, then motioned for them to mount up again. As fascinating as it was, it wasn't bringing them any closer to the others.

'Mount up.' Armand pointed to the wooden leg. 'Pass that around. I want everyone to know those names by heart.'

'YOU LOOK LIKE shit that someone's taken a dump on,' Erik said as Tomas dropped gracelessly onto the bench.

'Piss off,' he replied half-heartedly, sniffing at the cup his brother pushed towards him. 'What's this?'

'Bitterleaf.'

'It smells like boiled sweat.'

'Drink it,' he said, lifting his own steaming cup. 'You'll get used to it. It'll help you feel better than you look.'

Tomas took a tentative sip and had to battle the urge to spit it across the table. The second was marginally less awful. 'That's disgusting.'

'If it tastes bad it's usually good for you,' Erik rumbled. 'So, talk.'

'About?'

'About why it looks like you just emerged from the south end of a northbound vulture.'

Tomas looked around, but the inn wasn't open yet and there was nothing to divert Erik's unwavering and expectant gaze. He took another sip of the tea instead, then sat back.

'What do you want me to tell you?'

'How about you start with why it sounded like you were dismantling the room last night?'

'I'd rather drink the rest of this.' He set the cup down when Erik only continued to watch him. 'Fine. I had a bad dream. There. Are you happy now?'

'What was it about?'

Tomas swore and hunched forward, resting his elbows on his knees.

'We were on the road, the four of us. Just heading home, you know? I looked back, and there was a swarm of something rolling towards us. I told them we need to run, but they all just kept talking and acting normally and telling me I'm overreacting. And all the way it's getting closer behind us.' He took a sip from the cup and didn't wince. 'I try and run, but the mud's too deep. Then I look back and the swarm's there. These things, all black and shiny, they cover Stef and they're eating him, just chowing down on him like he's a wedding feast. They're biting holes in him and burrowing inside of him. I can see them moving inside him. And all the while he's still just talking as if he's out on a fucking stroll, calm as anything. And then they're landing on Hayden, and he's doing the same, just telling me about goddamned deer trails while these things are eating his eyes and crawling down his throat. And I can't run, as much as I try and try, and then they're landing on me.' He rubbed his face and sat back. 'And that's about when I woke up on the floor.'

'That's rough,' Erik said, earning a coarse bark of laughter from Tomas.

'You reckon? And then to make it worse I come downstairs to this.' He rattled the now empty cup against the table.

'Give it a moment,' Erik said. 'So was it the same dream the time before that?'

Tomas have him a sour look. 'Shouldn't you be cleaning tankards or something?'

'No. We're talking now.'

'I'm hungry and I don't want to.'

'Fine. I'll do us some eggs, but then we're talking.'

'If you're going to be a dick about it you can do up some of those spicy sausages too.'

Despite his protests, with a heaped plateful of egg, sausage and toasted bread in front of him Tomas found himself going back to what had been waking him from his sleep for past few days, slowly at first as he struggled to make sense of it himself. Perhaps it was easier because he didn't have to look at Erik, who for his part only replied with an occasional 'Go on' or grunt.

The pieces came back to him slowly, quietly arranging themselves into something recognisable as he tried to describe them. By the time he was mopping the last of the grease from his plate with a crust, he was fairly sure he'd remembered all that he would. He half expected Erik to shake his head and call him the new village idiot, but his brother simply folded his meaty arms and nodded.

'You're being chased,' he said before the silence became uncomfortable. 'Although that could just be how your spirit is interpreting guilt about something. And it sounds like you blame Stef and Hayden for it.'

'What? When did you become a sage?'

'Being smarter than you hardly makes me a sage. But think about it. It's never wolves, or Yoggs, or anything you know that's attacking you. If it was memories of the war that were troubling you, the imagery would be clear, or at least recognisable as something. But it's something faceless, and something that always kills those two first.'

Tomas chewed the bread slowly. He'd not thought of it like that, and had in fact not thought of it all once he'd woken up. It was a bad dream, that was all, and he was a fool for having them: a goddamned grown-up man, back from a war that many didn't walk away from, sitting on the edge of his bed like a child, afraid to sleep.

'Firstly, why would the war bother me? I did my duty and I damn well enjoyed it too. I'm no murderer to be haunted, and neither are Stef and Hayden.'

'I didn't say you were, brother. I'm just trying to make sense of it. Look, I have to open the kitchen. Go for a walk, get a shave and a hot bath. It'll help.'

'Maybe.'

There was no maybe to it. What Erik had said stuck with him, and not just about the bath. He'd never had dreams like this, not even when he was a child, or certainly none that he had ever remembered in the daylight. But these were different, and they'd started while they were still on the road. He hadn't expected to feel as exposed as he did without the others at his side, nor too miss them as much as he did. He let his feet wander while his mind did the same, and when he stopped to pick some late season berries, he realised that he'd wandered to the edge of town and the meeting with the Turnandal Road. He looked down and found the spot where he'd said his goodbyes to Hayden and Orec, then sat down crosslegged, idly crushing the berries against the roof of his mouth as he considered the idea that had wormed its way into his thoughts. By the time he'd eaten the last of the berries, his mind was made up, and he was smiling as he stood up and headed to the bath house.

He scrubbed himself thoroughly and had the barber trim his hair and beard at the same time. It wasn't that he minded long hair, but he was terrible at keeping it in order, and that part bothered him. If you were going to do something, you needed to be able to do it properly, and stick to it. He'd broken his own rule, however unwittingly, in letting Orec ride off without having gotten to the bottom of why they had both had the same damned dreams. He needed to know if Orec still had them, and if they were the same. If he didn't, then it was for Tomas to sort his own head out, but if Orec was being troubled too then that was another matter entirely.

The inn wasn't particularly busy when he returned and Erik applauded as he walked back through the common room.

'Well, look at that,' he said. 'Amazing how a little hot water can work its own magic.'

Tomas hopped onto one of the bar stools. 'We need to talk.'

'Gods, what have you done now?' Erik asked, tossing his washcloth aside.

'Funny. No, nothing like that.' He looked around to make sure there wasn't anyone within earshot. 'I need to go away for a few days. To see Orec.'

'Your captain?'

'Sergeant. But yes, him. Pour me a drink, would you?'

'Keep talking,' Erik said, sliding a jug over.

Tomas poured a cup and drank half of it. 'Here's the thing. Orec, he had dreams like that too. On the road back. We both did, but although we didn't think anything of it. But I was thinking about what you said.'

'And?'

'And what? I'm thinking about it, but I want to go to Cambry and speak to Orec, to see if it's the same for him. If it's not, then I'm just mad and life can go on.'

'And if it is?'

Tomas swirled the ale in the cup. 'I don't know yet. You can only cross a bog one step at a time.'

'I'm not sure how I'll manage without you being here to sleep and empty the larder.'

'That's hardly fair. I stopped that fight the other night.'

'You mean the fight that you started?'

'Hey, he was being an arsehole. He brought it on himself.'

'Of course.' Erik helped himself to an ale as well. 'So, when are you planning on going?'

'Tomorrow morning. I need to get my gear together.' He quickly finished the ale. 'Put it on my account.'

Erik shook his head as he watched his brother walk away, hoping he'd hidden his relief as well as he'd hoped. That had been the most sober and animated he'd seen Tomas since he'd come back. Having heard the sounds coming from his room on the nights he didn't drink, it'd become harder to judge whether it was kinder to try and keep him from drowning himself in ale and wine every night, or just let him drink himself into a dreamless oblivion. Which may have been a choice on Tomas's part, even if he wasn't entirely aware he was making it.

'Are you the innkeeper?'

Erik looked up at the man standing in front of him. A

stranger, fresh off a few days on horseback if the scent was any way to judge.

'I am. What can I get you?'

'I'm looking for someone. A fugitive. About my height, long black hair going to grey. Carries a baldric of axes and goes by the name of Tomas.'

Erik shrugged. 'We get a fair few woodsmen in here, but none I care to know the names of.'

'He's no woodsman,' the man said, sliding a handful of freshly minted coins across the counter. 'He'd have been riding with two others, an archer and a bearded man named Orec. Carries a longsword.'

'What'd they do?' Erik asked with enough genuine curiosity to mask his hesitation as he poured the rider a cup from the same jug that Tomas had just used.

'Grateful,' the man said, taking a long draught. 'They're wanted for murder and theft. Killed eight good men upriver.' He looked down at the coins and leaned forward. 'There's more where that came from if your information proves good.'

'I'll speak to a few people,' Erik replied, scooping the coins into his purse. 'Where would I find you?'

'We'll be camped near the green, but we'll be about. Spread the word, and let your friends now that any who shelter them will share their crimes.' He finished the ale. 'Thanks for the drink.'

'Good luck,' Erik said after him, conscious of the quiet that had fallen across the room. He looked around, assuring himself that there weren't any others like him, then leaned on the counter. 'So. Has anyone seen such a man?'

He looked at each man in turn, nodding as they shook their heads. The ones he knew would hold their tongues, at least for a while, but there were too many new faces for him to feel entirely reassured. He beckoned to one of the men who were as much of a feature of the inn as the bar counter.

'I'm going to go check the storerooms. Why don't you pour everyone a drink while I'm busy? Wouldn't want them going thirsty.'

'Sure,' he said, a knowing smile creasing his face even further. 'You do that. Best to be safe.'

'What did you do?'

Tomas looked up from his bed as Erik's silhouette filled the door frame. 'Eh?'

'Don't,' Erik said, stepping inside and closing the door. 'There are men in town looking for you, and your sergeant. Asking for you by name.'

Tomas sat up.

'From your expression I take it that this isn't news to you. What have you brought to my doorstep?' He took a fistful of Tomas' shirt and pulled him to his feet. 'They say you're murderers, that you killed eight men.'

'Hold on, hold on. It's not like that.'

'So, what is it like? Explain to me why there are enough men chasing you that they've had to camp on the godsdamned green? That doesn't happen because someone's misunderstood something.'

Tomas pried Erik's hand from his shirt and stepped away to stare out of the window, half expecting to see the provosts gathering outside. Not far off.

'It's a stupid thing,' he said after a moment. 'Some innkeeper tried to rob us. We weren't having it, so there was a scuffle. Someone got killed, and they sent some itinerant provost after us. There was a fight.'

'Gods and stars,' Erik said, leaning against the wall, suddenly exhausted. 'And you killed them.'

Tomas shrugged. 'Well, what were we supposed to do? Go meekly into some lordling's dungeon and beg them not to string us up like geese?' He resisted the urge to spit on the floor. 'Fuck that. I'd do the same thing again.'

'You need to go, Tomas.'

'I just said I was.'

'I mean, now. There were unfamiliar faces downstairs, although I know their kind all too well. They'd sell their own mothers if the price is right, so they'll be singing to those men just as soon they finish the free booze I've just thrown at them.'

'Fine, I'll finish here and go.'

'You'll need to go on foot, through the fields. They'll have riders on the roads.'

'I'll go past—'

'Don't tell me.'

Tomas turned and looked at Erik, who had the good grace to look away. 'You're going to tell them.'

It wasn't a question, and Erik only nodded.

'If I don't, they'll think I'm in on it. It's going to be bad enough already.' He looked out the window but from this side of the inn there really wasn't much chance of seeing the kitchen boy he'd sent to the riders.

'How much time do I have?'

'Not long. Jaspar was to count to two hundred before taking the message, but the boy's no savant.'

Tomas clenched his jaw but didn't give voice to the curse waiting on his tongue. Instead he knelt and began stuffing everything into his pack, no longer bothering to fold or roll it neatly.

'There's a package waiting by the kitchen door. Food and such.'

'Is it poisoned?'

'No more than usual.' Erik yanked the door open. 'Go well, brother.'

Tomas shrugged the pack into place and picked up his axe. The curses were still on the tip of his tongue, but there was a truth in what he'd said and more than that, it was what he would most likely have done had their positions been reversed. Denying everything would only cause more trouble. He paused at the doorway and slapped a hand to Erik's shoulder.

'See you around.' He didn't wait for a reply and made his way down the stairs two at a time. *If only Hayden had shot that bastard.*

He turned at the bottom and made his way through the kitchens, pausing only to add the promised food package and an unattended bottle of wine to his pack. The kitchen opened into an enclosed herb and vegetable garden that was far neater than the appearance of the inn would ever have suggested. He ignored it all and pressed himself the far wall, listening for the sound of anyone waiting on the other side of the gate. He heard nothing out of the ordinary and slipped through, closing it carefully behind him and hurrying along the rutted lane, heading west out of town, a route that would take him into farmland with hedges deep enough to hide him from watching eyes. It was a long and rough detour, but any hunter worth their salt would have men on all the usual paths, and then some, if they had enough manpower with them.

He maintained a steady walking pace as he emerged from the lane and crossed the road it spilled out into. People who ran got noticed. He kept his hood up and head down, trying to make himself look like just another tired tinker carrying his wares to the next road along. The houses quickly became fewer, leaving the western watchtower as the last obstacle for his getaway. It was his first time seeing it, although Erik had told him about it and the arguments it had caused when it was first built; but it was far more impressive than the glorified treehouse he'd imagined. It was built from thick beams and heavily cross braced, and the watch house itself was well designed, with a reinforced viewing platform that went around it fully. It was a strange and incongruous thing, seeing it rising above the outskirts like it did.

He squatted in the lee of a ramshackle hut and watched the guards moving around in the tower. There were only three that he could see, and they didn't seem particularly agitated, which meant that word probably hadn't reached them yet.

Which was good, as all he had to do was not be memorable. He stood and began walking, moving slowly and deliberately, all the while resisting the urge to look back and see if anyone was even watching him. No shouts or horns were raised though, and he crossed onto a track in the fields that would eventually lead him to a small canal where'd he'd turn sharply away from the track, leaving only a few hundred yards of open ground before he reached the lanes and the relative safety that they offered.

He readjusted his pack, tightening it all, and moved his axe back to its usual carrying position. The time for mummery was over. He checked his throwing axes, then began walking, quickly falling into a ground-eating marching pace, not fast, but one that he knew he could maintain for hours.

# CHAPTER SEVENTEEN

CATT COULD FEEL them staring as he walked down the street, greeting everyone he passed with an amiable good morning, or at least a smile. As towns went these days, it looked clean and prosperous, and while the scars that the war had left were still visible, they were healing. He smiled to himself, enjoying the metaphor and making a mental note to use it in his diary that night.

He let his nose guide him to a small eating house next to the bakery, which made it near-perfect in his eyes. The serving girl was quick and polite, and it wasn't long before he had his teeth in a warm pastry. He hardly bothered chewing, letting it dissolve in his mouth before washing each bite down with a sip of hot, sweet tea. There was a storm coming to Cambry, but it wasn't there yet, and perfect moments like this were to be savoured. He resisted the urge to order another treat and instead dusted the flakes from his coat and beckoned to the serving girl.

He paid, then held up an extra coin. 'I wonder if might help with another matter? I'm looking for an old friend,' he said, making the coin walk across the top of his fingers. 'A man named Orec. Do you have any idea where I might find him?'

She looked away from the coin, but he could see the effort that it took her. 'What does he look like?'

'Stocky, with a big beard. He will have just returned home.' He smiled. 'We managed to become separated on the road, you see, and I have some important papers for him.'

She held out her hand. 'I might know something about someone like that.'

He pursed his lips, then put the coin in her palm. 'Do tell.'

She pocketed the coin in a flash. 'Go speak to Max.'

'And who's Max?'

'The baker,' she replied, tilting her chin towards the stone building over the road. 'He knows him too. Perhaps you can all have a nice catchup.'

'I'll do that.'

He finished his tea and, true to his word, headed straight towards the bakery. Unlike some he'd seen, it had a fair sized, purpose-built shop at the front, with shelves that offered delicate looking pastries and sweet cakes alongside the usual array of far less interesting breads. The man serving him was unexpectedly lean, which seemed impossible given the temptations that surrounded him, but he looked amiable enough. It didn't take much to convince himself that it would be easier to start a conversation if he bought something first. Catt paid for a sweet bun then adopted his most disarming smile.

'A good day to you. Might I enquire if you go by Max, by any chance?'

The baker paused and looked at him. 'To my friends, yes. Can I help you?'

'Well, firstly, let me say that these are delicious.' He waved the dusted bun. 'Second, and it's a far more pressing matter, I also need to speak to you about a man named Orec, who I understand you know.'

'Wait outside,' the baker said. 'I'm busy right now.'

Catt did just that, taking the time to enjoy his snack and consoling himself that it was a necessary deceit, rather than the onset of gluttony. He didn't have too long to wait before

Max joined him outside, looking far more imposing without a counter between them.

'So, who're you?' Max asked.

'That's a bit of a long story to relay on the street I'm afraid, but you will need to trust me when I say I have an urgent matter to discuss with your friend Orec. It would be no exaggeration to say that it's a matter of life and death, and I am indeed saying that. I have been led to believe that you will know where I can find him.'

'You're Cheriveni.' It wasn't a question, and Catt simply nodded. 'Which means it's probably about tax or an old fine for walking the wrong way down a street.'

'Technically, so are you,' Catt said, a wry smile pulling at his lips. 'But I'm afraid it's rather more serious than that though.'

'I can't help you.'

'Can't, or won't?' Catt held up his hands to forestall Max's reply. 'Rest assured, I'm not pursuing him. I'm honestly trying to help him, and forgive me for repeating myself, but it really is no exaggeration to say that he's in grave danger.'

'Trust me, Orec can look after himself. Whoever's after him is the one who should be taking warnings.'

'Well, while I'm sure he's very capable fellow, I haven't come all this way because some thug wants to settle some petty score. This is quite serious, Max. It's not only his life that's in danger.'

Max chewed the inside of his lip as he considered Catt, taking in the slightly formal—if outdated—travel suit he wore and the scuffed but well-maintained gear that he carried. As threats went, he looked more like a lawyer forced to visit a rural client against his will, and one that Orec could probably throw into a stream with one hand.

'What did you say your name was?'

'Doctor Catt, to my friends.'

'Well, Doctor, where are you staying?' Now it was the baker's turn to hold up a hand. 'I will speak to Orec, and if he agrees to hear you out, I'll take you to him.'

Catt folded his arms and huffed, largely without really noticing he was doing it.

'Those are my terms, Doctor.'

'Fine, then I suppose I have little option but to accept them. I'll be at whatever the closest inn is, if you would be so kind to point it out. But walk with haste, Max. Every moment you tarry brings Orec a moment closer to disaster.'

Max couldn't help but smile at the older man's dramatic words. 'The Woodsman is that way,' he said, pointing down a side road. 'It's clean. I'll find you there tonight.'

'Where are you going now though?' Catt asked.

'I have a shop, and paying customers to attend to. Good day, sir.'

Catt huffed again as Max vanished back into the shop. He at least he knew now that he was in the right place, so that was progress, but waiting had never been his strong point. And did no one but him understand what urgency meant?

He made his way to the Woodsman and sat down on one of the benches outside, propping his chin in his hand. If Max knew Orec, it made sense that others would too, but he couldn't ask everyone; and if he'd learned anything in his years, it was that strangers asking too many questions in a small town were prone to having accidents. He drummed his fingers on the table, looking down as his fingertips found a groove in it. He looked again, leaning in closer, then smiled and called the serving girl over.

It was a fine, mild evening, and Max took his time on the walk, stopping to greet a few people on the way on to Martina's cottage. *Orec's cottage now*, he corrected himself. He paused at the end of the footpath that led to it, admiring his friend's handiwork. The repairs were visible, even in the half light; the paler wood standing out like the scars that they were. But the cottage looked almost better than it had when Orec had left, and from the look of the new door, a lot sturdier. The front garden had been replanted too, and a few stubborn bees were still circling the freshly planted lavender that bordered it.

The door opened just as he was about to set foot on the patio steps, framing Orec in the light from within.

'Come on in,' Orec said. Somewhere behind him, Martina laughed, and he heard a muffled voice say something in return.

'If you have company, I can make it quick,' Max said.

'You'll want to see this one,' Orec said, ushering him inside. 'In the kitchen.'

Martina had made the kitchen the heart of the cottage, expanding it and creating space for the generously sized table that Orec had carved in the style favoured by the nobility, all curlicues and stylised fronds with forest creatures hidden within. Martina was sat at the table across from a man who he recognised as soon as he turned in his seat.

'Why hello, Max,' Catt said. 'How good to see you again.'

'Oh, you know each other?' Martina said while Max tried to order his thoughts. 'How wonderful!'

'I had the pleasure of making Max's acquaintance this afternoon,' Catt said, turning back to Martina. 'He really does make the most wonderful pastries. I had two just as an excuse to talk to him and my only regret was that our discussion was concluded before a third could be justified.'

'What are you doing here?' Max finally managed, absently handing the breads he'd brought with him to Orec, who only looked amused. 'How did you get here?'

'Your friend is a fine carpenter,' Catt said, running his fingers across the carved leaves that seemed to be growing around the table leg next to him. He tapped his fingers against the leg itself, near a darker bit of carving. 'And like any master craftsman, for that is what he is, and I said that as something of an expert, he takes pride of his work and puts his name to it. People are justifiably proud of knowing craftsmen like that, and are surprisingly willing to talk about them.'

'We were just getting to the why of it,' Orec said, setting the bread down before coming to pour them both a cup of wine. He sat down next to Catt and took a sip. 'Apparently it's a long story,' Orec said. 'And getting to it is just as long. But it's one that we're now going to hear all about.' His tone had cooled as he spoke, going from entirely amiable to threatening with an ease that surprised Max, and made him feel unexpectedly uncomfortable. 'Time to talk, Doctor.'

Catt for his part, seemed entirely oblivious to the not-quite-veiled threat. He sipped his wine, then rubbed his hands and crossed his legs.

'Tell me, sergeant, do your wife and friend know anything of Tulkauth?'

Orec shifted in his chair, largely unaware of the movement or how his knuckles whitened as he gripped his cup.

'What's that?' Martina asked. 'Tool cow?'

'Tulkauth,' Catt corrected her. 'It's a derivative of old Varran, and while I may be mistaken, I believe it would translate to something along the lines of *this marshy valley.* I suspect that some cabal of cartographers agreed that it sounds better if you don't translate it and I think I agree with their sentiment.'

'What of it?' Max asked, glancing across at Orec's now-grim expression.

'Until recent times there was little history written of Tulkauth, and certainly none worth sharing over wine and cheese. I see the question on your lips, so I will save you the asking of it. There was a quite a battle there some six months ago,' Catt said, also turning to Orec. 'Wasn't there, sergeant?'

'There was,' Orec said, not looking up from watching the play of light across the wine he was swirling. 'I led the Fighting Fourth up that valley. And yes, it's very marshy. It slowed us down, and we took a lot of casualties from their archers and skirmishers. We paid for every yard we advanced, but we kept going, and forced them to face us.' He looked up now, and took a drink. 'It was a goddamned stupid plan, we all knew it, but what else could we do?'

'But you won,' Martina said, reaching across to squeeze his hand. 'And now you're home, so what does it all matter?'

'Well, it's in the how of the winning where Orec's story truly starts,' Catt said, watching Orec closely. 'Tell me, do you remember the blow that split the sorcerer's crown?' He nodded as a twitch tugged at the corner of Orec's eye, then looked at Martina. 'Your husband struck down the enemy champion with a single, mighty blow. And yes, you should look as proud as you do, madam. He split the Yogg's head, and the crown he wore upon it. A magical crown, as it happened, and as we have discovered, when you destroy something magical, all the power it has within it releases in a single wave.'

'Meaning what?' Martina asked.

'It exploded,' Orec said. 'White flame burst from it, brighter than the sun. It was the last I saw of it or Tulkauth.'

'I've been there you know,' Catt said. 'It burned everything on the battlefield, and left a crater many times the size of the one down the road here. It turned sand to glass, and melted men and Yorughan like candles so that you couldn't tell where one ended and another began, or even what was metal and what was flesh. It—'

'Enough,' Orec said sharply. 'Get to your point.'

'As you wish. My point is that only you and your three companions walked away from an inferno that defied the laws of nature, sergeant. Scarred, yes, but alive.' Catt folded his arms. 'Some might describe it as a divine miracle, but I believe you were simply in the eye of the proverbial storm. Whatever the reason, the point is this: the crown was recovered from that scorched and no doubt cursed earth, and the creature it was summoning has been loosed.'

'I'm lost,' Max said. 'What creature?'

'Me too,' Martina added.

Catt kept his attention on Orec. 'The sorcerer that you struck down knew they were losing, and was summoning something very dangerous to try and turn the tide. To put it in terms we can all understand, the spell got stuck when you split the crown.' He sipped his wine. 'When the crown was found, it seems that someone may have tried to repair it and the spell became unstuck and was finally released. The creature was finally set loose.'

Orec waved a clearly-agitated Max to silence. 'What does this have to do with me?'

'Don't you see, sergeant?' Catt said. 'It was summoned with one purpose: to kill the sorcerer's enemies. And only the four of you remain.' The lie came out sounding entirely sincere, just as he had rehearsed on the way. To try and explain the extraplanar nature of the creature would have been too much, too soon, for simple soldiers. 'Four last enemies.'

There was a moment of silence as all save Catt set their cups on the table, their brows furrowing.

'Let me understand this,' Orec said. 'You've followed me all this way to warn me that some new creature is tracking me down because it doesn't know the battle, the war, is over?'

'How do we know you're not the creature?' Max ventured, only half-jokingly. 'Or that it's just following you?'

'Firstly, you're mostly correct. That is the essence of the situation.' He turned to Max. 'Do you think the creature stopped on its way to establish a well-reputed legal practice? Or perhaps visit its tailor? No, gentlemen, I'm afraid the threat is very real.'

'I've not seen all the horrors that Orec has, nor what makes his nights so restless, so perhaps I lack the imagination to see what sort of new terror it is you're telling us about,' Martina said, rubbing her knuckles as she leaned forward. 'But the part

I am struggling with is why a well reputed lawyer has traipsed over mountain and valley to tell us this? If it's because of the battle, why hasn't the army come?'

Catt took a sip of wine to buy himself a little time to order his thoughts. 'To the first part, I will admit that a concern for your husband wasn't the reason for my journey. I represent someone who's interested in the creature,' he said. 'And as for the second part, it may be best that you ask your husband that question.'

Orec didn't take the bait and simply watched the exchange, his expression magnificently neutral.

'So, you're being paid to come here? A mercenary then,' she said. 'Who is it that's so interested in this creature?'

'I'm not sure that you appreciate the gravity of the situation, and perhaps that's my fault, at least in part,' Catt said, laying his hands flat on the table and looking across at Orec, who still had his arms folded and an unreadable expression on his face. 'The creature should be your priority. It is quite real, and it is very dangerous. It has tracked you across rivers and hills, and I'm sorry to be the one to tell you this, but it has already taken your young friend, Stefan.'

Orec flinched as if struck then, his arms dropping and his chair scraping and creaking as he pushed himself backwards. Martina's hand found his, anchoring him.

'Say that again?' Orec said.

'I'm sure you heard me well enough. I was with him when it happened.'

The confusion that had played across Orec's face vanished as quickly as it had come, replaced by something darker.

'That's not something to joke about.' His tone was flat.

'I assure you, no part of this is a joke.'

'Where?'

'In the woods, a few miles outside of Pulcek. I met him on the road, in answer to your next question. I arrived as he was leaving.'

'Stef wouldn't leave,' Orec said. 'Not again. You're lying.'

'I am not,' Catt said, indignant. 'He was fleeing the provosts, who had unfortunately arrived before I did. He said it was the same captain who had escaped your ambush.'

Orec's face coloured, but Catt couldn't tell if it was shame or anger. His wife's hand was on his arm again and she was looking up at him, questioning. He didn't say anything right away, only sat back and ran his fingers through his badly cut hair. 'Shit.'

'Orec?' Martina asked. 'What is he talking about?'

He told her of their ambush then, haltingly, and not looking up as his hands idly traced the carvings on the side of the table. She and Max both listened in silence, oblivious to Catt's careful scrutiny of each. 'It was stupid, and we didn't want any part of it. We just wanted to come home.'

With that, he finally looked up, searching Martina's face for any sign of forgiveness or at least, understanding.

'Couldn't you have talked to them?' Max said, his voice loud after Orec's quiet confession. 'Explained the situation?'

'It's not that simple,' Orec said.

'Didn't you even try?' Max persisted. 'Those were eight good men. They also had homes to go back to.'

Orec was on his feet in a flash, leaning across the table, fists clenched and his face inches from Max's.

'Do you think I don't know that? Do you think I wanted that?'

Max flinched away, hands held out. 'I was just—'

'Just what? Just go bake a fucking cake, how's that?'

Orec shrugged off Martina's hand and thumped his way out of the cottage, slamming the door hard enough to make the crockery behind them rattle and Martina gasp.

Catt pursed his lips. 'This simply won't do,' he said, more to himself than them. 'Please excuse me.'

He rose, but now Martina grabbed his wrist.

'Don't. Leave him be, it will pass. He just needs a little time to cool off.'

'I'm afraid he no longer has that luxury, madam.' He gently twisted his arm free and followed after Orec, marvelling that the door still opened and closed without any sign of damage. The light in the small barn was lit, so he let himself in.

Orec spun to face him as he came in. 'Get out.'

Catt ignored his protest and looked around, enjoying the soft scent of sawdust, before focusing on Orec. 'You need to pull yourself together, sergeant. The creature is real.'

'I said, get out.' He took a step towards Catt, knuckles creaking as he clenched his fists.

Catt again ignored the threat and made a show of examining a section of wood on the workbench.

'Stefan spoke very highly of you,' he said. 'I actually had to stop him talking about you to get anything else out of him. His every sentence either started or ended with Orec this and Orec that. He was very fond of you.'

Orec stood where he was, arms hanging at his sides.

'He spoke of you like an older brother. And it was you he was fleeing towards, even now that the war was over and he had gone home.'

'What happened?' Orec's voice was quiet, and rough edged.

Catt leaned against the bench and told him, sparing him no detail of how it had burrowed into and feasted on his innards and bones, but without embellishment. He needed to understand but deserved better than sensationalism.

'I, we, didn't know,' was all Orec said when Catt finished.

'Of course not. How could you? And if it offers any consolation, remember that if the provosts were not pursuing you, then he would have been at home when it struck. I'm sure he would not have wanted that.'

'This creature,' Orec said, stepping into the candlelight and looking down at his hands. 'Can it be killed?'

'Yes, but I have a better idea.'

'No.' Orec's stare was flat and cold. 'It dies.'

* * *

OREC HAD BEEN awake for some time, having eventually fallen asleep sometime in the early hours, exhaustion finally overcoming the hundred or more thoughts ricocheting around inside his head and dragging him into a short but satisfyingly deep sleep. There was a lot that he needed to do, but he was loathe to disturb Martina. Last night's revelations had come at them all thick and fast, undoing the care he'd been taking not to mention anything about the war or her own ordeal since they got back.

Contrary to his expectations, she hadn't shown any signs of being troubled by it, and this morning he had woken with her nestled behind him and her arm over his chest, which he was enjoying it too much to end.

'Good morning,' she finally mumbled.

'Good morning,' he said, still not moving.

'Have I found the secret to stop you thrashing about?'

'Seems like it,' he said, kissing the back of her hand. 'We should try it again, just to check.'

'I'd like that,' she said in a husky voice, her lips brushing the back of his neck, and he definitely enjoyed that far too much. 'Now go. I know you're itching to get up and do something.'

'I could stay here and do something.'

'Ha,' she said, slapping his shoulder. 'Go.'

He sat up and swung his legs from the bed, then quickly dressed. 'I'm going to have another talk with our guest.'

'Try not to break the door this time,' she said, watching him from the bed as he dressed, the light playing across the scars that marred his chest and back. It was very evident that he had other things on his mind, despite his awkward attempt to hide it, and she felt a pang of guilt at how she'd pushed him away.

Again, a voice in her chided. Keep at it and you'll lose him.

She absently hugged the blanket to her and only smiled as he protested against her accusation, as if being able to make another door was an excuse to break it. He closed the bedroom door with exaggerated care, which did make her laugh. He was still a good man, but a troubled one. There was a darkness in him that wasn't there before. It had shown itself a dozen small ways, and she could see him fighting it every day, burying under an unending stream of tasks to be done. But what would happen when all the work that needed doing was done?

Orec wasn't made for guile, and she could see the moments where he became aware of what he was doing as clear as day. He had always been terrible at lying or keeping secrets, but by the same token he was equally terrible at masking things like disappointment and frustration despite his best efforts. And by the gods, she loved him for how hard he was fighting to overcome both.

She shook her head and got out of bed. To sit there and stew in the same circle of thoughts was an invitation to lose herself to the darker thoughts that haunted her mind too, and she had made a promise to herself and the other survivors to never let Dimka win. She grimaced at even the thought of his name, steadying herself against the dresser as her muscles clenched and squirmed within her.

She closed her eyes and remembered his final moments, and the stupid, unbelieving look on his face as Orec rammed the black sword through his head. It was the perfect antidote to her other memories, and she stood a bit straighter for it. She would not have missed that moment for all the pollys in the world.

She dressed quickly and pulled on her shoes. She had a feeling that today was not going to be a good or easy day, but she was surprised to discover that she wasn't afraid of what may come, despite the lawyer's insistence that they were all somehow doomed. If there was any fear, then having Orec standing beside her was the tonic for it. She smiled to herself and headed to the kitchen. She was suddenly ravenous, and a decent breakfast would hold them all in good stead, whatever happened.

CATT WOKE TO the sound of muffled voices and the thump of heavy feet. He lay in the cot for the first few minutes, trying to remember where he was and how he'd gotten himself into this situation. He rose and opened the shutters, taking a deep breath of the fresh morning air, then checked himself for flea or bedbug bites. Satisfied that his fears hadn't come to be realised, he quickly dressed, pleased that he'd had the foresight to bring his travelling bag with him.

*What am I actually doing here?*

'That's a far question,' he muttered. Rather than fleeing, it seemed that the sergeant's first instinct was to hunker down and resist, which was ridiculous, and complicated the job of snaring the beast even further. He'd seen its speed for himself, and he had no illusions about getting more than one chance to nullify it—and that was only if he played his cards right. As much as he hated to admit it, he really wished Fishy was there, even if it would mean enduring a prolonged 'I told you so' speech. Adventures were easy to talk about with wine and the comfort of a good chair, but the reality was that moments of fear and boredom far outnumbered those of any real excitement.

A single rap on his door broke his train of thought and he looked up as Orec leaned into the room.

'Ah good, you're up,' he said. 'Come, we have much to do.'

With that he was gone again, leaving the door open. Catt hung the waistcoat he'd been considering over the chair and followed him into the kitchen, where the sergeant was blowing new life into the small terracotta oven.

'Tell me about how it moves,' he said, not looking at Catt. 'What sort of animal does it put you in mind of?'

'You're going to try and fight it, aren't you?'

'Of course,' Orec said, dusting his hands off as he rose. 'What choice do I have?'

'There are alternatives.' Catt sat down and tried to remain

nonchalant. 'We could trap it. There are parties who would pay handsomely for such a specimen.'

Orec's smirk was almost hidden by his beard, but not quite. 'So now we come to it.'

'I'm not sure I know what you mean?'

'Don't insult me by pretending otherwise, *Doctor.* You said as much last night, You're here for the beast, not us. Stef's death may have been an inconvenience to you, but it's another matter entirely for me.' He looked down at his hands, flexed them. 'I worry for the others. What if it goes to them first?'

'I didn't know where to find the others, so I'm afraid I can't answer that question.'

'I would have died for any of them, and they in turn for me. It came close to that, at least once. We all bear scars that were meant for other men.' He brushed his beard. 'I can't simply sit by and wait. And don't tell me to pray.'

'Who should I tell you to pray to?' Catt said. 'The gods are lost.'

'They were never much help to anyone anyway.'

'You shouldn't say that,' Martina said, walking in.

'I'll say it because it's true,' Orec said. 'The gods are as useless as the Guardians, if not more so.'

'Orec!'

'What? Are you telling me you did not pray?' He tilted his head towards the window, and while the gesture baffled Catt, Martina grimaced as she clearly took his meaning. 'I thought so.'

'Yes, I did, and there's no shame in that. You came.'

'For you, not because some face in a cloud told me to.'

'We really need to focus on the matter at hand. Prayers don't really matter anymore,' Catt interjected. 'The Kinslayer saw to that.'

The seemed to quell the argument, although there was a stony silence for several minutes while Martina busied herself with cutting slices of ham and bread for toasting.

Catt, unable to bear it, filled the silence with a retelling of the myth how man stole the secret of wine from the gods, questioning Orec on whether this was what he was portraying in the carving the along the edge of the table.

He shrugged. 'Vines are easier to carve, and I like wine.'

'So,' Catt sighed. 'Shall we discuss what you're planning to do about the otherworldly creature and the angry provost and his company who are no doubt all on their way here now?'

'After breakfast,' was all that Orec would give him, but he at least went to help Martina and the two of them spoke in quiet tones as they prepared the rest.

The breakfast was simple fare, and enough to feed twice as many, but Orec ate like a bear preparing for its winter sleep.

'Food is strength,' he said over a mouthful of ham when he saw Catt watching him take another piece. When they were eventually done, he sat back and dusted crumbs from his beard. 'I'm done running, Doctor. The beast is flesh and blood, and if it isn't going to stop, then it needs to be stopped.' He smiled at Catt, and there was little humour in it. 'And as for the provosts, well, I just so happen to have a lawyer to help me with that.'

'And while you two clean the plates and dig your holes and whatnot, I'm going to go apologise to Max on your behalf,' Martina said, folding her arms.

'For what?' Orec asked.

'You know full well.'

'What a load of rot,' Orec said. 'He's a grown man, he'll get over it.'

'You need his help.'

'She has a point, Orec,' Catt said. 'You were rather blunt, and another sword would be useful.'

'*She* has a name,' he replied. 'And I suppose he could be useful. But he owes me an apology more than I do him.'

'Honestly,' she said, rising. 'You're both grown men. I wish you'd act like it.'

Orec waited until she'd left before holding his hands up and shaking his head, but Catt remained carefully neutral.

'Come on, lawyer. There's work to be done.'

'WHAT DO YOU think happened here?'

Quental nudged his horse up alongside Armand's and sat looking at the rings of fallen trees.

'War spell, for sure,' he said. 'See how it's cratered there? I reckon whatever it was went off above ground. Anything else would have left a deeper impression.' He whistled softly. 'Wouldn't have liked to have been standing anywhere down there.'

'Seems a bit much for fighting a bunch of clerks and farmers.'

'Maybe. But after Athaln most militias weren't the walkover they used to be. They found their backbone.' Quental dismounted and walked to the edge of the area, then knelt and grabbed a handful of soil. It crumbled in his hands and blew away, fine and dry. 'Nothing's going to grow there until after our grandchildren are grandparents,' he said as he dusted his hands.

They both looked over at the sound of approaching hooves. Two men came riding up, slowing their horses amidst a cloud of the same fine, choking dust. Both fired off crisp salutes as they came to a halt.

'And?'

'It's confirmed, sir. There is a man named Orec, who fits the description on all points.'

The second scout nodded. 'He lives on the edge of town, with just his wife.'

Armand smiled and had to stop himself from clapping his hands. 'Excellent work. We have that bastard now.'

The scouts exchanged a look, one that Quental didn't miss. 'Spit it out,' he said.

'The story, and we heard this from three separate people, is that he singlehandedly rooted out a gang in the woods. Rescued a bunch of kidnapped women, including his wife.'

'So?'

'Local sentiment, sir,' the first scout said. 'Bit of a hero here. There was already some hostility when we asked for his whereabouts.'

The other nodded. 'It's true, sir. I thought the baker was about to pull me from the saddle.'

'You were scared off by a baker?' Armand shook his head. 'Gods and stars, man. Have some pride.'

'Yes sir.'

'Go get the boys up,' Quental said. 'We ride as soon as they're ready.'

'Yes sir,' they said in unison, before wheeling their horses and heading back along the road.

'How do you want to do this?' he asked Armand, looking up at the sky. 'We'd still have daylight if we go now, but not much.'

'We go. If he's been warned, he's more likely to run in the dark.' He stared out along the road, considering. 'Let's keep it simple. Three good shield men to the back, the rest in a fan out front. I'll take the lead.'

'What about the locals?'

'I doubt we'll be there long enough for them to rally. If they do, we'll deal with them. Put two men on the road.'

Quental nodded but didn't give voice to the concerns that he was mulling over. The last thing he wanted to do was see his men dragged into a heated squabble with the townspeople, and the gods help them if any got hurt. Cambry was on the edge of Cheriveni land, but that relative isolation would count for little if word got back that innocent parties had been worked over. Speed would be of the essence.

'They're coming,' Armand said cheerily, adjusting his surcoat and sitting a bit taller in the saddle. 'It's time.'

'Let's get this done.'

They moved out into the road and coaxed their horses into a canter, Armand in the lead while Quental hung back to pass instructions to the men as they caught up.

Armand smiled and took a deep breath of the afternoon air. He'd had his doubts on the road, and although Quental had kept a lid on it, not a few of the men had been grumbling too after so long on such a vague trail. They, like him, would be feeling energised by the prospect of putting an end to it and returning to their base. He indulged himself with the thought of his first visit to a decent bathhouse, all but salivating at the idea.

'I hope you're not counting chickens,' Quental said amidst a jingle of harness as he caught up again.

'Not all of them,' he admitted. 'But I am looking forward to a drink when this is done.'

'Now that's a thought I wholeheartedly support.'

The road curved around a densely vegetated hill that they kept a wary eye on, and then split shortly after, the troop taking the right- hand path. It wasn't long before the cottage came into view and the sight of its cheerful ordinariness woke a bitter anger in Armand. A lone figure was stood in front of it, too small to be their mark. The wife.

'Go,' he said, waving the troop forward, his teeth bared in a savage glee as they charged forward, hooves sending the neatly planted garden flying in a cloud of dark earth and sweet lavender. The woman disappeared into the cottage and the door was slammed shut almost before her foot was fully over the threshold.

The three lead riders dismounted to the side of the cottage and headed around to the back, shields and axes in hand. Three more kicked their way into the oversized shed and the remainder took up position around Armand, arrows nocked to their small but powerful short bows. There was no shouting or barging into each other, only an efficient ordering of the troop and a glance was enough to confirm Quental's obvious pride in the smooth operation. Armand stepped forward and threw his cloak back.

'Orec, known as Blackblade! You are bound by law for wilful murder,' he called out, his voice strong and true. 'Come out, and let justice be done upon you.'

There was no reply, but then none of them had ever imagined that he would simply surrender. It had to be done, though.

'Looks sturdy,' Quental offered. 'It's going to take a while to chop through that.'

Armand grunted. 'Shame it's only made of wood then. I'm not risking any of our men trying to get in. Let's get some oil and kindling.'

'I like where your thoughts are going.' Quental looked over his shoulder. 'You heard him. Smash that fence up, and check the barn for extra lamps or oil.'

A pair of the shutters on the ground floor swung open as one of the riders set to work on the fence. Three bows swung towards the window but Armand waved them down.

'A word please, captain?' called a voice with a light northern accent.

'Who is that?' Armand called back. 'Is that you, Blackblade?'

'I'm afraid not, captain. I'm assuming you're a captain, although I've never actually spoken to one before. That I know of, obviously.'

'And who're you?'

'Doctor Catt, at your service. And before you ask, I am in fact his lawyer.'

Armand looked at Quental, who looked equally taken aback.

'Then I suggest you tell him to come out before we drag him out.'

'I'd like to review the proposed charges and your reason for suspecting my client before commencing any discussions regarding the terms of a possible surrender and guarantees of safe passage.'

'Buying time,' muttered Quental, earning a considered nod from Armand. 'Most likely for the townies.'

'You heard me well enough. Eight murders. He's still under oath and bound to martial law.' Armand stepped forward. 'Tell me, *Doctor,* what rank do you hold?'

'Sergeant Blackblade was a member of an official militia, and has fulfilled and discharged the condition of his oath, but I'll get to that presently. But captain, on another matter, I must tell you that you're all in grave danger and need to leave the area right now. I give you my word that Sergeant Blackblade will present a full statement at an address of your choosing as soon as the present danger has been contained.'

Quental and several of the others chuckled behind him.

'You'll need to try harder than that.' He waved the riders with the wood forward. 'If that curtain moves, shoot,' he said to the archers.

The men moved forward and unceremoniously dumped the splintered wood in front of the door, kicking it right up against it before emptying a clay pot over it all.

'What are you doing?' called the lawyer. 'This is private property held on personal title and there is no martial law in force. As such, you have no right to damage or trespass therein. I must insist that you withdraw and expect a claim for damages.'

'Ever opened a beehive?' Armand replied, almost conversationally. 'You need a bit of smoke if you're to avoid a bunch of annoying little pricks.'

On the porch, the rider scraped flint and steel, caught it on a bed of dried moss, then coaxed it into a hungry flame. He looked to Armand, then placed it amongst the wood and stepped back. Smoke curled upwards behind him, first light in colour, but then darkening as it found the lamp oil.

A woman's voice could be heard as the shutters swung closed, an arrow slamming into them a moment too late, eliciting a yelp from inside.

'And now we wait,' Armand said.

'And if the mob arrives?'

'Then they get the same speech, and a couple of arrows. A mob only works if there are no personal repercussions. Make them remember they're individuals and you deflate them faster than a jester's bladder.'

'In the legs? It won't sit well, killing civilians.'

'That would do it, I believe.' He looked around. 'We may be here for a little longer than expected, so let's get some of that timber spread out. It's not much but it could slow them down a bit.'

'Of course,' Quental said, which was what he always said when he didn't entirely agree with an order. A few planks might trip the careless up at night, but doing it now took the focus off the mission at hand, and making it look like they were settling in for a longer time would probably encourage those inside. He didn't say any of this, though, because having an argument with the officer in charge would create a far worse impression.

'THEY'VE SET THE door on fire!' Martina shouted, not letting go of Orec's shirt. 'Can't you smell it?'

'Gods and stars, Martina,' he said, prising her hands loose as gently as he could. 'It's just outside. The door isn't on fire.'

'Yet,' Catt added helpfully, earning a filthy look from Orec.

'It's unseasoned wood, so it's going to smoke a bit but we've got time.'

'Time for what? There's so many of them.' She turned away from him. 'We should have left.'

'You did really well, coming back so fast with the warning,' he said, pulling her into an embrace and stroking her as she leaned into him. 'But we couldn't outrun cavalry, so we're safer inside for now.'

'I'll pour another jug under the door,' Catt said as they stood there quietly, quickly making his way back to the kitchen, where he took the opportunity to slump onto one of the benches and rest his head in his hands. This mess wasn't what he'd expected, nor wanted, and quite honestly he just wanted to go home and forget about it all.

*So, what did you expect?* He could hear Fisher's voice perfectly, and even visualise the cocked eyebrow as he said it. *That it would walk meekly into your cage and be carried off like a wayward house cat? Remember why you're doing this.*

He rubbed his face, wincing at the feel of the stubble that was emerging, then filled the jug from the crank handle and carried it back to the door. Martina had left and Orec was carefully peering through the slats in the shutters, his heavy black sword on the table next to him.

'Pour it on the door,' he said, not moving.

Catt did as he asked, then set the jug down next to the sword. 'Can you see what they're up to?'

'Putting up some sort of barricade on the path,' Orec said. 'I've been trying to straighten that wood for days and those bastards are just dumping it in the mud.'

'Is this your sword?' Catt asked, wincing as the words came out of his mouth. Orec didn't dignify it with an answer, which was worse. 'May I pick it up?'

The soldier glanced over at him, giving the smallest nod. 'Don't touch the blade.'

There was a small snapping sound as he touched it, like when he dragged his feet over the rugs, making him flinch. The sting faded quickly and he lifted the sword from the table, impressed by how light and well balanced it was, compared to how it looked, which was like nothing more than an overgrown cleaver that had seen too much use. He took it in the two-handed grip it was meant for and moved it through a block and counterblow, impressed both by how natural it felt and that he hadn't hacked a divot out of the furniture.

'Remarkable,' he said, setting it down again and leaning closer to the blade with an appraiser's eye. 'I thought it crude, but this is simply a classic design, and the blade is quite striking. Did you take it from a museum? It's not an accusation, by the way. I do some trade in antiquities.'

'What's remarkable is that you didn't cut your own leg with that overhead nonsense.' Orec turned the sword over and tapped a section with his fingernail. 'It was bequeathed to me, you might say.'

Catt only grunted as he peered at the faint sigils that Orec had pointed at. They must have been little more than hair thin to start with, and years of polishing and rubbing inside of scabbards hadn't been kind to them. 'They almost look like Tzarkoman hieroglyphs, but that's hardly likely, is it?' He straightened. 'Now that's more the sort of mystery that I like. Where did you say you got it?'

'That will need to wait. We can't stay in here,' Orec said. 'The smoke's already doing its work.'

'Do you think your friend will bring help?'

'Who, Max?' Orec smiled mirthlessly. 'Perhaps. At least in time to save Martina.'

'How do you mean?'

'Never mind that.' He waved the question away. 'The rear door is my best bet. There are three, maybe four out there, I think, so better odds.'

'Horsemen, remember?'

'About a quarter mile out that way the path gives way to rocky scrambles into the valley that won't do for horses. It's nearly dark, so they'll not find me, not even if they had dogs.'

'So,' Catt said, looking up from the sword, 'you would only need to fight your way through four men, and then outrun a dozen horses for, say, half a mile?'

That earned him a momentary glare. 'Fair. We need a distraction, something to keep those horses right where they are.'

'Why are you looking at me? I'm not about to attack anyone, even if I knew where to start. That archer nearly took my eye out, you know.' He straightened. 'And there's still the question of the beast. Even if you get away, it will find you.'

'One problem at a time.'

'Quite honestly I'm not sure that we have that luxury.'

'So, what's your idea then?' Orec growled. When Catt didn't reply, he shook his head. 'Thought so. You remind me of Tomas. A bit gloomy, and always finding problems, never solutions.'

Orec smiled at the idea of him throwing Catt out of the door halfway through his story, but it faded swiftly. The truth of it was that he didn't have anything more than running away to offer. This was his home and he just wanted to stay there, but the provosts weren't going anywhere without his head in a noose. He felt the anger rising inside him, sudden and swift, not the grumbling anger that dogged him most days but the pure, forge like heat that took him into battle, and it was so very tempting to surrender to it. To make everything simple again.

'Orec.' Catt's voice. 'Orec, look.'

He looked across at Catt, teeth clenched as he fought to keep his reason. His gaze followed Catt's arm and pointed finger to where his fist had closed around the hilt of his sword, something he didn't remember doing. An angry retort was forming on his tongue when he saw a filament of vibrant purple light flicker across the dark metal, leaping along it in diminishing arcs before vanishing.

'It's here.'

# CHAPTER EIGHTEEN

OREC LET GO of the sword and took a half step away from it. *That purple light*. It was the colour of his dreams, and the last thing he saw before he woke gasping and sweating in the deep watches of the night.

He felt a ghost of that same terrible fear and confusion upon him now, because if that was real, then his dreams were surely more than just the ramblings of his fevered mind. He fell into a chair and nearly out of it again, and rubbed his face, grinding his palms into his eyes until the dark was replaced by a sea of lights.

He let them fade again before sitting back and folding his arms.

'Any ideas?'

Catt, who was seated across from him with a concerned look on his face, simply shook his head. Orec hadn't expected much from him, not after his disastrous and most half-hearted attempt to stymie them with his 'I'm his lawyer' stunt.

'Maybe we'll get lucky and it'll eat them. That'll simplify things.'

'Well, I don't think it feeds like a normal animal. You see the—'

'No,' Orec said, cutting him off. 'The problem is *I do see.* I see it every other night, when it vies with everything else in my head to torture my sleep.' He tapped his forehead. 'It's in here, it and that goddamned light. It kills because it enjoys killing.' He smirked at the look on Catt's face. 'Do you think his sorcerers would do all of that to bring them into our world if they weren't steeped in violence and misery, like every other damned thing they touched?'

'Sorry, but did you say that you see it?'

Orec tapped the hand guard of the sword and watched it rock back and forth. 'I am it,' he said in a quiet tone. 'I see through its eyes, and can do nothing but watch it stalk and kill.' He sank deeper into the chair. 'I dreamed of Hayden three nights ago.'

'Oh,' Catt said. 'I am sorry, truly. Forgive me for being so bold, but might I ask about the nature of the dream?'

'He was camping. Gods, that man hated being indoors,' Orec continued, a smile pulling at his beard, swiftly gone. 'You could offer him a palace and he'd ask if it had a garden so he could pitch a tent. But a roof wouldn't have saved him anyway. You say it took Stef swiftly, but it didn't offer the same to him.'

Catt was staring at him now, and for once it didn't look like he was wishing he was somewhere else.

'It toyed with him. Ripped the sides of his tent and drove him out, then pounced and ran, time and time again, like a bored cat playing with a mouse. Eventually it cut his spine.' He rocked the sword again, and watched it as he spoke. 'He could do nothing as it began.'

When he did look up, Martina was standing in the doorway behind Catt, her hand over her mouth.

'Oh, Orec,' she said. 'You should have told me.'

'How could I?' he said. 'How could I explain that? You already think me some kind of monster.'

'I don't!' she said, rushing forward and kneeling beside him, her hands finding his. 'Never. Not for a moment.'

He looked at her, and she prayed that he took the colouring

of her cheeks for something other than the shame she felt for the lies that were coming so easily to her. For a moment then he smiled too, but it was his old smile, the one that reached his eyes as if all him were smiling, not the swift half-grimace he managed to conjure once a day as a greeting.

'Truly?' he asked, squeezing her hands back and nearly making her gasp at the strength in them. Before she could reply there was a sharp pop and she flinched away as an arc of violet light leapt from Orec's hand. He let her go and she fell backwards, rubbing at the back of her hand.

'Go to the bedroom,' he said, rising and taking up his sword. 'Bar the door. It's here for me, so I'll try and draw it off.'

'And what about me?' Catt asked.

'You're the expert, so you stay close to me. We—'

Martina stepped between them and, rising to her toes, pulled Orec into a long kiss that nearly made him drop his sword. She sank back down and embraced him, head on his chest, and now he did drop the sword back onto the table and return the embrace.

'Be careful,' she said quietly. 'I can't lose you again.'

He kissed the top of her head and she felt the knot that she carried inside her shift and fray. She held him even tighter, suddenly afraid of the seething emotions that it held bound within her, and desperate for the security that his arms offered.

Neither wanted the moment to end, but a sudden, piercing scream from the backyard took that decision from them.

Orec released her and reluctantly pushed her arms away. 'You must go,' he said as gently as he could. 'Please.'

'Be careful,' she repeated, as surprised by her tears as he was before she turned and ran back towards the bedroom. He'd fitted bars to each of the internal doors too, and she dropped this into place now, loud enough for him to hear. Hiding felt like a betrayal, but she would only be in the way and she had no appetite to see any more death, or perhaps more truly, to see the other Orec again. The one who made her feel safe with one breath and scared her witless with the next.

She flinched as the scream came again, weaker now, and accompanied by the sound of men shouting. She reached under the pillow and brought out the knife she'd taken from Dimka's ruined body, tugging the blade free from the sheath and holding it in both hands, the solidity of it reassuring.

'THE ROAD'S STILL clear,' Quental said, sitting down alongside Armand on the bench they'd dragged from the barn. 'I've sent a man up the hill. If they do come, they'll have torches or lanterns, so we'll see them easily enough.'

'Good idea,' Armand said around a mouthful of apple. It had been in his saddlebag for weeks and was finally wrinkled and soft, the way he liked it, and tasted like honey. 'We've another fire going at the rear door, and it's working. I reckon we'll crack this nut before midnight.'

'Suits me. Are we clear to start a cooking fire then?'

'Might as well. As long as Ballan isn't cooking that godawful sludge again.'

Quental grinned. 'You mean his famous stew?'

'More like infamous,' Armand said, snorting. Everyone complained about the food, but no one else ever volunteered to prepare the evening meal. The only positive thing he could say about it was that it made anything that an inn served them taste that much better. 'We should be arresting him as well.'

'Who knows, maybe he'll add seasoning this time,' Quental said over his shoulder.

'My kingdom for a pinch of salt,' Armand called after him. He licked his fingers and wiped them on the hem of his shirt as he stood. Everything was finally coming together, and by morning they'd have Blackblade trussed up like a bug in a spider's web. It would be a long ride back and they'd make better time if they simply strung him up here, but Armand was no savage. Blackblade would be sentenced before a court and then hung properly, surrounded by the friends and comrades of the men he'd butchered so that the last thing he heard would be their curses.

The thought was almost as warming as the brandy waiting in his saddlebag, but before he could do more than think about fetching it, a terrible scream came from the rear of the house, sharp and sudden.

Quental, the gods bless the man, broke into a run almost mid-stride, and two of the other riders followed him a moment later.

'Get those damned torches lit!' Armand called to the others, silently cursing them for not thinking of it earlier. He turned to the two archers. 'Watch the windows. You nail that bastard if you see him.'

He was at the side of the house when the scream came again, weaker this time. He pushed past two of the riders and found himself standing over one of the younger men who was sprawled in the grass, pale hands desperately trying to stop the rest of his guts snaking out from the raw gash across his stomach.

'Oh gods,' the man screamed, his voice rising. 'It hurts! Gods, help me.'

Quental looked across and shook his head, and Armand felt his own gut turn. The smell confirmed the sergeant's opinion moments later. Gut wounds like that were terrible enough, and a skilled surgeon could save a man, but not when the guts themselves had been split.

'Who did this?' Armand asked, dropping to a knee and turning the man's face away from the wound. 'Who did this?'

'Didn't see,' he half sobbed. 'The s-shadows, oh gods it hurts, the shadows came to life.'

'We'll get it, don't worry.' He looked up at the men standing over them. 'Go to your posts. Now.'

They lingered for a moment, saying their own silent goodbyes, then walked away in a grim silence. He nodded to Quental before turning back to the injured man.

'Hey now, we'll get you fixed up. You're going to be fine.' He didn't look away from the man as Quental knelt behind him. 'Look at me, son. You're going to be fine.'

He looked up at Armand just as the blade went into the back of his head. His eyes widened, and then he was gone, a long breath escaping his still-trembling body.

Quental pulled the knife out and sat there looking at the body. 'No one saw anything. The door didn't open.'

'Well he didn't bloody well do it to himself.' He stared down at the man. 'The shadows. What the hell does that even mean?'

'Help me move him,' Quental said. 'We can put him in the barn for now.'

Armand hesitated, but only until he saw the grim look on Quental's face. He nodded to the sergeant, who unceremoniously pushed the man's spilt guts back into his middle and roughly tied the ends of his cloak over the mess. There was something about the wet sound of it that brought a sour taste to Armand's mouth and forced him to focus on his breathing so as not to empty his own gut across the body, an act which he knew would be unforgivable in front of the stony-faced sergeant.

They lifted him, grunting under the weight, and had gone perhaps ten steps towards it when the man on guard outside fell to the ground, his legs folding beneath him as if he were too heavy for them to bear. He seemed surprised as he toppled and didn't even think to let go of his sword or the torch he held as he hit the ground.

The torch swung wildly as the fallen man sat up, his stunned expression clear to Armand as he stared at his boots, which were still standing by themselves, the nub of the severed bones within stark against the red flesh that surrounded them.

When he was a child, Armand had seen an unwary rabbit's legs crushed by a passing cart, and the sound of its screams had put him off meat for years afterwards. The scream that came from the man was like that now, inhuman and piercing, and pure in its terror.

Armand glanced at Quental and they both dropped the body they'd been carrying so solemnly a moment before. Across from them the fallen man was clutching the gushing stumps of his legs, his face growing visibly paler with each spurt. Then he keeled sideways and was still, eyes open and staring at nothing.

Behind him, the darkness seemed to shift and swell, solidifying into sharp angles under the diffuse torchlight. If it made any sound, it was lost to the man's screams.

Quental saw it too, and reached for his sword. The blade had almost cleared the scabbard when the creature launched itself at him, its legs kicking divots of dirt away under it as it threw itself forward, the impact sending a shower of purple sparks into the air and the impact throwing the sergeant backwards as if he weighed no more than a child.

Long, curved claws raked his armour, tearing away handfuls of the iron rings with flashes of purple light on every pass, and found flesh before Armand could even think to draw his own weapon. The claws ripped into the sergeant's exposed chest and tore handfuls of flesh away as if he were nothing more than wet clay. Quental stabbed at it, having somehow managed to draw one of his knives, but to little effect.

For Armand, it seemed as if time had slowed down. He could feel himself moving forward, his sword levelled, desperately trying to drive it forward before those claws could land again, but he was too slow. He watched as they punched into Quental's breastbone, then flexed and threw his chest open, exposing the slick, undulating organs within.

And then time found him again and his blade caught it with a blow that would have skewered a man's head. The creature flinched away as if he'd done nothing more than slap it, and he quailed as its molten eyes turned to him. A strange chirruping noise came from it, and then it was gone again, powerful legs launching it across the yard and into the waiting dark.

New torchlight flooded the area as others came rushing up, slowing to a uncertain walk as they saw the two men lying dead, and Quental sprawled on the ground before them with his gleaming organs and still-labouring lungs visible to all. One of them threw his torch aside and dropped to his knees alongside Quental, pressing the hilt of the dying man's sword into his grasping fingers. The sergeant, who hadn't screamed once, closed his eyes in gratitude as if this was all he had been waiting for and, with one final spasm, his lungs deflated for the last time.

One of the men standing near his feet staggered away and emptied his guts onto the lawn.

'What the fuck is going on? Sir?' asked the man who'd given the dying sergeant his sword. Alsan was an older man and a sergeant too, but had always been content to follow Quental's lead without protest, an attitude which to Armand had always smacked of indifference. He'd never liked the man, and he certainly wasn't keen on his tone.

'What does it look like?' he snapped back. 'Blackblade has let some sort of creature loose. Get the men together. We're going into that house and ending this.'

Alsan stood and bent his arm in his best imitation of a salute. 'You three to the rear, and stay together. Two men with axes on that door, the others keep those torches up. Go.'

Armand straightened and saluted the dead sergeant before turning back to the house. 'Right lads. Let's go get this bastard.'

'HERE,' CATT SAID, beckoning Orec over to the shutters he was pressed up against. 'They're standing over someone.'

Orec bent the slat in front of them and peered out into the dark. There were at least half a dozen men standing over an unmoving figure, with another two bodies lying motionless to one side and the other. Two of the soldiers were talking, and it didn't look friendly. Soon after the group split into two and headed towards the front and rear, both moving with purpose.

'They're coming in,' he said, releasing the slat. 'Get ready.'

Even as the words were leaving his mouth they heard the sound of something hammer into the door, then another, as the men outside adopted a rhythm with their axes. Orec grimaced at the sound of the wood cracking. He hadn't had time to make new doors from scratch and had shored up the broken doors with what he'd had to hand. They were better than they had been, but still no match for heavy axes.

'Where are you going?' he called after Catt, who didn't even turn around before vanishing into the spare room. He half-expected the door to slam shut behind him, but it remained ajar, which—if he was totally honest—was more than he'd expected. The lawyer, or whatever he really was, had no place here, and would either get in the way or get killed in short order when the fighting started. And it would start, for he had no intention of giving up and going to his death meek as a lamb.

He rolled his shoulders and neck, loosening them up, then checked his weapons. The sword would be good for the first one or two through the door, but then it would be knife work, close and bloody. The familiar fear and excitement was settling on him now, making his heart race and his gut squirm uncomfortably. Some men never made it through that stage and would stand there, pale and palsied until they were cut down. He almost hadn't escaped it the first time he'd gone into a life or death fight, and it was only the deep roll of the battle drums that had saved him, a steady beat that forced itself into heads and hearts until they were all crashing their spears or swords into their shields and chanting in time to it. It had broken fear's grip, and even though the chaos that followed had nearly been overwhelming, it was still better than the despair that had so nearly seduced him.

A knife fight was a terrible thing, but so be it. This was his home and his life, and anyone who came for either would have to win it from him.

'Come on,' he growled at the door.

A thump and scrape on the ceiling answered him and he swore again. He hadn't expected them to try that. Admittedly, the roof of the cottage wasn't particularly high, but neither were the eaves, and anyone climbing through the roof would be forced to their hands and knees and so unable to bring any leverage to the boards, leaving them no option but to move to the one point of access. He moved to the kitchen doorway and looked up as the panel there slid back.

He drew back the sword and prepared to thrust it upward.

'Nice place you've got here,' a voice said from the darkness above him. 'You mind putting that thing down?'

He lowered the sword, more out of confusion than anything else. 'Tomas?'

A pair of boots came out of the hatch, followed in short order by the rest of the axe man and a shower of dirt and dust that forced them back into the front room.

'What the fuck are you doing in my roof?'

'I just like watching you sleep,' Tomas replied, then thumped Orec on the shoulder when he stared at him in confusion. 'For these bastards,' he said, nodding towards the door. 'They came crawling up to the inn, so I figured they'd be carrying torch for you too.'

'You're mad,' Orec said, pulling him into an embrace and slapping his back hard enough to send another cloud of dust into the air. 'But I'm glad to see you.'

As he spoke, a sharp crack sounded from the back door. Unlike the front, he hadn't had a chance to do more than fit a slightly heavier bar to it, and it would be the first to give way. It was a narrower entrance, though, and anyone coming through it would be hemmed in by shoulder-high shelves on their right for the first few steps. It would hold them up and make the defence a little easier, at least until they pushed past the counter and into the kitchen proper.

Tomas stepped back and pulled out an axe of his own as Orec took up a position at the end of the counter.

'There's a weird kind of lion or something out there,' he said, almost conversationally. 'It took down two of their men. Pulled them away from their perimeter so I hopped up on to the little shed at the side and onto the roof from there.'

'It's a something, not a lion,' Orec said. 'And it's here for us, not them.'

Another crack came, louder, followed by the squeal of someone working an axe head back and forth.

'How do you mean?'

'Ask him,' Orec said, jabbing a thumb over his shoulder towards Catt, who had emerged from his room again, now wearing a bulky leather jacket with matching gloves, and holding a rod of some sort with what looked like a meat fork at one end.

Tomas stared at him, forehead creased and mouth open.

'You must be Tomas,' Catt said, holding out a gloved hand. 'A pleasure to meet you, despite the circumstances.'

Tomas stared at his hand, and then back at him. 'Who're you?'

'I'm his lawyer.'

'Long story,' Orec interjected. 'But he's here for the thing outside.'

Half of the kitchen door gave way with a crash and a single upwards stroke of an axe sent the bar tumbling away. The man who'd cleared it filled the doorway, switching his axe to his left hand as his shoulder scraped the shelves. Orec didn't wait for another chance and brought his sword chopping down at an angle, the dark blade shearing through the man's wrist and deep into his unprotected neck. Blood exploded from the wound, painting the ceiling and wall as the stricken man turned under the blow and fell to his knees, trying to staunch the flow with a hand that was no longer there.

An unseen arrow cut a burning line across Orec's cheek and slammed into the wall behind him, and then another man was forcing his way in, a short sword in one hand and a small shield in the other. Orec swung again as the soldier stepped over his fallen comrade, but the shield came up and his blade was knocked wide. He skipped back as the lunge came through, low, aiming for his groin. He rolled his wrists, turning the sword and bringing it chopping down across the soldier's forearm as he withdrew for another lunge. There wasn't enough behind the blow to break anything, but it drew a sharp curse. His attacker lunged again, his bleeding arm covered by the shield now, forcing Orec back again.

'Down.' The command came from behind Orec and he dropped low with no hesitation.

If the man was surprised to see Tomas, he didn't get a chance to show it before the throwing axe smashed into his face. Any thought of attack or defence was forgotten as he staggered backward, a hoarse cry bursting from him. Orec took a step forward and kicked him squarely in the chest, sending him heels over head as he tripped over the fallen man, ruining whatever shot the archer outside might have had.

The front door splintered as Orec was probing the seeping gash on his cheek, grateful that it wasn't above his eye and blinding him. Tomas darted back towards the noise, a hatchet in each hand, and Orec swore. He risked a look outside, trying to spot the archer, but there was only a dark shape sprawled next to a fallen, guttering torch.

The space between that sputtering torch and the door was a band of unbroken darkness. He peered around the doorframe, wary of arrows, but the yard was quiet, the only sounds coming from the room behind him. He edged forward, and saw another body laying sprawled amongst the cooking herbs, unmoving and silent.

The flickering light of the torch vanished in a stroke, plunging the yard into darkness. He flinched backwards, and heard a chirping noise from the band of darkness in front of him. A ripple of light surged along the length of the sword and arced away from the tip, disappearing into that same deep shadow.

He tightened his grip and took a careful step backwards into the house as the darkness shifted and began taking on form, like an inky blanket slowly being draped across an angular frame. It was only when its eyes lit with a golden light that he could really make sense of the shape, and even then it was wrong in ways he couldn't explain. It took a step forward, then another. Painless arcs of light flickered along his arms and back along the sword, growing in brightness as the creature stalked towards him, body held low between raised haunches and its tail whipping back and forth.

Orec moved backwards, his foot hitting the dying man who Tomas had dropped. He gurgled as Orec stepped over him, spitting his last words, and then his eyes rolled to the whites. It had barely been a second to glance that way, but when Orec looked up again, the creature was gone. The swordsman shook his head and then raced to the front room, where Tomas was bellowing obscenities.

The axe man was stood near the door, holding the soldiers at bay with wild swings, the hatchets either abandoned or thrown. The lawyer was to his side, his rod now the length of a javelin and the tip crackling with its own energies. One of the attackers was down in the doorway, making the entry difficult even without Tomas' energetic defence.

The attackers surged forward again then, the man in the doorway covering himself with a shield as his fellows helped push him forward. It was a desperate gambit and Tomas moved quickly, reversing his axe and hooking the blade over the rim of the shield and pulling it away from the soldier's body.

Catt jabbed his rod forward into the opening this created and the man gave a garbled scream as the energy in the tip was released. He stiffened and fell as Catt pulled the rod back, and in that moment neither of them saw the spear until it was too late.

It plunged into Tomas' side just above his hip and came out red. He staggered back, leg already stiffening and the spear shot forward again, this time fouling in his chainmail but still striking him hard enough to send him reeling backwards.

Orec managed to knock he shaft away before they could finish him, but by then it was too late to stop them surging into the cottage. Catt all but threw himself backwards to avoid a probing sword, the end of his rod connecting with the floor and spinning from his hands. The provost's men crowded forward, and Catt scrabbled back until his back hit the wall, raising his hands as a sword hovered over his head.

'Drop it,' another of them snarled, his sword levelled at Orec.

Orec knew it would be an easy matter to knock that sword away and take the man's hand with it, and he knew he could get another with the reverse, but the bloody spear and another two swords were in striking range. He knew his chances were vanishing with every heartbeat, but if he could win some space he still had a chance. Surrender would be the same as slipping the noose around his own neck. Even as Orec tightened his grip on the sword and readied himself for the final attack, a dark and glistening form sprang onto the porch, as yet unseen by any in the cottage.

One of the soldiers was knelt in the doorway, trying to rouse the man that Catt had dropped, when it landed behind him. He turned at the sound, but its jaws closed on the back of the neck and then it was shaking him like a terrier would a rat, that same purple light leaping across his body. He had no time to scream before his neck cracked under the terrible power of its jaws.

THE PROVOST'S MEN turned at the sound of their comrade's garbled scream, incomprehension slowing their reactions. The creature flung the stricken man away in a spray of blood and leapt away a moment before the spearman could release his weapon.

The provost captain spun to face Orec, extending his sword until the point hovered scant inches from Orec's neck, the blade steady. Behind him the spearman took up position near the door, holding his spear like a fisherman.

'Call it off,' the captain snarled. 'Or I swear to whatever god is still listening, I will make you and your wife beg for death before morning.'

'It's not mine,' Orec replied, stepping over Tomas, who was slowly dragging himself away, hands pressed to the wound in his side.

'Last chance,' the captain said. 'Call it off.'

'It's not his I can assure you of that, Captain,' Catt said from across the room, keeping himself as far from the sword levelled at him as the walls allowed. 'I can attest to that. You see, I have—'

'Drop your sword, Blackblade,' the captain said, not even glancing in Catt's direction. 'You've killed enough good men. It's over.'

Orec's sword wavered. It would be better to die here and now than choking at the end of a rope, but from the look of him, the provost captain wouldn't be beyond keeping his threats. He'd dragged Martina into this by coming here, and in the captain's eyes she'd made herself guilty by not throwing Orec to the law. Whether she knew of his guilt from the outset or not would not matter, and he didn't need some overdressed lawyer to tell him that. He glanced down at Tomas, who lay propped against the wall, hands red and his face almost as pale as his gritted teeth.

He flinched as something moved in his peripheral vision, but he was too late. One of the captain's men had launched himself forward as soon as Orec looked away and hit him shoulder first in the gut, arms wrapping around Orec's legs and tipping him over. He tripped backwards and landed heavily onto his back, cursing with what breath he had left. There was little time to do anything before the captain's sword touched the skin of his throat, stilling his struggle at a stroke.

'You're mine now, you bastard,' he said.

Orec held his breath as he felt the point move to press against the soft skin under his jaw. He felt it break the skin, and the hot trail of his own blood snaking over his neck. The captain's sneer was a hungry one, and he could see the battle between desire and duty raging within the man. He kept still and closed his eyes. It was easier to kill a struggling man than a meek one. For several long moments the sword remained where it was, burning like a hot coal pressed to his neck, and he wondered what it would feel like when it went through him. He'd seen men have their throats torn out and their passing had been neither dignified nor painless, and he could only hope that it severed his spine and saved him from that kind of terrible gasping and thrashing.

The pain flashed once more, and then the awful pressure was gone. He opened his eyes as the captain spoke.

'Bind them,' he said, looking as if the words left a foul taste. 'If either so much as looks at you, cut their throats. Alsan, help me block these doors.'

'Sir,' the spearman said, setting his weapon down.

Orec watched them tie his hands with a strangely detached misery, while the others hastily tipped the tables over to form a crude barricade to both the front and rear doors. He felt defeated and tired, so terribly tired, and the anger and need to fight back had dimmed within him, replaced by a desire to simply get it all over with. Nothing that he had thought he was fighting for was as it seemed anymore, and the last of his only true friends was bleeding out next to him.

'Looks like you just found a turd in your dumplings,' Tomas said as Orec looked over at him.

His first instinct was to shrug, but the man was dying and deserved a reply, even if it took him a few moments to muster the energy to do it.

'Feels a bit like it,' he managed.

He looked across as Catt twisted away from the man who was attempting to bind him.

'Just let me try help him,' he was saying. 'We're not going anywhere.'

The soldier had his knife drawn, and looked to the captain as Catt spoke, arm poised to strike. Orec was surprised by how pleased he felt when the captain shook his head.

'Let him try,' he said as he passed by to the front shutters.

The man gave Catt a surly look as he lowered the knife and stepped away, leaving Catt to scuttle over to Tomas.

'Thought you were a lawyer,' he said as Catt rolled his sleeves up and buttoned them in place.

'I am,' he replied. 'But one can wear many hats in this life. Biology has always been more of a hobby, if I'm honest. Fascinating stuff. I tried taxidermy once, but I really didn't care for all those little glass eyes. Now, move your hands.'

'Now who's found that turd,' Orec said, finding a smile at the filthy look Tomas shot him.

Catt pulled a small folding knife from his pocket and quickly cut Tomas' tunic away, revealing a neat but steadily bleeding wound.

'I'm afraid this will hurt a great deal,' Catt said, slipping his finger into the wound.

Tomas grabbed his arm and gritted his teeth hard enough that Oreo heard them grinding together like dice in a clenched fist. Ignoring the captain and his men entirely, Catt stood and walked to the lamp that one of them had lit, rubbing the blood between his fingers and sniffing it.

He returned to kneel next to Tomas with a smile. 'It seems that he missed the intestine,' he said. 'That is however the extent of the good news.'

'And the bad?' Tomas panted.

'You're still bleeding like the proverbial stuck pig. That wound will need stitching, and quickly.'

Before either of them could say anything, a loud thump sounded from above them, followed by a loud rustling. Everyone in the room stopped what they were doing and craned their necks, tracking the sounds.

'It's coming through the roof,' the captain said, moving to put his back against the wall. 'Be ready.'

Orec glanced towards the doorway that led to the bedroom, then took a steadying breath. 'You aren't going to stop it,' he said, loud enough for all to hear. 'Let me up. I'll stand with you.'

'Shut your trap,' Alsan growled, feinting a blow with the brass-tipped butt of his spear and sneering when Orec flinched away.

Dust fell from the ceiling as the creature pulled its way through the thatch and landed on the crossbeams. Wood creaked above them, then went silent. Alsan tilted his spear up and, taking care to walk softly, positioned himself directly under the last place the noise was heard.

Catt reached over and tapped Orec's arm. He ignored the first but not the second, more insistent tapping. He turned and Catt simply pointed to where his sword lay, kicked aside when they had been pushed back against the wall. Arcs of purple light were skipping along the blade, making it rock as they discharged into the floorboards.

He looked back at Catt, held up his roughly bound hands, and shrugged. They'd all seen it before, and they already knew the beast was there. The way his hands were tied he'd only be able to get one hand on its hilt, and for the fight it would result in, he needed both. However, if it came to that being the only option to get it away from Martina, then so be it.

Catt reached over Tomas' torso and grabbed Orec's arm like a mother holding onto a recalcitrant child.

'It's the sword,' he hissed at Orec, a strange light in his eyes. 'Don't you see? It's not come for you.'

# CHAPTER NINETEEN

OREC STARED AT him as if he were speaking a foreign language, then looked back to the dark blade of his sword. His sword, given to him by a dying knight who had mistaken his cowardice for courage and offered it to him with his last breath, as if passing the blade on was more important than any attempt to save himself from the swamp's deadly embrace. That solitary, unseen act had given Orec back his courage and strength, and he had carried within him ever since, earning a name for himself. A name that came from it and one, now that he thought about it, that was perhaps more astute than he had ever considered. Blackblade. He never seen its like amongst all the misshapen creatures and howling mobs that he and the company had been thrown into, nor among the men that he had stood with since.

He looked up as Alsan drew his spear back for a thrust into the ceiling, his movements seemingly as slow as resin oozing from a tree. He closed his eyes as the memories of the tumult at Tulkauth filled his mind one more.

The Yogg counter-attack had broken against their shield wall and he had raised his sword and, against all common sense and his orders, he had led the company forward again. It was the right moment, he knew that much. The enemy was in disarray, with those Yoggs who had survived the initial barrage of arrows and javelins having slowed or were jostling their way back through their own lines. There was no time to seek orders or argue with commanders who led from the rear.

They hit the Kinslayer's mob hard, paying for every yard with blood, but the momentum remained theirs. The Yogg warlord sent his elites forward, towering hulks in thick armour that did nothing to slow them down. Hayden took the first with an impossible shot that sped through a narrow gap in their ranks, his arrow burying itself to the fletching in the visor of a mottled helmet. He and Tomas took the next one together. He kept the Yogg busy with his sword while Tomas rolled past and split its ankle tendons with his axe. It didn't so much die fighting as lay there to be butchered as his men swarmed over it, their knives finding the gaps in its armour and cutting it to pieces. He couldn't remember how they got through the last of them, only that his armour had ended up crumpled like unwanted parchment and his right arm was left numb from the amount of hacking that it took to bring the guard to its knees.

And then the sorcerer was in front of them, tattooed face creased in what could have been any of anger, hatred or fear and quite possibly all of them together. His eyes had been lit with that same purple light as Orec knocked his thrusting staff aside and spun, the sword rising into the hawk strike position and then coming down with his full weight behind it. He could still hear the clang of the circlet breaking and the porcelain crack of the Yogg's head splitting.

His strike had ended at the sorcerer's collarbone. Tomas was to his right, Stef to his left and Hayden behind, like the prow of a warship with the sword as its ram. In his mind, he saw the explosion forming where the sorcerer's head had been, a dark hole that had drawn light in at first before vomiting it out in a single sun-bright moment, broken only by the outline of the sword that he kept in front of him, a dark stripe held against that killing sun.

He looked at the sword seeing it as if for the first time. As ever, the hilt was plain and unadorned, and like the blade itself, fashioned in a type from a hundred years ago or more. The steel was unmarked save for the few faded sigils he'd shown Catt, that he had always taken to be the maker's mark; and it looked as if the smith had somehow plunged it into a sack of charcoal dust as he finished it. He'd heard of enchanted swords, but few of the stories he'd heard made him want one. A sword that cut through anything it touched would be handy in a tight spot, but it wouldn't make you popular if you were fighting in a line. And how would you even carry such a thing? No, that was all a nonsense and the province of heroes, not common soldiers.

It had been the gift of a nameless, dying knight in armour as out of date as the sword he bore. A man no one else had recognised or remembered seeing. The thoughts ran through Orec's head in the space of mere heartbeats as he watched the sword rocking on the floor, harder and louder with each passing moment although no one had touched it.

A dull crash sounded from the bedroom, followed a breath later by Martina's scream, a sound that cut him to the bone, snapping him back to the present and firing the restive anger within him into a new heat. His feet were under him before she had finished screaming and he was diving on the sword, a calloused hand slipping around the hilt even before the spearman, Alsan, had spun around.

He was on his feet when Alsan's thrust came with killing intent, the sort of thrust you saved for the first clash of shields or particularly angry boar, and it would have punched through his mail had it landed. But he was already turning, guiding it away with a hard parry. Alsan was trying to use the length to stay out of reach, but not only was it the wrong weapon for fighting indoors, but the certainty of the kill had made him overbalance into the thrust.

Orec rolled his wrist and whipped the blade along the haft of the spear and the back of Alsan's lead hand, cutting all four fingers away at the knuckles. The spearman staggered forward and into a reverse cut that left a thin red line across his throat. His eyes widened and he reached up to the cut as it yawned open, his eyes widening with the knowledge of his own death, and whatever he tried to say was drowned in the blood that burst from the slit.

Orec shouldered the dying spearman out of his way as the other men turned, caught between rushing toward the bedroom and the sight of Alsan bouncing off the table in a ruby spray.

'Get out of my way,' Orec growled, advancing on them. 'My wife's in there.'

The captain squared off against him. 'Then she's already dead.' He sneered as Orec faltered. 'Probably gutted like a deer.'

In that moment, he attacked, his sword snaking forward. Orec was caught mid-step and barely managed to turn enough to have the point meet mail rather than skin. It hadn't been any feint either, from the impact he felt. Another thrust followed, faster than he'd expected, and again he had to flinch away, losing ground.

'Just let me get her out of here,' he said, taking another step back into the front room, where he had more space to move. 'I'll come quietly.'

'Too late for that,' the captain said, eyes flashing to the bloody ruin of Alsan's body. He lunged again, but this time Orec met it with a parry and a return cut that saw the captain hurriedly lean away.

'But not too late for that,' Orec said, making a show of looking over the captain's shoulder.

'Oh please,' he sneered. 'As if I would fall—'

The captain stiffened as Catt jabbed his lightning rod into the back of his leg. His legs and arms straightened, his sword falling from numb fingers as a strangled cry burst from his lips, ending only when he hit the ground.

Another scream came from the bedroom and Orec hastened towards it.

'Get out of my way,' he shouted.

The two remaining soldiers looked at him and then each other, and both stepped away, slipping past him as he strode by. He ignored them and the voice in his head that was screaming warnings about knives in his kidneys and struck the door with the pommel of the sword.

'Hey! You want this? Come get it, you bastard!' He kept pounding on the door, knowing it was futile to even try barge it down. He'd reinforced it to make it a refuge, never imagining that he'd be the one trying to get in.

Something heavy slammed into the other side of the door and he heard the sound of breathing, whistling like a bellows. It quietened, and then that strange chirping noise came again, except now he felt it in his chest as much as he heard it. Claws scraped across the wood and he heard wood land on the ground. *It had lifted the beam.*

It was inviting him in. He stared at the door for a moment, considering, but then what choice did he have? He spun the sword and cut through his bonds, then stepped back and kicked the door open, throwing his weight behind it.

It flew back, catching the creature a glancing blow as it leapt away. He raced inside, sword held out towards the creature as it righted itself and, gods help him, leapt aside and landed on the wall like an oversized spider, eyes glittering with that otherworldly light.

He dared a glance towards the shape sprawled on the bed. Martina was pale, but breathing and unmarked as far as he could see.

Wood creaked and snapped as it began slowly moving towards him, still on the wall, the chirping becoming more insistent and akin to a chorus of agitated crickets. He stepped sideways, keeping the sword between them as coruscant energies started to skip along the length of the blade, more than he'd ever seen. They leapt across his hands and up his arms, their touch unexpectedly light and cool.

It leapt at him without warning, tearing great chunks out of the wall as its powerful hind legs launched it forward. He jerked the sword down clumsily, cursing himself for being distracted. He clipped its arm, but not enough to stop it. Ebon claws raked his armour, showering him with purple sparks that were hot enough to blister the skin they touched, and fragments of broken rings which had been shattered as if made of pottery. Though glancing, the blow was powerful enough to send Orec stumbling backwards, a dull ache blooming under his gambeson as his ribs protested.

It was coming forward again and he all but threw himself sideways before it could trap him between the bed and wall. He feinted with the sword, hoping to gain some distance back from it, but it didn't flinch in the slightest.

'All right then,' he said, rolling his neck and eliciting a satisfying crunch.

Even though he was expecting it to attack, the speed that it moved with almost left him foundering. It was as if it was there one moment, and then in front of him the next, without ever being in the space in between. He managed to tilt the sword, catching one of its arms and batting it away, but the other caught him on the right hip, ripping through the mail and tearing the gambeson into strips. It was a bruising impact, and with it came the sharp heat that told him he'd been cut. There was no time to look how bad it was but he could already feel the blood running down his leg.

The creature circled him, eyes burning bright and the chirruping sound growing louder. And there, on its arm, a brighter patch of something. Something that flowed and dripped like the blood on his leg. Orec grinned and pushed all thought of the wound from his mind. Worrying about getting hurt was the first step to losing a fight, and he had no intention of doing that.

He hunkered forward, switching the sword from hand to hand like a knife fighter: needlessly showy, but it got the creature's attention. He switched again, then feinted forward. It swayed out of the way, but not by anything more than it needed for the thrust to miss, which he had counted on. As it moved, so did he, the lunge becoming a twist as he snaked his lead foot forward and pivoted on it, turning the thrust into a looping cut that caught the snarling beast across the shoulder before it could twist out of the way. The energies skipping along the blade brightened as it hit, and while it wasn't as solid blow as he'd hoped for, the creature still yelped, a shrill sound that sounded like it came from a dozen mouths. The arcs of energy followed it as it leapt away from him, landing on the opposite side of the bed, a bright gash on its shoulder.

He bared his teeth as he advanced on it, forcefully ignoring his stiffening leg. It in turn flexed its claws and narrowed its eyes, and he felt more than saw the pattern of the energy running through the blade change, drawing the blade towards the beast like a lodestone.

It hissed at him, then stepped backwards through the wall and was gone.

He stared at the space where it had been, then swung the sword through it, but the blade only met air. Something scraped across the floor behind him and he spun. He had a glimpse of a figure behind him, crackling rod in hand. He barely managed to turn the sword in time and chopped it into the bedpost instead, but then his leg gave out and sent him to the floor.

'Where did it go?' Catt asked, offering him a hand.

Orec ignored him and pulled himself onto the bed where Martina was stirring. She came to as he took her hand, her breath coming in a quick gasp before she realised who it was.

'Is it gone? Is it gone?'

'Are you hurt?' he asked her.

'No, I'm fine.' Her voice trailed off as she saw the blood smeared across his armour. 'But you are! Doctor, come quick!'

'I really need to reconsider my introductions,' Catt muttered, then louder, 'Where did you say it went?'

'Through the goddamned wall,' Orec said, wincing as he laid back to let Martina expose the wound. The look on her face wasn't encouraging.

'Through?' Catt asked, rapping his knuckles against the offending but entirely solid wall. 'Are you sure? How interesting. I should have considered that possibility, especially after it tried the portal in the woods. Fascinating.'

Martina give Catt a filthy look, then turned back to Orec. 'I need to stitch this.'

Orec sagged back against the bed, suddenly bone tired. He stared up at the sword embedded in the bedpost, tutting to himself at the work it would take to repair the damage. A strange heaviness was pressing down on him, forcing his eyes to close. He wanted to give in to it, but even as he thought about it a sharp agony exploded on his side. He hissed and half rose, but a slender arm pushed him down again.

'I thought that might wake you,' Martina said, pulling the thread through the hole she'd just made. 'You have to stay awake.'

His reply was a garbled string of curses he'd have been too embarrassed for her to hear any other time, but to his surprise, she only laughed. She ignored the rest of his complaints as she worked her way along the gash, not being rough but working steadily, every now and then glancing up at the ragged hole in the ceiling. When she was done she picked an ugly-looking knife he'd not seen before up off the floor and cut a strip from the bedsheet she'd been so proud of.

'Hips up,' she said, wrapping it around him and pulling it tight. 'It's going to be quite a scar.'

'Well done, Martina. Impeccable timing too,' Catt said, peering out of the bedroom. 'The commander is just about back on his feet too. Should I zap him again?'

'Thank you,' Orec said, taking both of Martina's hands in his own. 'I'm sorry I've brought this down on us.'

'You owe me a new bed,' was all she said, but it was said with something akin to a smile. She helped him onto his feet, bracing him until he felt steadier.

He looked down at the improvised bandage and raised his leg. He could feel the stitches pulling, but evenly. 'Good job,' he said. 'Better than the company sawbones.'

He stepped past her and yanked the sword from the bedpost as footsteps sounded in the hallway. The two soldiers came in first, swords in hand but held low, followed by their captain, who shot Catt a nasty look before turning his sour mien on Orec.

'What the fuck is going on here?' he said, tapping his sword against his leg.

Orec lowered his sword but resisted the urge to lean on it like a cane. 'That thing is one of the Kinslayer's pets. I killed its master, and it's been hunting me since.'

'And you?' He turned to Catt, eyes narrowing as if seeing him for the first time. 'You're the man in the cart.'

'Chariot,' Catt said. 'But that I am, captain. Mister Blackblade is telling the truth about the creature. I was there when it came for Stefan of Pulcek. And you've seen what it can do.'

'Martinsson,' Orec said, fighting the urge to sit on the edge of the bed.

'With all respect, captain, it wasn't the creature who killed Alsan,' one of the other men said, his distaste for the whole conversation obvious. 'Nor your company.'

'No it wasn't, and that matter will be settled once this thing is dead. Where did it go?'

Orec inclined his head to the wall. 'Through that.' Before the captain could say anything else he turned to Martina. 'Can you go check on Tomas, please? He took a spear in nearly the same place.'

'Of course,' she said, hurriedly repacking her sewing kit and gathering up the rest of the sheet, with Dimka's knife wrapped within it. She stepped between the men and hurried to the front room.

'Through the wall?' the captain said. 'Are you sure?'

'Sure as shit.' He gestured to Catt. 'The expert over there says it's from another world, so if it can do that, maybe walls aren't much of a challenge.'

'But then why—'

'We don't know,' Catt interjected. 'But I suspect such endeavours require more energy than it wants to spend.'

'How do we stop it then?'

'Same way as anything else,' Orec said. 'Steel and courage. It bleeds, so it can die.'

'If I can strike it but once we should have a better chance,' Catt said, lifting the now-quiet rod. 'Sorry about earlier, captain, but you understand.'

That earned him another sour look. 'Indeed. But do we know if that will be enough to stop it?'

Catt smiled and tilted the spear to show a small copper lever on the side of it.

'What you felt was a quarter charge, captain. I intend to use a full charge for our uninvited guest.'

'How're you feeling?'

Tomas opened his eyes and looked up at Orec. 'Better. Your wife has good hands,' he added with a wink. 'Couldn't keep them off me.'

'Dream on, grandad.'

'She's washed it with your good booze and stitched me up,' he said with a chuckle, lifting his tunic to reveal a tightly wrapped midriff. 'It's oozing a bit, but not much. She saved my life, I reckon.'

'And there will be a thousand new chores found for you to pay it off.'

'So what's the plan?' Tomas asked, looking past Orec and to where the riders were moving around inside the kitchen, blocking the rear door.

'It'll be back, so we're setting a trap for it.' He patted Tomas on the shoulder. 'You've been promoted to bait, first class. Congratulations.'

'You're trusting them? This is a stupid plan.'

'We're out of choices.'

'It's still a stupid plan. Even if you kill it, they'll kill you. And more importantly, me.'

'Would you prefer it came for you while they had you trussed like a bird for the fire?

Tomas stared up at the ceiling and sighed. 'Shit.'

Orec glanced over his shoulder to make sure no one was watching, then reached under the remains of his gambeson and pulled out one of the hatchets, quickly slipping it under the blanket. Tomas' scowl lightened as he tucked it under his leg.

'Nicely done. So what's the real plan?'

'Simple. It goes down, and then they do. I'm not swinging from a branch for them.'

Orec felt his fingers tingle as he spoke, and lifted his hand just in time to see an arc of violet light leap onto his sleeve and vanish.

'It's back. Be ready.' He rose and gave a short, sharp whistle that was answered by a curse from the kitchen. Martina emerged from the bedroom as the captain took up his position by the doorway.

'Are you sure you want to do this?' Orec asked, taking her hands in his.

'It's fine. It didn't hurt me before, it won't now. I'm not a threat to it.'

'There's no telling—'

She silenced his protest with a kiss and pushed past him, giving his hands a last squeeze as she let go. He watched her slip around the corner.

'She has a point,' the captain said from behind him. 'It killed everyone else on sight, but left her alone. Focus.'

Orec only grunted in reply and took up his position on the other side of the doorway, testing his leg and wincing as the stitches pulled sharply. It wouldn't hold for long, but then they probably only had one chance to do this anyway. If they missed the chance, a bleeding leg wouldn't matter.

He could hear the murmur of Catt's voice from the kitchen but resisted the urge to tell him to be quiet. If anything, him being quiet was a sure way to announce that something was afoot. A lot depended on him now, and knowing that his future now largely hinged on the overdressed lawyer was disconcerting. He lifted the sword as the violet arcs began skipping along his arms again and looked across to make sure the captain had noticed.

*This is a bad idea*. He pushed the thought away.

A soft impact came from above him, followed by the creaking of wood as it moved towards the front of the house where Tomas and Martina sat waiting. A collective breath was taken, and Orec transferred his weight to his uninjured leg, ready to rush in the moment it broke through. From the corner of his eye he could see Catt readying himself too. Another creak, following by a muffled clicking and chirping.

None were expecting the thumping on the door.

'Captain Armand? Captain?'

The scraping above them went silent. Next to him the captain, Armand, swore loudly and ignoring Orec's glare, stepped into the front room as the door was pulled open to reveal a stocky rider. He brightened at the sight of Armand but that only lasted as long as it took him to notice the two other bodies wrapped in blankets.

'Sir,' he said, offering a slack salute, 'there's a group moving up from the village.'

'Get in here and close that damned door,' Armand said, slamming his sword back in its scabbard and turning away.

'Sir?'

The ceiling bulged and exploded as Armand turned away. Plaster, straw and dust almost veiled the dark shape that followed the detritus down. The gawping soldier had no time to react before the claws raked him from neck to hip, opening him to the bone and sending him flying back through the open door. Armand's hand found his sword again just as its tail hissed through the air and cracked him across the face, sending him spinning him away and stumbling over the bodies.

Orec stepped forward, sword raised and the blade glittering with purple light that arced along its length and leapt towards the beast which now stood before him, claws held wide and its head low, eyes burning with that eldritch fire.

On the porch, the stricken rider found breath to scream once, the sound shrill and terrible but mercifully short-lived.

'You want this?' Orec said, slowly switching the sword from hand to hand as he had before. The beast mirrored him as he limped to the side, drawing it away from Martina and putting its flank to the kitchen entrance. The beast's slick hide rippled as another arc of purple light flashed from the sword, and its tail began to twitch behind it, whipping like a cat's.

'Now,' Orec said, holding the sword still before him.

Behind the creature, Catt threw himself forward, his rod flashing into life as he lunged towards the beast. Impossibly, it was already turning away as he did so, claws digging splinters from the floor. The rod hit its hindquarters and with a loud crack it discharged, momentarily replacing the purple light with a sharp, white brilliance.

The creature flinched away and one of its legs buckled beneath it, breaking the contact with the rod. As it stumbled, Orec felt the balance of the sword in his hands shift. He had little time to think about it before several vines of violet light flashed from the dark steel and raked his chest. He expected nothing from them, but these burned like reddened pokers being dragged across his skin and set his gambeson to smouldering. The killing stroke he wanted to deliver vanished from his mind as they burned their way across his chest, blackening and blistering his skin.

Catt pressed forward after the creature, but the second strike of his rod flashed for only a moment before the creature hissed like a scalded cat and turned on him, bony tail slicing a furrow across Orec's shins as it spun.

Catt stepped back, face paling as it flexed its claws, its shimmering eyes fixed on him.

For Orec, pushing the sword away was like trying to push a mountain away. It felt as if his arms belonged to someone else, and the only sensation was the hot agony of the violet light pouring into his body, burning its way up towards his face and neck.

*Not pouring. Draining.*

The thought was hard to hold onto as the waves of pain crashed through him, robbing the strength from him with every passing moment. Through the purple haze he saw the creature swat the rod from Catt's hands, sending it spinning into Martina's face. She fell back with a cry.

*Son of a bitch.*

He took a step forward. Unlike his arms, his legs still obeyed, however uncertain they were. The creature's tail whipped him again, but the sensation was lost to the experience of his own flesh cooking. Another step, and he felt that shift in the blade again, as if there was a weight sliding from hilt to tip. He focused on that, willing it away from him and gasped out loud as the crackling energies left him and leapt to the creature. It spun on him again, but if anything its eyes looked brighter and clearer, the cruciform pupils now distinct.

He could feel the power moving through the sword, and for the first time he felt an inkling of what it held. The fires that had killed so many at Tulkauth were a fraction of what had been unleashed by the catastrophic discharge of the ancient magic that had powered the sorcerer's crown, and the worst of it had been drawn into the blade.

He could feel it moving in there. He could feel the traces of it in his own body and that of Tomas responding, like metal filings being drawn to a great lodestone. Pushing and pulling.

*Draining into him*. They didn't belong there. The thoughts flashed through his mind as the creature drank the energy in, glutting itself. He tightened his grip on the sword. Behind the creature, Catt was shaking his head and mouthing words he couldn't hear over the sound of the energy leaping from the sword, a different note with every pulse. He felt that shifting weight in the blade again and willed it back towards himself, teeth gritted and grinding as he felt the lashing filaments begin to retreat from the beast.

There was a moment where he felt it start shifting back towards him and he focused on holding it there, held somewhere in between, trapped in the steel. The runes on the blade, once hair-thin and all but lost to sight, began to shine with violet light, and the honed edges of the blade followed suit a moment later.

The creature shook its head, but neither its gaze nor its toothy maw instilled the fear it once had. He lifted the sword, and he felt its muscles bunch. He could almost see the blur of its movements already, the way it would duck low beneath his swing and the sweep of its claws that would follow as it made to hook his guts out. *I see you*.

He feinted forward and then pivoted on his back foot, turning him out of the way as the creature moved forward, throwing the momentum into the sword and bringing it chopping down on the base of its neck as it ducked.

Violet energy exploded as the blade connected, sun-bright and blinding, and he felt himself flying backwards, sword lost to numbed hands. A sudden impact told him he'd hit the opposite wall. He lost his wind as he bounced off the floor and could only lay there whooping for breath, his eyes burning and weeping like he was a professional mourner.

Sound returned to him first, an arrhythmic thumping and scratching. He felt hands rolling him over and a voice joined the sound, a woman telling him to let her see. *Martina*. He let his hands fall away from his chest and rolled onto his back, a sharp breath whistling through his teeth as his burned flesh stretched and tightened. The drumming and scraping quietened rapidly.

'Open your eyes. Orec, listen to me.'

He opened them, squinting like a drunk whose windows had just been thrown open. Of all things, he'd always feared the vulnerability of blindness the most, and he squeezed her hand with painful force as a new panic started rising within him. 'I can't see!'

'Your eyes are going to be fine, you hear me? They're reacting, so they just need a little time.'

He closed them again and sagged back, releasing her hand. 'Is it dead?'

'Dead as fuck,' Tomas said from somewhere to his left. 'But that captain is eyeballing us again. If he tries it on, I'm going to split his head.'

'Captain, they're coming,' a voice called from the porch.

'How many?'

'Dozen or so.'

Footsteps approached. 'You, outside with me.'

'I'm staying with Orec,' Martina said, but then yelped.

'On your goddamn feet.' Armand's voice.

'Leave her alone, damn you,' Orec said, his voice dry and whispering. 'It's over.'

'Shut your mouth,' Armand replied. 'Nothing's over until I say it is.'

Martina yelped, then cursed, and Orec heard the scuff of reluctant footsteps. He could only curse and pull himself closer to where he knew Tomas lay.

'What's happening?'

'Hold on, I'm standing up.' He grunted and cursed as much as Orec had, but eventually managed it. 'Fine pair we make, eh?'

'Shut up.' Orec gently massaged his eyes. They were still watering like meltwater springs but no longer stung, and small pinpricks of light were bursting across his vision.

'They're standing on the porch. There's a proper little mob coming up the path.' He gave a pained laugh. 'I've always wanted to see a mob.'

'They're going to get themselves killed.'

'Their choice, not ours.' He felt Tomas shrug as he always did, a habit that had annoyed Orec to no end when he tried to give him an order.

'They're my neighbours, damn it.'

'You won't be anyone's neighbour if that prick hangs you. One of them's coming forward. Strapping chap with blond hair.'

'Max.'

'Wait, is that *the* Max? I thought you said he was fat.'

'He was.'

'He's not anymore.' He paused. 'Did he stay in Cambry throughout?'

Before Orec could tell him to mind his own business, he heard Max's voice, although he couldn't make out the words. He could understand Armand's though as he recited the binding of law and their crimes. Hearing it said out loud like that made it sound tawdry and terrible, and he felt a pang of shame. Whatever happened, they would always remember this of him.

'Here,' Catt said from close by, startling him. He pressed something cool into Orec's hand. 'Drink that. Careful, it's open.'

Once he would have asked him what it was, but he was beyond caring now. He tipped the small bottle into his mouth, fully expecting some vile tincture but instead only tasting apples. He smacked his lips.

'The apple flavour was my own invention,' Catt added. 'A huge improvement, if I say so myself. I won't tell you what else was in there for your peace of mind.' He deftly plucked the vial from Orec's hand. 'Waste not, want not. Now, be ready.'

'For?'

The word has just left his lips when Catt plunged an icicle into each of his eyes. Or so it felt. It started at his eyes and snaked through his body, as if that icy meltwater was pouring from his ruined sockets. It had all but passed by the time he'd rolled onto his side and clutched at his face, fully expecting to feel gaping holes where his eyes had been.

'Outstanding,' Catt said as Orec straightened, carefully opened his still whole eyes and hesitantly squinted at him. 'Just about good as new.'

Orec blinked again, and the four images of Catt that had been rippling across his vision slowly coalesced into one. He shook his head and sat up, gently probing the still smouldering gashes in his gambeson. The flesh beneath was tender and tight, as if he'd fallen asleep in the sun for far too long, but it was whole. He grunted in surprise, and then quickly pushed himself to his feet, holding onto the wall as he tried to find his balance again.

Outside, Armand was issuing a warning to Max about interfering in the execution of justice, and from the sound of it, was really getting into his stride. Orec staggered past Tomas and onto the porch.

Armand turned as Orec stepped out, surprise warring with distaste across his expression. There were more than a dozen men gathered in the front garden, lanterns held in one hand and entirely functional looking swords and axes in the other. Max was at the head of them, a chain tunic and matching gambeson adding inches to his shoulders. He had a shield that he'd painted a loaf on, probably as a joke and to hide the heraldry of whichever body he'd taken it from, and his falchion was in his other hand. They all turned as he stepped out.

'Speak of devils and they shall appear,' Armand said with a sneer. He had his hand around Martina's arm and she looked entirely miserable. 'Ask him yourselves if you do not believe me.'

Max took a step forward. 'Is it as he says?'

'I wouldn't trust him to tell you if it was raining or not,' Tomas said, stepping up next to Orec. 'A man who hides behind a woman with a knife at her back? Who tries to burn down a man's home in the night?' He spat on the grass. 'I've stood with Orec in the bloodiest fighting this war had to offer. He's saved my life ten times over, and never flinched at the asking. Crooked words will never change that.'

He stopped beside Orec, trying not to show how heavily he was leaning on the railing.

In the garden, Max turned to the men around him and an urgent conversation began, one that Armand was not pleased with.

'This is not open for debate!' he called. 'They're coming with us, and you're going home. Anyone who interferes can share their scaffold.'

'Can't help but notice there are a score of us, and only four of you,' Tomas called back.

The riders who were flanking Armand shifted at this, raising their swords a fraction, but enough for Max and his men to notice. Their conversation quietened.

'You are bound by law,' Armand said. 'You cannot interfere here.'

'Whose law?' Orec said, taking a step forward and forcing the other rider to turn and face him. 'The law of the same generals and lords who abandoned Cambry to the horde? Who left its defence to those men and women, even children, who remained? Is it that law?'

Armand shot him a look of pure hate at that. He'd almost

had them, but he could practically feel the townspeople's attitude shifting against them. It was in the way they stood, in the raising of their lanterns and how they looked from Orec to him, as if he was the murdering bastard in this scenario.

'Put your weapons down,' he said, keeping his voice calm and steady, as if he was trying to pacify an angry dog.

The blond leader looked at the falchion in his hand, but didn't lower it. 'I don't think we will,' he said. 'And I suggest you leave. We will bury your dead with honours.'

'I'm not leaving here without them in chains, or hanging from a branch,' Armand protested. 'Go back to your homes, or you'll share their fate. That's your final warning.'

'No, it's yours,' Tomas called out, earning himself another murderous glare from the captain. 'Leave this place while you can, and take your threats with you.'

The riders who were standing on either side of Armand looked distinctly uncomfortable now, and while they were holding their place, they were looking at Armand now as much as they were the townsfolk. From where he stood, Orec could see them talking to the captain, their voices too low to hear. Tomas walked forward as the silence grew heavy, slipping the hand axe he'd concealed behind him into his hand.

As he had expected, the movement didn't go unnoticed and the rider nearest him lifted his sword.

'Drop it!' he called. 'Drop it, you bastard.'

'What, this?' He held up the axe. 'Come and take it.'

'Drop it,' Armand called from behind the rider. As he spoke he pushed Martina forward, her arm cranked up behind her. His other hand came around her body and set a knife to the underside of her chin. 'Do it.'

Orec straightened and drew his own knife. 'Move that blade. You hurt her and I'll gut you like a deer.'

In the garden the townspeople followed Max and took a step forward, the murmured conversations falling silent once more.

'Get back,' Armand said, glancing over his shoulder and edging back down the steps at the far end. Martina stiffened as they moved, her head thrown back to ease the pressure of the knife.

The riders followed him, shields up and swords levelled as Orec and Tomas followed. 'They're going for the horses,' Tomas said. 'If they make it, they'll go get more of their kind.'

'I know that,' Orec snapped, his eyes not leaving Martina. As Armand edged her back, he saw her free hand slip into the jacket she wore. The riders had their backs to her and Armand was watching Orec as keenly as he was watching her.

Metal gleamed in Martina's hand for a moment as she pulled Dimka's knife free. Both Orec and Tomas slowed as she turned the knife and drove it backwards into Armand's thigh.

He yelped like a kicked dog and flinched, and as the blade left her neck she kicked herself away from him and sprinted towards Orec. One of the riders took a swing at her as she passed, missing by inches, and then staggered back as Tomas's axe caught his helmet and careened off into the gloom.

The other rider turned and ran, and like a pack of hounds finally set free, the townspeople launched themselves forward with a wordless and almost animalistic cry. The rider who'd swung at Martina went down screaming, his shield and helmet wrenched away, two axes and a sword quickly silencing his pleas.

The other turned and began scrambling up the hillside, his shield cast aside, running for his life with the crowd at his heels. Armand was limping towards the horses, looking over his shoulder with every other step as Orec advanced on him with Max, Tomas and Martina in a line behind him.

Behind Armand, the horses began whinnying and stamping their hooves, agitation growing rapidly. Armand turned at the sound of the wood splintering and the drumming of their hooves as the horses broke free. Two came tearing up the path as if their tails were on fire, forcing them all to dive aside or being trampled.

Armand landed with a pained cry and incoherent curse that both Orec and Tomas echoed as their own wounds protested.

Max was back on his feet first and striding towards Armand, but Tomas, who had been staring at the patch of ground the captain had fallen on, reached out as he passed and grabbed his arm.

'Wait,' he said, repeating it in an unusually stern voice when Max tried to pull himself free. 'Don't move. Nobody move!'

AHEAD OF THEM, Armand pulled himself to his feet. His leg was throbbing more painfully with every minute that passed but he didn't dare pull the knife out. That bitch. He looked back at the group, who had now stopped and were simply watching him, no doubt expecting him to fall over and give up. Or maybe they just wanted to watch him suffer. They knew as well as he did that without a horse they had him cornered.

He'd never leave this cursed valley alive, no matter what oath he swore or how sweet their promises would be. He might have struck a bargain if it was just Orec, but there was no way that all of them would agree to risk it.

He started walking again, teeth gritted at the impact of each step, no matter how carefully he trod, feeling the trapped blade saw at the flesh around it as the leg flexed and pulled around it. Blood was pooling in his boot, squelching and slippery, slowing him even further. He rounded the corner of the house, shuffling past the gate that led out and up in to the hills—the route he would have taken had that bitch not stabbed him. They were all the same, a rats nest of vicious scum, and deserved each other.

And then he saw the horse standing at the rear of the house, still saddled and the reins hooked on something. Hope rekindled within him and he limped towards it, forcing a soothing note into his voice. It snorted and shook its head in response, stamping its hooves aggressively. He could see its nostrils flaring, and it shook its head again. It took some time for the thought to penetrate the fog in his mind but, like the rest of their horses, it was war trained, so it wasn't the blood it was reacting to, but something else.

*Had Orec not slain the creature?* He took up the reins and began working them loose from the old stump they'd caught on, looking around desperately as he did. The horse had at least stopped hammering its hooves into the ground but was standing there shivering, whites showing in its eyes.

'Easy boy,' he said softly.

Several things happened as he grabbed for the saddle. The horse flinched and turned away, sending him sprawling with the weight of its hindquarters. And then the earth exploded around him, clumps of mud and grass shooting upwards and spinning past him. Pale, segmented legs shot out as he crashed to the suddenly uncertain earth, folding over and caging him for a moment before they curved inwards, chitinous tips burrowing deep into his chest, the sound of his ribs snapping masked by the dull rumble of the earth shifting beneath him. He opened his mouth to scream but dirt filled it before he could draw that last, long breath, and then there was only darkness and the feel of soil and roots scraping past him.

MAX STAGGERED TO a stop and was still staring at the crater when the others caught up to him.

'Was that—?' Orec started.

'A grabber,' Tomas finished for him, beaming like his prize stallion had just won the race of his life. 'You bet your life it was. Big one too.'

'A what?' Max mumbled, stepping back from the edge of the churned earth.

'Grabber,' Tomas said. 'It's like the bastard child of a mole and a jumping spider. I've been telling the boys about it for a year now and they didn't believe me. Did you, Orec?'

'No, I suppose I didn't.'

Orec let out a long breath and leaned on Martina. He looked at the earth and raked his fingers through his beard, a nagging thought rising in his mind. What was it that the witch had said? *Beware the shifting earth when it finds you.* He'd forgotten all about it, but then he'd had a lot on his mind. He pursed his lips at the thought. He would need to tell them, and Stef's mother too, and that would hurt more than his hip. Next to him, Tomas' grin widened as he saw Orec's sour expression.

'See? I was right. It's about time you started listening to me. You've still got so much to learn.'

'How'd you know?' Max asked.

'Felt it swimming through the ground under us. If Martina hadn't poked a hole in that bastard, it would be one of us down there now.'

'Gods and stars,' Max said, looking pale. 'I never want to see or think of that ever again.'

'Careful now,' Tomas said, touching the side of his nose. 'They travel in packs, so you might get well another chance to.'

Max wasn't the only one to blanch at that, and Martina's suggestion that they go back into the house was welcomed despite Tomas's laughter and assurances that he was joking. Orec stopped her at the door.

'It's not a pretty sight in there at the moment. I need a couple of you to come in and help drag the bodies out.' He gestured to he and Tomas's bloody clothes by way of explanation.

Max sheathed his falchion and gestured to two of the men, one whom Orec recognised as the innkeeper.

'Thanks,' he said. 'I'll get a lamp on.'

He stepped into the room, which was darker than the gardens and fumbled his way to where the lamp should be, eventually finding it by stepping on it. The matches were at least still on the shelf and struck the first time.

'You could at least have lit some lamps,' he said as he worked, but there was no reply from Catt. He turned with the lamp and stared at the blood-soaked floor where he had left the creature. It, like the Doctor, was gone.

'What's wrong?' Max asked behind him.

'It's gone,' Orc said, holding the lamp high. The dead riders were as he had left them, but there wasn't so much as a drag mark or bloody hoof print where the beast had lain.

'Oh shit,' Max said. He shoved the innkeeper and drew his falchion again. 'Go warn them.'

Orec turned, then turned again. 'My sword's gone too.'

He bent and picked up one of the fallen rider's swords, cursing as the crude stitches in his hip pulled painfully, then moved forward, Max close behind. It didn't take them long to confirm that all three of Catt, beast and sword were missing without a trace.

Martina found him sitting on the end of their bed, borrowed sword on the floor next to him, while Max directed the clearing out of the house. She sat next to him and rubbed his back.

'It's over,' she said. 'We'll get the place back in shape in no time.'

'I just don't understand it,' he said.

'Hey,' she turned his face towards her. 'It's over. You're alive, I'm alive, and everyone and everything that wanted to change that is gone.' She forced the image of the pale legs erupting from the ground and pulling the captain under from her mind as she spoke, but was an image that would return to haunt her whenever she went into the rear garden for the rest of her life.

'I had a magic sword,' he said, pushing himself further onto the bed and laying back slowly.

'I know you did,' she said, gently touching the side of his face. She sat next to him as the exhaustion and blood loss finally dragged him into a deep, healing sleep.

# CHAPTER TWENTY

When he woke, he was naked and under a blanket, and sunlight was streaming through the shutters. He lay there for several minutes before doing anything as the memories of the previous day rearranged themselves in his mind.

He pulled the blanket away and propped himself up on his elbows. The stitches in his side were lying on the sheet, and the few drops of blood around them were the only sign that they were once in him. The wound itself was a curve of silvery skin, a delicate curlicue that was hardly worth noticing compared the knotted whorls that stretched across his chest and shoulders. Whatever was in the tincture that Catt had given him, it had certainly worked a magic of its own.

He dressed quickly and after a quick stop to relieve the terrible pressure in his bladder, he staggered into the kitchen, where Martina was filling a bowl with hot porridge.

'Welcome back to the land of the living,' she said.

'How long was I out?'

'A day and half,' she said after a moment's thought.

He sat down and the smell of the porridge made his stomach growl loud enough for both of them to laugh.

'Slowly,' she said, ladling a dollop of butter on top of the steaming porridge. 'It's hot.'

He grunted his agreement and stirred the butter in. 'Where's Tomas?'

'Max took him to the surgeon, and he's going to stay there for a while. He and the others stayed until well after first light to help clear the house out, you know. They took the bodies away for burial too, on old Compton's cart. I told them to take the horses as well, and to share out anything they got for them. As thanks.'

Orec spooned porridge into his mouth as she continued on about how helpful they had been, but he was only half listening. His thoughts were centred on the so-called lawyer, the missing creature, and his sword. He had no use for the creature, but the sword had been his, damn it. Gifted to him and him alone. It wasn't that he ever wanted to use it again, but it was his, and a magic one as well. Gods, if nothing else, he could have sold it and bought them more land, or kept the money for their older years, which were not so far down the road anymore.

'Are you even listening to me?'

'Yes,' he said automatically, blinking as he focused on her again. 'About the fences.'

She looked mollified by that. 'Yes, the fences. Do you think you're well enough to make a start on those?'

'The fences.' He pushed the bowl aside and wiped his beard. 'Well, I'm going to go see Tomas first.'

'He's fine. We need to—'

'He nearly died for us. You can nag about the godsdamned fences when I get back.'

He set his spoon down and stood, but the protest he'd been expecting didn't happen. Martina watched him as he spoke, and as he finished, she erupted into tears, doubling over where she sat and sobbing harder than she had at her own father's funeral.

Orec stood fixed on the spot, utterly bewildered, then slowly stepped around the table and pulled her into an embrace. She resisted for a moment, then leaned into him.

'Everything's all right,' he said in a kinder tone. 'I promise. I'll fix the fences.'

She pushed him away, fists beating at his shoulders. 'That's not what I want.' The words came out thick, and bracketed by heavy sobs. 'You damned fool.'

He did the only thing he could think of, which was hold her again, tighter this time. Her fists slowly opened again and she held him as tightly. He stood there, rocking ever so slightly, until her sobs quietened and her grip relaxed.

'What is it?' he asked quietly, gently brushing the hair from her face.

'I don't want to lose you. I can't, not again,' she said quietly.

'Why do you say that? Everything I did, I did so I can be here. With you.'

'But everything I say is wrong, and at night,' her voice trailed off, and she hiccoughed before starting again. 'I lay there wanting you to touch me, but… but afraid that you will,' she finished miserably. 'What man would stay with a cold, nagging harpy like that?'

'A man who loves her,' he said, gently stroking her cheek with the back of his fingers. 'A man who apprenticed as a carpenter solely because he knew her father was looking to extend his house, and he wanted an excuse to be around that man's daughter, even if he was too fat and shy to speak to her.'

'Orec, I—'

'Let me finish,' he said. 'I know I'm different, inside and out. We all are, and the world is too. But different doesn't mean bad, it just means it will take time to get used to the new bits.'

She wiped her face and took a steadying breath. 'I could do without the giant mole-spiders.'

'Me too,' he said, smiling. 'But mole-spiders is what we have.'

'Is it really over?'

'It's over.'

'Go see your friend,' she said, stroking his face. 'Buy some bread and wine on the way back. Lots of wine.'

'Lots of wine?'

'Lots,' she said. 'The healing starts tonight.'

THE PARCEL ARRIVED a week later. Tomas brought it to the house as part of the daily walk that the surgeon had recommended, and was warmly received. Orec needed scant excuse to set aside the repairs he was working on and sit on the porch as Martina bought out a jug and three mugs. The parcel was sealed with an impressive blob of wax that glittered as he broke it, giving him pause. He opened it slowly, but found only a leather bag and letter within. He opened the letter first, reading it in silence while Martina opened the bag and gasped as glittering coins spilled out.

'It's from Doctor Catt,' he said, dropping the letter into the open box. 'There was a bounty on our heads, it seems. A bounty that he's claimed on our behalf, less an appropriate fee of course. He says it's fair recompense, and that we're legally free now. Officially, we're dead criminals, but we're free.'

Tomas grinned and spread the coins out. 'I wonder who was worth more.'

'This will pay for everything,' Martina laughed. 'Isn't that great? Orec?'

Orec set the box down, turning it so she could see the marks impressed on it. 'See that? That's a municipal coat of arms. Cinquetann would be my first guess.'

'So?' Martina asked.

'We know where he is now.'

'Again, so what?'

'So,' he said, pausing to take a long drink from his cup, 'now that we know where he is, I can go get my bloody sword back.'

# ABOUT THE AUTHOR

**Mark de Jager** isn't sure if his love of writing led to his love of gaming or vice versa, but his earliest memories involve both. He now spends his time trying to find a balance between these and working a full-time job in the City, a process made slightly easier by his coffee addiction.

An ex-MP in the South African army, Mark now lives in Kent with his wife Liz (herself a published author) in a flat that is equal parts library and home. His first novel, *Infernal*, was published in 2016. Follow him on twitter and Instagram as @Gergaroth.

AFTER THE WAR
REDEMPTION'S
BLADE
ADRIAN TCHAIKOVSKY

# *Credits*

"New Home Isn't Pretty, but I Came from Hell Anyway" and "Fishing Trip to Boundary Waters" both first appeared in the *Saint Paul Pioneer Press*. "Drinking and Flying" and "Faegre's 'Women Who Run with the Wolves'" both first appeared in *Corporate Report Minnesota*. "Brian Coyle's Secret" first appeared in the May 1991 issue of *Minnesota Monthly*. Reprinted with permission. "Even in Facing AIDS, Coyle Served Truth and His City" first appeared in the Aug. 27, 1991, issue of *The Star Tribune*, Minneapolis, MN. Reprinted with permission. Eight essays in Chapter 2 were originally contributed as part of "Because I Said So . . . ," a recurring column in *Family Times*. "Prodigal Clown," "Paranoid or Positive?," "IR Queer," "Still Life with Alien," "Indictment City," "Jackpot City," and "Public Dis'course" all first appeared in *Twin Cities Reader*. "Andrew Sullivan Out at *New Republic*," "Good News Traveling Too Fast," "Gored," "Sidney Blumenthal," "Sally Quinn on Vernon Jordan," "Kids Say the Darnedest Things," "Road Trip," "Crash Course," "Death March," "People (Not) Like Us," "Who Asked You?," "One Last Hitch," "Goodbye to All That," "Oral Exam," and "Oh Say, Why Can't We See?" all first appeared in *Washington City Paper*. "Slower Than a Speeding Bullet" first appeared in the Oct. 2001 issue of *Washington Monthly*. Reprinted with permission. "*Details* Reborn," "Me, Me, Me™," and "Who Needs Writers and Actors When the Whole World Is Your Backlot?" all first appeared on Inside.com. "The Futility of 'Homeland Defense'" and "A New Mask" were first published 2001–2002 in *The Atlantic*. Reprinted with permission. "18 Truths About the New New York," "Gathering to Remember," and "That's All, Folks!" all were first published 2001 in *New York Magazine*. The articles "Neil Young Comes Clean," "Both Hero and Villain, and Irresistible," "At Flagging Tribune, Tales of a Bankrupt Culture," "Ezra Klein Is Joining Vox Media as Web Journalism Asserts Itself," "When Fox News Is the Story," "Deadly Intent," "Been Up, Been Down. Now? Super," "Before They Went Bad," "Calling Out Bill Cosby's Media Enablers, Including Myself," "All Hail the Helix," "View, Interrupted," and "Breaking Away, but by the Rules" all originally appeared in the *New York Times*, are copyright The New York Times and used here by permission. "The Wrestler" and "Press Play" first appeared on Medium .com. "All That You Leave Behind" was first published in the Oct. 2013 issue of *Bicycling*. Reprinted courtesy of Hearst Magazine Media, Inc. "Cats" is from the collection *Cat Is Art Spelled Wrong*. Used by permission of Coffee House Press. "Untitled Essay" first appeared in *Worn Stories* edited by Emily Spivack. Copyright © 2014 by Princeton Architectural Press. Reprinted by permission. "The So-Called Artist's Lifestyle" is from the collection *The Art of Wonder*. Used by permission of Minneapolis Institute of Art.